Brides of
IOWA

50 States
of *Love*

Brides of
IOWA

Three Loves Are Sweet Surprises along Willow Creek

CONNIE
STEVENS

BARBOUR BOOKS
An Imprint of Barbour Publishing, Inc.

Leave Me Never ©2011 by Connie Stevens
Revealing Fire ©2011 by Connie Stevens
Scars of Mercy ©2011 by Connie Stevens

Print ISBN 978-1-62836-235-0

eBook Editions:
Adobe Digital Edition (.epub) 978-1-63409-909-7
Kindle and MobiPocket Edition (.prc) 978-1-63409-910-3

All scripture quotations are taken from the King James Version of the Bible.

This book is a work of fiction. Names, characters, places, and incidents are either products of the author's imagination or used fictitiously. Any similarity to actual people, organizations, and/or events is purely coincidental.

Published by Barbour Books, an imprint of Barbour Publishing, Inc., P.O. Box 719, Uhrichsville, OH 44683, www.barbourbooks.com

Our mission is to publish and distribute inspirational products offering exceptional value and biblical encouragement to the masses.

 Member of the
Evangelical Christian
Publishers Association

Printed in the United States of America.

Contents

Leave Me NEVER

Chapter 1

Looking into Mama's face had always been like looking into a mirror, but not anymore. The skin on Mama's face hung over her cheekbones, creating gaunt hollows where beauty once resided. Tessa wiped her tears with the hem of her apron. For the first time in months, the lines between her mother's brows smoothed out. Her struggle was over.

"Mama." Tessa's own whisper echoed within the wagon canvas. "Oh Mama, please don't leave me here. Take me with you." Brokenness more cruel than anything she'd ever known invaded her heart with an onslaught so brutal she couldn't remember how to breathe. She straightened out her mother's fingers and laced them together in a posture of prayer, hoping against hope those fingers would squeeze hers once more. They didn't.

With leaden legs, Tessa slid to the end of the tailgate and lowered herself to the ground. Dawn had broken, but the morning mist still lingered over the unfamiliar town. Papa hadn't returned to their rickety wagon all night. Why wasn't he here? No doubt he drank himself blind again.

God, I need help. I don't know what to do.

She forced her eyes to scan her surroundings—for what, she wasn't sure. The edge of town where Papa left the wagon yesterday didn't offer much of a vantage point. A giant elm tree and thick underbrush offered meager privacy from the nearest building, the livery. Horses dozed in the corral, uninterested in her plight. The rest of the town seemed set apart, as though a line had been drawn in the dirt that she and her family weren't permitted to cross.

Farther down the street, a patchwork of brick and board buildings lined up like mourners in a funeral procession. An occasional sign, hitching rail, or picket fence broke the monotony of weathered storefronts, but the silent buildings offered no hint of the people residing within. Was there anybody in this town who could help her do what needed to be done?

Under different circumstances, she might consider this a pretty little town. She moved forward and crossed the space between the wagon and the corral, stopping at the watering trough in front of the livery. Her reflection in the still water startled her. A stranger—weary and disheveled—looked back at her. She dipped her cupped hands into the trough and lifted cool water to her face. With wet fingers she smoothed her hair. The cramped muscles in her back protested as she straightened to look down the street. Papa was nowhere to be seen.

Tessa's feet balked. Part of her heart was back in the wagon, stilled and unbreathing. Her constant source of unfailing love was now silent. Gentle, uncomplaining Carly Langford, her precious mama, would never call her "honey girl" again.

As she stood anchored in place by her grief, the gradual sights, smells, and sounds of a town awakening from slumber stretched their arms and yawned a greeting to the sun. Frying bacon and fresh-perked coffee wafted on the air. Then a rooster crowed. Strange sounds seeped into her awareness, and she realized it was birds chirping to each other in the trees. Eventually shopkeepers opened their doors to welcome the start of a new day. The comforting music of a town where everything was as it should be.

How could such cheerfulness exist? What was the matter with these people? Tessa wanted to scream for everyone to stop. Didn't they care that her mama just died?

"Miss?"

Tessa turned.

A tall, dark-haired young man stood behind her. His image wavered through her tears. "Miss, are you all right? Can I call somebody for you?"

She blinked back the tears and drew in the deepest breath she could manage. "A preacher. I need a preacher."

The stranger took her by the elbow and guided her to the board sidewalk. "Why don't you sit down here, miss? I'll go find the preacher and bring him. Can I get you anything?"

Tessa shook her head. The movement felt numbed and disconnected. As soon as she sat, the stranger strode away down the street. A slight breeze lifted the wisps of hair that lay along her cheek. "Oh God, I wanted to go with Mama. Why couldn't You take me, too?"

The rooster crowed again. A pair of little boys ran down the boardwalk, their laughter trailing strangely in their wake.

The wide doors of the livery opened, first one then the other. A wiry, whiskered man in a leather apron propped a rock in front of each door. He returned inside but reappeared a few moments later, dragging Papa by the arm. "Get on outta here. This ain't no hotel for drunks."

Papa stumbled over his feet, hitting the dust with a thud. His half-empty whiskey bottle broke on impact. Curses spewed from him as he got to his knees, contaminating the air with vile oaths. He squinted in her direction. "Tessa! Tessa, that you?"

Tessa squeezed her eyes shut, wishing she could block out the sound of her father's voice. Where was he when Mama needed him? "Yes, Papa, I'm here."

Papa staggered to his feet and kicked the remaining shards of broken glass. "What're you doin' just sittin' there, girl? Get me some breakfast."

A dull throb at the base of her skull caused Papa's demands to ring in her ears. "There is no breakfast, Papa. Nothing but the corn dodgers left from yesterday."

Storm clouds built behind her father's eyes. "Whadja say to me?" His voice slurred, and his watery, bloodshot eyes narrowed into slits. "You miserable little brat. How dare ya talk that way to your papa!"

He drew his hand back and slapped her across the face, sending her sprawling into the dirt. The metallic taste of blood touched her tongue, but she didn't care. Nothing Papa did mattered now. Her heart was numb.

Papa lurched over to where she lay in the dirt. He grabbed her arm and yanked her up then backhanded her again, knocking her backward against the livery door.

"Hey! Stop that!" The unfamiliar voice seeped through her daze. "What's the matter with you, mister?" The same stranger who told her he'd get the preacher stood before her. "Miss? Are you all right?"

She blinked and realized two men held Papa up by his arms and that another older man stood beside the dark-haired stranger.

"Are you all right, miss?" The older gentleman with thin, silver hair echoed the younger man as he bent to peer at her.

What difference did it make? "Yes, I'm all right."

"I'm Pastor Witherspoon. Gideon here says you need a preacher."

Gideon? Tessa slid her gaze to the tall young man. His dark scowl was fixed on Papa, but when he turned to look at Tessa, his eyes immediately softened into something foreign. Is that what sympathy looked like?

"Do you know that man?" His voice was low and even. The young man's finger pointed at Papa, who stood with splayed legs, swaying as though the breeze would blow him over.

"He's my father."

"Where is your mother, child?" Pastor Witherspoon touched Tessa's hand.

In order to answer the preacher, she would have to give voice to words she didn't want to speak. Loathsome, ugly words. But the preacher awaited her answer.

"Mama. . .Mama's in the wagon. She's. . ." Tessa couldn't allow the word to cross her lips, as though holding it back would erase the reality. If she didn't speak it, it simply wasn't so.

The man called Gideon strode across the yard in front of the livery to where the wagon sat partially concealed by low-hanging branches from the elm and drew aside the flap. He stepped up and leaned inside the canvas then exited slowly. "She's dead, Preacher."

"Dead!" Papa roared. "I told you!" He pointed his finger at Tessa. "This is your doin'. It's your fault. If it weren't for you, I'd still have a wife. You killed her, sure as I'm standin' here. Your mother's death is on your head, you no-good, miserable—"

"That's enough!" The dark-haired man drew back a fist.

Before he could throw the punch, the preacher grabbed his arm. "Gideon!" Pastor Witherspoon turned him away from Papa. "This young lady needs our help now, and her mother needs a Christian burial. Let's get busy and do what needs doing."

Gideon nodded, cast another withering glance at Tessa's father, and motioned to the livery man in the leather apron. "Cully, can you take him back behind the barn and let him sleep it off?"

"I ain't sleepin' now. I got things to do." The familiar belligerence of Papa's tone stung Tessa's ears. She knew better than to believe these men could change his mind.

Pastor Witherspoon stepped forward. "Sir, your wife's funeral is going to take place in just a little while. Why don't you go clean up and get some coffee, and when we're ready for the burial, you can—"

"I don't have time for no buryin'." He threw a glare at Tessa and pointed his chin at her. "*She* can do that. I got business." He shrugged off the men on either side of him. "Leave me alone. I got things to do."

He stalked down the street, leaving the small group staring after him.

All except Gideon. He looked at Tessa with such sympathy and compassion that she nearly lost control of what little resolve she had left.

She looked away and stiffened her spine. Papa would be drunk the rest of the day. It was up to her to see to it her mother was treated with the respect and caring she deserved. "Pastor, can you help me bury my mother?"

The elderly preacher took her hand and patted it. "Of course, child."

Gideon stepped forward. "I'll take care of it, Pastor. If you can look after Miss. . ."

"Langford," Tessa supplied. "Tessa Langford. My father is Doyle Langford, and Mama. . .Mama's name is Carly."

The preacher turned to Tessa. "Come with me, child. Mrs. Dunnigan at the boardinghouse will give you something to eat and a place to freshen up."

Tessa hesitated. "I have no money. I can't even pay for a decent burial for my mother."

Pastor Witherspoon waved his hand and nudged her ahead of him like the declaration of her poverty wasn't anything he hadn't heard before.

Two hours later, a small group stood around the freshly dug grave on a rise beyond the edge of town. A scattering of makeshift crosses and headstones dotted the grassy area where butterflies played tag among the wildflowers and cicadas provided the funeral music.

Mrs. Dunnigan from the boardinghouse stood beside Tessa and patted her shoulder. Gideon and two other men, each holding his hat in one hand and a shovel in the other, stood opposite the mound of dirt. They listened while the preacher read from the Psalms.

Tessa thought it fitting that he read from Mama's favorite book of the Bible. She felt a brief wave of relief that Papa saw fit to stay away, but guilt immediately assaulted her for thinking so. Despite Papa's hateful words and drunkenness, something within her longed for his approval. Couldn't he see she'd tried her best to take care of Mama? He'd always blamed her for Mama's illness and told her she was a sorry substitute for the son Mama never had. Was she the reason he sought solace from a bottle?

After the preacher finished reading and praying, Gideon approached her with a bunch of yellow daisies and blue cornflowers. "Here." He shuffled his feet and handed her the flowers. "I thought you might like to put these on your mother's grave."

When she lifted her eyes to his face, the tenderness she saw there unsettled her. Other than Mama, she couldn't remember anyone ever defending her or extending kindness to her. She barely knew this man. Only his name: Gideon.

She accepted the wildflowers and mumbled a thank-you. Bowing her head, she closed her eyes so she wouldn't have to watch the body of her mother lowered into the hole. Oh, how she longed to feel the comfort of Mama's arms around her one more time.

She held the flowers to her face while the men filled in the grave. Then she sank to her knees and laid the flowers on the fresh mound. "Mama," she whispered through her tears. "What am I going to do without you?"

Gideon watched as Mrs. Dunnigan coaxed the poor girl away from her mother's grave and walked her back to the boardinghouse. With her father a drunk and her mother gone, what kind of life would she have now? She appeared to be close to his sister's age, and he hated to imagine Martha being left in such a depressing situation.

When he'd placed the bouquet of wildflowers in her hands, her fingers reminded him of the delicate bone china he sold in the mercantile. Her red-rimmed hazel eyes tore at his heart, and her wheat-colored hair escaped its sorry scrap of a ribbon and wisped in a dozen different directions. He was sure Mrs. Dunnigan would help her clean up, but what good would it do if she was destined to fetch and carry for a drunkard?

The image in his mind made him grateful he'd been able to keep the family business going after his father died two years ago. Running the mercantile might not be what he wanted to do, but at least he and Martha had a roof over their heads. Gideon sent a quick prayer heavenward to thank God his younger sister was about to be married in just a few months to a fine, godly man.

The sun was high in the sky by the time Gideon reached Maxwell's Mercantile. He unlocked the doors and propped them wide open to invite customers. If only opening the doors was all it took to bring in business. The reason for the recent decline in his sales clomped down the sidewalk at that very moment.

"Maxwell." Henry Kilgore puffed out his chest to display the ornate watch chain hanging from his vest pocket. The ever-present cigar stuck in his teeth made the man sound like he was trying to talk with his mouth full.

Gideon ignored the man and entered the store, pulling his dark blue apron from its hook as he passed the storeroom door. The last thing he needed right now was another visit from Kilgore.

"Maxwell, didn't you hear me?"

"I heard you, Kilgore. What do you want?" As if he didn't know.

"I was wondering if you'd given any consideration to my offer to take this place off your hands. You'll have to admit I've offered you a fair price. You don't really want to stand behind a counter waiting on people the rest of your life, do you? I thought you were a bright lad. You could do better than being nothing more than a shopkeeper. But maybe I was wrong."

Ire grabbed Gideon's gut at the implied insult, but he refused to give Kilgore the satisfaction of seeing the effect of his offensive remark. He picked up a feather duster and began flicking it over the glass jars lining the counter. "My father was nothing more than a shopkeeper, Kilgore, until you pressured him into an attack of apoplexy. He worked hard, earned an honest living, and managed to provide quite nicely for his family."

Kilgore threw his head back and guffawed. "You call this providing quite nicely? I don't see the customers beating down your door."

Gideon turned to confront the accuser standing in the middle of his store. "I think we both know why that is, Kilgore. Ever since you came to town a couple of years ago, you've been buying up as many businesses as you can get your hands on. Many of my longtime customers are now trading at your Willow Creek Emporium. I know you can't possibly be turning a profit from the prices you're charging there, especially since you have to pay someone to run the place for you."

Kilgore pulled a match from his vest pocket, struck it on the bottom of his boot, and lit his cigar. He puffed several times in rapid succession until the foul-smelling smoke caused Gideon to take a step backward.

"I don't need to make a profit. I'm making enough money from my other enterprises. I can afford to lower my prices for the fine citizens hereabouts."

Gideon snorted. "It's not the fine citizens you're concerned about, and we both know it. You think if you take enough business away from me, I'll be forced to sell out and then you can charge whatever prices you want. You don't just want to own Maxwell's Mercantile. You want to own the town. Well, let me tell you, Kilgore, if I ever plan to sell, it won't be to you, seeing as how you probably sent my father to a premature grave." Gideon jerked his head in the direction of the entrance. "There's the door. Use it."

Kilgore laughed, but no mirth filled the sound. "I'm a patient man. . .for now. In another few months you'll be singing a different tune." He withdrew the cigar from his mouth and flicked the ashes on the floor. "Don't wait too long though, Maxwell. I make a practice of getting what I go after, and I just might lower my offer. Remember, I can buy and sell you ten times over if I want to." An arrogant smirk filled the man's face. He took a long draw on the cheroot and blew the smoke in Gideon's direction before sauntering toward the door.

Ordinarily Kilgore's barbs found their mark and Gideon chewed on the crust of the man's arrogance all day. But today was different. Maybe because the distracting picture of young Tessa Langford at her mother's grave stuck in his head.

Chapter 2

Tessa fought her way through the grogginess. As she struggled to sit up, the ragged edges of sleep fell away, and she realized two things: It was daylight, and she didn't know where she was.

Needles of panic pricked her stomach. Her glance skittered around the simple furnishings in the room, from the clean, white curtain on the window to the closed door. Like pieces of a puzzle coming together, Tessa extracted a sense of time and place. She remembered now. That nice lady who ran the boardinghouse tried to get her to eat something and then invited her to lie down and rest.

Along with the understanding of her surroundings came the resurgence of grief. The ache blew through her like a searing-hot prairie wind, and a sob escaped her tight throat.

She almost didn't hear the soft tap on the door. The boardinghouse lady poked her head in. The woman reminded Tessa of a schoolmarm with her severely pinned, iron-gray hair and creases around her eyes. Tessa guessed the woman either laughed a lot or frowned a lot.

"I thought I heard you crying, poor thing." The woman came into the room. Tessa's dress hung over her arm. "You were so exhausted I didn't have the heart to wake you last night for supper. You needed to sleep."

Last night? Supper? Bright sunlight streamed in the window.

The woman draped the dress across the foot of the bed. "I hope you don't mind, but I washed out your dress. There's fresh water in the pitcher, dear, and I saved you some breakfast."

Confusion fought with grief for first place in Tessa's mind. "I'm sorry. I don't mean to be stupid, but what time is it?"

The woman lifted the dainty watch pinned to her bodice. "It's almost ten thirty. You take your time freshening up." A soft smile deepened the creases in her face as she turned to leave.

Tessa scrambled from the bed and realized she was wearing only her chemise. She snatched up the dress and held it in front of her. "Uh, Mrs. . . . .uh,

17

ma'am, how long have I been here?"

"I'm Pearl Dunnigan, dear. We met yesterday, but I don't blame you for not remembering. After the funeral, you swallowed a few sips of tea before you collapsed on that bed, and you've been asleep ever since."

Tessa gasped. Papa would be furious. Heedless of Mrs. Dunnigan standing there, she lowered the dress and stepped into it. "Mrs. Dunnigan, I'm so sorry. I had no right to stay here. I told the preacher I had no money—"

Mrs. Dunnigan held her hand up. "It's perfectly all right, dear. You needed a quiet place to rest. Now come and eat something."

"But my father will—"

The woman's expression changed from sunny to stormy in an instant. "Your father will just have to wait a few more minutes." She clucked her tongue. "His behavior yesterday was deplorable. And such vile language! Didn't even attend his own wife's funeral, and the way he treated you. . .tsk-tsk."

As if suddenly realizing her words might be offensive, the woman's cheeks turned bright pink. "Well, anyway, come eat some breakfast. I think there's still some apple butter left." She slipped out the door.

Tessa's fingers fumbled with the buttons down the front of her dress. She pulled on her shoes—Mama's shoes, actually. Mama told her to wear them a couple of months ago when her own were beyond repair. A simple pair of secondhand shoes, certainly not much to look at, but tangible proof of the footsteps Mama left for her to follow.

After a quick washing of her face and arms, she pulled her hair back and secured it with a frayed scrap of old ribbon. How might she excuse herself and hurry back to the wagon without appearing ungrateful? She couldn't, in good conscience, take advantage of Mrs. Dunnigan's generosity and accept food without paying for it.

She followed the heavenly mingled fragrances of coffee, bacon, and biscuits and found the kitchen.

Mrs. Dunnigan turned from the stove when Tessa entered. "Here, dear, you sit down while I pour you some coffee." She reached for the coffeepot. "How about some bacon and eggs?"

"Thank you, ma'am, but I'm not hungry." She regretted the lie. "You've been so kind. I just wish I could pay you for your trouble."

Mrs. Dunnigan set a mug of coffee in front of her. "You need to eat something, child."

Tessa took several tentative sips of the steaming brew. The aroma of breakfast made her stomach growl, but she set her jaw and stiffened her spine against the temptation. The overriding fear of her father's wrath bullied every other thought—her grief as well as her hunger—out of the way. Despite Mrs. Dunnigan's kindness, she couldn't linger at the woman's table.

She took one more sip of coffee and stood. "Thank you, ma'am, for everything. You've been more than kind, but Papa will be furious if he's had to wait for me."

Mrs. Dunnigan's eyebrows dipped in disagreement, but she simply nodded and patted Tessa's shoulder. "All right, dear. You take care now. And I'm so sorry about your mother."

The lump in Tessa's throat prevented her reply, so she forced a smile and returned the woman's nod. She slipped out the door and scurried down the boardwalk, past the livery to the giant elm tree at the edge of town where Papa left the wagon yesterday—or was it the day before?

She arrived at the place beneath the giant elm tree, but the only evidence of the wagon's presence was the trunk Tessa shared with her mother, Mama's treasured hand-carved cabinet, and a crate containing a crude assortment of household items strewed in the bushes.

Tessa's feet froze in place as she stared at the belongings littering the ground. Beside them, a set of wagon tracks led away from town in a westerly direction. She forced her eyes to cast a wide search of the area. Reality laughed in her face. Papa dumped everything he didn't want or need off the tailgate and left without her. He'd discarded her like a piece of unwanted baggage.

She sank down in the dirt beside the trunk. Her mother's cabinet lay sideways in front of her, one door askew. A cracked teacup, a broken crock, Mama's apron—evidences of a meager existence, tossed aside in the dust. Tessa picked up each item by turn, wiped it clean, and cradled it in her lap. Papa may have viewed these things as worthless and unnecessary, but they belonged to Mama. They were priceless.

She employed some muscle and set the cabinet upright, noticing that the collision with the ground had broken one of the hinges. How could Papa treat Mama's cherished cabinet with such carelessness?

Placing each item exactly as Mama kept them in the cabinet, she let her hand linger on each one. Caring for her mother's things was a privilege.

When she opened the opposite cabinet door, she saw Mama's Bible wedged into one corner. She withdrew it and traced the edge of the worn leather

19

cover with her finger. Mama taught her to believe and pray from the time she was a young child, but a troubling thought now clouded her mind. Mama always said God would never forsake them. Yet here she sat, in a barren patch of dirt, with nothing more than a handful of belongings and a bewildered heart full of memories. Was this the way God cared for His children? Leaving them alone in the midst of strangers?

She pressed the Bible against her chest. "Mama, I miss you so much. Papa's left me, too. I wish you could tell me what to do."

The tears she'd held back for the last two days finally released as her grief and fear sought expression. She fell on her face beside the cabinet, clinging to the Bible and sobbing into Mama's apron. The surrounding trees and underbrush afforded enough privacy to erase any fear of onlookers, and she no longer cared to control the emotions she'd kept hidden far too long.

By the time her sorrow was spent, her eyes burned and raspiness grated her throat. She lay on the ground hugging the Bible and apron for a time. There was no hurry. She had no place to go. Perhaps if she stayed right here, God might decide to reach down and take her, too.

꙰

After an undetermined time, Tessa pulled herself to a sitting position and leaned against the trunk. If wishes could undo circumstances, she'd wish enough to erase her entire life, but whims didn't affect reality. She could choose to sit under this elm tree and die, or she could choose to survive.

The memory of Mama's voice whispering encouragement and telling her how precious she was despite Papa's tirades invaded her heart. Mama didn't choose to die. She didn't give up. She gave out, but not until she'd fought as hard as she could. Tessa could do no less.

Carefully brushing the dirt from Mama's Bible, she returned it to the cabinet and tucked the apron into the trunk. She dug past the few articles of worn clothing and located a small leather pouch buried at the bottom of the trunk. It contained a few coins Mama managed to keep hidden from Papa. Tessa untied the strings and dumped the contents into her hand. A pitiful amount of money, but it was enough to buy a handful of crackers and a bit of cheese.

Tessa rose and brushed off her skirt. She walked to the livery watering trough where she dashed some water in her face and smoothed her hair. After she retied the old ribbon holding her hair away from her face, she headed down the street looking for a general store.

She passed a half dozen buildings, some freshly painted, others weatherworn, until she came to Maxwell's Mercantile. The place looked similar to the store where she and Mama traded back home. The brick front encased a large window displaying assorted kitchenware and household items. Barrels of apples, milk cans, and brooms lined the boardwalk outside. A neatly lettered sign proclaiming the store's name hung overhead. Double doors with slightly chipped green paint stood open in a friendly invitation.

She stepped inside. The storekeeper, his back turned, measured coffee beans into the large grinder behind the counter. Two ladies chatted as they examined yard goods. Nobody noticed her, so she wandered through the store and sniffed the aroma of freshly ground coffee. The storekeeper spoke to his customers, but Tessa paid no attention as she fingered the cuff of a blue calico dress hanging next to a small display of bonnets.

"May I help you?"

Tessa jumped at the nearness of the voice, spun around, and came face-to-face with the man who'd handed her the wildflowers yesterday. Surprise registered on the man's face as well. What was his name? Her mind was too muddled to think.

"Your name's Tessa, isn't it?"

Tessa nodded. She forced words past her lips. "Yes sir."

A wide smile filled his face. "It's Gideon. What can I get for you today, Tessa?"

Tessa reached into her skirt pocket and extracted a nickel. "Is this enough to buy some crackers and cheese?"

Gideon's gaze traveled to the coin in her hand. His eyebrows lifted, and Tessa could only guess what he must be thinking. He crossed to the counter and pulled layers of cheesecloth away from a large, waxed round of cheese. With a deft motion, he cut a generous wedge, too generous to cost only five cents. He wrapped the cheese in paper then scooped a handful of crackers into a paper bag. "Here you go." Gideon slid her purchase across the counter.

She laid her nickel beside the paper-wrapped cheese. "Thank you."

"I want to extend my condolences again for the loss of your mother."

The tears that consumed her earlier threatened again. She pressed her lips together and drew in a tight breath to deny any show of emotion in this public place.

Another customer entered the store, and Gideon greeted the woman politely. He glanced about the store. "Is your father with you?"

The mere mention of Papa set her stomach spinning. Fear and grief collided in her chest. Should she tell Gideon her father had up and left her? What kind of explanation could she give? That she was worthless and her father had no use for her? That she was alone and had no idea how she was going to survive? "No, he must have had something else to do."

"So where are you folks from, and where are you headed?"

She wasn't headed anywhere—now. Harsh truth accosted her, but courtesy required she answer Gideon. "Papa had a farm back in Indiana. But he didn't like being a farmer."

"Indiana, huh? Good farm country there. Why didn't your pa want to farm?"

"Work was too hard, I guess. He raised hogs and grew corn, but he said he couldn't make enough money to keep body and soul together."

Gideon nodded like he understood. "Farming isn't easy, and that's a fact. Your crop can depend on a lot of things—weather, insects, blight. Anything can turn a harvest sour no matter how hard a man works."

Tessa felt heat crawling up her neck. Papa failed to turn a decent profit because he drank more than he worked the fields or cared for the pigs. He'd charged her with the animals' care and railed at her when the porkers brought a lower than expected price. How could she tell Gideon the embarrassing truth?

"Has your pa come west to try farming here in Iowa?"

She didn't know why Gideon was interested, but she didn't wish to be rude. "Papa heard some men talking about gold strikes in the Black Hills country. He figured he could get rich if we went there and dug for gold."

Gideon's brows dipped into a V. "A few folks pulled some gold out of there several years back, but not many got rich. There's been no report of gold strikes up there for a long time. Maybe the man at the land office can give your pa information about farmland hereabouts. Lots of farmers here in Iowa have harvested bountiful crops of corn and wheat, and for the past several years, there's been a lot of farmers raising porkers and cattle, too. Your pa could do well here."

If Papa could've stayed away from the bottle long enough to devote time and energy to their farm, they'd still be in Indiana. Maybe Mama would still be alive. Instead he'd decided to chase a harebrained dream of getting rich, while putting Mama through the rigors of traveling to goldfields that were nothing more than a mirage. Tears burned their way to the surface and spilled over. Her throat convulsed when she tried to swallow back the sobs.

Gideon's eyes widened, and his brow furrowed. "I'm sorry, Tessa. I didn't mean to—"

Tessa didn't wait to hear any more. She ran out the door, mortified at her lack of control in front of Gideon.

She picked up her skirts and escaped back to the seclusion of the elm tree and dropped down beside the trunk, her chest heaving more from anger at Papa and shame over her tears than from running. At least she didn't have to admit Papa had abandoned her. If Gideon knew what a worthless person she was, he likely wouldn't be so kind to her.

Despite her humiliation, her stomach still complained of its emptiness. She unwrapped the hunk of cheese and broke off a few small bits. It wouldn't do to eat too much. The cheese and crackers would have to feed her for a few days, at least until she could find employment.

She nibbled slowly to stretch out her mealtime as long as possible. She closed her eyes and imagined the fragrance of warm yeast bread fresh from the oven and savory roast beef with tender potatoes and carrots. If she played this game of imagination each time she ate a bit of cracker or cheese, her mind might convince her she wasn't as hungry as she thought.

The lengthening afternoon shadows indicated there wasn't much daylight left. She couldn't impose on Mrs. Dunnigan again. The canopy of branches overhead would be her roof tonight, and the underbrush would serve as her walls.

Dread washed over her at the prospect of spending the night outside and alone, at the mercy of whomever and whatever might be lurking in the darkness. But if Mama was right, God would spend the night with her.

Chapter 3

Tessa grunted as she pushed Mama's cabinet between the fat tree trunk and a dense juniper. Tangled underbrush snagged her sleeve as she dragged the crate across a patch of thorny weeds. The heavier trunk required all her strength to shove into a position where the shadows of the big tree and the thick juniper and yew bushes concealed it from anyone who happened by.

Straightening, she scrutinized her hiding place. Anyone milling around the livery at the edge of town was unlikely to see her through the brush. It was the best she could do.

The descending sun marked the signal for most of the businesses in town to close their doors. Most, but not all. Down the main street at the center of town, the Willow Creek Hotel with its fine brick facade attracted a steady stream of people coming and going.

Boisterous clamor increased at the saloon. A shudder rippled through her when she imagined the amount of whiskey consumed there each night and its effect on the families of the men who patronized the place.

Tessa wrapped the remains of her dinner in the store paper. When she opened the door of Mama's cabinet to tuck her provisions into a safe place, the Bible she'd hugged earlier begged to be picked up. Why, she didn't know. What could God possibly have to say to her? Still, perhaps reading the same words Mama read might offer comfort.

She extracted a tattered quilt pieced from flour sack scraps from the trunk and arranged a makeshift pallet under the broad limbs of the elm. She peered around the juniper boughs, searching for signs of snakes then made herself as comfortable as possible and opened the Bible. The waning light fell on the pages of the Psalms. Mama's favorites were dog-eared and underlined. Extra marks by the verses of Psalm 27 indicated Mama found solace in them.

With the book positioned to use all the light available, she began to read what her mother found comforting. One verse spoke of hiding her in the time of trouble. Did that mean God would conceal her from prying eyes during the night? She read another verse.

"Leave me not, neither forsake me, O God of my salvation."

Was God aware that she was alone and frightened, hiding in the bushes like some kind of animal? Did He know about the fear knotting her stomach as the noise from the saloon built to a raucous din? In the dim glow of the final ray of light, she held up the book and squinted at the next verse.

"When my father and my mother forsake me, then the LORD will take me up."

The Bible slipped from her grasp and fell to her lap. Mama always said God kept His promises. If that verse was a promise, it surely wasn't meant for her. Only people worthy of God's love received His favor, and Papa always said she "wasn't worth nothin'."

૨

The morning sun fell across the ledger as Gideon added up the last column one more time. He totaled up the net profits and frowned at the number. The grim number remained the same no matter how many times he reworked the figures. Every month since Kilgore bought the Willow Creek Emporium, that number shrank a bit more.

He blew out a noisy sigh and slammed the journal shut. The bell on the front door jingled, and Gideon looked up to see the preacher entering the store. "Hello, Pastor Witherspoon. What can I get for you today?"

"Morning, Gideon." The silver-headed pastor handed Gideon a scrap of paper. "Here's my wife's list. How's business?"

"Well Pastor, things are getting a little tighter all the time."

Fatherly concern deepened the lines around the preacher's eyes. "That a fact? Does this have anything to do with Henry Kilgore taking over the Emporium?"

Gideon pulled two cans of applesauce from the shelf and set them on the counter before pausing to look at the preacher. "I know every man has a right to make a living." He ran his fingers through his hair. "Kilgore is undercutting my price on just about everything. I understand that times are tough. If folks can save a few cents by going to the Emporium, I don't suppose I can blame them." He heaved a deep sigh. "But Pastor, he's pulling so many of my regular customers away from me, I don't know how much longer I'll be able to stay in business. And I've cut my own prices to the bare minimum."

Gideon cast a glance toward the boardwalk and lowered his voice. "For the past two years, Kilgore's been buying up businesses all over town. He owns the hotel and, of course, his saloons, the newspaper, the tannery, even seven or eight of the farms around here. He practically forced Mr. Lee to sell the Emporium last year. Cully told me Kilgore is trying to buy the livery. Why?"

The preacher frowned. "I can't understand why Kilgore is doing this. Besides the Emporium, seems like he owns half the town now, and I hear tell he's trying to buy the bank."

"The bank? Can he do that?"

Pastor Witherspoon scratched his head. "I suppose, if he's got enough money."

"No doubt about him having enough money." Gideon resumed filling the preacher's order. "He wants to buy me out."

"What? Gideon, you mustn't sell. If Kilgore gets control of this place, he'll fix prices and we'll all be at his mercy."

"I know that, Preacher. The fact is, my dream is to sell this place and start a horse breeding farm. I've been looking at some land, and I've sent out some inquiries about purchasing breeding stock." Gideon placed a box of lucifers beside the pastor's accumulated order and paused to search the kindly older man's face. "Pastor, I want to sell the mercantile to anybody but Kilgore, but his is the only offer I've gotten."

The preacher rubbed his chin. "I'll surely pray about this. You can count on that."

The bell on the door drew their attention as Tessa Langford walked into the store. Her faded green dress was clean, and her hair was neatly wound and pinned into a bun. When he smiled at her, she looked at the floor and twisted her fingers.

"Hello, Tessa. It's nice to see you again."

"Hello. . .Gideon. Hello, Pastor Witherspoon." Her voice was so soft Gideon barely caught her response.

"Tessa." The preacher smiled at her. "I heard you and your father had already pulled out. I guess I was mistaken."

Tessa's chin lifted a tad, and she straightened her shoulders. "No, Pastor, you weren't mistaken. I think Papa left yesterday morning."

Gideon and the preacher traded looks, and Pastor Witherspoon's brow furrowed. "What do you mean, you think he left? Are you saying that you didn't know he was leaving?"

Tessa blinked several times while her chin quivered, but she simply shook her head. "No, I didn't." She turned to Gideon. "I wondered if there might be a position available here at the mercantile. I am in need of employment."

Anger rushed through Gideon. He didn't understand the malice with which Tessa's father lashed out at her and could only attribute it to the man's drunkenness, but what kind of a father abandoned his daughter? He swallowed back the remark he wanted to make.

"Tessa, do you have a place to live?"

She dropped her gaze again. "Well, yes I do, sort of."

Pastor Witherspoon put his hand on Tessa's shoulder. "Child, you aren't old enough to be living on your own."

The tiniest hint of a half smile tilted one corner of her mouth. "I'm nineteen." She looked back at Gideon. "I'm old enough to take care of myself. All I need is a job."

Indignation filled Gideon's chest. Here she was, the same age as his sister who was engaged to be married. But Martha had a big brother to look out for her until her wedding day. Tessa had no one.

Her attempt to appear strong and composed was evident, unlike yesterday when her tears couldn't be hidden. An inclination to protect this young woman filled him. He didn't understand such feelings, knowing her only a few days. Someone certainly should be looking after her, but regardless of any willingness on his part, it didn't change the facts.

"I'm so sorry, Tessa. I'm sorry your father went off and left you, and I'm especially sorry that I can't hire you. I wish I could."

"I wish I could."

Tessa smiled. How she managed to smile in her position, he didn't know, but it endeared her to him. She thanked him and bid the preacher good-bye and walked out the door. When she stepped onto the boardwalk, however, Gideon noticed her shoulders slump. Oh, how he hated being the cause of her disappointment. He watched her walk across the street and wondered how many more places would turn her away.

❧

Tessa stared at the ornate decor in the hotel lobby while she waited for the clerk to finish checking in a gentleman. The room was fancier than anything she'd ever seen. Polished wood paneling and molding set off maroon and ivory wallpaper with gold filigrees. A crystal chandelier matched the sparkling wall sconces. Even the clerk behind the marble-topped desk wore a black linen coat and necktie.

When the transaction was completed, Tessa stepped forward.

The clerk, a middle-aged man with thin hair and a thick belly, swept a lecherous gaze over her from head to toe. "Well now, what can I do for you?" He arched one eyebrow. The corner of his mouth twitched in a salacious smile.

Tessa didn't like the way he looked at her, but her need for a job pushed her uneasiness aside. "I'm looking for employment, sir. I can do just about anything. I can scrub and make beds, do laundry and—"

"Just about anything, huh? Well, Willow Creek can use some new talent." His chuckle sounded purely evil. "But you're in the wrong place, darlin'. You need to go over to the Blue Goose."

"Blue Goose? What's that?"

The man threw back his head and belly laughed, slapping his thigh. "The Blue Goose Saloon. It's down the street a ways. Some fancy feathers and a little paint, not to mention getting you out of that flour sack dress, and you might be a real welcome addition to the stable down there."

When Tessa understood his suggestion, she sucked in a sharp breath. Her face flamed with indignation. "Sir, that's not the kind of employment I'm seeking."

She spun and nearly collided with a portly gentleman with an unlit cigar sticking out of his teeth.

"Excuse me. . . ." She attempted to step around the man, but he caught her arm.

"Whoa, not so fast there, young lady." The cigar waggled up and down as he spoke, and she didn't know how he managed to keep it from falling out of his mouth.

"My name's Kilgore. I own this place. I heard you tell my clerk you need a job. Why don't we go sit over here and talk?"

Hope sprang up in Tessa's heart. She resisted glaring at the desk clerk and followed Mr. Kilgore through an arched doorway to a table in the corner of the hotel dining room. The same wallpaper that adorned the lobby covered the walls in this room. Fancy tapestry drapes embellished the windows, and the tables boasted fine linens and crystal glassware.

He held the maroon tapestry-covered chair for her and called to the waitress to bring two cups of tea. After he lowered himself to the chair opposite her, he interlaced his fingers and tapped his thumbs together. "Now, young lady, tell me about yourself."

Tessa swallowed hard and fingered the edge of the ivory damask tablecloth.

"I'm Tessa Langford. I can clean, do laundry, and cook. I'm good with sums, and I'm sure I could learn any job quickly." The waitress arrived with the tea, and Tessa took the opportunity to smooth her faded dress.

Mr. Kilgore stirred sugar into his cup and sat back in his chair looking her up and down in the same manner as the desk clerk. "Have you ever waited tables?"

"No sir, but I'm sure I can learn."

"You'd have to be friendly with the customers. The friendlier you are, the more they buy. If they like you, they might stick around for. . .other services."

Confusion churned in her stomach. She glanced around the room. "I'm certain I can learn to wait tables, but I don't understand what other services you mean."

Mr. Kilgore removed his cigar and took a sip of tea. "Don't be coy, Miss Langford. I'm not talking about waiting tables here in the hotel. You're better suited to my other establishments. I own the two best saloons in town, the Gilded Lily and the Blue Goose. I'm always looking to hire fresh young women who know how to satisfy my clientele. The right girl can make good money. Of course, I take my cut, but you could do well."

Tessa shot a glance through the archway to the hotel lobby. The desk clerk leaned forward on his elbows and watched her with a nauseating grin. She wanted to slap the faces of both men. Maybe Papa was right; the kind of degrading employment Mr. Kilgore was offering her was the best she could do, but honoring Mama's memory prevailed. She'd rather starve than serve whiskey to men like Papa. She pushed her teacup away and stood. "I'm sorry, Mr. Kilgore, but I'm not looking for that kind of work."

Before she could take a step, the man motioned for her to sit down. She didn't sit but waited to hear if anything he had to say resembled an apology.

"All right, maybe you think this is a Sunday school picnic and you're one of those people who thinks they're better than anybody else. That's fine, if you want to be pigheaded. I'm telling you, you could do a lot better, but if that's what you want, I can use someone else here in the kitchen and dining room. Thirty-five cents a day."

Tessa lifted her chin. "I need a place to stay, and I can't pay rent on thirty-five cents a day."

Kilgore scoffed. "I suppose you expect me to put you up in the grand suite?"

She stood her ground without blinking.

"Sassy little thing, aren't you? All right, there's a shed out back you can stay in, and I won't charge you rent. But I have to warn you—the tips you'll get here aren't even close to what you'd make at my other establishments."

Tessa remained standing. "Working in the kitchen and waiting tables in the dining room is just fine with me."

Kilgore stood and looked her over again, then he called the waitress over. "Tillie, take Miss Langford here to the kitchen, and tell Flossie she's the new worker."

As Tessa turned to follow the girl, Kilgore called after her. "You think about what I said, and let me know if you change your mind."

She paused and half turned. "I thank you for this job, Mr. Kilgore, but I won't change my mind."

The man hooked a thumb under his suspender and snorted. "Suit yourself."

❧

The woman named Flossie stirred a large pot of thick stew while she studied Tessa. With her free hand, she pushed back drab brown hair that had escaped its loose bun. Crow's-feet framed her eyes. Suspicion steeled her gaze into a defensive wall. "Old man Kilgore might've said you was hired, but I ain't gonna train anyone to take over my job."

The cook's declaration took Tessa aback. "Oh no, ma'am, I'm not here to take anyone's job. It's my understanding I'm supposed to work *with* you."

The waitress, Tillie, crossed the kitchen. "Flossie, you keep askin' how Kilgore expects us to do everything. Maybe she's just here to help, like she says." She took biscuits from the warming oven and added them to her tray. "Give her a chance."

"Flossie, that's all I want—a chance."

The cook grumbled under her breath and turned her back to Tessa. "There's an apron on the hook in the corner. You can get started scrubbin' those pots. Don't have to show you how to scrub pots, do I?"

"No ma'am."

"Ma'am? Nobody calls me ma'am."

Tessa poured hot water from the reservoir on the side of the huge stove into a bucket. "My mama taught me to show respect when I meet new people."

Flossie just grunted and continued stirring. "Don't know that you're strong enough to be of much help. You're a scrawny little thing."

Tessa didn't look up as she scrubbed a greasy pot. Arguing wouldn't convince Flossie. She'd need to pray for an opportunity to prove herself to the woman.

Pray? She supposed she should pray, but it was hard enough just reading Mama's Bible. If she asked for help, would God listen?

Chapter 4

Tessa hung her apron on the peg and glanced once more across the spotless kitchen. Her raw hands stung, and her feet ached, but she had a job. Her body begged for rest, but she needed to go back to the elm tree and gather her belongings before she found Mr. Kilgore's shed.

She tried not to think about the fact she'd be living in a shed. Even without having laid eyes on the place, she presumed it wouldn't be more than a shack—probably unlivable when the cold weather arrived, if Iowa winters were as cold as Indiana winters. If she was frugal with her earnings for four or five months, surely she'd be able to save enough to afford a small room at Mrs. Dunnigan's place, at least for the winter.

She stepped out the side door into the alley. Lengthening shadows lined her way as she hurried down the street. The heightening noise from the saloons carried on the evening air, piquing her uneasiness. Drunken men always meant trouble.

As she passed Maxwell's Mercantile, the door opened and Gideon exited. When he looked up, recognition lit his eyes. "Tessa, good evening. I hope you had some luck finding a job." The same apologetic tone he'd used earlier colored his voice.

"I did, thank you. I'm working at the hotel."

Even in the deepening shadows, she saw him scowl. "You're working for Kilgore?"

"Yes." No sense humiliating herself by telling him of Kilgore's first offer. "I'm working in the kitchen and dining room. If you'll excuse me, I'm very tired, and I still have to move my things."

"Your things?"

"Yes. Mr. Kilgore was kind enough to give me a place to stay behind the hotel. I need to move my belongings there."

When she started around him, Gideon stopped her. "Please, allow me to help. I can't stand by and let a lady carry her own luggage, especially after she's worked hard all day."

Tessa's jaw dropped. A lady? Papa would hoot with laughter to hear her referred to as a lady. She couldn't fault Gideon for his mistake. He was merely being polite, and in her weariness she couldn't turn down his offer. "All right. I would appreciate the help."

She led the way past the livery to the elm tree. In the gathering twilight, she glanced at Gideon, and a butterfly hiccuped in her stomach. Her nerves stood at attention. He'd already demonstrated kindness, but trust wasn't given away easily. Vulnerability invited contempt. She drew in a tentative breath. "My things are over there." She pointed toward the underbrush.

Gideon stared at her. "You mean to tell me you've been staying outside? I thought you were at Mrs. Dunnigan's."

She shrugged and continued toward the elm. "I was for one night, but I couldn't stay there indefinitely. I have no money."

"And you wouldn't take charity, is that it?"

She didn't look at him but sensed he wore the same sympathetic expression he'd worn earlier.

"You know, Tessa, there's nothing wrong with accepting help from a friend."

She wasn't sure what that word meant. She had no friends. Everything she loved was buried in the cemetery.

"Tessa?" His voice coaxed her gaze in his direction. "I thought we were friends. Friends help each other. But you can only have a friend if you be a friend."

She hardly knew what to say. He was offering something she'd never had. "Gideon, you don't know anything about me."

He walked back to the livery and picked up a lantern hanging on a post. The glow of the flame sent fingers of light dancing across his face as he returned to where she stood. "I know you loved your mother and your heart is broken. And I know you need a friend." He shifted the lantern to the other hand. "I'd like the chance to get better acquainted with you. But for now, let's get your things moved to your new place. I don't think Cully will mind if we borrow his wheelbarrow."

She was too tired to argue.

Gideon handed her the lantern and pushed the wheelbarrow from the side of the corral close to the elm. He hoisted the trunk first and balanced it over the hand grips. As he loaded the cabinet, he ran his hand over the carving on the front. "This is fine work."

"My grandfather carved that cabinet for my grandmother when they were first married. Mama brought it with her when she and Papa left Kentucky to move to Indiana. It's the only thing Mama had to remind her of her parents."

Gideon traced the intricate detail with his finger and gave a low whistle. "Your grandfather was a fine craftsman." When he turned the cabinet to steady it, the right side door wobbled. "It looks like this hinge is broken. I'd be happy to fix it for you."

Tessa shook her head. "I don't have the money."

Gideon turned with an exasperated sigh and put his hands on his hips. "There you go again. Can't you just let me fix it because I want to?"

Wariness prodded her. Nobody put themselves out without expecting something in return. She wondered if he expected favors she was unwilling to give. "Why are you being so nice to me?"

He picked up the lantern, and the light played across the space between them. His eyes studied her, but not the way the hotel clerk's did. Even in the flickering light, she saw something different about Gideon, but she couldn't distinguish what it was.

"The Bible says, 'A man that hath friends must shew himself friendly.' I just want to be your friend, Tessa. There aren't any strings attached." He handed her the lantern and picked up the handles of the wheelbarrow. "C'mon, let's go find this place Kilgore was so generous to *give* you."

When they reached the corner of the alley bordering the hotel, Tessa halted. "If you'll please put my things right here, I can manage. Thank you for your help."

Gideon frowned. "But—"

"*Please.*"

❧

Gideon chafed at the memory of Tessa setting her jaw and insisting he leave her things at the corner. Her stubborn stance declared there was no use arguing the point. He'd done as she requested, deposited her belongings and left, but he'd fought with his pillow all night thinking about it.

The following morning as Gideon swept off the boardwalk, a friendly voice hailed him.

"Hey Gideon."

Gideon looked up.

His friend, Ty Sawyer, set the brake on his wagon and hopped down. A thatch of blond hair stuck out in a dozen directions when he removed his sweat-stained hat, and his lopsided grin reminded Gideon of the trouble they used to get into together in their childhood days.

"Hey Ty. Haven't seen you in town for nigh onto a month."

They tromped into the store where Ty promptly helped himself to a handful of gumdrops from the jar on the counter. "Came in for supplies. A pound of coffee, cornmeal, couple pounds of bacon, beans, some white sewing thread, and some ten-penny nails." He popped an orange gumdrop in his mouth and looked around. "Where is everybody?"

Gideon propped the broom in the corner. "Probably over at the Willow Creek Emporium."

"Hmph, Kilgore's place? It's not likely I'll ever do business with Kilgore again. That land deal soured my opinion of him."

Gideon scooped a handful of nails and dumped them into a sack. "Is this enough?"

Ty glanced into the sack. "That'll do. I had the down payment for that piece of bottomland I'd been looking at. You know the place where we used to hunt rabbits?" Without waiting for Gideon's reply, Ty continued. "Mr. Sewell said the bank would carry a loan for five years." Ty shook his head. "A week later he turned me down, and I found out it was Kilgore who denied the loan."

"How could he do that? Mr. Sewell's the bank president, not Kilgore."

Ty chewed another gumdrop. "I heard Kilgore's bought out fifty-one percent of the bank stock."

Gideon scowled. "But why would he refuse you a loan?"

Ty snorted. "Never got a straight answer on that, but you know who owns that piece of bottomland now?"

Gideon raised his eyebrows. "Not Kilgore."

"Mm-hmm."

"Why? He's not a farmer."

"No, he ain't. Mr. Sewell told me the *new owner* might sell me the property, but the price suddenly tripled."

Footsteps on the boardwalk drew Gideon's attention. Kilgore stood in the open door, an arrogant smirk on his face. He puffed his stubby cigar and ambled inside.

Ty counted out his money and handed it to Gideon before picking up his purchases. "See you around, Gideon." He headed toward the door.

"Thanks, Ty."

The young man sent a stiff nod in Kilgore's direction. "Mr. Kilgore."

Kilgore stuck his thumbs in his suspenders and replied with a condescending snort. "Sawyer." Kilgore sauntered to the counter. "Say, Maxwell, you should come to the hotel and see the pretty little tart I just hired to wait tables. She's sassy and holier-than-thou, but I'll tame her in short order."

The disrespectful reference to Tessa set Gideon's teeth on edge. "That's no way to talk about a lady, Kilgore."

Kilgore sneered and blew a puff of smoke in Gideon's direction. He turned and cast a wide glance around the store. "When you get ready to unload this dump, you know where to find me." He exited and strolled down the boardwalk.

Self-accusation burned in Gideon's chest. If only he could have hired Tessa himself. The prospect of Kilgore paying Tessa an honest wage for an honest day's work filled him with misgivings.

❧

Tessa's feet throbbed as she bumped open the kitchen door with her hip. Her stomach growled at the aroma of the beef stew, pork chops, steak, and fresh biscuits on her tray. She forced a smile as she placed steaming platters before three men at a corner table.

"You're new here, ain't ya?"

Tessa set a basket of warm biscuits on their table and started toward the next table where a party waited to order, but the man in the plaid shirt and leather vest grabbed her hand.

"Hey now, don't be in such a hurry." The dark-haired cowboy waggled his thick eyebrows. "Why don't you stick around, and maybe me and you can get better acquainted."

Her breath caught in her throat, and her heart accelerated as she twisted her arm trying to extract her hand.

He tightened his grip.

Her stomach constricted, and nausea rose to her throat. "Please excuse me. I have other customers."

The man's laughter drove chills down her spine, and he reeked of whiskey. "We was gonna order dessert. Maybe you can"—he cast a surreptitious glance over his shoulder and leaned toward her—"offer some suggestions."

She yanked her arm free and took a step backward. "Our dessert menu for today is"—her voice trembled—"apple pie, chocolate cake, or raisin pudding."

"Tessa!" Mr. Kilgore's voice boomed across the dining room, and every patron in the place turned in his direction.

Tessa scurried over to her boss. "Yes sir?"

"I'm not paying you to stand around and chat. If you can't attend to your duties, I don't need you."

Tessa felt every eye in the dining room on her as she stood under the lash of Kilgore's upbraiding. Her face burned, and she couldn't gulp enough air to satisfy her lungs.

"I'm sorry, Mr. Kilgore. I tried to—"

"If your trying isn't good enough, I'll find someone else. Now get back to work, and don't let me catch you lollygagging again."

Her tongue seemed stuck to the roof of her mouth. She'd listened to Papa's tirades for as long as she could remember and survived them. Subjecting herself to Mr. Kilgore's abuse wasn't any different except that Mr. Kilgore was paying her. She needed this job.

She took orders from two other tables and scurried to the kitchen to find Flossie at the sink pumping water over her hand and groaning. "Flossie, what's wrong?"

The cook growled under her breath and continued to pump water.

Tillie spoke up as she filled the orders Tessa left on the serving counter. "She spilled hot grease over her hand. I told her to pour cold water over it."

Tessa peered over Flossie's shoulder. Angry blisters already formed on the inflamed skin. Tessa grimaced, imagining the pain.

Flossie dipped her head to one side and wailed. "What am I gonna do? If I tell Mr. Kilgore I can't work for a few days because of this, he'll fire me. This job is the only thing keepin' us goin' since our wheat crop got flooded out last year."

Tessa's heart broke for the woman. Her hands mechanically filled coffee cups and cut slices of pie as she tried to think of a way to help Flossie. Sympathy shuddered through her as she left the kitchen with her loaded tray.

As she set two plates of apple pie before a lady and a gentleman, an idea gradually formed in her head. She cleared off adjacent tables and hurried back to the kitchen where Flossie leaned forlornly against the big worktable, holding her hand in obvious agony while Tillie applied goose grease to the blisters. "Flossie, I'd like to help you."

"Why?"

Tessa blinked. Why indeed? Maybe the way Gideon helped her had something to do with it. When everyone in her world had left her, Gideon stepped forward. She remembered the verse about having friends he quoted to her.

Mama taught that verse to her when she was a little girl afraid to go to school for the first time. Gideon brought it back to her memory.

She smiled at Flossie. "Because the Bible teaches if we want friends, we must first be a friend."

A furrow dented Flossie's brow. Maybe she wasn't familiar with the scripture, or she simply didn't trust Tessa. Perhaps both.

She'd have to show Flossie she was serious. "When do you usually do your baking?"

Flossie cast a doubtful look in her direction. "Early in the morning, before the breakfast crowd starts coming in. Why?"

Tessa looked at both Flossie and Tillie. "If we work together, I think everything can still go smoothly and Flossie can keep her job." She turned to look directly at the cook. "Flossie, you can still cook. It will just take you a lot longer to do things with one hand. But we can help, can't we, Tillie?"

Tillie shrugged. "Sure. I'll help wherever I can."

Tessa gave Flossie an encouraging smile. "Tillie can lend a hand cutting up the vegetables and preparing the meat. I'll come in early, the same time you do, but I'll do the baking, and you can get started on the day's menu."

Flossie stared at Tessa while she cradled her injured hand. "You would do that for me?"

It felt good to smile. "Yes. I don't want you to lose your job, Flossie. And besides, I really enjoy baking."

Flossie grunted. "And I hate to bake. I only did it because I had to."

Tillie glanced toward the door. "What if Mr. Kilgore finds out?"

"He never comes into the kitchen, and as long as the work gets done, why should he care?"

Flossie hesitated then nodded her head. "I don't know why you're doin' this for me, but I appreciate it."

"C'mon, let's get the kitchen cleaned up and ready for tomorrow." Tessa plunged her hands into the soapy water and made short work of the dishes. In less than an hour, she slipped out the side door and made her way to the shed.

The ramshackle, lean-to structure constructed partially of sod blocks and partially of irregular widths of boards wasn't much to look at, but at least it had a roof. Unexpectedly, Gideon came to mind. She wasn't sure why it mattered to her, but she was glad he hadn't seen the place the night he helped her carry her things.

She pushed open the door. "In a few months I'll have enough saved to afford a room at Mrs. Dunnigan's place for the winter."

She pulled the much-mended quilt from the trunk and spread it on the earthen floor. Flossie had given her a leftover biscuit and a spoonful of cold gravy to take home. She added the last bit of cheese and a few crackers to finish out her meager meal. As she nibbled, she pretended the biscuit was still hot and fresh and the gravy warm and savory instead of cold.

She wrapped the last two crackers in the paper to save for her breakfast, but when she started to return the bundle to the cabinet, something caught her eye. She stared hard through the shadows, trying to determine what it was. Then it moved—no, it scurried. She bit back a scream.

Chapter 5

"S cat!" Tessa banged her hand on the trunk lid to scare the mouse away. She wasn't inclined to share either her quarters or her food with rodents. A shiver sent gooseflesh up her arms.

If she planned to read Mama's Bible, she'd best hurry. Night shadows loomed, driving the rays of sun behind the horizon.

Tessa took a seat in the doorway with the book angled to catch every bit of available light. She flipped pages until she came to Psalm 27. Her eyes scanned the verses she'd previously read, and she turned the page. Her lips formed the words as she read the rest of the psalm in the dusk. Her finger traced the last verse.

"Wait on the LORD: be of good courage, and he shall strengthen thine heart."

She closed the book carefully and laid it in her lap. The last bit of light faded, but the words she'd read echoed in her mind.

"It sounds like a promise. God, Mama always told me I could trust the words of this book. It says You will take me up since Mama and Papa are both gone. Does that mean You'll take care of me? Is that what I'm supposed to wait for?"

She leaned against the doorframe. "And what about Gideon? He says he wants to be my friend. But what if he goes away, too?"

God's answer didn't echo from heaven.

Fatigue draped around her like a heavy cloak. She scooted aside and started to close the door only to realize she'd be closing the mice in with her.

A shudder rippled through her. Which was better—sleeping with mice or leaving the door open so anyone could enter? She shrugged at the obvious. The mice could come and go as they pleased whether she shut the door or not, and a closed door didn't offer security since there was no latch. Tomorrow she'd find a stout stick to brace the door closed.

She stretched out on one side of the quilt and pulled the other half over her. Her eyelids grew heavy as she listened for the skitter of tiny feet.

❧

A cacophony of laughter accosted her ears. Faces of men loomed before her, their leering eyes hungry as they reached out to grab her.

She pulled away from one only to bump against another. She gasped and whirled in the opposite direction where another man closed in. Her breath caught in her throat, strangling her screams. The men laughed as she pushed against them.

In the middle of the encroaching sea of intimidating faces was Mr. Kilgore. His stubby cigar waggled up and down as he repeated his declaration of the wages she'd earn working at the Blue Goose.

She strained for breath as panic filled her. "No, I won't! Leave me alone!"

Kilgore guffawed. "The friendlier you are, the more they buy, and if they like you, they might stick around. . .stick around. . . ."

"A man that hath friends must shew himself friendly." Gideon's smiling face came into view. "I thought we were friends. You can only have a friend if you be a friend."

She almost took a step toward him but halted abruptly when another face in the crowd pushed forward.

"You ain't worth nothin'." The hateful accusation spewed from Papa's lips. "It's your fault. You ain't worth nothin'. . . ."

Tessa lurched awake with a cry. Sweat dripped from her temples and slid down her cheek. Or was that a tear?

She consciously slowed her breathing and lay back down on the quilt. Without a clock, her only means to gauge the time was the level of noise coming from the saloon. The earlier fever pitch was now silent. She didn't know what time the establishment closed, probably the wee hours. If she allowed herself to go back to sleep, she might rise too late to help Flossie with the baking.

She rose and shook the quilt, hoping her unwelcome visitors found someplace else to spend the night. The door squeaked as she pushed it open. No illumination from the street lanterns reached the shed. Blackness enveloped the alley.

Her hands groped along the brick wall as she made her way toward the side door that opened to the hotel kitchen. Once inside, she struck a match and found the lamp hanging over the worktable. The wick caught easily, and she slid the glass globe back into place. After she fed the banked coals in the cookstove, she crossed to the cavernous pantry.

From the shelves she gathered spices, sugar, and a crock of lard. Three large baskets of apples sat beside the flour barrel.

By the time Flossie came in the side door with her hand wrapped in a clean rag, three apple pies wafted their cinnamon fragrance through the kitchen, while Tessa crimped the crust of three more on the worktable.

"Good morning, Flossie. How is your hand feeling today?"

The cook looked down at the makeshift bandage and shrugged. "Don't help to complain. I just hope it don't get no fever in it."

Tessa started to suggest Flossie have the doctor take a look at the burn but held her tongue. Doctors cost money. She bit her lip and returned to her task.

❧

A week after taking over the baking, Tessa's apple pies and chocolate cakes earned numerous compliments. Working the dough with her fingers gave her satisfaction, and pulling fragrant pastries from the oven brought a measure of contentment she'd not known for a long time.

Tillie stuck her head in the door. "Tessa, there's a girl out here who wants to know if you can make a wedding cake."

Tessa looked up from the chocolate cake she was frosting and thought for a moment. "Sure." She considered the cost of the supplies and the extra time involved. "Tell her. . .two dollars and a half."

Flossie smirked as Tillie left to deliver the message. "Don't reckon Mr. Kilgore knows about our arrangement yet, but if folks keep asking for special orders, he might wonder why."

Flossie unwrapped her hand, and Tessa crossed the kitchen to inspect the wound. The inflamed red flesh didn't appear to be healing as fast as Tessa hoped. "Flossie, you must go see the doctor."

The woman shook her head. "Even if I had the money for a doctor, I couldn't take the chance of Kilgore finding out."

Tessa wondered if Gideon carried a burn remedy at the mercantile. It couldn't hurt to ask.

The thought of Gideon ignited a warm rush of feelings—the same feelings she'd experienced when his face appeared in her awful dream a week ago. Having Gideon close by felt comfortable. Maybe because he wanted to be her friend. She refused to entertain thoughts of his being anything more.

❧

The bell on the door jingled, and Gideon looked up to see his sister, Martha, entering the mercantile. A radiant blush glowed on her cheeks, and her green eyes sparkled. "Good afternoon, big brother." She planted a kiss on Gideon's cheek.

He grinned at her. "You certainly look like there's nothing wrong in your world today."

"What could be wrong?" Martha extended her arms and pirouetted. "God has answered my prayers, and in a few weeks, I'll be Mrs. Theodore Luskin."

Gideon smiled as peace filled his heart. Martha was marrying a fine, hardworking, Christian young man who adored her. "So what brings you to our establishment today?"

"This week's mail." She pulled the envelopes from her reticule and laid them on the counter.

She pressed her palms against the worn wood and beamed. "I just came from the hotel dining room. Their desserts are wonderful. The chocolate cake. . . mmmm." She closed her eyes and smiled as though she could taste the confection from memory.

Gideon leaned against the counter. "Did you and Ted have lunch there?"

Martha shook her head, and the gold tendrils that framed her face danced. "No, his mother came to town today so we could discuss the wedding with Pastor Witherspoon, and she took me to the hotel for lunch. We asked if the cook could make a wedding cake, and she said yes."

Gideon frowned. He didn't wish to deny his sister, but even the smallest luxuries cost money. "Did you happen to get a price for this cake?"

Martha's countenance fell, and her voice lost some of its joy. "She said two dollars and a half."

Gideon felt like a cad. His declining business wasn't Martha's worry. How could he rob her of her happy anticipation? He reached over and patted her hand. "Go ahead and order the cake, honey." *I'll manage to pay for it somehow.*

His sister came around the counter and hugged him. "Oh, thank you, Gideon. I'll see you tonight at supper."

He bid her good-bye and watched her dash up the stairs to their living quarters. He wished his parents could have lived long enough to see their daughter married. How pleased Pa would have been to walk Martha down the aisle.

Troubling thoughts of Tessa arose once again. The way her father hurled horrible accusations at her sickened him. Gideon puzzled over Langford's unreasonable attack on Tessa. How could the man possibly blame her for her mother's death? He couldn't imagine his own father telling Martha she was worthless. On the contrary, his father adored his daughter. He shook his head and breathed a prayer for Tessa's safety and comfort. Her welfare had become a regular request whenever he communed with God.

He sorted through the mail. The return address on one envelope made his heart leap—the long-awaited answer from a horse breeder in Illinois. He tore open the flap and extracted the missive. A smile climbed into his face as he read. The man was willing to sell him a Belgian stallion at a reasonable price. The letter included terms and suggestions for taking delivery.

The only thing standing between him and his dream of owning a spread and breeding horses was the sale of the mercantile. Now with the promise of a stallion, he allowed himself to daydream about a pasture full of fine animals, bred especially for the needs of farmers—powerful horses that could pull a plow or a heavy wagon and help a farmer clear a field of rocks and stumps, yet gentle enough to take the family to church on Sunday. If he accepted Kilgore's offer, he could move ahead with his plans. Despite the foul taste left in his mouth whenever he thought about the man, Kilgore's offer looked better all the time.

The door's jingling bell interrupted his thoughts as Pearl Dunnigan walked in. "Good afternoon, Gideon."

He tucked the letter away. "Hello, Miss Pearl. What can I do for you today?"

The smiling woman reached into her reticule. "It's pretty much the same list every week. Whenever I try to change the menu, my boarders complain that they'd rather have the same fried chicken and pot roast."

Gideon grinned. Miss Pearl's fried chicken was legendary, and her pot roast was fork tender and juicy. "I don't blame them."

She shook her head. "It gets tiring sometimes, especially since I'm getting older. Standing in the kitchen for hours isn't as easy as it was ten years ago. I thought I'd try to get some fresh fruit for dessert instead of having to prepare something."

Gideon glanced at her as he weighed the amount of sugar she needed. "I hear tell the hotel dining room is turning out some pretty good pies and cakes. Martha's planning to order her wedding cake from there. Maybe you could give yourself a break and pick up a couple of pies."

Miss Pearl put her hands on her hips. "Why, Gideon Maxwell, what an excellent idea. You know Mr. Clemmons who boards at my place thinks Mr. Kilgore must have hired himself a new cook."

Her observation gave Gideon pause. Kilgore said Tessa was waiting tables. "That a fact?"

Mrs. Dunnigan laughed. "You know what a gossip Mr. Clemmons is, so anything he says is purely speculation."

Gideon scooped dried beans into a bag to weigh them. "I might go over there myself and sample some pie. Maybe I'll take Martha along so she can see what an apple pie is supposed to taste like."

"Oh Gideon, shame on you. You shouldn't pick on Martha so. She'll be a fine cook someday."

Gideon didn't put much effort in his attempt to appear repentant. "If I didn't pick on her, she'd think I didn't love her."

"Tsk-tsk. Gideon Maxwell, you're terrible." Miss Pearl shook her head.

Gideon winked at her. "Did you want any molasses or bacon to go with these beans?"

"Hmm, five pounds of bacon, and go ahead and throw in a tin of molasses. Maybe I'll bake some cookies next week."

Gideon accommodated her request and tucked in a couple of the dear lady's favorite peppermint sticks.

Miss Pearl counted out her money, and he carried the loaded box out to the little cart she always pulled along behind her when she ran her errands. "Thank you, Gideon. Now don't you be a stranger. You come and see my Maggie's new batch of kittens."

Gideon grinned. "Haven't you told Maggie she's too old for such nonsense? How many years have you had that old cat?"

"Oh, nigh onto fifteen years, I think. Anyway, this is the cutest litter she's ever had. Maybe Martha would like to pick one out. She's going to be living out on the Luskins' farm. They'll need a good mouser."

"Yes ma'am, I'll ask her. You have a nice afternoon now." He paused in the doorway and considered Miss Pearl's comment about Kilgore hiring a new cook. Could it be Tessa was doing more than just waiting tables?

He glanced up and down the boardwalk. No throngs of customers demanded his attention. It wouldn't hurt to run over to the hotel for a piece of pie.

He locked the door and hurried down the boardwalk. His long strides covered the distance to the hotel in no time. Most of the lunch patrons had already departed when he entered the archway that led to the dining room. He sat down hoping for a glimpse of Tessa.

Instead the regular waitress came over to his table to take his order.

"Hello, Tillie. Do you have any apple pie left?"

Tillie smiled. "It's been going fast these days, but we're turning them out as fast as we sell them. Is that all you want, just pie?"

"And coffee. Thanks."

Tillie hurried away and returned moments later with a generous slab of apple pie and a steaming cup of coffee. "Fifteen cents."

Gideon pulled out two dimes and told Tillie to keep the change. The spicy aroma teased his senses, and his mouth began to water before he tasted the first bite. When the still-warm apples and cinnamon wrapped in flaky crust hit his tongue, he closed his eyes and savored the sweetness. It was beyond any doubt the best apple pie in the county. Would it be too bold for him to ask who made it?

Tillie returned a minute later. "More coffee?"

"No, thanks. But I would like to compliment your cook on this wonderful pie." He waited with hopeful anticipation to learn the identity of the baker.

Confusion traced lines across Tillie's forehead, and she cast a glance over her shoulder. "We all pitch in and share the kitchen duties."

Disappointment pricked him. He'd hoped Tessa was the one turning out the delectable desserts. "Did you make this pie? It's certainly the best I ever ate."

"N–no, it wasn't me." After another nervous glance from side to side, she leaned down to whisper to Gideon. "Actually, we have a new girl who was hired to wait tables, but she's been doing the baking since our cook burned her hand."

So it *was* Tessa! But why did Tillie seem to think Tessa's baking skills should be kept secret?

"If Mr. Kilgore finds out Flossie hurt her hand and isn't doing everything she's supposed to do, he'll fire her. Tessa, the girl who's doing the baking, came up with a plan for her and me to help out so Flossie won't lose her job. In fact, we were wondering if you have anything at the mercantile to use on burns."

Gideon's heart smiled at the thought of Tessa stepping up to help the injured cook, but outwardly he frowned. "Hasn't she seen the doctor?"

Tillie shook her head vehemently.

He pressed his lips together and thought for a moment. "Let me see what I can do."

The waitress smiled in obvious relief. "Thank you."

Gideon shoveled the rest of the pie into his mouth and pressed his fork on the remaining crumbs, unwilling to waste a single morsel. He drained his coffee and rose to leave.

On his way out, his eye caught a glimpse of motion from the second-floor balcony. When his gaze darted upward, he discovered Kilgore standing at the railing, watching him walk across the lobby.

Chapter 6

Gideon itched to contact the man in Illinois regarding the purchase of the stallion, but first things first. A piece of acreage he'd looked at awhile back, land perfectly suited for his dream, called to him. As far as he knew, the parcel remained available.

When he and Martha returned home from church and finished eating Sunday dinner, he walked over to the livery. "Howdy, Cully!"

The old curmudgeon snorted as he startled awake. "Gideon! Why you sneakin' up on a body like that? It's plumb dangerous to come up behind a man, y'know."

Gideon grinned at the gray-haired old coot. "You don't look too dangerous to me, sleeping in that haystack, Cully. Now some of those swayback, lop-eared nags in the corral are another matter. How much do you charge to rent one of those prized steeds?"

Cully brushed off his overalls and picked hay from his scraggly beard. He waved a gnarled hand in the direction of the corral. "Take your pick. If you saddle him yourself, I won't charge you nothin'."

"Thanks, Cully."

Gideon snagged the halter of the nearest horse. Minutes later he tightened the cinch and mounted. Reining the animal through the corral gate, he set off toward the east at a lope.

It'd been months since he'd looked over this piece of land. As he rode, he pictured in his mind every draw and grassy slope and the small creek that meandered through the prime grazing pasture.

He scanned the landscape and found the outcropping of boulders that served as the landmark. He reined the gelding in the direction of what he hoped would someday become his spread. A grove of aspens quivered in the breeze along the northern boundary of the parcel, and the slope was dotted with cottonwoods and birches.

He walked the horse along a line where he imagined sturdy fences for a corral and a large barn for housing his brood mares. Beyond that, the perfect spot for a house came into view, up on a rise surrounded by scrub junipers and sheltered by a stand of white pines and cedars. The creek sang as the water tumbled down the slope and leveled out into the grazing land. If he could have painted a picture of his dream, this would be it.

First thing Monday morning, he planned to be at the land office to confirm the availability of the land. If his dream was to be reality, however, the sale of the mercantile still hung over his head. Kilgore's smug smile tainted his ambition.

He lingered awhile longer, turning his plans over in his head. No need to hurry back since it was Sunday. He dismounted and looped the reins around a low-hanging branch. After taking a moment to inhale the fragrance of the thick spring grass, he hiked up to the spot where he thought to build the house.

The area was elevated just high enough to overlook the acreage spreading out before him. He needed nothing grand in a house but hoped one day to bring a wife to this place and raise a family. There was plenty of room on the rise for a good-sized house, a kitchen garden, a chicken coop, and a grassy area for children to play. In his mind's eye, he saw smoke coming from a stone chimney and a woman hanging laundry on the clothesline with a toddler clinging to her apron. Unexpectedly Tessa's face eased into his thoughts.

Startled, he blinked and the image melted from his mind. When he stopped to consider the idea, he realized Tessa's tender heart and uncomplaining spirit had already endeared her to him. She possessed a spirit of determination that made him smile.

He paused and invited his mind to once again entertain the possibility. Was it so unreasonable to ponder? True, he didn't know a great deal about her other than the love and respect she'd had for her mother and that her father abused then abandoned her. But the very fact that she wasted no time seeking employment and resisted help bespoke of her character. She was unspoiled, wanted a handout from no one, and didn't hesitate to befriend the hotel cook when the woman had a need.

He strolled across the imaginary front porch and leaned down to pluck a few daisies growing where he thought the fireplace ought to be built. He envisioned a warm, comfortable room with a rocking chair beside the hearth. Once more Tessa appeared in the picture, taking her ease in the rocker with a small babe in her arms.

"This is ridiculous. I hardly know the girl." He was glad there was no one about to read his foolish reflections.

But why were they foolish? He and Tessa were friends. What was to stop him from getting to know her better? The idea was not at all unpleasant.

A winsome thought wandered through his mind. "I wonder if Tessa likes daisies." His mouth tweaked with a smile. "Only one way to find out." He bent to add a dozen more flowers to his few and then pulled some long prairie grasses to tie the bunch together.

As he strode back to where the horse was tethered and munching the sweet meadow grass, Gideon's step hesitated. Did Tessa work on Sunday? How should he approach her to hand her the flowers? Knock on the kitchen door? The horse turned his head and gave Gideon a woeful look. "How should I know if she's working today?"

The horse gave an answering snort and shook his head as he pawed the ground. The only thing that interested the beast was heading back to the barn.

"Come on, horse. Let's go." He tucked the stems of the daisies inside his shirt and swung into the saddle. All the way back to town he accused himself of getting off track. After all, the purpose of his excursion was to take another look at the parcel of land he wanted to purchase, not daydream about the woman with whom he might one day share that land.

Gideon shook off the guilt. It wasn't unimaginable to want a wife and family one day as long as he didn't allow his priorities to become out of order. Wanting the kind of marriage his parents had was a fine aspiration. But his first priority was selling the mercantile and purchasing the land. Next, he'd strike a deal with the man from Illinois to purchase a stallion. Finding a wife should come later, after he had a place to offer her.

When he arrived back in Willow Creek, the first person he spotted was Henry Kilgore. Why did it always seem like the man was watching him? Kilgore thrust out his chest and hooked his thumbs in his suspenders, the ever-present cigar hanging out one side of his mouth. As Gideon rode past on his way to the livery, Kilgore nodded to him with a half smirk, like he knew to whom Gideon planned to give the daisies.

Walking into the dining room and handing Tessa the flowers was a stupid plan anyway. The last thing he wanted to do was embarrass her or jeopardize her job. If he couldn't think of a better idea, he'd wind up taking the flowers home to Martha.

≥≥

"I'm telling you, I think you should open a bakery. Just look at these orders. Three whole cakes and five whole pies, and that doesn't include all the servings we sell to the diners every day."

Tessa brushed a floury hand across her chin and continued rolling out piecrusts. Tillie's imagination was running away with her. "Where would I get the money to start a bakery? Sure, I like the idea, and I truly do enjoy baking, but just think of everything I would need."

Flossie snorted. "It ain't likely you'll ever make enough money here, working for Kilgore."

It was true. Her wages barely covered her thrifty needs. The old sock she used to tuck away a bit of savings toward her winter rent remained pitifully slack. How she wished she could afford to look elsewhere for a better paying job. When she made up her mind to survive, she took the first job that came along. Now she feared finding anything better was a fairy tale.

Tillie shrugged. "It's nice to dream."

Tessa had to admit it was an admirable goal, albeit an impossible one. She lifted her shoulders. "I appreciate your compliment. It was a very nice thing to say."

Flossie turned her head to look at Tessa. "We've got a problem, you know."

"What problem?"

Flossie held up her hand. "My hand is getting better since I started using that Porter's Liniment Salve Gideon Maxwell gave me. I can't keep expecting you to do all the baking. But the customers didn't rave about my desserts like they do yours, and if I start doing the baking again, we'll start losing business."

Tessa barely heard Flossie's description of what she deemed a problem. Her focus hung on the cook's first statement. "Gideon gave you that salve? I thought you'd gone to the doctor."

Flossie shook her head, and another lock of mousy brown hair escaped its pins. "No, Gideon brought it from the mercantile. I tried to tell him I didn't have money to pay him, but he just said I needed the salve now and I could pay him later. He told me to soak my hand in eucalyptus tea, too." She turned her hand over to show the healing blisters to Tessa. "See how much better it looks?"

Tessa arched her eyebrows. "That was a very kind thing for him to do." But Gideon's kindness wasn't a surprise. She'd already been the beneficiary of his thoughtfulness more than once. Perhaps it was true that not all men were like Papa. They weren't all drunkards, nor did they all care only for themselves.

"What do you think?"

Tessa's face warmed. What did she think? She thought Gideon Maxwell was a very nice man. Very nice indeed. "About what?"

"Weren't you paying attention? I asked you what you think we should do now that my hand is getting better. Fact is, I should be able to start doing the baking again in another day or two."

Tessa folded the pastry dough over and laid it into the pie plate in front of her. "I haven't given it much thought. I rather like doing the baking. Tillie does more of the serving than I do, although I help her as much as I can. You really do have your hands full just cooking the meals."

Flossie put her hands on her ample hips and stared at her. "Tessa, you're only getting paid thirty-five cents a day because Mr. Kilgore still doesn't know you're doing all the baking."

Tessa shrugged. "The tips have gotten a lot better."

Flossie laughed. "That's because folks love your desserts, not to mention your biscuits, your white bread, and your yeast rolls. The tips won't be as good when they start eating the stuff I bake again."

Tessa and Tillie exchanged looks. "Flossie, you aren't thinking about telling Mr. Kilgore, are you?"

Worry lines dug trenches across Flossie's forehead, and she turned back to the stove. "I don't want to. But it's not right that you're doin' so much work and not gettin' paid for it, Tessa. Before you came here, I'd never had anyone do something so nice for me like you did."

Tessa heard a sniff coming from Flossie's direction. She didn't know what to say. The feeling Flossie described was familiar to her. The day they buried Mama, she experienced more kindness than she'd ever thought existed in the world, and she didn't know what to do to repay the people like the preacher, Mrs. Dunnigan, and Gideon. Especially Gideon.

"Why don't we just continue the way we are? I'm not complaining. I keep trying to tell you I like to bake. It's more enjoyable than waiting tables and dodging rude men." She slid three pies into the oven and wiped her hands on a towel. "As soon as those pies come out of the oven, these loaves of bread will be ready to go in. I'm going to go help Tillie clear tables."

Several diners lingered at their tables over second cups of coffee.

Tessa removed plates and bowls and collected as many compliments as she did tips. She smiled and thanked the patrons and encouraged them to come again. With her tray loaded, she balanced it carefully through the kitchen doors and traded it for a clean, empty one. "Flossie, can you check the water reservoir to make sure we have plenty of hot water? I'll be right back and start these dishes."

Tray in hand, she pushed the kitchen door open again and headed for the other side of the dining room. At the second table, she came face-to-face with Gideon Maxwell.

"Hello there."

"Hello, Gideon. It's nice to see you. Did you enjoy your meal?"

Gideon smiled. "I ate dinner at home. My sister, Martha, is trying to learn to cook before she gets married in a couple of months, and I'm her victim. That is, I'm her loving big brother, so I have to—I mean, I *get* to—eat everything she cooks."

His smile as well as his teasing comment about his sister warmed her and made her wonder what it might be like to sit across the table from him and listen to his rich voice and watch his eyes twinkle. She'd wanted to know him better from the first day she met him, but it hardly seemed appropriate, his being a business owner and her nothing more than a serving girl.

"Do you need more coffee?"

"No, thanks. I just stopped in for a slice of the best apple pie this side of the Mississippi River, and I don't want to wash the taste out of my mouth with coffee."

Heat filled her face, and she couldn't keep from smiling. She lowered her eyes and reached to take his empty plate, noting there wasn't a single crumb left on it.

"I understand you are the one doing the baking."

She caught her breath and glanced to the right and left. "We'd rather nobody knew about that."

Gideon gave her a knowing look. "You mean you'd rather Kilgore didn't know about it."

She didn't know how he'd become privy to the information, but she merely nodded. Gideon could be trusted. "I really like doing it. Tillie even told me I should open a bakery. Of course that's ridiculous. Opening a new business takes money, and I don't make that much. But it was fun to think about."

Gideon nodded. "That does sound like an interesting idea. You should give it some consideration. Maybe you could get a loan from the bank."

"Pfft! Me? Why would the bank want to loan me money? No, it's silly to even allow myself to dream about such a thing."

Gideon appeared to be about to disagree when his expression darkened abruptly.

A hand grabbed Tessa's upper arm and jerked her around. Mr. Kilgore's ferocious expression bore down on her like an awakening grizzly in springtime. "Didn't I tell you not to stand around dawdling?" His fingers dug into her flesh so hard she winced.

Gideon was on his feet in an instant, grabbing hold of Mr. Kilgore's arm. "Let go of her, Kilgore!"

Her boss pulled away from Gideon so forcefully she nearly dropped her tray and lost her footing. "Gideon, please. It's all right. I shouldn't have stopped to talk. I'm sorry, Mr. Kilgore. It won't happen again."

Gideon grabbed the man's jacket lapel and necktie all in one powerful grip. "I said let go of her, Kilgore."

"Who do you think you are, ordering me around in my own hotel? I have half a mind to call the sheriff and have you thrown out of here."

The man's bluster didn't make Gideon back down an inch. As soon as Mr. Kilgore released Tessa's arm, Gideon turned loose of the man's garments.

Mr. Kilgore swore and pointed to the door. "Get out, and don't you set foot in here again."

Tessa's heart pounded in her ears. Fear dug cruel claws up her throat, as she held her breath, anticipating the men coming to blows.

Mr. Kilgore whirled around to growl in her face. "You're fired. Clear out of here." He tossed a few coins at her feet. "That should cover whatever I owe you."

The flinch that shuddered through her felt too familiar.

Chapter 7

Tessa stooped and picked up the coins with a trembling hand. When Papa left her, she thought groveling at a man's feet would become nothing more than an ugly memory, but she was wrong. She could feel Mr. Kilgore's glare boring into her, but the man wouldn't have the pleasure of seeing her cry.

Ignoring the stares of the diners, she fixed her eyes on the kitchen door and walked resolutely between the tables. No more exchanges between Gideon and Mr. Kilgore roared behind her, so she assumed Gideon had left as well.

As soon as the kitchen door closed behind her, she sagged against the worktable and let the tears come.

Flossie and Tillie came immediately to her side.

Flossie patted her on the back. "We heard him bellowing all the way in here."

Tillie slipped an awkward arm around Tessa's shoulders. "I'm so sorry, Tessa."

Tessa dried her eyes with the corner of her apron. "Those pies ought to be just about ready to come out, and the bread is ready to go in."

"Oh, who cares? Let the old buzzard bake his own pies."

Tessa shot a glance at Tillie. "Don't let them burn, or Flossie might get fired, too. Remember, he thinks she's doing the baking." She hung up her apron and exited the side door, only to run squarely into Gideon.

Remorse defined the lines carved in his forehead. "Tessa, I'm so sorry you got fired. But I couldn't sit there and let him put his hands on you."

She stared at him in astonishment.

He must have taken her silence for anger, because contrition filled his tone. "I apologize. It doesn't change anything, and it's my fault you got fired. Please allow me to help you find another job."

Words failed her. Never in all of her nineteen years had she ever seen a man apologize for anything, much less for losing his temper. Twice now Gideon had sprung to her defense. Her eyes remained riveted on his face, and the words she wanted to speak refused to line up in the right order.

"I. . . It. . .it wasn't. . .your fault. I. . .I—"

Gideon grasped both her hands. "Did he hurt you? Is your arm all right?"

Lucidity finally made its way back to her brain. "Yes."

"Yes, he hurt you?"

"No, he didn't hurt me, and yes, my arm is all right. Gideon, why?" Her hands seemed to not have a purpose. She clasped them together and held them to her chin. "*Why* did you get angry? Why did you grab him? I'm not worth your trouble."

Gideon jerked his head up, his eyes darkened. "Don't say that, Tessa. You shouldn't believe those things your father told you. You're a lady, and I will never stand idly by while a lady is treated disrespectfully." The anger on his face softened. "And besides that, you're not just any lady. You're. . .well, you're special."

His face flushed crimson. Perhaps he didn't mean to say what he'd just said. Maybe, like her, he had a hard time putting words together when he was upset. At any rate, his hangdog look spoke volumes. He regretted what happened—but did he regret defending her, or was he just sorry she'd lost her job?

"Well, thank you, Gideon. Don't worry. Something will work out. Mama always said tomorrow will be brighter."

He gave her a tiny smile, lifted his fingers in a half wave, and walked away.

She turned and walked toward the shed. Maybe Mr. Kilgore wouldn't care if she stayed there tonight. She hadn't planned on having to look for a new place to live so soon.

She turned the corner at the end of the alley and stopped short. Stuck in the door handle of the shed was a bouquet of daisies. They looked rather forlorn and slightly wilted, but they seemed to echo Gideon's words. She was worth something, even if it was just a bunch of wildflowers.

If they were from Gideon, it meant he knew where she was living, but somehow it didn't seem to matter. She reversed her direction and trotted down the alley to see which way Gideon had gone.

Just as she reached the boardwalk, Mr. Kilgore stepped out the front door of the hotel. "Ah, there you are."

What did he want? Whatever it was, it couldn't be anything good.

"I suppose you've learned your lesson. In fact, I wondered if you had given any more thought to my previous offer. If you can't manage to serve tables efficiently in the dining room, maybe you're better suited to a different type of establishment. You know, standing around and flirting with my clients at the Blue Goose might make you one of the favorites over there. They like it when the girls are nice to them. What do you say?"

Her mouth dropped open at his audacity, and she snapped it shut before she said something she'd regret. Did he expect her to lick his boots for telling her she could work serving whiskey? Besides, according to Tillie and Flossie, the girls who worked at the saloon did more than just serve drinks. Tessa didn't want to think about what other duties they might have to perform. Maybe the kind of work Mr. Kilgore suggested was the best she could be, but the unceasing tug on her heart reminded her that Gideon thought her to be a lady. She took a deep breath and met Mr. Kilgore's icy eyes. "No, Mr. Kilgore. I will not work in your saloon. Good day."

She started to go around him, but he stretched out his hand to stop her. Her feet froze, and she glared at his hand touching her arm, then up at his face, and back down at his hand.

Mr. Kilgore lifted his hand from her arm and held it slightly aloft, scorn coloring the sneer on his face. With methodic motion, he splayed his fingers and slid his thumbs down his suspenders and cleared his throat. "I understand you're the one who's been doing the baking."

Her pulse skipped a beat. They'd been so careful to keep their secret. She feared for Flossie's job, but she lifted her chin and tried her best to appear poised. "That's right. Flossie burned her hand, and she was afraid you'd fire her. I didn't want to see her lose her job, so I helped out." She again started around him.

This time he had the good sense to keep his hands to himself. "Miss Langford, I've changed my mind. I'm feeling rather generous today, so you can have your job back."

Tessa cocked one eyebrow at him. "At thirty-five cents a day?"

"Well, since you're doing the baking, I could raise you to forty-five cents."

She turned to face him squarely. "Fifty cents and Flossie gets to keep her job."

Mr. Kilgore's face reddened. Though a vein popped out on his neck and his lips tightened around his cigar, she didn't blink.

"All right! Fifty cents." He yanked the stubby cigar from his mouth and pointed it at her. "But you remember one thing. Nobody tells me what to do. Not you or that hypocrite Gideon Maxwell. I don't take that sanctimonious rot from anybody, and don't you forget it. You watch your step." He huffed and stalked down the boardwalk.

An odd mixture of laughter, tears, relief, and disgust welled inside her. Her pulse drummed in her temples, and she couldn't decide whether to look for Gideon or return to her humble dwelling. Instead she did neither. Her knees began to shake, and she sat down on the boardwalk, her lungs heaving like she'd just run a race.

❧

Gideon slammed the door of the living quarters above the mercantile. Fortunately Martha wasn't home to witness his tantrum. Anger seethed through him at the thought of Kilgore manhandling Tessa. His feet refused to stay still, so he paced back and forth across the front room. He wished he could have thrown at least one punch—just one—square in the mouth.

"He's insufferable!"

"Henry Kilgore may not have behaved like a gentleman, but you're not behaving like one either. Kilgore has an excuse. He's not a Christian. You are."

Gideon flopped down on the settee and sighed. "I know, Lord. Now Tessa's lost her job, and it's my fault."

He slid to the floor and knelt, leaning his elbows on the settee and holding his face in his hands. "Father, please help Tessa find another job. I hated that she was working for Kilgore, but now she has nothing. She probably won't accept any help from me. Whatever the solution, it will have to come from You." He remained on his knees for a time, asking God to forgive his display of temper and praying for Tessa's situation.

After a while, he felt the urge to go downstairs and work off some of his aggravation.

He'd been meaning to rearrange things in the storeroom for a long time. If the place was better organized with increased shelf space, the mercantile might be more attractive to a buyer.

He rummaged around, pushing and shoving crates here and there, and sketching some shelving ideas on a tablet. A large lumpy object hid under an old canvas in the corner, and Gideon groaned when he remembered the cookstove his father had ordered three years ago for a customer who never came back to get it. The thing took up so much space out front that Gideon finally dragged it back to the storeroom and covered it, thinking he could at least stack bales of fence wire on it.

He pulled off the canvas and scowled at the behemoth. Maybe if he put a reduced price on it and hauled it back out front, someone might take it off his hands. He gripped the thing and pushed and pulled, grunting until sweat popped out on his forehead and dribbled down his face.

Finally, after twenty minutes of wrestling, he straightened up and glared at the stove. The monstrosity simply didn't want to move.

Whatever the solution, it will have to come from You.

An idea began taking shape in his mind. He grabbed the tablet that bore his rough sketches and crumpled the page. With pencil in hand, a new plan unfolded on a fresh sheet of paper. He sketched efficient shelving and storage, a work space, and a new display area.

An hour later, the plan lay before him on the tablet. "Lord, if this is what You want me to do, You'll have to make all the details work. But don't let me run ahead of You, Father. This has to be Your plan, not mine."

Gideon slapped his hat on his head and bounded out the back door with the tablet in hand. The next step was to speak to Pearl Dunnigan. He took the stairs leading to her back porch two at a time and rapped on her door.

She opened the door and smiled broadly. "Why, Gideon! How nice of you to drop by. Please come in."

He swept off his hat. "Afternoon, Miss Pearl. Would you have a few minutes to talk?"

"Of course. Come sit down at the kitchen table." She bustled about pouring two cups of coffee.

The aroma of Sunday pot roast lingered in the spacious kitchen. He wiped his feet on the braided rug at the door. Cheery red-checkered curtains framed the wide window from which sunlight flooded the room. Clay flowerpots lined up like fence posts along the windowsill.

Miss Pearl ushered him to a bare, work-worn table in the middle of the room. Gideon sat on a creaking chair and laid his tablet in front of him, while Miss Pearl set out a plate heaped with molasses cookies and joined him at the table.

He took a tentative sip of the steaming coffee. "I have something I'd like to discuss with you." He pushed the tablet over so she could look at his sketches.

Thirty minutes later, Miss Pearl shared Gideon's excitement. She clapped her hands. "Oh Gideon, I can't tell you how I'm looking forward to this."

Gideon emptied his coffee mug. "Tessa can be in business for herself, and she can have a decent place to live here while she helps you out with the baking. Plus, the baked goods she'll sell from the mercantile will be her source of income while it brings more customers into the store."

"I have a little room behind the kitchen stairs that will be perfect for her." Miss Pearl blotted her lips with the hem of her apron. "I've been using it for storage, so it will take me a few days to get it ready."

Gideon rose and picked up the tablet. "There's no rush since it will take me at least a couple of weeks to construct the work area and install the stove." Even as he spoke the words, he wished he could make it happen today.

"When will you tell her?"

He paused by the door. "I'd like to get the storeroom organized into a work space first. That way, I'll have something to show her." Guilt still hounded him over the events of the afternoon. "I just hope she doesn't think of it as charity."

Tessa darted out the door and made straight for Maxwell's Mercantile. Telling Gideon she still had a job wasn't the only reason for her errand. When she'd opened up the cabinet this morning to retrieve the leftover cinnamon bread she'd brought home, she discovered little ragged holes chewed through the paper, and only a few miniscule crumbles of bread remained. The little beasts had also made a feast of the crackers she'd bought just two days before.

The mercantile door stood open, inviting her inside.

"Hello, Gideon."

When he looked up, his normal polite smile he used to greet all his customers deepened into something she didn't dare try to interpret. "Hi, Tessa."

Her heart skipped. "I wanted you to know that Mr. Kilgore gave me my job back."

"Oh?"

The scowl on his face surprised her. She thought he'd be happy she still had a job. "After you left yesterday, Mr. Kilgore came looking for me. He said he knew I'd been doing the baking and he'd changed his mind about firing me."

Gideon shrugged. "Hmph. More likely he was afraid he'd lose business without you doing the baking."

"I don't know about that, but he gave me a raise."

"That a fact? But Tessa, if he ever dares to lay a hand—"

She stopped him. "Don't worry. I don't think he will." She tilted her head to one side. "By any chance do you know who left a lovely bouquet of daisies at my door yesterday?"

If the red stain filling Gideon's cheeks was evidence, she had her answer.

"Thank you. They're lovely. You keep doing things that puzzle me. I can't understand why you want to be nice to someone like me."

Gideon bristled and put his hands on his hips. "Now don't start that again." He held his hands out, palms up, in an entreaty. "Tessa, I just can't understand why your father railed at you so, and I certainly can't understand why you believe the things he said to you."

She lifted her shoulders in a resigned shrug. "It seemed like I heard him say things like that all my life. I was...well, a disappointment to him." She dipped her head. "Mama had a very difficult time—" Heat filled her face. "After I was born, she never regained her strength. I don't ever remember Mama being healthy." Her voice became raspy. "She was never able to give Papa the son he wanted, and it was because of me." The memory of Mama's soft whisper in the night after Papa's tirades, telling Tessa how much she loved her, stroked her heart. But Mama feared Papa, too.

Gideon shook his head. "Tessa, he was wrong. You are a lady, and you don't deserve to be treated otherwise. Please believe that."

She lifted her shoulders. "I don't know. It may take some time."

"We'll work on it." His grin nearly knocked her breath from her. "Was there anything you needed?"

"Well, yes. I need to know the price of a crock or a canister, something with a lid tight enough to keep out a mouse."

His expression turned sympathetic, and he pulled two sizes of crockery off a high shelf and set them before her on the counter. "This larger one is twenty-eight cents, and the smaller is eighteen cents. Which size would suit your needs?"

Her hand felt around in her pocket for the coins Mr. Kilgore tossed at her yesterday. She hesitated. The smaller one would do nicely, but she wanted to put the coins in her pocket into the old sock she was using to stash away her savings toward her winter rent. Now that Mr. Kilgore had given her a raise, perhaps she could part with eighteen cents later in the week.

She ran a finger around the edge of the smaller crock. "I think I'll wait for now."

"Look, Tessa." He pushed the crock toward her. "Why don't you take this with you now. You can pay me later."

She stiffened and shook her head slightly, nudging the crock back across the counter to him. No, she'd not take anything without being able to pay cash for it. "When I get my pay this week, I'll come back and get it. Meanwhile, could I get five cents' worth of cheese and crackers, please?" She fished a nickel from her pocket.

He sighed. "Sure." He went behind the counter and sliced a generous wedge from the large round of cheese.

"That's too much, Gideon. I said five cents' worth."

He put one hand on his hip in mock indignation. "Are you trying to tell me how to run my store?" He wrapped the cheese in paper and went over to a wooden barrel to scoop out a large handful of crackers. "Tessa, is this all you're eating? Cheese and crackers?"

"No. Flossie said I can take some of the leftovers home at the end of the day." She pushed the nickel across the counter and picked up the paper-wrapped bundle. "But Flossie has a family to feed, so I usually make sure she takes home most of the leftovers."

She thanked him and started for the door.

"Tessa?"

She turned.

"God says you are precious in His sight, and I agree with Him."

Chapter 8

Gideon watched as the bank president glanced over the statement from the land office. When Gideon learned the land was owned by the bank, he'd stopped by to speak with Roland Sewell to inquire about the price and terms.

The portly man behind the desk cleared his throat. "This is a fine piece of land. The man who intended to farm it had a run of bad luck and defaulted on his loan." Sewell stroked his gray whiskers. "The board of directors meets Wednesday. I will bring your request before them at that time."

Gideon picked up the document and folded it. "The final agreement will have to wait until I have a buyer for the mercantile."

Mr. Sewell stood and offered his hand. "That's fine. There's no rush."

Gideon shook the man's hand and exited the bank.

Down the street, the stage pulled up to the depot amid swirling dust. The door opened, and a man wearing a tweed suit with a fancy vest and bowler hat disembarked. Gideon didn't recall seeing the man before. He'd surely remember a dandy dressed like that.

Gideon simply shrugged. None of his concern. He unlocked the mercantile doors and turned the sign over that declared the store open.

He set to work measuring and marking the walls for the new shelving in the storeroom. His carpentry skills wouldn't win any prizes, but he'd learned enough from his father to know which end of a hammer to use.

"Hello, anyone about?"

Gideon hurried from the storeroom to greet his customer. To his surprise, it was the fancy gentleman he'd seen earlier getting off the stage. The man's neatly trimmed mustache and side muttonchops were sprinkled with silver. "Good morning, sir. Welcome to Willow Creek."

The man smiled broadly. "Ah, you Westerners. Such a friendly lot, you are. My name is Behr, Hubert Behr." Mr. Behr's curious accent sounded European. "You're pretty well stocked here, I see. I need several articles— shaving soap, some pipe tobacco, writing paper, and a pot of ink. Linen handkerchiefs, if you have them. Also, I need some footwear more suitable to this area."

"Of course. Right this way, sir."

When Mr. Behr made his choices, Gideon tallied up the man's purchases. "Shall I deliver these for you, or would you like to take them with you?"

"You deliver, do you? Well, then just deliver them to the hotel down the street. I'll pick them up at the front desk after I've finished my business." He handed Gideon an extra silver dollar. "Take this for your trouble, young man."

When Gideon started to protest, Mr. Behr waved his hand. "I insist. You're saving me an extra trip." He touched the brim of his bowler in farewell as he exited.

He was a pleasant enough fellow. A smile tweaked Gideon's lips at the man's attire. His fancy suit, vest, and hat were as out of place in Willow Creek as a cattle rustler at a tea party. He slipped the silver dollar into his pocket with a grin. *That'll help pay for Martha's wedding cake.*

For the next two hours he worked feverishly on the shelves. When he finished, he stepped back and admired his work. The simple pine planks were plain, but they were serviceable, sturdy, and within easy reach for Tessa.

The bell on the front door sounded.

Gideon laid his hammer down and exited the storeroom to serve his customer but halted in the doorway. "What are you doing here, Kilgore?"

Kilgore smirked and looked around. "It appears your customers are staying away in droves. Your creditors will be knocking on your door before long with their hands out. I'd like to be around then, when you regret not taking my first offer to buy this place."

"Kilgore, I'll never regret not selling to you." Gideon gritted his teeth to keep from saying more.

Kilgore guffawed as though Gideon's reply was the funniest thing he'd heard all week. "Will you regret having to board up the place and not getting a dime out of it? Think you'll be able to buy that piece of land if you don't sell this dump?" His belly shook with laughter again. The sound grated on Gideon's ears.

How did Kilgore know about the land he wanted to buy? Gideon narrowed his eyes and fixed his gaze on the pompous man. "My affairs are none of your business, Kilgore."

Kilgore pulled his cigar out of his mouth and pointed it at Gideon. "I thought you were smarter than that, but you're a fool, Maxwell. You still haven't learned that I'm the most important man in these parts. But you'll learn it now because my offer just dropped two hundred dollars."

Before Gideon could retort, both men were drawn to the sound of footsteps. Tessa stood just inside the door. Gideon saw her expression change from friendly to apprehensive the moment she laid eyes on Kilgore.

At the sight of his employee, Kilgore gave another humorless laugh. "Birds of a feather, as they say." He jerked his thumb in Tessa's direction. "I offered this girl a job making good money at the Blue Goose. You'd think she'd rather work where she could sashay around and dally with the customers, but she turned me down flat." His tone turned dramatic, laced with sarcasm. "I guess she thinks she's too good to serve whiskey. She'd rather bake bread and make half the money rather than soil her hands on demon drink." He laughed, but then the snide mockery drained from his face as he narrowed his eyes at Tessa. "She doesn't understand that I don't take no for an answer." He stuck his cigar in his mouth and took a puff. The smoke shot from his lips in a derisive jeer.

He turned to Tessa and gestured toward Gideon. "Here's just the man for you, girl. You're two of a kind. Both of you are too stupid to know a good deal when you hear one."

He flicked his ashes on the floor and walked out.

◈

A flood of humiliation crashed over Tessa. Flames shot up her throat and consumed her. Bad enough Mr. Kilgore extended such a degrading offer to her in the first place, but to repeat it in front of Gideon made her wish she was invisible, especially if what Tillie and Flossie said was true. What must Gideon think of her? She couldn't even raise her eyes to look at him.

"Tessa, just ignore him. He's nothing but a windbag."

She appreciated Gideon's attempt to brush off Mr. Kilgore's crude remarks as inconsequential, but mortification still choked her. Her eyelids stung, and she bit her lip trying to halt the tears that wanted to further humiliate her. After several slow breaths, she wrangled her emotions under control.

She dared to glance at Gideon, and his warm smile sent tingles through her stomach, which only served to accuse her further. If she experienced such foolish flutters over a smile from a man she'd only known for two months, maybe she was no better than the girls Mr. Kilgore employed at the Blue Goose.

Gideon jerked his head toward the door. "Kilgore was just telling me how foolish I am for not taking his offer."

Was he trying to make her feel better by changing the subject? "What offer is that?"

Gideon pushed his shirtsleeves up higher on his arms. "He wants me to sell him the mercantile. Of course, I do want to sell, but not to him."

Tessa glanced around the store with a frown. "Why would you want to sell the mercantile? This is a good, steady business, and I'm sure you make a good living here." She pressed her lips together. It wasn't her place to make such comments.

But Gideon didn't seem to care. "My dream is to sell this place and start a ranch for breeding farm horses. Once I purchase the land and acquire my breeding stock, I'll be the only breeder in these parts."

Tessa stared at him. "My papa sold our farm to come west and dig for gold that didn't exist. It could have been a good farm, but he wanted to chase a mirage."

Gideon raised his eyebrows.

Regret niggled at her. Perhaps she shouldn't have blurted out the comparison. Regardless, she needed to complete her purchase and get back to the hotel. "I need a bar of lye soap, please."

Gideon retrieved the green paper-wrapped block and set it on the counter. "Anything else?"

She dug in her pocket for the few coins to pay for her purchase and managed a smile as she laid them on the counter. "That's all, thank you."

As she turned to leave, Gideon came around the counter. "Tessa, everyone has dreams and goals. This has been my dream for a long time. I kept the store going after my folks died so I could support my sister. Now that she's getting married, it's time for me to pursue my goal."

She looked up at him, an apology on her lips. Only days ago, she'd flirted with the idea of having her own bakery, but she'd dismissed it as foolishness. She wasn't making much money at the hotel, but at least she knew she'd receive a wage every week. After seeing what Papa put Mama through, chasing dreams left a bad taste in her mouth. "I need to get back to the kitchen. Good day, Gideon." She turned toward the door.

"Wait, Tessa. My sister and I would like you to join us for church on Sunday."

She halted. The idea sounded tempting. Mama always wanted to go to church when they lived in Indiana, but she was too weak and sickly most of the time—and of course Papa would never allow it. Whenever Tessa voiced a tentative request to attend church, Papa scoffed and told her the church folks wouldn't let the likes of her sit at worship with them. "Th–thank you, but I don't think so."

"Why not?"

The scuffed tips of her shoes drew her attention. "I don't have anything nice to wear, and besides, I'm not the kind of person that churchgoing folks associate with. But it was kind of you to ask."

Gideon kept step with her as she started toward the door. "Tessa, most of the folks in our church are farmers. Lots of them wear the same clothes to come to church that they wear to work in because that's all they have. There's nothing wrong with that."

A memory slipped through her mind. "My mama used to sing some of the church songs to me when I was little." The memory darkened. "But my father told me I could never go to a church because they don't let people like me in."

Gideon's face registered puzzled disbelief, and before he could argue the point, she beat a hasty retreat out the door.

❧

Gideon's heart ached at Tessa's reasons for refusing his invitation. He believed she wanted to go, but the image Tessa had of herself was stained with the memory of her father's ugly accusations.

He returned to the storeroom and appraised his work. Whenever he did find a buyer for the store, the bakery would only enhance its value. He decided to get started installing the stove. Surely he'd be finished well before closing time.

He measured the diameter of the section of pipe that would fit through the wall and marked the place for its installation. While he worked, he recalled the prayer he'd prayed last week, asking God to send him a wife so he could have the kind of marriage his parents had. At the time, he wondered if Tessa could be that woman, but now an element of doubt pricked him. As much as he disliked Henry Kilgore, Gideon couldn't shake the memory of the man offering Tessa a job working as a saloon girl.

"Is that what she meant when she said people like her?" His hands slowed. "God, I know I promised if You ever sent me a woman to love, I'd not question Your choice."

Gideon shook his head. He hadn't known Tessa long enough to be in love

67

with her. Why was he even thinking in terms of love? True, he had feelings for her, but they were purely of friendship, weren't they? Isn't that why he was going to all this trouble? He felt sorry for her. Anyone else would do the same. Of course he hoped his plan would make things better for her, as well as enhance the mercantile in the eyes of a potential buyer.

"Hmm, I may run this store forever if You don't send me a buyer besides Kilgore." He immediately regretted his words and sent a repentant glance heavenward. "Sorry, Lord. I didn't mean to tell You what to do. If You want me to be a storekeeper, I'll be content to stay here for as long as You say."

He pushed the coping saw into motion. If he didn't stop woolgathering, he'd never get this job finished. He made the last cut and picked up a section of the stovepipe to test the fit. After a few more minor adjustments, he slid the section of pipe into the hole and nailed it in place. But when he began trying to connect the sections of pipe, something was wrong. Perhaps he should have connected the sections first, before installing the outside piece.

"Well, how was I to know? I've never installed a stove before." He continued muttering as he pried the nails out. Sweat trickled down his neck as he pulled the piece out and laid it on the floor with the others. He stood with his hands on his hips, glaring at the assortment of tin scattered on the floor.

"What in heaven's name are you doing?"

Gideon startled and jerked his head up.

Martha stood in the doorway, mirroring Gideon's stance with her hands on her hips and a smirk on her face.

"What's it look like I'm doing?" he snapped.

His sister pressed her lips together, and he got the distinct impression she was trying not to laugh. "Going into the scrap metal business?"

Gideon sent her a mock glower. "Think you're clever, don't you?" He spread his filthy hands and reached toward her. "Come here, and I'll show you something clever."

Martha squealed. "Ooh, Gideon, you're dirty. Don't touch me."

"Ha!" He retreated a step. "And you're going to be a farmer's wife? You'd better get used to dirt."

She made a face at him. "I was just coming to tell you that I'm going out to Ted's place. His mother and I are going to pick strawberries and make jam."

He grinned. "And you don't want Ted to see you dirty, since you'll be working in the garden and all."

Martha heaved an exasperated sigh. "Ted will bring me home later this evening, so you're on your own for supper."

"Oh, thank goodness, a reprieve."

"Gideon!"

He gave her a contrite smile. "Sorry. Have a good time, and bring me some strawberries."

After she left, a thought occurred to him. What if Tessa considered accepting Kilgore's offer of the saloon job? If Kilgore's portrayal of Tessa was accurate, he'd have no choice but to rethink the plans for the bakery. He not only had a business reputation to think of; he had a sister to protect. Despite their brother-sister banter, he adored Martha and couldn't allow her respectability to be sullied.

"I'm letting my imagination get carried away. Kilgore said Tessa turned him down flat." Besides not trusting any of Kilgore's implications, something in Gideon's heart told him Tessa simply wasn't that kind of girl.

He directed his attention back to the task at hand. These wretched sections of pipe must fit together in a particular order before he could get the whole assembly into the hole he'd cut in the wall. It appeared he might not finish this job today, and he still needed to deliver Mr. Behr's order to the hotel.

He sucked in a deep breath and blew it out. He knelt beside the collection of stovepipe pieces and tried putting sections together, but after experimenting repeatedly, they didn't fit the way he thought they should. One piece seemed too big, while another appeared too small. No matter how he attempted to join them, he always ended up with an extra length of pipe. The part he thought should fit into the wall didn't seem to fit any of the other pieces.

He didn't want to swallow his pride and ask for help, even though Cully probably knew how to put this puzzle together. He leaned against the wall and sighed his exasperation. This contraption wasn't going to get the best of him!

Chapter 9

Tessa remembered the last time someone invited her to church. It was the itinerant preacher in Indiana. Papa had run him off with a shotgun. Gideon's invitation made her heart smile even if she couldn't accept. But the fluttery sensation she got every time she laid eyes on him perplexed her. She shouldn't allow such feelings.

Grabbing a towel, she slid her pies from the oven and placed them on the cooling rack. "Who am I kidding? I get butterflies every time I *think* about him."

"Every time you think about who?"

Tessa jerked herself back to awareness and glanced over her shoulder at Flossie.

The woman's eyebrows arched in speculation.

"Oh, nobody."

Flossie laughed. "You get butterflies thinking about nobody?"

As she struggled to think how to answer, her face grew hot. Finally the stretched-out silence apparently answered for her.

"Okay, I can take a hint. You don't want to talk about it."

She'd have to remember to keep her ruminations to herself. The pies cooling near the window wouldn't last through the dinner crowd, so she set to work mixing more piecrust.

As she did so, she allowed her mind to think back to Gideon's invitation. Perhaps she could wait outside the church until the service started then slip in and sit in the back. As soon as the service was over, she could slip out again before anyone noticed her.

What was she thinking? Gideon said he and his sister wanted her to join them. He must intend for her to sit with them. No, she was right to refuse his invitation, regardless of how much she wanted to accept.

Tonight she planned to open Mama's Bible and read awhile. After all, that's the way she and Mama used to worship together. The only thing wrong with that plan was by the time she returned to the shed there was little or no

70

daylight left, and she didn't have an oil lamp—or even a candle—by which to read.

Gideon crushed the brim of his hat in his fist as he strode down the boardwalk toward the mercantile. Something didn't add up. He'd stopped by the bank full of anticipation to learn the price and terms for the land about which he'd dreamed.

Only a few days ago Mr. Sewell seemed eager for the transaction to take place. *Why is he now telling me the land isn't for sale?* It didn't make sense for the bank to hold on to a parcel of land acquired through a defaulted loan. No, something certainly wasn't right.

He slapped his hat against his thigh as he stomped up the steps to the mercantile. The memory of Mr. Sewell repeating himself numerous times and glancing nervously at the door to an adjoining office that stood slightly ajar raised Gideon's suspicions that their conversation hadn't been entirely private.

As he propped the door open, a voice hailed him from the street.

"Gideon."

He turned. "Hey Cully. Boy, am I glad to see you. I've been itching to get this stovepipe hooked up."

"Waall, I sure am sorry it took me so long to git here. Old man Kilgore had me puttin' new shoes on his matched team of buggy horses, and then I had to replace the wheel rims on that fancy carriage of his."

Gideon set aside his unanswered questions about Mr. Sewell's odd declaration and turned his attention to Cully and the stove. "The stove is back in the storeroom." He led the way, hoping his inability to install the contraption didn't make him look completely incompetent. If Cully could finish the job today, he could show Tessa this evening.

Cully followed Gideon and grinned at the assortment of tin pieces lined up on the floor in the corner. He picked up several pieces, scrutinizing the edges and comparing sections, tapping his finger on each piece and grunting like he was inventorying the lot. "Where's your thimble?"

Gideon raised his eyebrows. "Thimble?"

"You gotta have a thimble piece to fit these two together. Otherwise, your chimney ain't gonna be tight." Cully held up the section Gideon had nailed into the wall and then pried out. "You wasn't tryin' to nail this piece up in that hole, was ya?" Cully started to chuckle.

"Well, I was just going by the way our stove upstairs looks."

Cully's toothy grin punctuated the man's amusement. "You'd best stick to runnin' the store, Gideon. You ain't never gonna make a living installin' stoves." Cully cackled.

Gideon pressed his lips together and decided not to embarrass himself by offering to help. He set to work rearranging the displays out front.

"Hey Gideon, what's going on?"

Gideon turned. "Mornin', Ty. What are you doing in town again? I usually don't see you more than once a month."

Ty stuck his hand deep inside the gumdrop jar. "I heard from one of the stage drivers that he dropped off a guy here who might be willing to make a land deal. I came in to see if I could find him."

Gideon scratched his head. "There was a man who got off the stage the other day. Name was Behr. He mentioned something about attending to some business."

Ty chewed thoughtfully for a moment and tossed a couple more gumdrops in his mouth. "He didn't say what kind of business?"

"No, it was none of my concern. I was just happy to make a sale."

Ty nodded like it all made sense to him. "One of the stage drivers said this guy might be connected with the railroad."

"Railroad?" Gideon frowned. "I read in the paper awhile back that the Chicago, Kansas and Nebraska decided to route that connecting line about fifty miles south of here. There was some talk for a while of the Illinois Central taking over that line."

After gathering up another handful of gumdrops, Ty shrugged. "I know as much as you do. Figure I'll ask some questions and see what the answers sound like."

Gideon propped one foot on a crate of canned goods. "I had a real strange meeting today with Mr. Sewell."

"Roland Sewell at the bank?"

Gideon nodded. "You know that parcel of land east of town that I've been looking at?"

Ty arched his eyebrows and swallowed. "You finally gonna buy that piece? Hey, that's great. Nice stretch of land. A little too hilly for planting wheat and corn, but you've always wanted to breed horses. That's some mighty pretty pasture land."

Gideon scratched his head. "When I checked at the land office last week, they said the bank owned it. But today, Mr. Sewell told me it wasn't for sale.

Don't you find that a little odd?"

Puzzlement drove Ty's eyebrows into a furrow. "That doesn't make sense. Why would the bank want to hold a piece of land?"

Either insight or speculation—Gideon didn't know which—fit some tentative pieces into place. "Unless. . ." He rubbed his hand over his chin and looked straight at Ty. "Are you thinking what I'm thinking?"

"Talk of the railroad coming through might drive up the price of land sky-high."

Gideon caught the corner of his lip between his teeth. "If the rumor is true, it might. When you get done talking with Mr. Behr, can you drop by and let me know what you found out?"

Ty tossed his hat on his head. "If it's anything worth passing on, you'll be the first to know."

"Thanks, buddy."

"Sure thing." Ty started for the door.

"Uh, Ty?"

"Huh?"

"That'll be four cents for the gumdrops."

"Put it on my account."

"You don't have an account."

"Oh. Well, could I open an account?"

"For four cents' worth of gumdrops?"

Ty pulled out his pocket linings and raised his shoulders, chagrin on his face.

Gideon laughed and shook his head. "Get out of here, you gumdrop thief."

"See you later."

"You better have a nickel on you when you come back."

"A nickel? You said four cents."

"I charge interest."

"Gideon, you got a catalog for stove parts?" Cully's request rang like a dirge in Gideon's ears. He pulled the catalog from underneath a shelf and pushed it across the counter to the old gent. Cully flipped through the pages and turned the book around for Gideon's perusal.

"This part right here." Cully's grimy finger tapped the page of the catalog. "You gotta have this here thimble connector, and you gotta have a collar piece before you can put that stove to work."

Gideon's shoulders slumped. Ordering parts would certainly hinder his plans. "Thanks, Cully. I'll order these parts right away."

Cully nodded and sucked on his teeth. "Sure 'nuf. See ya in church." He strolled out the door, leaving Gideon to stand in the middle of the storeroom and chafe in frustration over the delay. More than anything, he wanted to see Tessa leave Kilgore's employ and have a decent place to live.

"Just like everything else, I need to wait on God and let Him work things out."

"A sound plan, young man."

Gideon spun around to see Hubert Behr standing in the doorway. "Oh, I'm sorry. I didn't hear you come in, Mr. Behr."

"I apologize, young man. Eavesdropping is an unseemly pastime. But I must say, it's refreshing to find such wisdom in a person your age. If more people would follow God's leadership, they'd make far fewer mistakes and experience far less heartache."

Gideon followed his customer to the front of the store. "You sound like you know what you're talking about, sir."

Mr. Behr nodded slowly. "Indeed."

Gideon wiped his hands on his apron. "What can I get for you, sir?"

"I spoke with a friend of yours earlier—a young man, Mr. Ty Sawyer. He told me your general mercantile was for sale."

Gideon nodded. "Yes sir, it is."

"May I ask the price?"

The man's inquiry might mean nothing if the bank wouldn't sell the land he wanted to buy, but Gideon gave him the figure.

Mr. Behr stroked his chin. "That seems like a fair price."

Gideon watched the gentleman scan the displays of merchandise and examine the rows of bins. "Does that mean you're interested in buying the place?"

Mr. Behr ran his hand along the counter. "I need to study the feasibility of such a venture. I'll be in the area for some time, and I'm not in any hurry."

A glimmer of hope surged. Now if only he could persuade Mr. Sewell to sell him that land. . .

&

"Flossie, do think it would be all right if I'd bring my Bible back to the kitchen tonight and read? I don't have any light at my place." Tessa hung her apron on the peg near the door as the three women were leaving.

Flossie shook her head. "That ain't a good idea. Kilgore don't like burnin' the lamps for an extra minute, the old skinflint. Iffen he sees the light burnin' and comes in here to check, he'll fire you for sure."

Disappointment slumped Tessa's shoulders, but she bid Flossie and Tillie good night and made her way out into the alley that led to her humble dwelling. Her feet came to a halt as soon as she turned the corner behind the hotel. Sitting beside the door of the shed was a small crockery vessel with a wooden lid. *Gideon.* She picked up the container and hesitated. Should she march straight to the mercantile this minute and plunk down eighteen cents? She frowned. The store was probably closed by now. Gideon was just being kind, like when he brought the burn salve to Flossie. Humility poked her. God would want her to respond in gratitude and graciousness. Very well. She'd wait and pay him for it first thing in the morning.

The moment she opened the shed door, little trespassers skittered along the wall behind Mama's cabinet. Nasty critters.

She stamped her feet and thumped her fist against the lid of the trunk. "Shoo! I'm home, you wretched little beasts. You better not have been into my food again." Her fingers groped in the cabinet to locate her bundle containing a corn muffin, an apple, and the cheese she'd purchased yesterday. Sure enough, there was another hole despite several thicknesses of paper. She touched course crumbs littering the shelf in the cabinet. The miserable rodents didn't even have the manners to clean up after themselves.

Her stomach shuddered with distaste and at the same time complained of its emptiness. The cheese, apple, and muffin were all she had. She'd simply have to break off and discard the nibbled edges. It was that or go hungry. Whatever remained after she'd eaten would be safely protected in her new crock.

After the long day of standing at the worktable and waiting on the dining customers, her body begged for rest. Despite her weariness, she'd thought about Mama's Bible all afternoon. Gideon's invitation to church kindled a spark within her to renew her fellowship with God.

If she couldn't use the kitchen lamp, perhaps there was another secluded corner where she'd find some light. The hotel lobby was for paying customers, not the likes of her. Tessa could only imagine Mr. Kilgore's reaction if he found her sitting and leisurely reading like a grand lady. But it was the only place that offered a source of lamplight in the evening.

Well, not the only place. The saloons were open, and though there was plenty of light there, the idea of sitting in a saloon made Tessa's flesh crawl.

The reek of whiskey along with memories of her father's drinking habits sent shivers of loathing down her spine. Her stomach clenched at the thought of entering a saloon for any reason, even just for the purpose of taking advantage of the light.

She splashed water in her face from the bucket in the corner and ran a broken comb through her hair. If she made herself more presentable, might she dare take Mama's Bible and sit in the hotel lobby to read?

The Bible clutched under her arm, she walked down the alley toward the front of the building. When she reached the boardwalk and peered in the front window, the first person she saw was Mr. Kilgore. There was no chance of entering unnoticed.

Disappointment struck her again. Why did she think she could elevate herself to the level of the hotel patrons when she was nothing more than hired help?

She edged closer toward the front of the hotel. Perhaps there would be enough light coming from the window. She no sooner opened the book and found the broom straw she'd used to mark her place than the front door opened.

Mr. Kilgore stepped out and struck a match on the post to light his cigar.

She shrank as close to the shadow of the building as she could. He puffed away for a moment, and the noxious smoke floated in her direction, burning her eyes and throat. She tried to hold her breath, but as the smoke slithered around her, a cough escaped despite her effort to be invisible.

"What do you think you're doing there, girl? You can't loiter around here," Mr. Kilgore's voice boomed. "Employees use the side entrance. My clientele doesn't need to see the likes of you dawdling by the front door. Run along."

The stares of passersby and Mr. Kilgore's glare gave her feet wings. The cool night air blew against her burning face as she scurried down the street. She didn't stop until she was well away from the hotel.

Tinny piano music and coarse laughter accosted her ears. Just ahead on the boardwalk, patrons of the Blue Goose saloon came and went by way of the swinging door. There was certainly plenty of light coming from those front windows. Tiptoeing inside the establishment undetected seemed as unlikely as slipping past Mr. Kilgore in the hotel lobby. The longer she stood in the shadows staring at the saloon's glow, the more she longed for a place where she could sit and read the passages Mama had underlined.

She sidled up next to the window and leaned against the building. She'd dropped the broom straw when Mr. Kilgore bellowed at her, but she had little trouble finding her place. The page was so dog-eared and its edges so worn from use that it had to be one of Mama's favorites. The yellow glow from the window fell across the words her mother loved.

"The LORD is my strength and my shield; my heart trusted in him. . .with my song will I praise him."

Tessa doubted the discordant music coming from the saloon was the kind of song the psalmist had in mind, but she was reminded of the songs her mother taught her from the time she was a little girl. A sweet hum of memory seeped into her mind, and the words of Mama's favorite hymn caressed her heart.

"Fairest Lord Jesus, Ruler of all nature. . ."

Tessa tried to recall the rest of the words, but the noise from the saloon was so loud and distracting it was impossible to block it out. How Papa would laugh if he could see her now.

She pushed the thought from her mind. She was here to take advantage of the light. There would be time to recall those precious memories of hymn singing with Mama later. Maybe when she went to the mercantile to pay for the crock, she could also purchase a candle so she could read in the privacy of the shed. Regardless, she was determined to use this time to satisfy her hunger for worship. She read further down the page. Some of the psalms were familiar. She remembered her mother reading them to her.

"Thou art my hiding place. . . ."

The idea of God hiding her comforted her heart. She read it over again. Was a promise that precious meant for someone like her? Did she dare claim it? She closed her eyes and envisioned God covering her with His hand.

"Looky here. C'mere, little darlin'." A hand seized her arm and yanked her from her reverie. The unshaven face of a man she didn't know loomed before her. His menacing eyes swept up and down her frame. "You 'n' me's gonna have a little party, honey." His sour breath was so vile she nearly retched.

Her heart pounded, and her mouth was devoid of spit as the lecherous brute tightened his grip and pulled her toward the swinging doors. She planted her feet squarely, pulling away from the drunken man with all her strength. When she opened her mouth to protest, nothing came out except a raspy hiss.

Chapter 10

Gideon knocked on Miss Pearl's door as the crickets and cicadas were tuning up for an evening serenade. When she opened the door, Gideon noticed small, pinched lines around her eyes and a lock of gray hair that had escaped its pins.

"Hello, Gideon. Come in."

"Evening, Miss Pearl. I'm sorry to come by so late, but I needed to let you know we've run into a problem. Cully said we're missing some parts for the stove. I sent the order today and stated it was a rush order, so I'm hoping it won't take too long."

The woman brushed her hair back as she nudged Gideon toward a kitchen chair. She sliced a large piece of gingerbread and set it in front of him with a glass of milk. "I'm certainly ready for Tessa to come and take over the baking." Miss Pearl sat opposite Gideon with a cup of tea.

Gideon took a gulp of milk. "The challenge will be getting her to agree to our plan without thinking she's taking charity."

"Charity? Why, that's silly. She'll be working for her room and board by doing the baking for me. And what a blessing that will be!"

Gideon let out a rueful chuckle. "She's got a streak of pride, and that's for sure." He pressed his lips into a thin line and recalled Tessa's response when he urged her to take the food crock. He wondered if she'd found it on her doorstep yet. "She won't take anything that she can't pay for or thinks she hasn't earned."

Miss Pearl rolled her head from side to side and reached up to massage the back of her neck. "Do you think she'd agree to move in here right away while we're waiting for the stove parts?"

Gideon forked up a piece of gingerbread and paused with the tempting morsel balanced an inch from his lips. "I'd like nothing better than to move her in here tonight. But if we have every detail of the plan in place before we present it to her, it will make it harder for her to say no." He shoveled the large bite of gingerbread in his mouth and washed it down with another swallow of cold milk.

The thought of Tessa working herself into exhaustion every day at the hotel with nothing more than a ramshackle shed to call her home troubled him more deeply than he cared to admit. Gideon shook his head. "Every time I think of her over there in Kilgore's kitchen, I could bite a horseshoe in half. I don't like the way he treats her."

"Henry Kilgore is a scoundrel, and that's a fact."

Gideon snorted and sank his teeth into the last bite of gingerbread. "I've got to get going. Martha will be wondering where I am." He rose and moved toward the door but stopped abruptly. "Say, Miss Pearl, do you have any of Maggie's kittens left?"

"They're out on the back porch. Take your pick."

He crossed the kitchen to the porch.

Three kitties curled up, overlapping each other in a basket. Maggie assumed a regal pose beside them and switched her orange-and-white tail while she surveyed him with aloof detachment.

Gideon scratched the top of the mother cat's head. "You have some mighty pretty babies there, Miss Maggie. Would it be okay with you if I take this one with me?" He stooped down and gently eased a sleepy white kitten with orange patches into his arms.

The kitten, which was the image of its mother, immediately nestled against his chest.

"Much obliged, Maggie. I promise your baby will have a good home."

The mother cat craned her neck as though telling her offspring good-bye and curled up with the remaining kittens.

Gideon returned to the kitchen and held up his choice for Miss Pearl's approval.

"That one's real playful. Martha will like her."

Gideon grinned and rubbed the kitten's chin. "She's for Tessa. I hope this little one will be a good companion for her."

Miss Pearl arched an eyebrow as she walked him to the door. "Why not just leave the kitten here? Tessa will be moving in here shortly."

Gideon lifted his shoulders. "She has an urgent need for a cat's hunting abilities."

Miss Pearl shuddered and frowned. "Ooh, Gideon, we need to get her moved out of that awful shed and over here as soon as possible."

"Believe me, I wish I could convince her this very minute. I telegraphed the order and left word for the agent at the freight depot in Dubuque to notify me as soon as the parts are on their way. I'll let you know when they arrive. Thanks for the gingerbread and this little mouser." He tucked the kitten inside his shirt as he descended the stairs and headed home.

Just as he turned the corner, his attention was drawn to the boisterous activity across the street at the Blue Goose Saloon. The raucous shouting and bawdy revelry shattered what should have been a peaceful evening. His irritation mounted when he thought of the immorality taking place inside. He skewed his face into a frown. Some of that activity seemed to be spilling out onto the boardwalk. Then his feet froze in place.

Tessa? Was that Tessa out in front of the saloon? The man she was with left her and staggered back into the saloon while Tessa disappeared into the shadows, but the noise emanating from the place prevented Gideon from hearing anything they might have said to each other. The feelings he'd kept telling himself were purely friendship exploded in his chest, and something twisted in his gut. Did Kilgore convince her to take the saloon job?

ॐ

Tessa locked her fingers around Mama's Bible and ripped her arm from the drunken oaf's grasp. Her feet flew down the alley, carrying her away from the nightmarish scene. She didn't stop until she reached the shed.

Tessa slipped inside the dark refuge, pushed the door closed, and sucked in great gulps of air. Her own heartbeat pounded so loud in her ears that she was certain the despicable man would only have to follow the sound of it to find her. Beads of cold sweat dripped down her neck and back. The skin on her wrist burned where the man's fingers had scraped when she pulled her arm from his grip. Dizziness washed over her trembling frame, and she allowed her weakened knees to buckle and lower her to the floor. Pressing her back against the door, she closed her eyes and braced her feet against the trunk.

The lingering stench of the man's sour breath smelled just like Papa's after he'd come home from town with a bottle in his hand and rage in his heart. She swallowed back the nausea the memory evoked. Uncontrollable shudders spilled over her like a bucket of icy water, and she let go of her tears.

All she'd wanted was some light by which to read Mama's Bible. Still clutched in her cramped fingers, the book flopped like a half-stuffed rag doll. Even in the darkness, she could feel the torn pages and broken spine. "Mama, I'm sorry. I should have taken better care of your Bible." Salty tears slid across her lips. Guilt over the damaged Bible hung its accusing weight around her.

She reached out to feel for the trunk's latch. Her fingers found the leather flap, and she lifted the lid, tucking the Bible inside with a heavy heart. Wrestling the trunk's bulk across the small space, she wedged it against the door.

Tomorrow's daylight would no doubt point further condemnation at her when the full measure of harm to the Bible became apparent. For now, she'd lie on her quilt and listen for staggering footsteps and a slurred voice.

&

Darkness still hung its heavy curtain over the town, but Gideon hadn't been able to close his eyes all night except in prayer. He tiptoed in his stocking feet down the back stairs to the solitude of the mercantile.

Despite trying to deny what he saw, the fact remained Tessa was consorting with some disreputable-looking man in front of the saloon. True, she disappeared into the shadows and the man entered the saloon without her. But what if things were as they appeared?

Tessa seemed repulsed by the idea the day Kilgore blurted out his sordid offer. Either she'd been pretending, or she'd swallowed her pride and accepted the job.

Gideon raked his fingers through his hair. Two pictures tangled in his mind—one of Tessa standing in the doorway of the house he hoped to build someday and the other of Tessa outside the saloon with that man. The two couldn't be reconciled to each other. If God was going to answer his prayer for a good marriage, the Lord certainly wouldn't draw him to a fallen woman.

"God, I'm confused. Were You truly leading me to Tessa? Should I continue working on the bakery if she's made the choice to work in the saloon?"

The sign he'd finished painting yesterday lay on the shelf in the storeroom, ready to hang in the front window of the mercantile. The cheery yellow and green letters he'd painted were now dry. TESSA'S BAKERY. When he'd spoken the words yesterday, he'd done so with excitement. Now they sounded hollow. His heart ached with the possible truth of what he'd seen.

"God, I thought maybe Tessa was the woman You've chosen for me. Maybe I was wrong. Please make things clear for me, so I can follow the path You want me to take." A verse in Psalm 5 came to mind. *"Make thy way straight before my face."*

No audible voice responded, but an unmistakable nudge moved in his heart—God's admonishment to not judge but simply wait.

Wait? All right, Father, I'll wait. Please reveal Your will to me one way or the other. I thought setting Tessa up in her own bakery was Your plan. Maybe it wasn't. I thought maybe You had chosen Tessa for me. Maybe You didn't. All I can do is wait.

"At any rate, maybe it's a good thing I found out about this before I started having real feelings for her." Incrimination prickled in his middle. Whether he admitted it or not, his heart was already drawn to Tessa.

He propped the front doors open and displayed the OPEN sign.

He spent the morning moving stock from one shelf to another, muttering as he went. Sometimes having no customers in the store was a good thing. He could talk to himself without anyone thinking he was daft. There was more than one reason a man could go loony, and he suspected most of those reasons had to do with women.

He worked his way along the shelf, until he came to his inventory of crocks, the ones with the snug lids. He picked one up and stared at it. If he felt nothing for her, why did it matter to him that she needed a vessel to keep mice out of her food? Why did the prospect of Tessa working in the saloon fill him with an ache so painful he could barely draw a breath? He returned the crock to the shelf.

"That's the problem. I do feel something for her, and the way she's living bothers me more than I can put into words." He dropped his arms to his sides. "That's not the only thing I can't put into words."

Light footsteps on the wood floor made him turn. If there was a day that he didn't want to look at those hazel eyes, this was it. The morning sun gilded her hair, turning it the color of sun-ripened wheat. She sent him a shy smile, and he nearly choked on his thoughts.

"Good morning, Gideon."

He let out the breath he was holding. "Morning."

She walked up to the counter and laid down eighteen cents. "Thank you for bringing the crock. That was very kind."

Gideon detected a hint of strained humiliation in her voice, but she didn't utter a word of anger over his deed.

"Do you sell candles?"

His tongue simply lay there, paralyzed between his teeth, and refused to function. *Answer her, you idiot, or she'll think you've lost your mind.*

At that moment he was quite certain he'd lost his heart, but God's instructions were to wait. He had a hundred questions to ask her, and he feared the answers. Impatience hammered inside his rib cage.

But in the meantime, she was standing there waiting for an answer. What was her question? "I'm sorry, what did you need?"

Tessa sent him a skeptical look. "Did I come at a bad time?"

Gideon kicked his brain into motion. "No, not at all. What can I get for you today, Tessa?"

Her brows lowered into an uncertain frown. "Candles?"

"Sure. I carry several sizes." He forced his feet in the direction of the shelf that contained the large divided tray with a variety of candles. He scooped up a handful of the most popular size. "These are two cents apiece. How many do you need?"

"Just one, please."

Gideon paused in midmotion. "One candle?"

She straightened her shoulders. "Yes, please." She laid two pennies on the counter.

"You sure that's all you need?"

She leveled her gaze straight into his eyes. The hazel eyes darkened a bit and erected a stubborn, defensive barrier. "Yes, I'm sure."

"One candle it is." He laid her purchase on the counter and picked up the pennies. "Before you go, I have a surprise for you. Wait right here." He hurried to the storeroom. As he picked up the kitten, he allowed his gaze to drift over the stove, worktable, and shelving. This would be the perfect time to show her the work he'd put into the project on her behalf. No, he needed answers to some of his questions first. And besides, God told him to wait. He returned to the front with the kitten in his arms.

The guarded look in her eyes fell away. "Oh! What a sweet kitty." She reached out and gathered the ball of orange-and-white fluff against her chest. "Just listen to that purr. It's like she's singing." She caressed the kitten's head, and the little cat reciprocated by rubbing against Tessa's chin. "You mean you're giving her to me? To keep?" Her eyes glistened.

"I thought she might keep you company."

Her smile put the rays of the morning sun to shame. "Oh, thank you, Gideon." She buried her nose into the kitten's silky fur. "We had barn cats back in Indiana, but Papa wouldn't let me pet them. He said their only purpose was to keep down the mouse popula. . ." The word faded on her lips, and she gave Gideon a knowing look.

"Cats are good for that, too, I suppose."

She raised her eyebrows at him. He hadn't fooled her at all. "Whatever your reason for giving her to me, thank you, Gideon." She scratched the kitty under the chin. "I think I'll name her. . .Daisy. But now I really must hurry and get back to work. I told Flossie I'd only be gone a few minutes. It's all I can do some days to keep up with all the orders for cakes and pies."

Uncertainty and impatience drove all good sense from his head. "Cakes and pies? I thought you changed jobs."

Tessa shook her head. "No, I'm still working at the hotel kitchen. Why would you think I'd gotten another job?"

Heat climbed his chest and burned its way up his neck. "I saw you—last night. In front of. . ."

Her eyes widened, and the color drained from her face. Apparently she didn't know she'd been caught.

He hated confronting her, but he had to know the truth. If her stricken expression was any indication, he must be right.

Tears filled her eyes, and she hugged the kitten close. "You saw me out in front of the saloon so you supposed that I was working there?" Mortification permeated the curves of her mouth, and fire lit her eyes.

What he first thought to be tears of shame, he now realized were tears of anger. "Well, I—"

"You what? You assumed I was the kind of girl who would take a job like that?"

"No, I—I mean, I saw you, and I—I just wondered. . ."

"You wondered what I was doing there."

"Well, yes. Tessa, why?"

Her jaw muscle twitched, and her eyes narrowed. "Not that it's any of your business, *Mr.* Maxwell, but I was looking for some place where I could read my mother's Bible."

Gideon blinked. "Oh, so naturally you would go to the saloon to read the Bible." He couldn't keep the sarcasm from his voice. "Tessa, that makes no sense. Why would you do that?"

She sucked in a breath and blinked rapidly, but a tear escaped anyway as her voice trembled. "Mr. Kilgore wouldn't let me sit in the hotel lobby or use the lamp in the kitchen. The only other place where there was enough light to read by was the saloon. I didn't go in. I stood outside by the front window. But it was so noisy, and the men were so—so vile, I decided—" She lifted her chin. "I decided I would simply have to buy a candle so I could read in the shed." With that, she picked up her candle, snuggled the kitten onto her shoulder, turned on her heel, and marched out the door.

Gideon's voice failed him. God had directed him to wait, but instead he blurted out what was on his mind. Why couldn't he learn to listen to God's instruction? He kicked the corner of the counter and strode to the door. "Tessa! Tessa, wait!"

He caught sight of her skirt as she disappeared around the corner of the alley. He stood there staring, hoping she would come back—but she didn't. Nausea stung his throat. He owed both Tessa and God an apology.

He was about to turn to go back to the storeroom for a heartfelt talk with God when something farther down the street caught his eye. Standing out in front of the land office was Hubert Behr, and walking up to greet him was Kilgore. The two men shook hands, spoke for a moment, exchanged a piece of paper, and then stepped inside the land office together.

Chapter 11

Tessa stormed down the alley toward the shed, huffing each breath out in rhythm with her pace. If Gideon Maxwell thought for one minute he could stand there and accuse her of being a wanton woman, he could just go soak his head in a horse trough.

She'd believed him when he said he was her friend and even felt fluttering tickles in her middle when she thought about him. The confusing ache in her heart tugged her first one way then another.

Realization swept over her. The flutters she experienced every time Gideon entered her thoughts were more than simple attraction. The comfort and warmth of being in his presence grew stronger each time she saw him. To think he assumed she was a woman of loose morals made her eyes water as surely as if he'd slapped her.

The kitten in her arms protested her tightening grip.

"I'm sorry, Daisy. I'm not angry at you." She ran a gentle caress over the kitty's head.

Daisy leaned into Tessa's stroking and purred.

Tessa scooted the kitten into the shed and closed the door. The mice were in for a surprise.

Perhaps she'd been surprised as well. Maybe Gideon wasn't the man she thought him to be.

She hastened back to the kitchen and grabbed her apron. Working would take her mind off Gideon. A basket of apples sat beside the large mixing bowl on the worktable. She thumped an apple on the table and stabbed at it, hacking it in half, then in quarters, taking pleasure in chopping the hunks into thin slices.

"What's the matter with you?"

Looking up, she found both Flossie and Tillie staring at her.

Tillie shrugged. "You seem kinda moody. Something wrong?"

Gideon's question rang in her ears. *"Why would you do that?"* Yes, there was something wrong, but she forced a smile and shook her head. "I'm thinking about adding a buttermilk spice cake to tomorrow's menu."

Flossie wasn't fooled. "Is that what you went to the mercantile to talk to Gideon Maxwell about? Spice cakes?"

Tessa riveted her eyes on her task as she continued to slice the apples. "What would Gideon Maxwell know about dessert menus?" *What does Gideon Maxwell know about anything?* "I was also thinking about making a peach cobbler. Can we get peaches from any of the local farmers?"

"You can buy canned peaches at the mercantile."

Tessa tightened her grip on the handle of the knife. "I'd rather use fresh." She pushed the blade of the knife through the apples with increased energy.

Flossie reached out and patted her shoulder. "Whatever's wrong between you two, you need to talk it out."

The apple slipped from Tessa's hand, and the knife took a tiny nick from her finger. She sucked in a breath. "I don't know what you're talking about." She stuck her finger in her mouth.

"Yes, you do. You were happy as a lark when you left here. You came back with fire in your eyes. What happened?"

Tessa examined her finger. Not much damage. On the other hand, her heart was bleeding. How foolish to allow herself to daydream about a man like Gideon. Hadn't Papa always told her not to get any highfalutin ideas about attracting the attention of an upstanding man? She could still hear his bitter laughter when he told her she might as well fall in love with one of the pigs.

Fall in love? The notion of love was a will-o'-the-wisp. Nothing there to grasp and hold. Oh, how she wished she could talk to Mama.

Tears burned the inside of her eyelids, and she stiffened her spine. Daydreams might be fine for schoolgirls, but she had a job to do. Swallowing hard, she picked up another apple and quartered it.

Flossie still waited for an answer.

"Nothing worth talking about, and I need to get these pies in the oven."

&.

By two o'clock the lunch crowd dwindled. Tessa began clearing dirty dishes and changing table linens in the dining room.

Mr. Kilgore walked in with a man whom she remembered seeing once or twice.

Tessa did her best to avoid following the pair with her eyes. Her face still heated when she remembered the way Mr. Kilgore embarrassed her in front of Gideon. Not that it mattered anymore. Gideon already thought the worst of her.

"Tessa! Bring coffee for myself and Mr. Behr to my office."

Hurrying to do his bidding, she set cups and a coffeepot on a clean tray with spoons, cream, and sugar. She carried the tray to the back of the dining room where the door to the office stood open and deposited it on the small table beside the gleaming mahogany desk.

Not wishing to linger in Mr. Kilgore's presence any longer than necessary, she poured the coffee and returned to the dining room to finish cleaning. The tables along the back wall all needed to be cleared and she couldn't help hearing snatches of the men's conversation as Mr. Kilgore's voice carried into the quiet of the nearly empty dining room.

"I understand you've made inquires about purchasing property in this area."

The other man's reply was drowned out as Tessa stacked dishes on her tray, but a few disjointed words pulled her senses to attention.

". . .young man. . .Maxwell's Mercantile. . ."

Mr. Kilgore's booming laughter rang out. "Gideon Maxwell is a fool. I already offered to buy that place of his, and he turned me down. You'd think he'd want to unload it."

Tessa continued to stack dirty plates and coffee cups, ashamed for listening but wide-eyed at Mr. Kilgore's remarks about Gideon. Taking more time than necessary for her chore, she straightened chairs and tablecloths. Mr. Kilgore wasn't making any effort to lower his voice. Was it wrong to tarry and hear more words that weren't meant for her ears?

"I already own several businesses in town." Kilgore's pompous tone irritated her. "I'm putting pressure on Jake Peabody who owns the gristmill. It won't be long before I own that enterprise as well. The Standridge brothers own the sawmill, but I don't think they'll give me too much trouble about selling out. Maxwell is the only nut I haven't been able to crack."

Tessa heard the sound of fingers drumming on the desktop, and the other man cleared his throat. "I see. Seems to me that you've already acquired a rather substantial portion of the town."

One of the men took a noisy slurp of coffee.

"Not only the town, Mr. Behr, but also some of the outlying areas. I have some inside sources who keep me apprised on. . ." He cleared his throat. "Well, let's just say I have access to certain opportunities. Of course you're privy to much of the same information—maybe even more so—working for the railroad as you do."

"It's true that I'm privy to a great many things, Mr. Kilgore. Some things may surprise you."

Mr. Kilgore's chuckle rang wickedly in her ears. "Ah Mr. Behr, that is precisely why I felt it might be advantageous for us to form a partnership." A chair squeaked. "I've already begun to make some strategic moves, but with the information you can provide, we could triple our assets by this time next year."

"Strategic moves?"

"You know that young man you were talking about, Gideon Maxwell? I happen to know he wants to buy a piece of land east of town. He's been downright pigheaded over refusing to sell the mercantile to me, so I bought that piece of land myself. Now, if he wants it, he'll have no choice but to sell me the mercantile first. Then, if he wants that land, he'll have to match the railroad's price, and he doesn't stand a chance of being able to do that. Not only will I have that prime stretch of land, but I'll have the mercantile as well."

There was a pause. Tessa heard clicking china. She wished she could see the faces of the men.

"Competition between land speculators is fierce, as you well know, Mr. Behr. A few creative adjustments of the survey maps will put us at a great advantage when it comes time for the contracts to be signed. In addition, business owners stand to turn a tidy profit by—shall we say—*unofficial* agreements with the railroad."

When the man named Behr finally replied, it sent a shiver down her spine. "Very shrewd, Mr. Kilgore. Very shrewd, indeed."

Tessa started to pick up her loaded tray when a water glass slid and tumbled to the floor.

A moment after the crash, Mr. Kilgore appeared in the doorway. "What's this? What are you doing, girl?"

Tessa caught her lip between her teeth as she stooped to pick up the shards of broken glass. A rush of blood filled her face with heat. "I'm sorry, Mr. Kilgore. I was just cleaning these tables and dropped a glass."

She didn't dare look up. It wasn't like she set out to eavesdrop on his conversation, but she didn't hasten to move out of earshot either. The pieces of broken glass jiggled in her trembling hand.

"This will come out of your pay! Now get this mess cleaned up." He stomped back into his office and slammed the door.

Relief wilted her shoulders. If he suspected her of listening to his conversation with Mr. Behr, he didn't let on. More than happy to comply with his orders, she hoisted her burden of dirty dishes and carried them to the kitchen.

Safely within the walls of the kitchen, she deposited the dishes by the sink and returned to her worktable. As she assembled the ingredients for tomorrow's spice cakes, Mr. Kilgore's words came back to her. Did Gideon know Mr. Kilgore had purchased the land he wanted? Her boss's other statements regarding the railroad made no sense to her, but the arrogance in his voice raised the hackles on her neck. It didn't take a Philadelphia lawyer to figure out that her employer was up to something unscrupulous. Now she had one more reason to dislike the man.

While she measured flour and spices into her mixing bowl, she entertained the inclination to go and tell Gideon what she'd heard. Conflicting notions collided in her head. Yes, she had feelings for Gideon. If she didn't, his reproachful questions wouldn't have hurt so much. On the other hand, uneasiness over what she'd heard made her wish she could run to the mercantile this minute and tell Gideon. But repeating information not meant for her ears was as unethical as eavesdropping. Why add to Gideon's low opinion of her?

Anger welled in her stomach. She'd let her attraction to Gideon grow, and he'd stepped on it and ground it into the dust. No good could come of seeing Gideon right now, much less talking to him. She clenched her teeth, realizing the anger she felt wasn't aimed solely at Gideon. Irritation crawled up from her gut, and she resented her own fickleness.

Just forget about it. There's nothing you can do.

Forgetting about Gideon, however, wasn't so easy. Despite her every effort to resist thinking of him, he still appeared in her mind's eye. The look on his face when she stormed out of the mercantile stayed with her as she poured the cake batter into pans and slid them into the oven. What exactly was that look? Disappointment? Suspicion? Gideon's expression didn't look anything like the accusation she'd been accustomed to seeing in Papa's eyes. Was it possible what she saw was regret?

Gideon's own words indicted him. *"If you want to have a friend, you have to be a friend."* She'd not had many friends in her lifetime, hardly even one if she didn't count Mama. But she knew enough to understand that friends didn't believe untruths about each other based only on appearances.

What hurt most was the growing realization that she already regarded Gideon as more than just a friend.

&

Daisy purred and rubbed against her ankles when Tessa opened the door of the shed. No scurrying sound fell on her ears upon her arrival.

The day's tension lifted as she picked up the little cat and rubbed its whiskers against her cheek. "I brought you a little bit of milk. Flossie said it would start to sour by tomorrow anyway."

She set Daisy down with the saucer of milk and smiled as the kitten cautiously sniffed it, took a few tentative laps, and then ignored the offering.

"I know it's not your mama's milk, but it's the best I can do." She glanced around the shed wondering if Daisy had encountered any of her roommates. Maybe they'd spread the news to all their rodent relatives that a cat now resided here.

Placing the folded quilt beside the trunk, she created a place where she could sit and have her supper. She unwrapped the cold biscuit and small bit of sausage she'd brought home and retrieved the remainder of the crackers and cheese stored in the crock. She thanked God for her meal, then she broke off a piece of cheese and popped it into her mouth along with a nibble of sausage.

As the rich flavors satisfied her hunger, she watched Daisy play with a corner of the quilt. Despite the strain of her day, she couldn't help smiling at the kitten's fierce little growls as she pounced on some imaginary prey. Then she realized Daisy had some kind of object between her paws.

Leaning over to get a closer look, Tessa's mouth dropped open with horror. Daisy's plaything was a mouse's tail. "No wonder you weren't hungry for milk. Your belly is full of. . .mouse!"

Tessa lost her appetite and tucked the rest of her meal away in the crock. With the edge of her shoe, she shoved the bodiless tail out the door with a shiver. "I know, Daisy, you're just doing your job." It was a good thing, she supposed, but somehow the kitten lost some of her innocence and took on the aura of a miniature predator.

As the shadows engulfed the shed, she lit her candle. A cracked coffee cup served as her candle holder. She held the candle aloft to search every corner of the shed for other remains of Daisy's lunch. Finding none, she breathed a sigh of relief and sat down on the quilt with Mama's Bible.

Instead of the Psalms tonight, she turned to the New Testament and began leafing through the pages, reading an underlined verse here or there. The marks showed her the words Mama read and loved then left as a legacy to her.

"Words to live by, honey girl. You can always trust the words in God's Book."

Tears welled in her eyes. If only Mama were here to answer some of the questions taunting her.

She turned a few more pages and found a folded bit of newspaper with torn edges. She carefully unfolded the yellowed paper and held it close to the candlelight to read the date. *"August 12, 1866."* Three days before her fourth birthday.

The article described the arrest of three men in Madisonville, Kentucky. One of the men stood accused of murder while the other two claimed to know nothing about it. Since they were in the company of the guilty man, it was at first assumed they, too, were guilty. During the trial, evidence proved the other two men innocent of the murder but suspected in various petty crimes. One of those two men had escaped custody before the verdict could be pronounced, and the name of the escapee caused her blood to freeze. "Doyle Langford." *Papa?*

She looked at the pages in First Thessalonians where Mama had tucked the scrap of newspaper. There was a verse underlined. *"Abstain from all appearance of evil."* Accompanying the verse was a dried smudge that appeared to be a water droplet. Or a teardrop.

"If Papa hadn't associated with the guilty man, he wouldn't have appeared guilty and would've had no reason to run."

Tessa's hand aimlessly stroked Daisy's fur. Being in the wrong place with the wrong person had brought suspicion down on Papa and heartache to her mother. In the candle's glow, she read the verse following the one Mama had underlined. Paul, the writer of First Thessalonians, prayed for the people he loved to remain blameless.

Tessa leaned back and closed her eyes. Had she done the very thing Papa did? By standing out in front of the saloon, she'd placed herself in the position of appearing guilty. Maybe Gideon's question wasn't one of reproach at all, but rather one of sorrow.

Chapter 12

Gideon stared over the top of his coffee mug. "Maybe she'll come into the mercantile today," he muttered aloud. Would speaking the words make them so?

"Did you say something?"

He turned to see Martha at the sink looking at him over her shoulder. She was probably afraid he'd bite her head off again like he'd done yesterday. They'd teased each other throughout their childhood, but the past several days, even Martha tiptoed around him.

"No, nothing important."

Martha wiped her hands on a towel and crossed the kitchen to sit at the table with him. "Gideon, just go and talk to her. What's stopping you?"

When had his little sister become so intuitive? He was the big brother. She was supposed to come to him for advice, not the other way around. But he'd certainly made a mess of things where Tessa was concerned. Maybe Martha was wiser in matters of the heart. Either that or she'd simply had enough of his grumpy disposition.

He set his cup down and leaned on his elbows. "It's not that easy, honey. I said something I shouldn't have, and now I don't know how to make it right."

Martha's eyebrows arched a little. " 'I'm sorry' usually works well. And if it's your pride that's keeping you from apologizing, remember living with nothing but your pride can be awfully lonely."

Oh, being wrong was tough, especially when one's little sister pointed out the obvious. A week's worth of loneliness grated on him with relentless condemnation.

His reasoning sounded completely logical to him: He couldn't leave the store. There wasn't enough privacy to talk at the hotel. Besides, the last time he spent a few minutes talking to her while she was working, she almost got fired. Going to speak to her after work at her little dwelling wouldn't be appropriate since it was located in a back alley. All those points made perfectly good sense during the day. But at night, as he fought with the bedcovers, the feeble excuses tormented him, and there was no one to blame except the man whose face peered back at him from the mirror every morning.

Martha rose and brushed a kiss on his cheek. "Don't wait too long, Gideon. The longer you put it off, the harder it will be. And from what you've told me about her, Tessa's a nice girl." She picked up her towel. "You're going to a great deal of trouble downstairs in the storeroom to give Tessa a place to work for herself instead of for Henry Kilgore. I don't suppose you were doing all that work just to pass the time."

Gideon leaned back in his chair, pressed his lips together, and narrowed his eyes. He was about to tell her to mind her own business when she sealed her case.

"I'm sure after you've prayed about it God will tell you what to do." She patted his shoulder and returned to the breakfast dishes.

How was he supposed to refute that? He stared into his coffee cup. Sure, he'd prayed about it. He prayed God would bring Tessa into the mercantile so they could talk. But she hadn't come in—not for a whole week—and he was beginning to get the idea God wasn't going to bring Tessa anywhere. Like Martha said, he just needed to go talk to her.

"But I don't know what to say to her," he mumbled under his breath. "I wounded her. She probably never wants to see my face again." He stood and scraped his chair back across the wooden floor, continuing to mutter as he descended the squeaky stairs to the store. "She was beginning to trust me, and I hurt her."

"You aren't the one she is supposed to trust."

He halted in midstep. "God, You must get awfully tired of me trying to handle things on my own."

He stepped inside the storeroom and knelt by the worktable he'd built for Tessa. "Father, I told Martha I didn't know how to make things right between Tessa and me, but that wasn't true. I know I owe Tessa an apology. I just don't know how to make it happen. I owe You an apology, too, Lord. You've nudged me in Tessa's direction, and if I'd listened to You, maybe I wouldn't have said those stupid things. I doubted You, Father, and I didn't wait like You told me to do. Forgive me, and please work it out so I can talk to her today."

❧

Business remained slow most of the morning, giving Gideon plenty of time to carry on a running conversation with God. Now, as he scowled at the paper in his hand, he had to admit God certainly had interesting ways to test his perseverance. Not that he was complaining. He'd simply have to exercise some faith and trust.

The bell jingled announcing the arrival of a customer.

A surge of hope quickened his pulse. *Tessa?* He looked up, but it was Pearl Dunnigan's sunny smile that greeted him.

"Good morning, Gideon."

His shoulders sagged in disappointment, and he mumbled, "Morning, Miss Pearl."

The woman chuckled. "What kind of welcome is that? Should I go back out and come in again?"

Gideon sent her an apologetic smile. "Sorry." He held up the paper. "The stove parts have been shipped."

"Wonderful. How soon before they get here?"

Gideon sighed. "That will depend on how soon I can go get them."

Miss Pearl frowned. "They're not coming here?"

Gideon handed her the telegram. "I wired the freight office in Dubuque to see if the parts had come in. They've arrived, but the next shipment for this area isn't due for another week and a half. I can get there and back in three days on horseback."

She looked over the missive and returned it to him. "Who would run the store?"

"Martha. She's worked in the store plenty of times along with Pa and me. She can do it for three days." He shrugged. "I'd like to get those parts as soon as possible. Even so, it may all be for naught."

"Why, Gideon? Didn't Tessa like the idea?"

Gideon pulled the pencil from behind his ear and thumped it on the counter. "I haven't had a chance to show it to her yet. Miss Pearl, I've really messed things up."

Miss Pearl arched her eyebrows. "You want to tell me about it?"

By the time he finished the whole story, she stood with arms folded, tapping her foot. "Gideon Maxwell, you should be ashamed of yourself."

"Oh, I am."

"I'm appalled that you've let an entire week go by without going to apologize. And you're waiting for God to simply do your bidding and bring Tessa to you?"

"But Miss Pearl, it's not—"

"How do you think that poor girl felt when you asked her if she was working at that awful place?"

"I didn't mean—"

"I know your pa taught you better than that."

"Miss Pearl, I—"

"If you don't march yourself over there this minute and talk to her, I'll go myself and bring her back here with me!" Miss Pearl ended her declaration with a snort and her hands on her hips. "Well?"

Gideon took in a breath and held it for a moment. Maybe Miss Pearl had something there. At any rate, Tessa would likely be more receptive to Miss Pearl than to him at the moment.

He reached out and took Miss Pearl's hands in his. "I think that's a wonderful idea. When are you going?"

༄

Tessa stood with her mouth agape, staring at the stove and the work space in Gideon's storeroom.

Large mixing bowls, baking pans, pie plates, and utensils lined the sturdy table. Sacks of flour and sugar crowded under the table while spice tins occupied one of the shelves. The stove sat proudly in the corner, polished and waiting.

She shook her head. "Gideon, I can't do this. You know I don't have the money to pay you for these things."

She watched Gideon glance at Miss Pearl who stood to one side. The woman smiled and nodded, and he took a deep breath like he was preparing to plunge headfirst into a rain barrel.

"Tessa, it's a business arrangement. You sell your baked goods out of the mercantile, and I get a small percentage until the cost of the materials and equipment is met. After that, your only expense would be your baking supplies. In addition, you supply Miss Pearl here with baked goods for the boardinghouse in exchange for your room and board. Not only can you quit your job at the hotel and work here full-time, you'll have a pleasant place to live."

Her mind staggered in an attempt to fully comprehend all Gideon had done on her behalf. Business arrangement or not, he'd gone to a great deal of trouble, and she only had one question.

"Why?"

His hopeful expression drooped. "Why? Well, because. . .you. . .you're. . ." His shoulders rose and fell.

She remembered the only other time she saw him so befuddled and speechless was a week ago when she stormed out the door. This simply didn't make sense in the light of his earlier assumption that she'd taken the saloon job. "Gideon, I don't understand why you would go to so much trouble for someone like me."

A grimace distorted his features. "Tessa—" He seemed to forget about Miss Pearl as he took a step closer. "Tessa, this might come as a surprise to you, but it shouldn't. I care about you. I care what happens to you, and I care how you're treated. You're a lady deserving of respect."

He fidgeted a moment, staring at the floor. "Tessa, the other day when I jumped to conclusions—I was wrong." He looked up and locked his gaze on her face. "I should've known you'd never do something like that. I apologize for even considering the possibility. Please forgive me."

Forgive? Gideon was asking for her forgiveness? It was too much to take in, and she turned toward the worktable. Of all the men she'd ever known or come in contact with—Papa, Mr. Kilgore, the hotel desk clerk, even the awful man outside the saloon—Gideon was the last man she believed needed to ask for forgiveness. Her gaze traveled over the equipment, the baking supplies, and the stove.

"Tessa, please?"

She pulled her attention back to the man standing before her. His eyes remained fixed on her as if willing her to accept his declaration. She believed he was truly sorry for the misunderstanding, but she couldn't let Gideon shoulder all the responsibility.

She glanced over at Miss Pearl who, judging by her smug though teary-eyed smile, was enjoying every minute of this. But Tessa had to clear up one thing. "There's something I have to say."

The anticipation etched on his face faded, but he didn't interrupt her.

"I found a verse underlined in my mother's Bible that says, 'Abstain from all appearance of evil.' If I had used better judgment, I would never have gone near the saloon for any reason. And if I hadn't been there, you wouldn't have drawn the wrong conclusion. So I'm sorry, too."

Tenderness spread across Gideon's countenance.

Her guarded hesitation melted away, and a slow smile crept into her face. Did she dare allow herself to hope?

"Ahem." Miss Pearl stepped forward. "Does this mean I have a new boarder?"

How did one say thank you for such generosity and kindness? "I just can't believe you did all this—for me." She couldn't keep the tremor from her voice.

Miss Pearl patted her hand. "For us, dear. You're helping me by doing the baking. I'm getting too old to stand in the kitchen all day. And you'll be helping Gideon by bringing more customers into his store."

She liked that idea. If she could repay Gideon for all the kindness he'd offered her, then it would be easy to agree to the arrangement. "It sounds like I'll benefit more than either of you. But if you truly want a three-way partnership, then my answer is yes."

Gideon pulled a small painted sign from a shelf and held it up for her approval.

"Tessa's Bakery. Oh my goodness!" She clapped her hands.

"There's just one small delay." Gideon crossed the space and pointed out an area on the stove and chimney, explaining that two connecting pieces were missing. "The parts are in Dubuque. I'm leaving first thing in the morning to go get them."

Tessa nodded, still barely able to take it all in.

Miss Pearl slipped her arm through Tessa's. "Since you'll be using my kitchen to do the baking for the boardinghouse, I'd like for you to move in today, if that's all right with you."

Tessa gave the woman an impulsive hug. Her throat was too tight for any other reply.

Miss Pearl beamed. "Gideon, can you help Tessa move her things to the boardinghouse this evening?"

He gave her a silly schoolboy grin. "My pleasure."

❧

Gideon loaded Tessa's trunk onto Cully's old wheelbarrow and dusted his hands on his pants. "Is that everything?"

Tessa stepped out the door of the shed with the kitten in her arms. Her smile set Gideon's heart tumbling. "Everything except Daisy."

He reached out and scratched the cat behind the ears. "You want to put her in the trunk?"

"Of course not," Tessa sputtered. She threw a defensive look at him and broke into a giggle at his teasing grin. "I'll just leave her in the shed, and as soon as I've finished talking to Mr. Kilgore, I'll come and get her."

The mention of Kilgore's name dampened the anticipation that had been skittering through Gideon's middle all day. "Do you want me to come with you?"

She shook her head. "No. You go ahead to Miss Pearl's with those things. This won't take long, and I'll meet you over there."

Doubt nipped at Gideon. If he knew Kilgore, the man would do his best to intimidate her. Gideon wanted to insist on accompanying her, but her independent spirit waved like a flag on the Fourth of July. "All right. But if you don't show up at Miss Pearl's place in a few minutes, I'm going to come looking for you."

The moment he arrived at Miss Pearl's back door, the woman bustled about, directing him to carry Tessa's things to a small but clean room just off the kitchen.

"This quilt has always reminded me of spring flowers," she said as she smoothed the cover over the bed. "I hope Tessa likes it." Miss Pearl fluffed up the pillow and straightened the rag rug on the floor.

Gideon nodded. The room was a startling contrast to the dismal shed. He set down the last of Tessa's belongings and left Miss Pearl to fuss over her preparations. As he descended the back porch steps, he caught sight of Tessa coming through the shadows.

She smiled a greeting and deposited Daisy on the porch. "Thank you, Gideon, for carrying my things."

"It was my pleasure. Did Kilgore give you a hard time?"

A tight-lipped smile tugged a dimple into her face. "He told me I couldn't quit because I was fired. Again."

He could only imagine the pompous man's bluster. "Either way, you don't have to deal with him anymore."

"Thanks to you."

The evening breeze lifted sandy strands of hair across her cheek, and an unseen hand pressed him a step closer. His fingers took on a mind of their own as they reached to brush the wisp of hair from her face. She raised widened eyes to his, and his heart rolled over in his chest. Twilight's fading rays fell across her, casting bronzed reflections in her eyes. Muted sounds of the evening hushed as he focused his gaze on her lips. The blood rushed in his ears. He gently cupped her chin and started to lower his face to hers.

When his lips were mere inches from hers, she turned her head and pulled back. "Thank you again, Gideon. For everything. Miss Pearl must be waiting for me." She darted like a scared rabbit up the porch steps and through the door.

Chapter 13

Tessa couldn't stop staring at the cozy, cheerful room that was her new home. It wasn't much larger than the shed, but the difference made her feel as though she'd just been released from a dungeon to live in the king's palace. The blue flowers on the pitcher and basin reminded her of the blue in Mama's eyes, and the colorful quilt smelled of fresh lavender. A crisp white curtain hung at the small window.

Miss Pearl stood in the doorway. "I hope it's not too cramped, dear."

"Oh no, ma'am. It's. . .it's. . ." Her eyes traveled around the space until they came to rest on the oil lamp on the small dresser. "It's wonderful." She crossed the room and touched the sparkling glass globe of the lamp. "May I really use this?"

Miss Pearl laughed. "Of course, dear. There's a box of wood matches in the top drawer of your dresser. Now, you must be tired, so I'll leave you to get settled."

Tessa thanked her and eased down on the bed, relishing its softness. She wondered if she'd be able to sleep on a comfortable bed after sleeping on nothing but her tattered quilt on the hard ground for so long. She looked forward to finding out.

There weren't many things in her trunk or cabinet to tuck away or hang, but she extracted each item and smoothed it with her hands before giving it a home on one of the wooden pegs or a dresser drawer. She reached into the cabinet and pulled out the cracked coffee mug that served as her candle-holder. The pitiful short stub of melted wax in the bottom of the cup was no longer needed now that she could sit and read by lamplight.

As she pushed the nearly empty trunk to the foot of the bed, the memory of Gideon touching her face crossed her mind like a web of silken threads. The touch of his fingers against her cheek sent flutters through her stomach. She could still feel his breath on her face.

She closed her eyes and tried to imagine how it might have felt if she'd not turned her head. Gideon's face lowering to hers caught her completely off guard. It never occurred to her that he might wish to kiss her.

"Why did I pull away from him?" No answer was forthcoming. "I wonder what was going through his mind." One thing was certain: She couldn't begin to describe what was going through hers.

❧

Tessa lay awake half the night tussling with worrisome thoughts. Her new bed was comfortable enough to invite sleep, but nagging images of Gideon loomed every time she closed her eyes. His tender expression and gentle touch lingered softly in her mind—like a melody she didn't want to forget. But her response to his touch drove her brow into a furrowed frown.

When she finally drifted off, she startled awake what seemed like only a moment later. The conversation she'd overheard between Mr. Kilgore and Mr. Behr prodded her conscience. She'd fretted all week, wondering whether or not she should tell Gideon what she'd heard. But then she'd have to admit to eavesdropping. She'd almost made up her mind to tell him last night when he carried her belongings to the boardinghouse. When he leaned down, appearing like he intended to kiss her, everything flew right out of her head. She hadn't given the overheard conversation another thought until now.

Giving up on sleep, she rose, dressed, and padded softly to the kitchen to stoke the fire in the cookstove. By the time Miss Pearl joined her, the fragrance of cinnamon spice coffee cake, fluffy biscuits, bacon, and coffee filled the air.

After the boarders finished their breakfasts, Tessa went to work kneading bread dough and setting it to rise. Later that morning, two warm, fresh loaves sat side by side and Tessa was taking cookies from the oven.

"I feel positively lazy!" Miss Pearl declared with a chuckle as she entered the kitchen.

Tessa hoisted a basket of apples to the worktable. "I thought I'd make an apple cobbler for dessert." She pushed a plate of cookies in Miss Pearl's direction. "Would you like some warm sugar cookies with your tea?"

"Mercy sakes, you're going to spoil me, child."

Tessa gave Miss Pearl a shy smile. "I'd like to spoil you. It's just my way of saying thank you."

Miss Pearl patted Tessa's shoulder. "Now, I haven't done a thing. It's all Gideon's doing." She picked up an empty basket from the pantry. "I'm going to pick some green beans from the garden." The woman stepped out the back door, leaving Tessa to work in solitude.

All Gideon's doing. The very mention of his name set her stomach to quivering. She wondered where he was now, how close to Dubuque and how soon to return.

Her unsettled heart pulled her first one way and then another when she invited last night's memory back to her mind. When Gideon's lips were inches from hers, she'd felt unable to draw a breath. His nearness paralyzed her, like time had stopped. When she'd escaped to the safety of her room and leaned against the closed door with her heart pounding in her ears, her legs barely held her up. Even now, as she recalled the touch of his fingers on her face, a shiver danced through her.

But why? Was it fear? Or something else?

When the drunken man outside the saloon grabbed her wrist that awful night, a nauseous, dreadful fear caused her to tremble. Gideon's touch was completely opposite.

"Why did I turn away from him?" Her own whisper accused her of being fickle. Her eyelids stung. She longed to talk to Mama. Miss Pearl was a sweet lady, but Tessa feared she didn't know the woman well enough to confide in her yet. Mama always knew her heart and could help her sort out her tumultuous emotions. To whom would she run now?

One of the psalms she'd read last night said God was a Father to the fatherless. The concept was almost too precious to ponder. If she claimed it, did that mean she could talk to Him when she was confused or lonely? Right now, she was both.

"God?"

She paused to gather all her tumbled thoughts.

"God, I don't know how to explain this, but I guess that's silly. I don't have to explain anything to You." She closed her eyes and sighed. "I'm so mixed up inside. Sometimes I want so badly to be close to Gideon that I ache. But when he's near, my heart feels like it's going to jump out of my chest, my hands won't be still, and all I want to do is run away."

She'd hoped speaking the words might help put her unruly emotions into perspective, but instead her own voice sounded hollow and her plea directionless. All she could do was pray God understood.

Daisy came tiptoeing into the kitchen with her tail held straight up like a tiny, furry flagpole.

Tessa scooped her up and sat on one of the kitchen chairs, settling the kitten in her lap. A twinge of envy pricked her. "God, sometimes I wish I could

102

curl up in Your lap."

Daisy purred and kneaded her paws into the folds of Tessa's apron.

"What if I hurt Gideon's feelings last night?" Her heart spun like a whirl-wind. "He's been so good and kind I can't stand thinking I might have offended him. But what I feel for Gideon isn't just because he's good and kind."

She looked out the window, beyond the yard, and through the trees. The distant hillside was dotted with headstones and makeshift crosses. Mama rested there.

"God, I don't know what to do. Help me understand. When I was a little girl and I was hurt or angry—or I couldn't understand why things were the way they were—I could always talk to Mama." Tears slipped down her face. "She helped me sort out my confusion when nothing in the world made sense. I wish she could tell me what to do about my feelings for Gideon."

She stroked the purring kitten in her lap, and Daisy pressed her head against Tessa's hand in a gesture of unfeigned love and complete trust. It reminded her of the times she'd spent as a little girl snuggled beside her mother.

"God is our refuge and our sanctuary, honey girl."

As a child, she hadn't known what those words meant. Maturing into adulthood, she walked the paths of adversity, grief, doubt, and confusion. When she found herself alone, the promises in God's Word offered sweet assurance that she could run to Him for sanctuary and comfort.

She lifted her face toward heaven. "God. . .Father. . .I love You."

❧

Tessa glanced at the clock ticking away on the parlor mantel. Two fifteen. Plenty of time to run to the mercantile for a few things.

She slipped into her room to wash her face and tidy her hair. Her appear-ance in the small mirror over the washstand disturbed her. Since she no lon-ger needed to save her money to pay rent for the winter, perhaps she could purchase a new hair ribbon or even a bit of lace to add to her collar. Such an extravagance might take some getting used to.

It wasn't hard to find Miss Pearl. The woman's humming could be heard coming from the front porch where Tessa found her sweeping.

"Miss Pearl, I'm going to the mercantile. Is there anything you need?"

Miss Pearl's broom halted as the woman placed a finger on her chin. "Yes, I need some laundry blue and a couple of pounds of coffee. Tell Martha to put it on my account. And if there is anything you need for your baking here, put that on my account as well."

Tessa hesitated a moment. "I thought I'd make a gingerbread cake for tomorrow if that would suit you. But I'll need some ginger and nutmeg."

"Gingerbread cake is one of my favorites—and Gideon's, too. Go ahead and get the spices, dear, and anything else you think we might need for the next few days." The woman resumed her sweeping and humming.

Tessa patted her pocket to ensure her own money was safely tucked away before stepping down the cobblestone walkway that led to the white picket gate. She might even purchase a hair clasp if it wasn't too costly.

The mercantile was a pleasant walk down the shady street and around the corner. Miss Pearl had told her of a shortcut through the back alley, but it was such a beautiful day that she had no desire to cut her errand short.

The house on the corner had hollyhocks growing beside the porch. The deep pinks drew her attention. She wondered if Gideon would find a hair ribbon that color becoming on her.

She turned the corner and proceeded down the main street through town. Just ahead, a door opened and a man exited an office. Tessa slowed her steps. The man had his back to her, but she still recognized Mr. Behr. He appeared to be speaking to someone behind him still inside. When the other person followed Mr. Behr onto the boardwalk, Tessa halted. She had no desire for a confrontation with Mr. Kilgore, given his ugly parting words to her the previous evening. The alley that bordered the building the two men exited provided a place for her to slip behind a stack of crates. She pressed her back against the wood-sided wall and waited for the men to pass. But they didn't pass by. They stopped right at the entrance of the alley, not ten feet from where she stood. Tessa peeked through the slatted sides of the crates that concealed her.

The sound of Mr. Kilgore's voice sent prickles up her arms. "I can assure you the Standridge brothers will see things my way. Once the sawmill is ours, the only other enterprise we lack is Maxwell's Mercantile."

"You're so certain of your persuasion with both brothers Standridge?"

A mirthless chuckle preceded Mr. Kilgore's reply. "Every man has his price, Mr. Behr. Ben and Earl Standridge both resent splitting their profits with each other. Once I convince each of them separately that his brother intends to sell his portion of the sawmill, it will just be a simple matter of drawing up a bill of sale. We'll take over that business for a fraction of what it's worth.

Taking ownership of the sawmill will give us the advantage with the land speculators."

Mr. Behr stood stroking his beard.

Tessa sucked in a slow, silent breath and held it. Neither man looked in her direction, but the guilt that plagued her earlier over listening to the men's conversation at the hotel now swelled with each passing moment.

"And young Mr. Maxwell?"

Tessa's lungs ached to expel the breath she held, but Mr. Behr's question locked it in place.

Mr. Kilgore struck a match on the bottom of his boot and lit his cigar. "Gideon Maxwell is in for a surprise. I'll let you know when I have the details worked out." He puffed on the cigar. "As soon as that mapmaker, Feldman, gets those altered land grant maps back to us, we can set our plans into motion. I just hope they'll look like the originals."

"You have nothing to fear, Mr. Kilgore. I've seen some of Mr. Feldman's work. He is truly an artist. The people with whom I work recommended him, and they are the best at what they do."

"Good. I don't settle for anything less, and I don't allow anyone to stand in my way."

❧

Gideon nudged the gelding through a wooded area and picked his way around a patch of scrub pines. His stomach rumbled a complaint, reminding him that breakfast was long past, but he pushed on. He hoped cutting through the woods would shave a couple of hours off his journey.

The memory of last night dogged him every mile. The alarmed expression on Tessa's face kept intruding across his mind. He couldn't run from it. "I practically forced myself on her. No wonder she ran off."

The horse twitched his ears and snorted like he agreed with every word.

"Why did I do that? If some guy had taken liberties with Martha, I'd have punched him in the nose." He pulled off his hat and wiped the sweat from his face with his neckerchief.

The warbling of a meadowlark provided the background music as Tessa's image slipped easily into his thoughts again. Her face felt exactly as he thought it would—velvety soft, like the supple kidskin gloves he sold in the store. No, softer than that. That loose wisp of hair that had grazed her cheek resembled the silk threads he remembered his mother using. The radiance of the sunset behind her had given her an ethereal glow. How could he *not* lean down to kiss her?

"But she turned her head and pulled away. Why did she do that?"

As he emerged from the stretch of woods, the road lay just ahead. He nudged the chestnut gelding into a mile-eating lope.

Minutes later, as he crested a hill, a group of three men with cumbersome-looking equipment appeared in the distance. One set a boxlike apparatus atop a tripod while the other two proceeded farther across the meadow with their gear.

"Surveyors." What were they surveying way out here?

Chapter 14

"S he was acting so strange."

Gideon listened as Martha told him about Tessa's visit to the mercantile.

"She looked at several different ribbons but didn't buy any. When I asked her if she was looking for a particular color, she acted like she didn't even hear me. Then she left the things she'd purchased for the boardinghouse sitting on the counter and walked out the door without them. I had to run after her to give them to her."

While it wasn't unusual for Tessa to be reserved and quiet, Martha's description of her behavior weighed heavily on his heart. Was she upset by the way he'd tried to kiss her the other night?

He took a sip of his coffee and cleared his throat. "Maybe she was just distracted. She might have had a lot on her mind." He made his voice sound as nonchalant as possible, but his heart grieved.

What if she was having second thoughts about working in such close proximity to him? He'd kick himself if his impulsive action ruined everything. Maybe she just didn't feel the same way about him as he felt about her. His gut wrenched at the thought. As soon as he stopped by the livery to see Cully, he'd make a visit to the boardinghouse.

Martha refilled his coffee cup. "Ted's mother and I plan to work on my wedding dress today, unless you need me here."

Gideon ran his finger around the rim of his cup. "I have two errands to run this morning, so if you could mind the store for about an hour, I'd appreciate it."

He descended the stairs and slipped out the back door of the storeroom. The cornflower blue sky promised a beautiful day. He hoped it would be beautiful in more ways than just the weather.

❧

Gideon walked around the boardinghouse to the backyard where Miss Pearl was hanging freshly washed sheets on the clothesline. "Morning, Miss Pearl."

The woman smiled through the clothespins held in her teeth. She removed the wooden pins and hugged Gideon. "You're back a day early. Did you get the stove parts?"

He grinned. "Sure did. I stopped at the livery and told Cully. He said he'd have them hooked up by this afternoon."

"Oh, that's just fine. But I don't suppose you came here to pass the time with an old lady like me." She gave him a sly smile. "Tessa's in the kitchen."

"You're beautiful, Miss Pearl, even with clothespins sticking out of your mouth."

She flapped her hand in his direction. "Oh, mercy sakes! Go on with you." She returned to her task, humming a tuneless ditty.

He took the porch steps two at a time and rapped lightly on the back door. When Tessa opened the door, he pulled his hat off and drew in a shallow breath.

She was a vision, even with strands of her sandy hair refusing to stay within the confines of their pins. Her cheeks were flushed a becoming shade of pink, but apprehension filled her eyes.

"Good morning, Gideon." She stepped aside so he could enter, then filled a coffee cup and set it on the table for him.

He took that as a good sign. At least she was willing for him to stay as long as it would take him to drink the coffee. "Morning." He lowered himself to the chair and watched her at the stove.

Her green-checked apron enhanced her hazel eyes as she placed a plate of fragrant cinnamon rolls on the table.

"Mm, thanks. Those smell great."

Silence hung between them as words eluded him.

Tessa appeared nervous, like she had something on her mind but didn't know how to begin. "Gideon, I have to tell—"

"Tessa, I need to—"

They exchanged uncomfortable smiles.

"There's something I heard—"

"Tessa, about the other night—"

Tessa twisted her fingers then gestured in his direction. "You go ahead."

Perhaps if he let her air out her feelings, he might be able to better address them. "No, please. You first."

She turned her back and picked up the corner of her apron. "There's something I need to tell you, but I'm afraid when I do you'll think ill of me."

The memory of the last time he jumped to conclusions stirred in his stomach. "Tessa, I won't think badly of you. I realize I did once, and I'm so very sorry I misjudged you."

She turned slowly to face him, the hem of her apron tangled around her fingers. "I didn't mean to eavesdrop, really. I was cleaning off tables in the dining room, and Mr. Kilgore left his office door open. He was talking so loud . . .I couldn't help hearing him. And then yesterday, when I saw him coming toward me on the boardwalk, I just didn't want to have an encounter with him, so I stepped into the alley behind some crates. I didn't know he would stop to talk with Mr. Behr right beside the alley."

Gideon reached over and pulled out the other chair at the table, inviting her to be seated. "Tessa, slow down. You're not making sense. Take a deep breath, and come sit down."

She gingerly slid down onto the chair, her eyes downcast. "I know it's wrong to eavesdrop. I didn't do it on purpose." She raised her eyes to meet his. "I don't want you to think I'm the kind of person who listens at doors or snoops around trying to overhear things not meant for me."

Gideon's lips twitched. It simply wasn't conceivable for Tessa to do anything sinister. She was too unassuming. "Tessa, nobody is accusing you of doing any such thing."

"But Gideon, I heard something by accident that you need to know about. I've struggled trying to decide whether or not to tell you. It feels like repeating gossip. But it's not gossip. Mr. Kilgore is planning something that isn't right, and I'm afraid it can hurt you."

"Hurt me?" Gideon frowned.

Anything Kilgore did wouldn't surprise him, but he was more concerned with Tessa at the moment. His attempt to kiss her didn't seem to be bothering her, but whatever she'd overheard upset her to the point she was even now mangling the edge of her apron.

"Tessa, it's all right. Whatever you heard wasn't your fault. It doesn't sound as if you set out to eavesdrop on purpose. But if Kilgore has something up his sleeve that you feel I should know, I'm listening."

She gave him a hint of a wobbly smile, and his heart rolled over. If relief was a tangible thing, it spilled over her countenance like handfuls of cold water.

He could clearly see she'd been worried about his reaction. To put her at ease, he broke a cinnamon roll in two and slid one half over to her. "Come on.

Share this delicacy with me, and tell me what's on your mind."

Fifteen minutes later, Gideon tried to make sense of everything Tessa had disclosed. His impression of Hubert Behr was that of a fine, upstanding, Christian gentleman. But if that was the case, what dealings did he have with Kilgore? "Did they say anything else? I don't understand what he means by altered land grant maps."

Tessa shook her head. "I don't either. He said you were in for a surprise, and his voice sounded so hateful when he said it. Do you think you should speak with the town sheriff?"

Everything Tessa had told him pinched his eyebrows into a V. "No, Sheriff McCoy is one of Kilgore's puppets. I doubt he'd do anything to help if he's in Kilgore's back pocket." He rubbed his chin. "If I telegraphed the US marshal, he isn't going to come all the way out here based on our suspicions."

Tessa set her elbow on the table and leaned her chin into her hand. "So what should we do?"

Gideon's heart did a little flip at her question, and he decided to tuck away the "we" for future consideration. "First thing we're going to do is pray about it. After that. . .well, I've made a mess of things too many times running ahead of God."

Tessa looked at him squarely in the eye, like she was weighing his answer. A hint of a smile tilted the corner of her mouth. "Prayer is a good start. I'll certainly be praying."

Gideon ignored the heat rising from his middle. "I. . .uh. . .I sort of thought, well, maybe we could. . .pray together."

Tessa's eyes widened, and she raised her chin off her palm. "Together?"

His breath constricted in his throat. If she had any discomfort or misgivings about spending time in close proximity with him, she would express it now.

She clasped her hands and dropped her gaze to study her fingers. At least she was no longer mutilating the hem of her apron.

He waited.

Finally she spoke. "Gideon. . ." Her voice was as soft as an angel's song. "Your invitation is very kind, but I think I'd best pray alone."

Gideon's shoulders slumped. She was, no doubt, trying to distance herself from him. A wave of self-condemnation crashed over him, but he pushed his disappointment away lest it color the tone of his voice. "That's all right." He filled his lungs slowly, deliberately, then released the air. "Tessa, about the other night. . . . I apologize if I frightened you or if my behavior was ungentlemanly."

He saw her stiffen, but she didn't raise her eyes.

"Forgive me?"

The tiny shake of her head was so slight he almost missed it.

No? She didn't forgive him?

She lowered her hands to her lap and began worrying the corner of her apron again.

Indecision gnawed at him. Should he excuse himself and leave? Should he wait to see if she had anything else to say?

Just as he sought God's advice, Tessa cleared her throat. "Gideon, you've never been anything but a gentleman. There's nothing to forgive."

If his heart could have burst free of his rib cage and taken wing, he'd have cheered it on. A fleeting thought sprinted through his head. Should he make another attempt to kiss her? Maybe not. Not yet, anyway.

She rose from the table, and he followed suit. "I stopped by the livery this morning and told Cully the stove parts are here. He said he could install them this afternoon, so your stove will be ready later today."

Anticipation filled her expression. "That's nice. Very nice." The corner of her apron hung twisted like a little girl's ringlet.

"We can hang your sign up in the window this afternoon if you'd like."

A nervous smile wobbled across her face. "I'd like that very much."

He stepped toward the door, but her voice lassoed him. "Gideon?"

He turned.

"I've never prayed *with* anyone before. Except Mama. I'm afraid I might not do it right."

A slow smile worked its way up from deep within his chest and spread to his face. "Tessa, there's no wrong way to pray. God just loves hearing from His children. Besides, if our prayers had to line up with a list of rules, I've been doing it wrong for years."

Tessa's laugh fell on his ears like music, and she nodded. "Okay, then. Maybe praying together would be all right." She lifted her fingers in a half wave as he headed toward the door. "I'll see you this afternoon."

He almost tripped over the threshold going out the door.

❧

Tessa dumped bread dough on the floured table and sank her fists into the soft, elastic blob. Methodically she pushed the air bubbles out of the mass, folded it over, and rolled her knuckles through it again and again, until the dough was satiny smooth. After dividing it into four equal parts, she greased the pans with lard and laid a portion of dough in each one.

Miss Pearl came in the kitchen toting her empty laundry basket on one hip. "I can't tell you how wonderful it is having you here doing the baking." The woman gave a pleasant sigh and dropped the basket by the door. "It's kind of nice having a friend in the kitchen, too. Coffee?" She withdrew two cups from the shelf.

"I just made a fresh pot." Tessa placed the pans of bread to rise at the back of the stove where warmth still lingered from breakfast. "There are a couple of cinnamon rolls left."

"You're going to spoil me for sure." Miss Pearl filled the two cups. "I don't suppose watching my figure is an excuse not to indulge." She bit into a roll and closed her eyes. "Mmm."

Tessa smiled at her landlady and took the seat opposite her. "I can check the laundry on the line for you and bring it in when it's dry."

"That would be a big help. I'm doing all the bedding today. It's a big job."

The steam from Tessa's cup sent fragrant tendrils wafting by her nose, coaxing her to take a sip. The coffee's bracing flavor lent her a bit of courage. "Miss Pearl, do you ever wish you had someone to talk to—someone special, someone you loved?"

Miss Pearl gave her a knowing look. "Missing your mama, are you?"

Tessa nodded wordlessly.

The woman took another slow sip of her coffee and set her cup down in front of her. "I'm not your mama, but if you've got something troubling on your mind, I'm a good listener."

Tessa bit her lip to command the stinging behind her eyelids to quit. She swallowed hard, forcing her emotions into line. Her eyes locked on to the dark liquid in her cup, and she willed her thoughts to fall into the right order so they wouldn't sound stupid. "Miss Pearl, did anyone ever try to kiss you?"

A snuffled sound came from Miss Pearl's side of the table. When Tessa looked up, the woman's eyes twinkled, her lips pressed together, and the corners of her mouth appeared to have the hiccups.

Miss Pearl cleared her throat and finally spoke. Her voice reminded Tessa of a tinkling music box. "Well, yes. I remember the first time my Jacob tried to kiss me. We were standing behind an old willow tree where he'd carved our initials. He leaned way over, his eyes all squinched closed and his lips pooched out like a guppy."

Tessa tried to paint the picture in her mind, and a smile tugged at her lips. "What happened?"

"Teacher rang the bell. Recess was over."

A laugh bubbled up from Tessa's middle, releasing the tightness in her chest. "How old were you?"

A faraway look crept into Miss Pearl's eyes. "He was eleven, and I was nine. But I knew from that moment he was the man I would marry."

"And did you?"

"Mm-hmm."

Tessa could see memory's pages turning backward in the woman's mind. "I was just sixteen. We married and worked side by side together for twenty-six years. Fever took Jacob twelve years ago." She smiled at Tessa. "Sometimes I can still taste that first kiss."

A flutter tickled Tessa's stomach, and she drew in a soft breath. How sweet would it be to hide a memory that special in one's heart?

"So"—Miss Pearl picked up her cup again and eyed Tessa over its rim— "may I assume Gideon kissed you?"

"No." She blurted out the reply as a rush of heat filled her face and burned her ears. She gentled her voice. "No—that is, he started to, but...."

"But what? Teacher didn't ring the bell."

Tessa blew out a stiff sigh. "I pulled away from him. And I don't know why."

Miss Pearl's smile crinkled the lines around her eyes. "Maybe you just weren't ready, child. A girl wants to know a man cares about her here." She laid a hand over her heart. "And she has to know how she feels about him, too. Do you know how you feel about Gideon?"

Tessa lifted her shoulders slightly. "I–I'm not sure."

"Well, there's one way to find out for sure." The woman reached across the table and patted Tessa's hand. "You talk to God about it. He'll reveal those feelings to you, so you don't have to wonder if it's right or not."

Tessa returned Miss Pearl's smile. "Seems like I have a lot to pray about."

"You take it to the Father. You can trust Him, honey girl."

Honey girl. She never thought she'd hear those words again. The sweet endearment wrapped around her heart like a warm quilt. The grief she felt at missing her mama suddenly wasn't quite so sharp.

Chapter 15

The reproach on Tessa's face took Gideon aback.

"Don't you like horses?"

Tessa's shoulders hunched with a slight shake of her head. "It's not that. . . It's really none of my business."

Gideon laid aside the letter from the breeder in Illinois he'd shown her moments ago. Judging by her frown, she didn't share his enthusiasm. Maybe her stony silence was because she feared she'd no longer have the bakery. "Hey, don't be concerned about the buyer not wanting to keep the bakery. Business has doubled in the past couple of weeks because you're here."

She fingered the wiggly ridges around the edge of a pie for several long moments. Not meeting his eyes, she pursed her lips before answering. "My father had a good farm in Indiana—at least it could have been a good farm if he'd worked at it. But he sold it and dragged Mama and me out here to chase an illusive dream of getting rich. Mama had been sickly for so long, and traveling was too hard on her. She might still be alive today if we'd stayed put. I don't understand how a man can throw away a perfectly good means of support for his family in favor of such an uncertain prospect."

An invisible fist punched Gideon in the gut. He swallowed the ire rising in his chest only to feel disappointment replace it. For weeks he'd wondered and prayed about Tessa possibly being the woman God had chosen for him. But her disdain of his dream was a bucket of cold water thrown in his face. How could she compare his plans to her father's drunken irresponsibility?

"Tessa, this is something I've planned for a long time. I'm not entering into this with my eyes shut." He wished she'd look at him. "There's a huge need in this area for sturdy, well-bred farm horses."

She cocked her head to one side. "But you told me your father started this business and that he supported his family well because of the dependable reputation he built as a merchant. Why would you cast that aside on a gamble?"

Defensiveness sprang up and grabbed control of his words before he could stop it. "I'm not casting anything aside, and I'm certainly not gambling away my father's hard work. Being a merchant suited him. He enjoyed the work. I just want something different." He didn't add that he'd hoped for her support of his dream. He'd sought God's guidance in this endeavor for three years and felt assured of the Lord's approval. But for weeks Tessa's image had begun entering into that dream as well, and it was an image he didn't want to dismiss.

"Mmm. Something sure smells good in here." Ty Sawyer strolled in the door. "What's this? You operatin' a bakery now?"

Gideon shoved his disconcertment down and greeted his friend. "Hey Ty."

Ty stopped short, and his eyes widened at the sight of Tessa in her green gingham apron. He yanked his hat from his head. "Don't believe I've had the pleasure."

The silly grin on his friend's face caused Gideon to grit his teeth, but courtesy demanded he at least make the introduction. "Tessa Langford, Ty Sawyer."

Ty swept his hand across his middle and executed a courtly bow. "Miss Tessa, pleased to meet you."

Gideon stifled a growl. "What brings you to town again so soon, Ty?"

Ty leaned against the counter. "I came in to make my loan payment at the bank. But I saw something while I was standing there waiting that I thought you'd be real interested in."

"What's that?"

Ty took off his neckerchief and wiped the sweatband of his hat. "I'd just stepped up to the window when the clerk asked me to wait for a minute and went into Sewell's office with a handful of papers. He left the door open, and I could see Kilgore and Behr sittin' in there with Sewell." Ty paused like he was waiting for Gideon's reaction. "I'd give a week's wages to know what was going on in there, wouldn't you?"

Gideon rubbed his chin. "Kilgore and Behr—both in there with Mr. Sewell?"

"Mm-hmm."

"Were they're doing anything illegal?"

Ty stuck his hand into the gumdrop jar. "What do you think?"

"I think I have work to do, and I think you owe me about twenty-five cents now for all the gumdrops you've eaten in the past month." He lifted a crate of sewing notions to the counter and pried off the top.

"Look, Gideon, if this guy Behr is doing business with Kilgore, you better watch your back."

A frown forced Gideon's brows downward. "I appreciate you telling me about this, Ty, but what can I do? Even if I thought they were doing something illegal, the sheriff isn't going to do anything since he answers to Kilgore."

"Gideon?"

He'd almost forgotten Tessa was standing there. The stricken look on her face indicated she'd all but forgotten their earlier disagreement.

"Gideon, I feel terrible. I should have told you sooner about what I overheard."

He took a step closer to her, deliberately moving between her and Ty. "Tessa, we don't even know what they're up to yet. It could be something completely legitimate."

"Pfft." Ty grunted. "You really believe that?"

Gideon shrugged. "Truthfully, no. But until we can prove otherwise, all we can do is wait and see."

Ty shrugged. "Suppose you're right." He turned and bestowed a huge smile on Tessa. "Miss Tessa, there's gonna be a barn dance next Saturday night over at the Johnson place. I'd be pleased to escort you."

Gideon's insides twisted. He sucked in a breath and shot daggers at the guy who was supposed to be his best friend. But Ty seemed oblivious, standing there twisting his hat, waiting for Tessa's reply.

No, Tessa. Tell him no.

Tessa's lashes dropped to her cheeks in a demure pose as a tiny smile curved her lips. "Why, Mr. Sawyer, that's so kind of you to ask."

If one could chew his own teeth, Gideon gave it his best effort.

A ridiculous-sounding chuckle came from Ty's direction, and Gideon suppressed the urge to throw the jar of gumdrops at him. *As soon as Ty leaves, I'm going to ask you myself, Tessa, so just tell him no.*

She gave Ty a sweet smile. "Martha was telling me about the barn dance just yesterday. I'm sorry, but I've already made plans to attend with someone else."

Ty's grin drooped, and he shuffled his feet for a moment. "Oh. Well, maybe I'll see you there." He plopped his hat back on his head and lifted a hand in good-bye.

Gideon barely acknowledged Ty's leaving. Instead his eyes followed Tessa as she turned toward the storeroom. Who had already asked her to the barn dance? "Tessa?"

Tessa turned in the doorway. "Yes?"

"Um, about the barn dance. . ."

"Gideon, if you don't mind, could we talk later? I need to get these pies in the oven, and the heat is just right."

His head bounced up and down. "Oh, sure. You go right ahead. Don't let me keep you."

꙼

The courage to inquire about the man with whom Tessa planned to attend the barn dance eluded Gideon for days. He'd managed to initiate topics about almost everything else, but he couldn't bring himself to speculate on the identity of the man who would hold Tessa in his arms and waltz her across the barn floor. Perhaps it didn't matter, since Tessa's opinion of his dream still left a bitter taste in his mouth.

The bell on the door jingled.

Gideon looked up to greet his customer, but the words stuck in his throat. He'd mulled over the information Ty gave him several days ago, as well as the conversation Tessa had overheard, but came to no conclusions.

Now Hubert Behr entered the store wearing the same dignified expression he'd worn the first day Gideon met him. "A pleasant afternoon to you, young fellow. Might I have a word with you?"

Warning signals shot through Gideon's head. "Good afternoon, Mr. Behr. How may I help you today?"

Behr cleared his throat. "First off, I must apologize for the delay in getting back to you. My business here has taken a bit longer than I expected. I do hope the mercantile is still available for purchase."

Gideon glanced in Tessa's direction and saw a frown flit across her face at the mention of selling the mercantile. With Ty's information in mind, Gideon exercised caution before replying. "I thought you might leave Willow Creek as soon as your business was finished."

One thick eyebrow lifted slightly as Behr silently questioned Gideon's response. "No, I'm not planning to leave anytime soon. I would like to make an offer on your place, but it will take at least a couple of weeks before I can finalize any plans." The man named a figure that matched Gideon's original asking price.

Gideon studied Behr's face, searching for signs of deceit or corruption. "Sir, if I might be so bold, may I speak frankly?"

Behr nodded. "Of course, young man. What's on your mind?"

The store was empty at the moment, but the presence of Tessa's Bakery had increased the number of customers coming and going, and Gideon didn't want to be interrupted. He spoke quietly and quickly. "Mr. Behr, you seemed like a decent sort when you first arrived. But I must say I've been more than a bit concerned to see you in the company of Henry Kilgore numerous times. I apologize if I'm out of line, but I feel I should warn you. You would do well to be careful in dealing with Mr. Kilgore."

Hubert Behr's gray eyes narrowed and scrutinized Gideon for a long minute. Just when Gideon was certain he'd not only overstepped his bounds but probably also ruined any chance of selling the mercantile, Behr finally spoke. "Young man, you seem to know more than you are letting on, so let me caution *you*. Employ discretion before proceeding."

Gideon glanced in the direction of the storeroom where he could hear Tessa humming as she worked. He wanted no confrontation with Hubert Behr with Tessa close by.

He took a deep breath and met Behr's steady gaze. "Sir, I have reason to believe you are engaged in business with Henry Kilgore. He's probably told you by now that I've refused to sell him the mercantile."

Behr showed no reaction.

"My decision not to sell to Kilgore is based on several reasons, both personal and ethical."

The front door opened, and two ladies entered carrying large market baskets over their arms.

Gideon threw Behr a pointed look before greeting his customers. "Morning, ladies. How may I help you?"

The women both declared they wished to purchase baked goods, and while Tessa filled their orders, they browsed through the bolts of cloth, exclaiming at the colors and choices.

Gideon motioned to Behr to step over nearer the door to put more space between them and the ladies. "Mr. Behr, I'm sorry, but I can only assume you're here as a proxy for Kilgore, trying to purchase the mercantile for him."

Behr lowered his head and slipped his hand inside his jacket pocket.

Gideon nailed an unblinking stare at Behr's arm, waiting to see if the man might pull out a derringer. His mind raced along with his pulse making lightning decisions how to position himself to protect Tessa and his customers.

Through the thick curtain of tension, one of the ladies called to him. "Mr. Maxwell, might I get a dress length of this cloth, please? And I'll need some thread and buttons as well."

Gideon didn't take his eyes off Behr as he replied in a voice he hoped sounded natural. "Of course, Mrs. Clary. I'll be right there." He paused to see if Behr would react. When he didn't, Gideon excused himself and went to meet his customer's need, hoping Behr would simply leave. He started to measure out the yardage the woman requested when he heard Tessa's voice.

"Would you care to sample some of these cinnamon cookies or perhaps some pound cake, sir?"

Gideon's eyes widened as Behr crossed to stand next to Tessa and accept a tidbit from her tray.

All spit evaporated from his mouth, and clumsiness attacked his fingers. After managing to cut and fold the material for the woman, he hurriedly added up the other purchases and finalized the transaction. "Thank you, ladies. Come again."

He turned to where Behr was still standing and chatting with Tessa.

She handed him a bag, and he paid her for his purchase. "I hope you enjoy it, sir."

"I'm sure I shall, young lady."

Gideon took Tessa's arm and gently pushed her toward the storeroom, positioning himself in front of her. "Mr. Behr, I doubt we have any more to say to each other, so I'll ask you to leave now."

He heard a soft gasp behind him. "Gideon!"

Behr's expression did not change, but his eyes shifted toward the door. "Mr. Maxwell, is there a place we can speak privately where we won't be interrupted? I fear I have given you the wrong impression."

Gideon folded his arms across his chest. "Mr. Behr, you've been seen in Henry Kilgore's company on numerous occasions, and you've been heard exchanging business plans with him. Earlier today you and Kilgore were meeting with Roland Sewell. Exactly what impression was I supposed to get?"

Behr glanced past Gideon's shoulder where Tessa still stood. "I can see you won't be satisfied until I reveal my true purpose for being here. If you will trust me, I'd like to meet with you anywhere you say, someplace private, so I can clear up this misunderstanding."

Gideon deepened his frown. "I have no reason to trust you, sir."

The thick mustache on Behr's lip tweaked. "Very prudent, young man.

But if you will allow me, I will prove I am worthy of your trust. However, we should not be seen leaving the store together. Tell me where you'd like to meet, and I shall be there."

"Gideon. . ." Tessa's frightened whisper tugged at him.

The man's odd statement aroused deeper suspicion, but Gideon slowly nodded. Without taking his eyes off Behr, he spoke to Tessa. "Tessa, would you mind taking care of the store for a short time? I don't think this will take long."

The silence was broken only by Tessa's sharp intake of air.

After probing Behr's face for a full minute, Gideon spoke. "Take the main street through the edge of town past the livery stable. There's a grove of cottonwoods and elm trees to your right. Beyond that, you'll see the town cemetery. Meet me by the pines on the far side of the cemetery. It's about a ten-minute walk." Gideon pulled out his pocket watch. "I'll be there by two o'clock."

Behr nodded and walked out the door.

Tessa gripped Gideon's sleeve. "Gideon, please don't go there alone. What if it's a trap? What if he brings Mr. Kilgore with him? When Mr. Kilgore said you were in for a surprise, his voice was so cold and hateful. Gideon, please don't go."

Chapter 16

Gideon berated himself as he approached the stand of pines at the far end of the cemetery. If Behr was luring him into a trap as Tessa feared, the spot was too remote to expect help to arrive quickly should the need arise. Indecision caused Gideon's steps to hesitate. Should he abort this meeting or see what the man had to say?

Hubert Behr stepped out of the shadows. "Thank you for coming, Mr. Maxwell."

Gideon gave the man a wary nod.

Behr reached into his coat pocket and extracted a wallet. "I should begin by telling you my real purpose for being in Willow Creek." He opened the leather folder and displayed the identification within.

Gideon studied the pewter badge and the words engraved around it, unsure whether to believe what Behr was indicating. "Pinkerton National Detective Agency. You're a Pinkerton agent?"

"I am." Mr. Behr's tone, though modulated, held the ring of authority.

Abrasive edges of puzzlement troubled Gideon. "What business would a Pinkerton have in a town the size of Willow Creek, Iowa?"

Behr tucked the wallet away. "The Chicago, Kansas and Nebraska Railroad received a most interesting letter from Mr. Roland Sewell describing some rather creative land deals Henry Kilgore was attempting to put together. Included were Mr. Kilgore's ongoing practices of intimidating business owners and landowners in this area to sell to him at deflated prices. The railroad contacted the General Land Office in Washington, which in turn contacted our Chicago office requesting that we investigate Mr. Kilgore's activities and gather tangible evidence of fraudulent transactions."

Skepticism tussled with relief in Gideon's mind. Behr seemed to use all the right words and phrases, and the identification he'd displayed moments ago bore silent testimony to the man's explanation.

Behr interlaced his hands in front of him and cleared his throat. "I might ask you how you knew I was meeting with Mr. Kilgore and Mr. Sewell earlier today, but that's not really important. However, I would like to prevail upon what I suspect is your sense of honor and request your assistance."

Gideon guarded his expression while he digested Hubert Behr's revelation of his identity. *A Pinkerton agent!* If that were truly the case, Gideon had a few questions. He steeled his eyes. "Mr. Behr, how do you explain the overheard conversations in which you indicated entering into a partnership with Kilgore?"

A slight shrug lifted Behr's shoulders. "One of the distasteful parts of this business, young man. Sometimes the investigating agent must employ a bit of fiction before the suspect will relax enough to divulge information we need to build a case. Speaking untruths is not something to which I aspire. Unfortunately, I've recently found it necessary to lead Mr. Kilgore to believe my occupation is procuring land for the railroad—with a willingness to engage in private land speculation on the side."

"And the reference to altered land grant maps?"

Behr's bushy eyebrows arched slightly, but Gideon didn't plan on naming Tessa as the one who overheard the conversations.

"The surveyors, as well as the cartographer hired by Mr. Kilgore, were taken into custody this morning without Mr. Kilgore's knowledge. My agency is now in possession of the maps, which were rather masterfully revised, I must say. The forgeries appear to be quite authentic. They were the last piece of evidence I needed. All that remains now is to take Mr. Kilgore into custody."

Gideon weighed the credibility of the man's answer. The memory of the slight tremble in Tessa's voice accompanying her urge for caution gave him pause. Another question nagged him.

"If all this is true, how does your offer to buy the mercantile fit in? How can I be sure you aren't making a deal for Kilgore?"

Behr didn't blink. "You can't, young man. Life is full of uncertainties. That's why God's Word encourages us to learn wisdom and discretion." His eyes remained fastened on Gideon, but his mustache twitched. "Even Pinkerton agents tire of adventure after a time and desire a bit of a slower pace. My investigating days are drawing to a close. I can assure you my offer is legitimate. I've shown my identification credentials and given an explanation. I can't make you believe me."

Gideon took a slow, deep breath. "Exactly what is it you're asking me to do?"

Behr smiled. "Send word to Kilgore that you've changed your mind about selling the mercantile to him and you now wish to discuss a deal."

ﻬ

Tessa glanced toward the door for the hundredth time since Gideon left, then she looked at the clock. Had it really only been twenty minutes since he followed Mr. Behr to the agreed-upon meeting place? Anxiety weighed in her chest where she knew faith should reside.

The scriptures she'd read in the past weeks about God's care and protection echoed in her mind, along with her mother's repeated admonition that God was worthy of her trust. Such trust was a choice, much like the choice she'd made months ago to survive to honor Mama's memory.

She finished sprinkling cinnamon sugar over the top of a pan of scones and slid it into the oven. Wiping her hands on a towel, she squared her shoulders. Those days following Mama's funeral, Tessa believed her survival depended upon herself and her own perseverance. Reading the precious words in Mama's Bible and remembering the faith she'd learned at her mother's knee birthed fresh understanding of God's care. Even now she realized she could do nothing to ensure Gideon's safety, and his well-being depended completely upon God's grace. She whispered a prayer for God's protection.

Her disagreement with Gideon earlier in the week made little sense now. Admittedly Gideon's well-thought-out plan of raising farm horses in no way resembled Papa's selfish whims. Furthermore, a man didn't share his dreams and goals expecting rejection.

After several restless nights, understanding had dawned. Gideon confided his plans to her because they were friends. No, more than friends. He'd almost kissed her.

Every time she was in his presence, contentment warmed her and there was nowhere else she wanted to be. When she was apart from him, she ached with a longing that only his return satisfied. The times she caught him gazing at her or when he sent her a toe-curling smile, an entire colony of butterflies turned loose in her stomach. How could she deny the connection that existed between them?

Shame filled her when she remembered the hurtful words she'd carelessly tossed at Gideon's dream. She determined to apologize for her thoughtlessness as soon as he returned. She glanced once more at the door, hoping for a glimpse of him.

Keep busy. He'll be back in a few minutes.

Miss Pearl had requested some potato rolls to serve with her pot roast, and they were popular items in the bakery as well. *Keep busy.* She blended softened yeast into the batter, adding flour with leftover mashed potatoes until the dough became stiff. Her knuckles plunged into the dough and began the rhythmic kneading action.

"Well, well. I'd heard you and Maxwell had a cozy little arrangement here, but I wasn't sure I believed it."

Tessa spun around. Henry Kilgore stood in the storeroom doorway. She hadn't heard him come in. A shudder rippled through her. "If you want to speak to Gideon, he's not here."

Kilgore sauntered into the storeroom, casting a disdainful perusal at the results of Gideon's painstaking work. "I don't need to talk to him. You're the one I came to see. I wondered if you'd given any more thought to my offer."

Offer? What offer? Surely he didn't mean. . . . "Mr. Kilgore, I made it quite clear when I quit my job at the hotel that I had no intention of working for you in any capacity. Ever."

Kilgore's laugh lacked even a shred of humor. "Never say never, my dear. I'm certain you'll come around to my way of thinking."

Nausea swelled in her stomach, and the air she tried to drag into her lungs suddenly felt thick. "That will *never* happen. And I'm *not* your dear. You can leave now."

He took two more steps in her direction. "I can't leave yet. We haven't had a chance to sit down for a nice talk. Why don't you come over to my place, and we can discuss a business arrangement?"

Was the man deranged? Did he honestly believe he could talk her into going anywhere with him? She backed away. Panic slid its tentacles around her throat, and her stomach threatened to retch. A chill unlike anything she'd ever known invaded her bones. "Mr. Kilgore. . ." She hardly recognized her own voice as suffocating fear restricted her air.

Another voice bullied its way into her memory. *"You ain't worth nothin'."*

The past few months, she'd begun to distance herself from Papa's assessment, even daring to reject the validity of his words. But the wicked gleam in Kilgore's eyes and the insinuation of all that his "offer" entailed brought the ugliness of her father's ridicule crashing over her again.

She took another step backward and bumped into the corner that formed where the worktable met the wall shelves.

Kilgore closed the space between them, his scrutinizing gaze lingering on her in a most ungentlemanly way. Was this what Papa meant? Kilgore reached out and ran his fingers down one side of her face. When she jerked away from him, he seized her jaw in a cruel grip. "I'm a patient man, but I do have my limits. You've been in this town long enough now to know that I get what I want." He released his hold and patted her cheek.

The prayer she'd sent heavenward for Gideon's safety crossed her lips once more, only this time the petition was for herself. "I told you, Mr. Kilgore. I will not work in your saloon. Now please leave. Customers will be walking in here any minute."

"No they won't. I hung the CLOSED sign on the door when I came in." A slow, sinister smile slithered across Kilgore's face, and he stepped back. "You know what I heard? Gideon Maxwell isn't the choirboy you think he is. In fact, the good people of Willow Creek might be interested to know that Maxwell is a regular over at the Blue Goose."

If Kilgore's presence hadn't initiated such revulsion, she might have laughed at the insinuation. The very idea was preposterous. Did he think she would agree to go along with his proposition because he tried to make her believe Gideon visited his saloon? "That's a lie! Gideon would never go there."

Kilgore sucked on his teeth. "Maybe not, but people love a spicy story. What do you think that will do to his credibility as an honest businessman, hmm?" A smug upturn at the corner of his mouth punctuated his question.

Tears burned her eyes, and she felt sick to her stomach. "Please don't do that to Gideon. What has he ever done to hurt you?"

All semblance of the smile faded from Kilgore's face. "He thinks he's better than me. Gideon Maxwell looks down his nose at me, just like his old man did. Holier-than-thou hypocrites, both of them. Just like the good people of the town where I grew up." A vein bulged on the side of his neck, and his chest rose and fell like the bellows in Cully's blacksmith forge. "Just because my old man was no good, all the important people in town—those fine, upstanding people who always acted like they were better than everyone else—said I had his bad blood." A grotesque sneer disfigured his face. "Gideon Maxwell is just like them. Well, I aim to teach him that nobody toys with Henry Kilgore. I will destroy Gideon Maxwell. Unless. . ."

Fear rose up to strangle her once more. Even without Kilgore finishing his thought, she knew what his conditions were. He moved close to her again and wrapped his fingers around a handful of her hair. She couldn't draw enough air to scream.

He leaned in so close she felt his hot breath on her face. "You come with me now, or I promise you, before the day is out, I'll see to it that Gideon Maxwell's good name and reputation are so sullied he'll lose the respect of everyone in this town. People will spit on him just like they used to do to me. But no more."

If Kilgore did what he threatened, the dream Gideon had shared with her a few days before would shatter at his feet. She couldn't let that happen.

Kilgore grabbed her arm and pulled her toward the back door. "You keep your mouth shut when we step out, or so help me, you'll wish you had."

He pushed her out the door in front of him, and when he did so, the gingham apron she wore—Mama's apron—caught on the hook Gideon used to latch the door at night. A ripping sound reached her ears. When she tried to rescue the garment, Kilgore clamped his fingers around her upper arm and twisted her flesh. She bit her lip to keep from crying out.

"You won't be needing that apron anymore." Kilgore's hateful gloat seared her heart. Papa's jeering words echoed in her head again, mocking the effort she'd made in the past months to live in a way to make her mother proud.

He dragged her along beside him as they stepped out from behind the telegraph office on their way across the street to the Blue Goose. When they entered the establishment, the odor of whiskey and smoke assaulted her senses. Jeering catcalls from the men leaning against the bar and indecent invitations from others seated at the tables brought tears to her eyes. A hand reached out and pinched her as they passed. It was her nightmare come to life.

God, protect me.

"Hands off, boys. She's off-limits." Kilgore tugged her up against him, out of the reach of the groping hands. A maniacal grin spread his lips. "At least for now."

One man wearing a dirty, sweat-stained shirt with missing buttons bellowed, "Ain't our money good enough for her?"

Kilgore forced her through a doorway at the back of the smoke-filled room. "In due time, gentlemen. For now, she's mine."

He pulled the door shut behind them and pushed her down a narrow hallway. Muffled voices and laughter came from behind a row of closed doors.

God, please help me.

When they reached the last door, Kilgore pulled a key from his pocket and inserted it in the lock. Thrusting the door open, he shoved her into what she assumed was his private room.

Heavy draperies hung at the window, blocking out most of the light. Whiskey bottles and glasses sat on a small table. A wooden chair took up one corner. Maroon velvet covered the bed positioned in the opposite corner.

He locked the door behind him. "Now then, you and I need to get to know one another. Sit down there." He indicated the chair.

Heavenly Father, don't let this man touch me. "Mr. Kilgore, please don't do this."

"I thought we had a deal," he hissed, raking his gaze over her in a way that made her feel like the deed he insinuated had already been done. "Not that it matters now."

Through her paralyzing fear, words she'd heard over and over in her dreams came back to whisper in her ear once again.

"Tessa, God says you are precious in His sight, and I agree with Him."

Chapter 17

Gideon cut through the alley behind the telegraph office mulling over Hubert Behr's words. As he approached the back door of the store, his steps slowed.

The door stood open, and smoke drifted out.

He closed the distance in a few long strides and leaped up the steps. A blue gray cloud filled the bakery area. Had she gotten distracted by customers out front? "Tessa?"

He jogged through the storeroom and past the store counter. Odd. Why was the front door shut and the CLOSED sign displayed?

"Tessa!" A sweeping glance told him she was nowhere in the store.

He strode back to Tessa's work area and yanked the oven door open. Smoke billowed from blackened lumps inside. Tessa wouldn't leave something in the oven like this, unless. . . "*Tessa!*"

Where could she have gone? He turned to head out the back door when a small green-checked scrap of cloth on the latch caught his eye. Tessa's green gingham apron. He shoved the shredded cloth into his pocket.

His heart in his throat, he lunged out the door and raced in the direction of the boardinghouse. There was no sign of her along the boardwalk. He catapulted over the picket fence surrounding Miss Pearl's backyard and bounded up the back steps. "Miss Pearl!" He hammered on the door, gulping air.

Scurrying footsteps approached from inside, and the door flung open. "Mercy sakes, Gideon. What's wrong?"

He pushed back his panic and wiped his sleeve across his forehead. "Is Tessa here?"

"Why, no. She likely won't be home until later this afternoon. Why?"

Without taking the time for an explanation, he bolted across the yard and hollered over his shoulder. "If she shows up, keep her here."

His pounding heart reverberated in his ears as he ran down the boardwalk, checking stores and offices as he went. The ache in his chest had nothing to do with his heaving lungs. Where could she be?

Maybe she'd gone to the hotel to see Tillie and Flossie. He dashed down the alley to the side door that opened into the hotel kitchen. Trying to keep his wits about him, he yanked it open.

The two women sent startled stares in his direction.

"Have either of you seen Tessa today?"

Tillie shook her head. "Not today. She stopped by yesterday to bring me and Flossie some—"

Gideon pushed away from the door and ran to the front door of the hotel, nearly plowing over two people who were exiting. He mumbled an apology and strode directly to the front desk. "Do you know if Mr. Behr has come in, in the last few minutes?"

The clerk behind the desk tossed Gideon a look of surprise. "Why, no. I've been here for the past several hours. If anyone had come in, I'd have known it."

Gideon lit out across the street, dodging passersby. Willow Creek's sheriff might be Kilgore's puppet, but if Gideon couldn't locate the Pinkerton agent, he was running out of choices. He found Sheriff McCoy leaned back in his chair with his feet on the desk and his hands interlaced over his chest, eyes closed.

"Sheriff!"

The man flung his arms out like he was about to take flight. He scowled at the interruption of his nap. "What is it, Maxwell?"

"The young woman who works in my store, Tessa Langford—she's missing."

The sheriff yawned and tipped forward in his chair, bringing the two front legs down on the floor with a thump. "How long has she been missing?"

Gideon frowned with frustration. "I don't know, maybe an hour?"

Sheriff McCoy snorted. "An hour? She's probably running an errand, or out galivantin', or maybe she's got herself a beau and it ain't you. Is that what's got you so riled up?"

Gideon resisted the urge to grab the man by his shirt. Instead he turned on his heel toward the door. "I'd appreciate your help, Sheriff, if you don't have anything better to do. Miss Langford wouldn't have just up and left while she was working." He stopped in the doorway to toss a hard look at the lawman. "Isn't that what you get paid for? Or does Henry Kilgore pay you more than the town does?"

Gideon didn't wait for a reply. He stepped out onto the boardwalk ticking off a mental list of places Tessa could have gone. If she'd visited her mother's grave, he'd have seen her when he met with Behr. He'd checked all the likely places.

What if she didn't go anyplace on her own? What if she was *taken?* He stood panting on the boardwalk for a moment, his stomach in a knot. Could her father have returned? Would he have forced her to go with him?

He'd need a horse to widen his search. Cully would help him.

As he ran past the hotel, he nearly collided with Hubert Behr coming out the ornate doors.

The Pinkerton agent grabbed his sleeve. "What's going on, Maxwell? The desk clerk just told me you were looking for me."

"Tessa's missing. After I met with you, I went back to the store, and she was gone. She had something in the oven, and it was burning, and I found this." He pulled the small green-checked scrap of cloth from his pocket. "Her apron was snagged on the back door latch. Wherever she went, I don't think she wanted to go."

Behr's thick eyebrows lifted. "You think someone took her against her will?"

Gideon lifted his shoulders. "I'm beginning to think so."

Behr scanned a practiced eye down one side of the street and up the other. "Where are you going now?"

"I've looked all over town. I thought I'd get a horse from Cully and start searching out past town."

The investigator pulled his face into a frown. "You haven't sent the message to Kilgore yet, have you?"

"No." Annoyance niggled at Gideon. How could the man think about Kilgore at a time like this?

Behr nodded. "Good. Have you notified the sheriff?"

Gideon pulled his lips into a grim line. "Hmph, for all the good it will do. He's about useless."

The Pinkerton's expression indicated he understood. "All right. I'm going to comb the town, every building, every house, every place of business, every alley." He pulled out his pocket watch. "It's almost three thirty. If we haven't found her by four thirty, I'll force the sheriff to organize a search party." Behr clapped Gideon on the shoulder and set off at a brisk pace.

Gideon continued toward Cully's place, grateful for the agent's help. What direction should he look, once he was mounted? Dozens of wagon tracks led in and out of town.

He prayed as he ran down the street. *God, please protect her. Where is she, Father? Show me where she is.*

He rounded the corner and had to stop short to avoid running into two men lounging against the building, sharing a bottle.

"Didja see that pretty little new girl at the Blue Goose?"

"Sure, I saw her, but Kilgore told everybody she was off-limits. Don't see why our money ain't good enough."

Gideon's blood ran cold. He grabbed one of the men by the shoulders. "What girl?"

The man scowled. "Hey, take your hands off me."

His friend laughed. "He just wants a date with that new girl, like the rest of us. Well, you're gonna hafta get in line, buddy. There's other gals at the Blue Goose."

The two guffawed as Gideon released his grip.

The Blue Goose! Looking there hadn't even entered his mind.

He sprinted across the street and pushed the swinging doors open. A sweeping scan from one side of the room to the other didn't reveal Tessa. He strode to the bar.

A heavyset man wearing an apron polished a glass and set it in front of him. "What'll it be, friend? Whiskey?"

Gideon brushed the glass aside. "I'm looking for a girl. She might have come in here earlier—maybe with Henry Kilgore."

The bartender smirked. "You ain't the only one who'd like to get to know her better. But Mr. Kilgore's orders are—"

Gideon lunged across the bar and grabbed the man's shirtfront. "Where can I find Kilgore?"

The man's eyes darted back and forth. "He's back there in his private room. I can't disturb him now."

"Well, I can. Which room is his? Tell me now, or I'll break down every door in the place."

A sneer slid across the bartender's lips, and he released a nervous cough. "Long as you don't tell him who told you, it's the last door on the left." He jerked his thumb toward an open door that revealed a hallway.

Praying he wasn't too late, Gideon shoved his way in the direction the bartender indicated. Ignoring all the other doors, he barged toward the last one. Without bothering to knock, he tried the doorknob. Locked.

"*Tessa!*"

Thumping and crashing noises, punctuated by a terror-filled scream, filtered through the door.

Gideon took a step backward and raised his boot, ramming it with all his weight against the door. The doorframe splintered and gave way.

The few pieces of furniture in the room were in disarray, broken chair pieces littered the floor. The shattered remains of a whiskey bottle lay strewed across the room.

Tessa stood in the corner, eyes wide with fear, tears streaming but unrelenting tenacity carved into her face. She gripped a broken chair leg like a formidable weapon.

Henry Kilgore leaned against the wall opposite her with his hands raised in surrender and blood trickling from his lip as well as a gash on the side of his head. "Get her out of here! She's crazy!"

Gideon plunged across the room and locked his hands around Kilgore's throat.

"*Gideon, no!* I'm all right. He didn't touch me."

Gideon threw Kilgore to the floor, his chest heaving with controlled rage and his fists clenched. He glanced up at Tessa and then to the busted door.

Hubert Behr stood in the doorway with the bartender just past his shoulder. The Pinkerton agent reached into his back pocket and extracted a pair of handcuffs. "I'll take over now, young man." He pulled Kilgore's hands around to his back and secured them.

Gideon climbed over the debris in the room and gathered Tessa into his arms. He held her trembling form tightly against his chest as she dropped the chair leg and her torrent of tears released. The fury drained from him. He tightened his arms around her and whispered against her hair, "Shh, it's all right."

Behr hauled Kilgore to his feet with surprising ease. "Allow me to reintroduce myself, sir. Hubert Behr, Pinkerton National Detective Agency, at your service. Looks like we can add kidnapping to your list of charges."

Kilgore's face registered first shock, followed by venom. "You can't do this," he spat. "She came here on her own accord."

Behr glanced at Tessa weeping in Gideon's arms. "Judging by the lady's reaction, the validity of that statement is in question. But not to worry, the charges of land fraud, falsifying official documents, and forgery will all stick." He sent Gideon a smile. "Since I plan to deliver Mr. Kilgore to the US marshal myself rather than relying on your sheriff, it might take a few days before we can discuss the purchase of the mercantile."

Kilgore glared at Behr over his shoulder. "*You're* buying Maxwell's place?"

Behr prodded Kilgore toward the door.

Gideon smiled and pulled his shirttail out to wipe Tessa's tears. "Come on. Let's get you home."

⚬

Tessa wasn't sure her shaky legs would carry her all the way to the boarding-house, but Gideon's comforting arm around her waist steadied her. He settled her onto a kitchen chair, concern knitting his eyebrows.

As she sipped a glass of cool water, she listened as Gideon filled Miss Pearl in on the events of the afternoon. She closed her eyes, grateful that Gideon relieved her of having to speak of those horrible moments.

Miss Pearl hovered over Tessa and bustled about the kitchen in turn. "Mercy sakes, Gideon. It's a pure blessing that you got there when you did. I shudder to think what might have happened." She pushed the coffeepot onto the hot part of the stove and set a pitcher of cream and the sugar bowl on the table, clucking her tongue.

"Actually, Miss Pearl, Tessa had the situation under control before I busted down that door." He reached across the table and gave Tessa's fingers a squeeze as his dark eyes locked on to hers. "You're quite a lady, Tessa."

A burning ache crept up her throat. She dropped her gaze to her hands, unable to look at Gideon any longer. How could he say such a thing? Papa always said she was worthless, unfit for polite company. Shame filled her at the thought of Gideon having to rescue her from the tawdry back rooms of the Blue Goose.

As if reading her mind, Gideon gave her hand a gentle tug. "Tessa, you are precious in God's eyes. You know it, too. You fought for yourself. You refused to knuckle under to Kilgore's demands. I'm so proud of you."

She slowly raised her eyes to meet Gideon's eyes again, comprehension dawning like the first light of day. "It's because of who I am in God's eyes. I'm His. Because He loves me and promised to never leave me, I'm not worthless."

Gideon pulled her hands across the small table and drew her fingers up to his lips. "You are God's treasure." He placed a gentle kiss on each of her hands.

Miss Pearl tiptoed to the back door. " 'Scuse me, I'm just going to go take the laundry off the line." She slipped out, leaving Gideon and Tessa alone.

Gideon rose from his chair and stood with his back to her, looking out the window. "Tessa, I know how you feel about my selling the mercantile and starting a horse ranch. It's been my dream for a long time. I've put a great deal of study into it, and I believe I have God's approval. It will take some time. I need to purchase some acreage, acquire breeding stock, put up fences, a brood mare barn"—he turned to face her—"and a house." He stared at the floor. One boot scuffed the other.

Sorrow pinched her. She'd intended to apologize to him for her hasty opinion, but with everything that had happened, her apology slipped through the cracks. "Gideon, I—"

"Tessa, do you think—"

She smiled. "You first."

Gideon didn't smile. He raised his eyes and held her gaze.

She couldn't look away even if she'd wanted to.

"Tessa, I'd like to ask you to reconsider your opinion."

Emotion swelled in her chest. She wasn't sure she could contain it. He wasn't just asking her to change her mind. He was telling her he valued her support of his dream. "Gideon, you and your father built a solid, reputable business through hard work and integrity. When your father passed away, he left you a legacy. But I see now that the legacy he left isn't the mercantile. It's the integrity he taught you. Your dream will succeed because of that integrity and hard work, but most of all because you have God's blessing."

A light from within slowly lit Gideon's face. "Tessa, there's one more thing I need for God's blessing to be fulfilled." He crossed the kitchen and lowered himself to one knee in front of her. Enfolding her hand in his, he spoke as solemnly as if taking a vow. "Tessa, I love you. My dream won't be complete unless you'll marry me."

A single tear slipped down her cheek. "Gideon, it's my dream, too. Yes, I'll marry you."

He rose and drew her up from the chair. Cupping her face in his hands, he leaned down and sealed their pledge with the gentlest of kisses.

She snuggled into his embrace, releasing the shackles of her father's accusations.

Gideon lifted her chin. "There's just one other question I need to ask you."

She couldn't imagine anything else being important enough to need an answer this minute, but she nodded. "What is it?"

He pressed his lips into a thin line and took a deep breath. "You said you've already made plans to attend the barn dance with someone." His dark eyes searched her face. "Who?"

Tessa threw her head back and gave free expression to the joy that overflowed within her. "Gideon, it's you. I always planned to go with you. I was just waiting for you to ask me."

Epilogue

Willow Creek, Iowa, 1883

Gideon wiped his hands on a rag and tiptoed out of the stall to stand beside his wife. If there was any doubt of God's blessing on his dream, the twin foals standing on wobbly legs beside their mother erased it.

Tessa leaned against him. "Just look at them, Gideon," she whispered. "Aren't they precious? Did you know she was going to have twins?"

Gideon grinned. "Well, I thought she was a mite plump, even for a pregnant lady."

His wife lifted her shoulders in a contented sigh. "I'm so glad I got to help bring those little ones into the world."

He slipped his arm around her as they made their way out of the barn to give the new family some privacy. "The two yearlings are coming along well. They're both broken to halter, and by this time next year, I'll start training them to harness."

A high-pitched whinny drew their attention to the small corral attached to the barn where another new mother with her month-old foal trotted along the fence. Beyond the fence, two more mares and their foals grazed in the meadow among the wildflowers.

Gideon paused to lean on the top rail and appreciate the blessings God had given him. "Five strong, healthy foals so far."

Tessa propped her arms on the fence beside him. "The miracle of birth is something I'll never tire of watching."

He grinned down at her and drew her close as they walked toward the house. "If God keeps blessing us like this, we're going to have to add on to the brood mare barn next year."

She cocked her head to one side but kept looking straight ahead. "I think we should add on to the house first."

When he cast a sideways glance at her and saw a twitch play at the corner of her mouth, he thought she was teasing. She'd not made mention before of the house being too small. In fact, she'd told him it was the most beautiful house she'd ever seen.

"Why would we need to add on to the house?"

She peered up at him in a demure fashion. "Think about it. You'll figure it out." She continued on toward the house, leaving him standing by the birch trees, scratching his head.

He watched as she stopped by the vegetable garden to pull a couple of weeds from the row of carrots. *I'll figure it out?*

She dusted off her hands and climbed the front porch step to their home, pausing in the doorway to send him a secretive smile.

Realization dawned, and he let out a whoop of exultation. "Tessa!" He ran and scooped her into his arms, his joyful laughter blending with hers as he twirled her in a crazy circle. When he let her slip to the ground, his arms surrounded her, and he lowered his face to smother her with kisses. God had blessed them with such an amazing love.

Revealing FIRE

Dedication

To all my sisters:
Those God gave me by birth—Pam and Chris
And those God gave me by grace—
Kim, Eileen, Margie, Susan, Ginger
I thank God for every one of you.

Chapter 1

Willow Creek, Iowa
May 1884

Oh, for mercy sakes! Stop flittering about like a silly schoolgirl!" Pearl Dunnigan glanced over her shoulder, thankful there was no one to hear her self-admonishment except Maggie, the cat. Perhaps she should have declined when Hubert Behr asked her to dinner. How preposterous for a woman in her September years to experience flutters over a man's attention.

She propped her hands on her hips and frowned at the two dresses carefully arranged on her bed. Her newest, a dark blue with tiny flowers, was simple, just an everyday housedress. No elaborate trim or fancy buttons adorned the bodice, no special tucks or decorative stitching embellished the garment. The other was her Sunday best. Dove gray with purple ruching around the neck and cuffs and exquisite little purple buttons; the dress was elegant. Every time she donned the dress for church, she pictured fine Eastern socialites sitting down to tea, holding delicate bone china teacups with gracefully gloved hands. The image always made her snort. She'd be as out of place at a fancy tea party as Queen Victoria at a hog-calling contest. But every lady should have something special to make her feel dressed up, even for just one day a week, and Pearl loved feeling like a lady. Cooking and cleaning all day for a house full of boarders provided her an income, but at the end of the day all she felt was exhaustion. When Hubert smiled at her, she felt. . .revived.

She picked up the gray dress and turned with it in front of her to face the small mirror over her washstand. What would folks think if they saw her on the arm of a gentleman like Hubert in the middle of the week, and in her Sunday best no less? She held the dress against her and smoothed her hand over the precise gray tucks, each one embroidered with purple silk thread. Glancing back at the dark blue still lying on the bed, she knew her mind was already made up.

A knock drew her attention. "Miss Pearl?"

She recognized the voice of Tessa Maxwell, a dear friend who was like a daughter to her. Hastily returning the gray dress to the wardrobe, she called out, "I'm in here."

The young woman with honey brown hair, holding a blond-headed toddler by the hand, poked her head in the door of the bedroom. "We stopped by to see Grandma Pearl while we were in town."

Pearl crossed the room with her arms held out. "Come here, punkin!"

"G'ma!" The little girl pulled away from her mother and ran to Pearl.

Gathering the child to her, Pearl inhaled the child's sweet scent. "How is my sweet little Susan today? My goodness, how fast she's growing."

Susan stretched her hand up over her head. "I dis big."

Tessa gave a sad little smile. "You know I've already had to pack away so many things that she's outgrown." The young mother heaved a deep sigh. "I wish she could stay little."

Pearl nuzzled the little one, her own sigh matching Tessa's. "I don't think I realized all I'd missed by not having young'uns of my own. But I'm grateful that you've let me be a step-grandma." Pearl planted little kisses all over the child's head, and the tot rewarded her with a smile.

"G'ma, cookie?"

"Not before supper," her mother admonished.

Tessa hugged Pearl's shoulders. "I just came from the mercantile. Mr. Behr asked if I could bring in some gingerbread cakes and sugar cookies to the store." She reached out to catch Susan's hand to keep her from investigating Pearl's bureau drawers. "Taking care of a home and a husband, and now this little sweetheart, doesn't leave me much time for baking like I used to do. But Mr. Behr said anytime I can bring baked goods in, he'd be pleased to have them to sell."

At the mention of Hubert Behr, Pearl's heart did a giddy flip and telltale warmth stole into her cheeks. Her mouth took on a mind of its own and stretched into a wobbly beam of pleasure.

Tessa cocked an eyebrow at her. "What's this? A smile through the blush?"

Pearl stroked Susan's yellow curls and shrugged. "Don't suppose I can keep it to myself much longer. I'd like to tell you and Gideon before the whole town knows about it. Hubert and I—that is, Mr. Behr has asked me to join him for dinner tomorrow night."

Tessa's eyebrows arched a notch higher, and Pearl decided to blurt out the rest before her friend's imagination got carried away.

"He—Mr. Behr—asked me two weeks ago if he could. . ."

"If he could what?"

Pearl bent and straightened Susan's pinafore to cover the nervous tremble in her voice. She cleared her throat twice. "He asked permission to—" Her voice cracked. "Oh mercy sakes! He asked permission to call on me."

Tessa's eyes widened along with her smile. "Call? You mean he wants to court you?"

"No, it's nothing like that." Her pulse tapped an erratic rhythm. "He just asked if. . ."

"Mr. Behr is taking you to dinner? That's so exciting." Her friend appeared genuinely happy at the news. "Mr. Behr is such a nice man. Where is he taking you?"

An involuntary smile tweaked the corner of Pearl's mouth. "He said he'd reserved the best table at the hotel dining room."

"Really?" A grin split Tessa's face.

Pearl took a deep breath. "Really. I was just trying to decide what I'll wear when you came in." She crossed to the bed and looked down at the dark blue dress draped across the end of the bed. "I think I'll wear this. It's new and quite serviceable."

Tessa's lips pursed and her eyebrows dipped as she looked over the dress. "Miss Pearl, you're not wearing a housedress for your dinner with Mr. Behr, no matter how nice it might look on you when you're sweeping the front porch." Her young friend opened the wardrobe and fingered through the garments hanging there. "Here. This will be perfect." She extracted the light gray with the purple trim.

"Oh honey." Pearl lowered her voice like she was telling a secret. "Don't you think people will think I'm being a foolish old lady, getting all gussied up to have dinner with a friend?"

Tessa gave Pearl a quizzical look. "A friend? Is that why Mr. Behr spent every minute with you at the church potluck supper a couple of weeks ago? Is that why he started stammering a little while ago when I told him I was planning on stopping by here, and why you blushed when I mentioned his name? Because he's your friend?"

Pearl took the gray dress from Tessa and laid it on the bed. "Honey girl, I'm more than fifty years old—too old for such nonsense." Susan cackled as though she understood Grandma Pearl's joke.

Tessa plunked her hands on her hips. "Who says you're too old? I don't ever remember hearing there is a certain age at which people are no longer allowed to enjoy each other's company." The two women watched as Susan sat on the braided rug and pulled off her shoes. "Besides, you're a lovely lady and. . ." She leaned forward and finished in a conspiratorial whisper. "And Mr. Behr is a handsome man." She straightened. "And furthermore, I think the occasion calls for a new bonnet as well. Mrs. Pettigrew is displaying some pretty new things in her shop. She could fashion something for you with some lovely purple flowers on the brim that will go with the trim on this dress."

"Oh, pshaw!" Pearl flapped her hands. "There are plenty of things I can spend hard-earned money on besides a new bonnet." She caught her reflection in the mirror and hesitated. Her hair used to be honey brown. Now there was much more gray than brown. A new bonnet might make her look like a girl again. As quickly as the thought crossed her mind, she dismissed it. Such nonsense. She picked up Susan's shoes. "Come sit on the front porch with me awhile."

The scent of the lilac bushes by the porch beckoned Pearl to spend time with Tessa and little Susan. They settled themselves on the swing, and Pearl reached to tickle Susan's tummy.

"I remember one time." Tessa's teasing smile pulled the corners of her mouth upward. "You told me once that I *needed* to buy myself some new hair ribbons. I think you *need* a new bonnet."

Pearl squirmed "That's not fair. You're using my own words against me." She reached through the railing and plucked a lilac blossom and held it to her nose. The sweet fragrance pulled a soft sigh from her, but the contentment that normally accompanied her brief respites on the porch swing surrounded by the scent of lilacs eluded her. She pushed against the railing with her toe and set the swing into a gentle motion.

"Part of me is afraid of what folks will think and part of me doesn't care what they think. Maybe I'm still trying to figure out what I feel." Out of the corner of her eye she saw Tessa smile.

The young woman laid her free hand on Pearl's arm. "Remember the day we sat at your kitchen table and I told you how confused I was about my feelings for Gideon?"

Pearl chuckled at the memory and halted the swing so Susan could scramble aboard. "Seems to me I recall you asking if anybody ever tried to kiss me."

Tessa giggled. "Yes, I suppose I did. But do you remember what you told me about how to sort out my feelings?"

Pearl shrugged. "I probably told you to take it to the Lord."

"Mm-hmm, that's exactly what you told me." Tessa picked up Pearl's hand and squeezed it. "I can't tell you what to do, but God can."

Pearl sighed. "When did you get to be so wise?"

Tessa's laugh filled the air between them. "Between my mama first and then you, I had two wise teachers."

Perhaps taking her own advice given through the heart of a friend wasn't such a difficult thing to bear. "How about a cup of tea."

"No thanks, we have to get home. Gideon will be looking for his supper soon." The younger woman hugged Pearl and bent to put Susan's shoes back on. "Tell Grandma Pearl she needs a new bonnet."

Susan chortled and shook a chubby finger at Pearl. "G'ma need a new bonnet."

Pearl captured Susan's finger and gave it a kiss. "You come back to see me real soon, punkin." Looking at Tessa and reading her eyes, Pearl added, "And I'll think about the bonnet."

After Pearl waved good-bye from the front porch, she walked back to the kitchen to push the kettle over the hottest part of the stove. New bonnet, indeed. It wasn't enough that she'd be making a spectacle of herself, dressing in her best dress to be seen on the arm of the dapper and distinguished Hubert Behr. Her friend thought she should have a new bonnet to mark the occasion.

She scooped tea leaves into the china teapot and waited for the water to heat. The truth was she wanted that new bonnet. But the sudden desire for the bonnet didn't surprise her as much as the unexpected quiet longing that tugged from deep within her. She'd never loved another man in her whole life but Jacob Dunnigan. She couldn't remember another boy in school who even remotely drew her attention. From the day Jacob kissed her out behind the old willow tree when they were children, she knew he was the one she would one day marry.

She fingered a gray tendril by her ear. After being a widow for fifteen years, this desire to be with another man—to be with Hubert—so startled her, she felt like she needed to ask Jacob's advice in the matter.

The kettle began to boil, and she poured steaming water into the teapot and set the tea to steep. She sat and propped her elbows on the kitchen table with her forehead in her hands. No, Jacob couldn't tell her what was right or wrong, but God could. She folded her hands and closed her eyes.

☙

"You are a doddering fool!"

Hubert Behr pulled the end of his bow tie loose and began retying it for the fourth time. When his thumbs got in the way again, he sighed and yanked the blue silk cravat from his neck and tossed it on the dry sink.

What was he thinking, asking Pearl Dunnigan if he could call on her? One thing was certain, he was supplying the town gossips with a new topic to occupy their tongues.

He could only imagine what people would say when they saw him parade into the hotel dining room with Pearl on his arm. Sitting together at the church potluck supper was one thing, but asking her to accompany him to a public place for dinner looked like. . .well, it would look like they were courting.

"Courting!" Hubert blew out a stiff breath. He hadn't courted a woman since—"Since Lucinda."

A familiar jolt shuddered through him again. He wasn't sure if it was still the pain of Lucinda's betrayal or the guilt he bore for driving her away that kept him from seeking female companionship all these years. Twenty years to be exact.

Should a man of his age even be thinking about enjoying the company of a lady? He stared at his reflection in the mirror. "Why not?" Was there a law written somewhere that forbade him to take a lady to dinner? The gray in his mustache and muttonchops reminded him he was no longer of the age when one commonly courted a woman.

"But isn't that what I intended when I asked Pearl for permission to call?" Hubert remembered Pearl had blushed to the roots of her hair, but it was her smile and her demure reply that made him feel like a schoolboy. He shook his finger at his reflection looking back at him from the mirror. "She said, 'Yes, Hubert, I believe I'd like that.' That's what she said." He nodded as if reconfirming Pearl's agreement.

"And what will Everett think?" His son's latest letter lay on the table. Hubert crossed the room and picked up the single sheet of paper. Many years had passed since Everett had willingly revealed his emotions to his father.

146

Doing so now indicated the young man cared what Hubert thought. Despite the years and miles that separated them, Hubert had never stopped caring about what Everett thought. He'd loved his son from a distance. Holding the missive in his hands brought a fresh wave of joy. The letter was tangible evidence that the desire of his heart—the restoration of the relationship between him and Everett—was truly coming to pass.

Hubert fingered the corner of the page, reflecting on the long list of missed opportunities that had escaped during the years his son was reared by his wealthy grandparents. If he could turn back the calendar, he'd do things so much differently. "Lord, You know it is my biggest regret not having been a godly influence in my son's life. If only I'd not let my own faith grow cold during those early years, Everett might have grown up in a Christian home."

Hubert sighed and turned his gaze to Everett's carefully penned words. *"Dear Father. . ."* He scanned down the page to the last two paragraphs.

I, too, am pleased that we are working to put our differences behind us and find a common ground on which to build a friendship. Of course Grandfather was a good man and I admired him, but I am now beginning to understand what I missed over the years by resisting your efforts to take your rightful place as my father.

I hope you are now comfortably situated in your new home. Your reasons for wanting to operate a general merchandise store since your retirement are still a mystery to me. I would think after years of moving around conducting investigations for the Pinkerton Agency and apprehending criminals, you would be ready to take your ease. I am trying to imagine you behind the counter of your establishment selling harnesses and work gloves to farmers, and cannot understand your desire to do so. Does your decision have anything to do with the woman named Pearl you mentioned in your last letter? Perhaps you can enlighten me in your next letter.

Everett

"The woman named Pearl. . ." Everett's question gnawed at him. He barely knew Pearl when he decided to purchase the mercantile, so he really couldn't say she was the reason for his decision. But after many months of filling her grocery orders and sitting across the aisle from her in church, listening to her laugh when she played with Gideon and Tessa Maxwell's little daughter, hearing her kind words for friends and neighbors, and finding himself included in that circle, it happened. So gradually he couldn't tell where or when it began. But there it was—the dawn of attraction, like a soft inhalation of fresh air in spring. The realization came upon him so quietly he was mesmerized by its onset until it enveloped him like a glove. The thought quickened his breath.

In hindsight, he suspected her blue eyes were probably the first thing that caught his attention. Watching her eyes when she spoke, he saw tender-hearted compassion and the kind of joy that one can know only through a relationship with God. Her eyes spoke to him even when she didn't say a word.

He ran his finger over the carefully inked words of Everett's letter—*"the woman named Pearl. . ."* His pulse accelerated at the thought of telling Everett about the lady who so captured his senses, he couldn't direct his fingers to tie his own cravat. But what should he say? It would take a sheaf of paper to tell Everett about the woman named Pearl.

Hubert pulled his watch from his pocket and his heart caught. Time to go pick up Pearl for their dinner date.

Chapter 2

The fireflies danced a captivating waltz in and out of the silhouetted garden, but Pearl shifted her eyes discreetly toward the front window overlooking the sprawling porch.

"They're staring at us."

Beside her on the swing, Hubert chuckled. "How can you tell when a firefly is staring at you?"

She lowered her voice to a whisper. "Not the fireflies. My boarders. They keep looking at us through the curtains."

"Well now, I suppose they've never seen such a handsome couple." Merriment threaded Hubert's voice, and she resisted the urge to poke him.

Pearl clasped her hands in her lap. "Every time I glanced up yesterday in church, Mrs. Pettigrew and Miss Frick were paying more attention to us than they were to the preacher. What do you suppose they're all saying?"

Hubert patted her hand under cover of the gathering twilight. "Does it make you that uncomfortable? Would you prefer that I not come and sit with you on your porch?"

Pearl jerked her head toward him. "No! I would not prefer that." Warmth crept up her neck. She certainly didn't want Hubert to think her forward. "But it does appear that we are the center of attention. It must seem odd for two people of our age to be seen. . ."

The word she started to say faded on her lips. What word should she use to describe their recent activities? Going to dinner at the hotel, taking strolls along the creek at the edge of town, and watching fireflies from the porch swing? Every Sunday for the past three weeks, Hubert had picked her up in his buggy for church, and instead of glancing shyly at each other from across the aisle, they now sat together. The picnic they enjoyed several days ago didn't go unnoticed, and Pearl was certain the town gossips had plenty to discuss over the back fence while they hung up their wash.

Being the talk of the town wasn't one of her ambitions. Lately, however, a feeling she couldn't label or explain away followed her like a shadow. After being so in love with her Jacob since childhood, marrying in their teens, and spending twenty-six years working side by side with him, how could her head possibly be turned by another man?

Hubert quietly cleared his throat. "I believe the word is *courting*."

Pearl's breath caught and her heart stuttered. A firefly pirouetted through the lilac bush, and Pearl followed its path as it laced its way across the yard. Would voicing her agreement with Hubert's assessment be a betrayal of all she and Jacob had together? Jacob was her first love—her only love. Did it blur the lines between right and wrong to welcome Hubert as more than a friend? When her heart looked heavenward, God's comforting nod of approval caressed her spirit.

"Yes," Pearl whispered. "I believe it is." They sat in silence for a few minutes, the gentle swaying of the swing keeping time with her heartbeat.

Hubert reached into his pocket. "I had another letter from Everett. He wants to know who you are."

"Mercy sakes, what are you going to tell him?"

Hubert's thick eyebrows rose slightly. "The truth. That you are a lady whose company I immensely enjoy."

A smile rose up within her chest and found a home on her lips. "Then I suppose you can tell him the feeling is mutual."

The fading light of the evening cast a soft glow over the pleasure on Hubert's face. He stroked his mustache with one finger and answered her smile. The late spring evening suddenly became unseasonably warm.

"Uh, why don't we go inside and read Everett's letter? I made molasses cookies this afternoon. Would you care for some of that tea you like to go with them?"

Hubert's deep, throaty chuckle tickled her ears. "You do know the way to my heart, my dear. Your molasses cookies and Earl Grey tea are my favorites."

Pearl composed herself as they rose and made their way inside. Crossing through the parlor on their way to the kitchen, she noticed two of her boarders peering at her and Hubert over the top of their books. She held back the sigh that gathered in her lungs.

"Miss Frick, Mr. Hogan, would either of you care for some molasses cookies?"

The prune-faced dressmaker pursed her lips and scowled. "No thank you." The woman's gaze flitted over Pearl for a fleeting moment before hiding behind her book again.

Mr. Hogan snorted and flicked a glance at the spinster in the adjacent chair. "I'd like to, Miss Pearl, but I'm full up." He patted his ample belly and gave Hubert a nod, waggling his eyebrows.

"I'll set out a plate on the kitchen table if you change your mind." Pearl stepped into the kitchen and checked the glowing coals in the stove before setting the kettle to heat.

"So, how is Everett?" Although they'd kept company for several weeks, she still knew little of Hubert's life prior to his arrival in Willow Creek three years ago, other than the fact he recently retired from the Pinkerton National Detective Agency. Perhaps his investigator background made him wary of revealing too much of his personal life, but Pearl found herself wishing to know more about this man to whom she felt drawn. "Didn't you tell me he mentioned in his last letter that his grandfather was ill?"

Hubert opened the letter and laid it on the table. "I'm afraid his grandfather passed away."

"Oh Hubert, I'm so sorry." Pearl set a plate of thick molasses cookies on the table. "Was this your father?"

He looked up at her. "No, his mother's father. Everett went to live with his grandparents when he was eight."

Not wishing to appear nosy, Pearl refrained from asking why Hubert's son was raised by his grandparents. If Hubert wanted her to know the details, he'd tell her.

"I imagine Everett is quite proud of you, in light of the number of criminals you've captured."

To her surprise, Hubert shook his head. "No, not really. My son and I haven't had much of a relationship for many years. Up until recently, I'm afraid he wanted little to do with me. He wrote me about his grandfather's illness a few months ago, and we have begun to correspond."

Sympathy filled Pearl's heart at Hubert's pained expression. "I had no idea. But you and he are exchanging letters now?"

Hubert's chin lifted and a small smile tweaked his mustache. "Yes. From what I gather, he has spent some time talking with a minister who came to see Everett's grandfather. It was this minister who encouraged Everett to write to me."

"You must be very grateful."

Hubert studied her, his gray eyes softening. "You have no idea how much this restoration means to me. I think I understand a bit how the father in the book of Luke must have felt when he saw his son coming from afar off. Not that Everett is a prodigal, but the long separation has been very painful."

Pearl poured steaming water into the china pot with Hubert's favorite tea and replaced the lid, letting the tea steep. "He was such a little boy—just eight years old. It must have been confusing for him. You mustn't blame yourself for the estrangement." She replaced the kettle on the stove. "Did his grandparents keep you apart?" She slipped a hand up to cover her mouth. "Oh, I'm sorry. That's none of my business."

Hubert smiled and waved her apology away. "Don't fret yourself. In some ways, yes, Everett's grandmother did have a tendency to stand between us, especially when he was still quite young." He took a bite of a cookie and chewed thoughtfully, as though weighing what to say next. "My wife's mother objected to our marriage, so when Lucinda—that was my wife—left Everett with her parents, her mother believed it was her duty to keep Everett from me. I suppose she felt she was protecting him."

Pearl sputtered. "Protecting him? From you? Why Hubert, you are a wonderful man. You would never harm your son. Why did she think she had to protect Everett from you?" She flapped her hands. "Mercy sakes, there I go again. I'm not usually this nosy. Don't pay any attention to me." She crossed the kitchen to take cups and saucers from the shelf and place them on the table.

She poured the tea into both cups and slipped down into the chair across from Hubert. A troubling thought wouldn't leave her alone, however, and nosiness had nothing to do with her question.

"Hubert, your wife—Lucinda?" She left the rest of her question unspoken, but hanging in the air nonetheless.

"She died some time ago. Her father, Everett's grandfather, wrote me about it. They. . .didn't know where she was. So by the time they learned of her demise, it was a few months after the fact." Hubert hesitated and rubbed one side of his mustache with his finger. "Lucinda left me for another man. After she left Everett with her parents, she didn't tell anybody where she was going. Her parents learned of her death when Everett was ten. Her father thought I should know, so he wrote me."

Pearl's heart ached for the little boy whom she'd never met as well as for Hubert whose wife betrayed him. "I'm so sorry. That must have been painful. I apologize for bringing it up."

Hubert shook his head. "Do not apologize. You have every right to know about my past if you and I are going to be"—the familiar smile found its way back into his eyes—"courting."

"Well, one thing is certain." Like they had a mind of their own, Pearl's hands moved across the table, and her fingers interlaced Hubert's. "You mustn't allow anything to stand in the way of reconciling with your son."

He squeezed her fingers. "I don't intend to."

✄

Hubert crossed another day off the calendar hanging behind the mercantile storeroom door and frowned. June 18. If his order didn't arrive within a few days, he'd have to do some quick thinking. Almost two months ago he'd ordered a silver music box from a distributor in Philadelphia. Mermod Freres created some of the finest musical boxes made, and Hubert chose one especially for Pearl's birthday. But he had another reason for wanting her birthday to be special—a reason that tied his stomach in a knot.

He'd imagined the delight in Pearl's eyes, but his plans to make the day memorable might turn out less than perfect if the music box didn't arrive. He rubbed his hand over his whiskered chin. For all he knew, the music box was sitting in some freight office in Dubuque. If only Willow Creek had a freight company, he'd likely already have his special surprise for Pearl in hand.

"Nothing to be gained by fretting."

Hubert set to work unpacking crates and restocking shelves. Despite exchanging pleasantries with townsfolk who came in to make purchases, Hubert's mind wasn't far from the twinkling blue eyes that held his heart captive. But a disturbing cloud hung over him. It wasn't the delayed delivery of the music box. This was deeper, more troubling.

As a Pinkerton detective, he'd learned years ago to leash his emotions. Masking the turbulence occurring on the inside made him a successful detective for the agency. Pearl considered him some kind of hero for apprehending the unscrupulous man who'd defrauded many of the folks in Willow Creek three years ago, but doubt gnawed at him and regrets swirled over his head like vultures. Forgiveness was something for which he hungered.

The mercantile was quiet for the moment. He stepped into the storeroom. "Lord, I never want to make those same mistakes again. I didn't listen to You when I should have, and remorse has been my constant companion all these years. Can You use me now if I wasn't usable then?"

Everett's letters, however welcomed, also reminded him of his shortcomings. He'd been able to keep the sins of his past buried for years to those around him, but there was one person who knew—Everett. The joy he savored over the reconciliation with his son brought with it a hint of bitterness.

The bell on the front door jingled, announcing the arrival of a customer. Hubert blinked the moisture from his eyes and reentered the front of the store. Pearl stood there smiling, a market basket over her arm.

"Good morning, Hubert." Every smile she bestowed on him was a gift.

His heart quickened and a tremble tiptoed through him. "Good morning. I was just thinking about you earlier, and I had an idea."

Pearl set her basket on the counter and adjusted her bonnet. "What kind of idea?"

He cupped his chin between his thumb and index finger. "A little bird told me that Sunday is your birthday."

Pearl's eyes narrowed. "Was the bird's name Tessa?"

A smile tipped the corners of Hubert's mouth. "Possibly." He clasped his hands together and laid them on the counter. "I would like very much to take you on a picnic to celebrate your birthday."

A small frown dented her brow. "But I have to make dinner for my boarders."

Hubert nodded and pressed his fingertips together. "Do you think they would mind fending for themselves just this once? Since it's your birthday?"

Pearl cocked her head and placed a finger on her chin. "I suppose I could ask Mrs. Russell to manage dinner. She keeps telling me what a good cook she is." She bit her lip. "I didn't mean that the way it sounded."

Hubert chuckled and took her hand, lifting it to his lips to deliver a kiss to her fingertips. "Then it's settled. If Mrs. Russell is agreeable, I will look forward to our picnic on Sunday." If she only knew how much. "Now what can I get for you today?"

She handed him her shopping list and browsed around the store. While he measured coffee beans, cornmeal, and sugar, he watched her finger the edge of a bolt of calico. When he was in the same room with her, he could barely take his eyes off her. When they were apart, loneliness ached in his heart.

He deposited the last item in Pearl's basket. "Was there anything else?"

"That's all for today." She paid for her purchases and gave him a modest smile. "Thank you, sir."

Hubert took the basket and walked her to the door. "May I pick you up for church at the usual time this Sunday?"

"Of course. I'm looking forward to our picnic."

"As am I." He handed her the basket. The memory of her smile would have to last him until Sunday. He prayed the music box would arrive in time.

≥

Hubert couldn't remember being this nervous facing the most notorious criminal. If the church service had gone on another five minutes, he might have jumped out of his skin. As it was, he could barely remember what the pastor preached about, spending the time instead praying God would calm his pounding pulse. When the final hymn was sung, Hubert escorted Pearl to the front door of the church where they shook hands and exchanged pleasantries with the pastor. After assisting her into the buggy, he drove to a quiet grove of birches near the edge of town beside the tumbling creek. Several huge willows hung over the water like a curtain. He pulled a quilt and a picnic basket from beneath the buggy seat and extended a hand to help Pearl disembark. When she was safely on the ground, he didn't let go of her hand but gave it a gentle squeeze as they selected a shady spot. Did she feel the tremor in his hand?

They spread out their picnic near the willow trees where they could watch the creek play over the rocks. Despite the delectable fried chicken and potato salad prepared by Tessa, Hubert could barely swallow a bite, wondering if Pearl could hear his galloping heart. When they finished their meal, he reached into the basket and extracted a small beribboned box wrapped in tissue paper and set it on the blanket in front of Pearl.

"For you, my dear."

Her mouth formed an O. "Mercy sakes, Hubert, you're going to spoil me."

"I hope so."

She opened the box and gave a soft gasp. She lifted the silver music box and found the tiny key on the side. Two gentle twists of the key and a Strauss waltz wafted on the breeze.

"Hubert, this is lovely." Moisture glistened in her eyes.

Hubert's breath shortened as his pulse raced. The time had come for him to reveal his heart to her. He took her hands in his. "I must tell you, dear Pearl, that this isn't really a birthday gift."

Pearl blinked and looked askance. "It's not?"

Hubert shook his head and started to rise but halted midway and went to one knee, Pearl's hand in his. Her eyes widened and her lips parted. His heart pounded like a blacksmith's hammer on an anvil. Sweat dampened his palms.

"I am hoping it will serve as an engagement gift. That is, if you will have me. I love you, Pearl Dunnigan, and I never wish to be parted from you. Will you consent to be my wife?"

Chapter 3

Pearl studied the floral print of the wallpaper in the boardinghouse dining room as she listened to Hubert's pen scritch-scritching across the stationery. Apprehension knotted her stomach. When she accepted Hubert's proposal one week ago, he suggested they write his son together, letting Everett know of their engagement.

Hubert reached across the dining table and patted her hand. "What date should I tell him we've set for the wedding? I'm not sure if he would be able to come, but if we give him enough notice, perhaps. . ."

Though he left the sentence unfinished, Pearl read his thoughts. "How long has it been since you've seen Everett?"

Hubert leaned back in his chair, the pen paused over the page. "Just over four years. I went to see him when I received word of his grandmother's death. The reception he gave me was rather cold."

"But that was before the two of you began corresponding. The letters you've shared with me sound like Everett is anxious for a restored relationship." Pearl hoped the optimism in her statement encouraged Hubert's heart, even while misgivings prodded her own. Given the fact Everett was an adult, would he think she was trying to take his mother's place? At the very least, he might consider her marriage to his father an intrusion into their fragile bond. She took a slow, deep breath.

"Hubert, you know I never had children of my own. I'd always hoped to give Jacob a son, but the Lord didn't see fit to allow it. Tessa Maxwell is like a daughter to me, and I'm delighted to play the role of step-grandma to little Susan." She paused and bit her lip. "But I must admit the idea of suddenly becoming a stepmother makes me a bit nervous, even if Everett is a grown man."

Hubert's thick eyebrows rose as he looked at her with surprise. "Now why should you be nervous?"

She tilted her head to one side and huffed out a soft breath. "He's never met me. His father is marrying a complete stranger. What if he doesn't like me?"

A mirth-filled chuckle bubbled from him. "That, my dear, is quite impossible." He dipped the nib into the inkwell. "So, today is June twenty-ninth. If you want a June wedding, we'll have to get married tomorrow or wait a whole year."

A June wedding. Dreaming of being a June bride was for young girls, not matronly women, but even as the romantic notion filled her mind, she giggled. "At our ages, waiting a whole year probably wouldn't be a good idea." She smiled and allowed the picture to form in her mind. Wouldn't it be lovely for her and Hubert to stand amid the apple blossoms in her backyard?

Her backyard. "Oh." She placed her fingers over her mouth. "Hubert, we haven't discussed where we'll live after the wedding."

A twinge of regret flicked across his features. "I'm sorry, Pearl. I've been making decisions for so long, taking nobody but myself into consideration. I suppose I need to work on changing my habits." A repentant grin tilted his mouth. "When I had my house built last year, I didn't exactly design it with the idea I'd one day bring a wife home, but it surely could use a woman's touch. When I first imagined asking you to marry me, I just assumed you'd move to my home." He laid the pen aside. "It was boorish of me to be so presumptuous. Did you have other thoughts?"

Pearl looked about the boardinghouse dining room. "It didn't occur to me until now, but I suppose I'll have to sell the boardinghouse."

Hubert's gaze turned apologetic. "Would that distress you?"

More than a decade of memories filled the walls of the old house. Some happy, others not so. Several of the boarders who'd resided there over the years had become like family to her, and the house itself symbolized God's provision, the means He gave her to support herself after Jacob's death. Running the place was hard work, especially after Tessa married and moved out. Even though Tessa had only resided at the boardinghouse for a year, Pearl enjoyed her help while she was there and missed it when she left. Every passing year new repairs had to be performed. Hubert's proposal meant a new chapter in her life. She contemplated the answer to Hubert's question. Would she regret selling the place?

"No, not really." Her spirit agreed with her response. "Sometimes it's hard to say good-bye to one's yesterdays, but I believe God is telling me it's time to build some tomorrows with you." She gave him a wobbly smile. "I'd love to be married as soon as possible, but what if it takes awhile to sell the boardinghouse?"

Hubert waved his fingers. "There's no need to fret over that." He stroked his chin. "What would you think about asking one of your lady boarders to take over the operation in exchange for free rent and a small stipend?"

She pondered the possibility and nodded. "Yes, I suppose that's a possibility. Miss Pendergrass, the schoolteacher, has moved out now that school has closed for the summer, so there are currently only four boarders. Mrs. Russell might be interested in such an arrangement. I'll talk to her this evening."

He returned her smile and picked up the pen. Speaking the words aloud as he wrote them, he continued the letter to Everett. "We are hoping to be married soon. I hope you can come, as I am anxious to introduce you to my bride. With warmest regards, Father."

Hubert blew on the page to hasten the drying of the ink. "Would you like to add a personal note?" He held the pen out to her.

Pearl's breath caught. What should she say to the young man she'd never met, but whose father had stolen her heart? She hesitated, then took the pen from Hubert and dipped it into the inkpot.

Dear Everett,

I am so grateful God has brought your father into my life. We both pray you can come to Willow Creek for the wedding. I look forward to meeting you.

Pearl Dunnigan

Hubert folded the letter and tucked it into the envelope. "You know, there were many days—many years, actually—that I thought I'd never be this happy again." A tiny muscle twitched downward on the corner of his mouth, and he rubbed his finger over his mustache. Pearl had grown accustomed to the gesture. It seemed to be an unconscious habit Hubert did whenever he contemplated a matter. She waited in silence for him to continue.

"The weeks and months after my wife left were terribly painful." He hesitated as though carefully weighing his words. "As the months turned into years, I thought it would become easier to deal with the loneliness. By the time I got word of Lucinda's death, Everett had already built up a rather formidable dislike of me." A troubled, faraway look crept into his eyes and the tone of his voice changed, like he was speaking to some unseen person. "I wondered if perhaps God had decided I wasn't worthy of happiness."

"Hubert, how can you say such a thing?" Pearl's heart pinched as she listened to Hubert's words. "You are as well-acquainted with God's love as I am."

As if someone snapped their fingers, Hubert abruptly returned his attention to her. He picked up her hand and kissed her fingertips. "Indeed, I am. What do you say we go for a walk to work off your delicious Sunday dinner?"

"Just let me get my shawl." She rose and hurried to her bedroom, anticipating the late afternoon stroll in the early summer air. But Hubert's pensive speculation echoed in her heart. How could he think God didn't desire his happiness?

Pearl gave the worktable one last wipe and hung the damp rag on the back of the pantry door. Hubert's troubling words dogged her thoughts all evening. When she'd attempted to bring up the topic again, he'd brushed it off as inconsequential, and she could only wonder at the past memories that must have prompted such a statement. He'd bidden her good night earlier than usual, claiming a headache.

"Lord, maybe I do understand a little of how Hubert must have felt." She slipped into her bedroom and closed the door. Lowering herself to the chair at her dressing table, she began unpinning her gray hair. "When Jacob went home to be with You, I never thought I'd love again." But she suspected it was something more than loneliness that induced Hubert's ponderings.

Her hands paused as she stared at the crow's-feet around her eyes. Anyone who'd lived long enough to have wrinkles had unpleasant memories of hurtful times. "I suppose everyone has things from their past they'd rather forget."

She pulled out the rest of her hairpins and picked up a maple-handled hairbrush. Pulling the brush slowly through her hair, she stared at her reflection in the oval mirror. Truth be told, Hubert wasn't the first to make her an offer of marriage since she became a widow. Seven years ago a man had attempted to court her while neglecting to mention he was already married. The very recollection made her sigh with the desire to erase not only the memory, but also the distrust that lingered from the experience.

She brushed a bit harder and pushed the dark image of the former would-be suitor from her mind. "And just because—it doesn't mean—" She drew her lips into a tight line, annoyed with her own thoughts. "Hubert has never been anything but a perfect Christian gentleman. I have no reason to imagine he could be deceitful about his past." She narrowed her eyes at her reflection. "He's told me about his first marriage, and I believe him."

She gathered her hair over one shoulder, and her fingers began deftly twisting it into a braid. "Lord, Your ways are far above my understanding. I trust You, Father. My heart is overflowing with happiness that the path You've designed for me includes Hubert."

She changed into her nightgown and robe, and sat in the old rocker with her Bible in her lap. "Father, the plain truth is I love Hubert, and because of my love for him, I want him to be happy. Thank You that You're bringing him and Everett back together after so many years. It fills me with joy to see his happiness. I pray that You will bless our marriage, and if it's Your will, let Everett come to Willow Creek so he and Hubert can be reunited."

🍃

Hubert stirred honey into his tea and crossed the room to sit beside the fireplace. Despite the mild temperature, he wanted the comfort of a fire. He stared into the flickering fingers that wrapped around the logs while guilt gnawed at him. Telling Pearl he had a headache wasn't entirely true. Oh, he had a headache now, but it wasn't the real reason he'd taken an early leave this evening. The annoying pain in his brow was born of regret.

When they were writing the letter to Everett, Pearl had assumed his hesitation about inviting his son to the wedding was because of their long estrangement and the uncertainty of Everett's reaction to the marriage. His heart pulled in opposite directions. His arms ached to embrace his son again. So much time—time he could never reclaim—had slipped away, and the father's heart that beat within him longed for reconciliation. Every letter that arrived from Everett flooded him with joy. Reuniting with his son was an answer to many years of prayer.

On the other hand, the one person in the world who knew why Hubert's wife left him was his son. If Everett came to Willow Creek for the wedding, would he disclose the details of that doomed marriage to Pearl? He'd felt like a fraud telling Everett in the letter that he was anxious to introduce him to Pearl. Perhaps he should rewrite the letter.

Reaching into his pocket, he extracted the envelope addressed to his son. The personal note Pearl had written was at the bottom of the last page—the same page that included his invitation for Everett to come to the wedding. He gazed at the graceful script of Pearl's hand. Sick in his heart, he slowly crumpled the page and tossed it into the fireplace and watched the flame consume it.

He stood and picked up his teacup and carried it across the room to the desk in the corner. Hubert uncovered the pot of ink and tapped his pen on the edge. Struggling to find the right words, he dipped the pen into the ink and carefully rewrote the last page, noting that he'd understand if Everett couldn't come to the wedding.

"Ah Lord, I've learned over and over that even if one is forgiven a transgression, the consequences remain." He closed his eyes and leaned back against the oak desk chair. God had blessed him on so many sides, but this thorn festered in his flesh. He never dreamed God would give him another woman to love, but doing so created a paradox. Reuniting with Everett fulfilled one longing of his heart, but it also ran the risk of Pearl learning of his past sins. If only he'd listened when God spoke all those years ago—if only he'd heeded God's direction. But being young and ambitious, he'd allowed the dream of success to blind him.

He took a sip of tea and discovered it had grown cold—just like his relationship with God had grown cold years ago. He'd long been comforted by the forgiveness God graciously bestowed and was diligent to never again permit the lure of worldly desires and aspirations to divide him from his loving heavenly Father. But the mistakes made during the broken fellowship could not be changed.

He returned to the fireplace and picked up the poker and prodded the logs, encouraging the flames to devour them. How he wished he could do the same with the regrets that had haunted him for twenty years. The loneliness that shadowed him for so long cast a reminder of the price of his disobedience. Sinking once again into the comfortable chair, he studied the blazing logs and pictured the sweet face of his intended.

"Pearl, my love, I want to be completely honest with you, but to do so, I have to admit that my failed marriage to Lucinda was the result of my selfishness and greed." Not exactly what a bride wanted to hear from her groom.

Chapter 4

Hubert engaged in mortal combat with the grime tracked from the street and up the steps in front of the mercantile. Using his broom, he attacked the miniature cloud of dust that billowed across the boardwalk and back down the steps. Impatience drove him as he slung the dirt back where it belonged. The activity served to work off some of the frustration of waiting to make Pearl his bride. Almost three weeks had passed since they'd written Everett telling him of their plans, and he and Pearl had still not decided on a specific date for the wedding. Since posting a For Sale sign on the front porch of the boardinghouse and sending advertisements for publication in several newspapers in the larger cities, they'd not received a single inquiry. He swiped the broom at one last spot of dirt and clomped back up the steps, dragging his grumpy disposition with him.

Two ladies with market baskets over their arms followed him in the door and he served them with his customary politeness, but the contentment he normally enjoyed operating the mercantile had vanished. He measured a length of cloth for one of the women and forced a smile as she looked over his supply of threads.

"Hubert!" Pearl bustled in the door. "Mrs. Russell just received a letter from her nephew and she said—" Pearl halted abruptly. "Oh, I'm sorry. I didn't realize you had customers. Good morning, Pamela, Christine."

The women chatted a moment with Pearl while Hubert gritted his teeth behind a pasted-on smile. His customers finally bid them both a good day and exited. He turned to Pearl. Her blue eyes danced like those of a young girl.

"You were saying?"

"I couldn't wait to tell you." She set her reticule down on the counter. "You remember I told you I had spoken with Mrs. Russell about taking over the cooking and cleaning at the boardinghouse in exchange for free rent and a small salary—just until we can find a buyer." Words bubbled out of Pearl like water from a spring. She clasped her hands as if holding them in check. "Mrs.

Russell corresponded with her nephew, the one who sends her money each month. He thinks it's fine if she wants to perform the duties, as long as she doesn't overtax herself."

Hubert's tentative smile beamed into a full-blown grin. "Does this mean we don't have to wait until the boardinghouse is sold before we can set a date?" His earlier grumpiness ebbed away like a vapor.

Pearl's laughter sounded like music. "That's what it means."

Hubert didn't hesitate another second. He grabbed Pearl, picked her up, and whirled her around, her skirts billowing like a sail in full tailwind.

"Hubert! Put me down! Mercy sakes! You're going to hurt yourself."

Hubert plunked her back on the floor, warmth creeping up his neck. Never before had he acted in such a demonstrative fashion. What in the world had gotten into him? Pearl clutched one hand to her chest and stared at him, speechless.

He tilted his head and gave her a sheepish grin. "I apologize, my dear, but your news has just made my day. No, my entire week." He took both her hands in his. As they locked gazes, a warm thrill rushed through him. He could hardly believe God had blessed him with such a wonderful woman. The idea of living out the remainder of his days with Pearl kicked his pulse up a notch. They shared a special smile—communicating more with a silent look than a thousand words could tell.

A hint of her lilac water teased his senses, and it was all he could do to keep from hanging the CLOSED sign on the door and running off with his intended to find the preacher that very minute.

He tucked her hand in the crook of his elbow and walked her to the door. The cheery red color of the flowers on her dress competed with the roses in her cheeks. His heart leaped within his chest, and he thanked God again that Pearl had said yes.

Hubert couldn't keep from smiling. "We need to discuss our plans."

Pearl's eyes twinkled. "Thinking about wedding plans makes me feel a bit giddy. Am I being foolish?"

He patted her hand. "If you are, then I'm foolish as well, because wedding plans have occupied a good portion of my thoughts."

She glanced up and down the boardwalk and lowered her voice. "Hubert, please don't think me selfish, but I'd rather have a small, quiet ceremony, something simple. Would you be terribly disappointed if we did that?"

A deep chuckle bubbled up from his middle. "Of course I wouldn't be disappointed." He leaned slightly forward. "The truth is I've been a little nervous about having a fancy wedding with all the trappings. Small and simple is fine with me."

Several doors down the street, the stage pulled up at the depot. Hubert glanced at his pocket watch and nodded. "Right on time. I always know when it's eleven o'clock, even if I've left my watch at home." He clicked the timepiece closed and slipped it back into his pocket. "Pastor Witherspoon usually goes home for lunch around noon, so we might stop by his house and ask him what day he can perform the ceremony."

Pearl nodded. "I'd like that just fine."

"Perhaps you'd like to have lunch at—"

The words caught in Hubert's throat. A single passenger disembarked the stage. The young man brushed dust from his coat and turned to reach up for his bag. Even at the distance between them, Hubert couldn't mistake the man's features.

"Hubert? What is it?" Concern colored Pearl's tone.

His mouth fell slightly agape, and he took a couple steps forward. Could it be?

"Everett?"

Hubert's feet moved of their own volition, and within seconds he was striding toward the stage depot. "Everett? Son?"

The young man halted and looked up. Recognition lit his eyes, and he set his bag on the boardwalk. "Father."

The two clasped hands in a strong handshake, and Hubert pulled his son into an embrace. Joy spilled over him in bucketfuls. Hubert clapped his son on the back, then grasped him by both shoulders.

"Son, I can hardly believe you're here." Emotion burned behind his eyes. Everett—his boy—had actually come to see him. How many years of regret passed between them, wasted years like water slipping through his fingers? But he held the answer to his prayers in his arms.

"It's so good to see you, son."

"It's good to finally be here." The timbre of Everett's voice carried the unmistakable ring of maturity—deeper, stronger. His firm, square jaw, inherited from his grandfather, was more pronounced now that manhood etched its mark over Everett's features. Adolescence had been left behind. When did that happen?

Everett glanced around, as if giving the town a cursory appraisal. His eyebrows dipped, drawn together by small lines above the bridge of his nose. Another family resemblance left its imprint on the boy—not a physical trait, but rather in his mannerisms. A hint of arrogance. "So this is Willow Creek."

Hubert's detective instincts kicked in without effort. If he didn't miss his guess, his son was less than impressed by the town. A tiny twist pinched his gut. Everett's arrival caught him by surprise, something that rarely happened. A sensation akin to anxiety swept through him. How many weeks and months had he dreamed of this day? Now that he stood face-to-face with his son, he wished he'd had more notice, more time to prepare.

"Hubert? Is this your son?"

He spun around. Pearl stood a few steps behind him, waiting to be introduced.

&

Pearl's heart accelerated in a rush of joy. What a blessing to witness Hubert's reunion with his son! She stepped forward, side by side with Hubert.

Hubert placed his hand on her shoulder. "Son, I'd like you to meet Pearl Dunnigan. Pearl, this is my son, Everett Behr."

Everett extended his hand. Pearl accepted his offer of a handshake. His brown eyes darkened as they scrutinized her face. Stiffness drew his shoulders back. "Mrs. Dunnigan."

Her breath hesitated. The formality of his tone and stately air gave her pause. Perhaps his upbringing in a wealthy home instilled the reserved manners and propriety. Regardless, he stood waiting for her response.

"It—it's so good to finally meet you, Ev—uh, Mr. Behr." She couldn't remember the last time she felt so awkward meeting a person.

Everett cast a cool glance over her and returned his attention to his father. "I made my travel arrangements as soon as I received your last letter."

Hubert smiled, but it wasn't the warm smile Pearl was accustomed to seeing.

"I'm so happy you could come, son. In fact, Pearl and I were just discussing the wedding." Hubert bent to retrieve Everett's bag. "You must be tired and hungry after your trip. Let's get you settled. We'll have plenty of time to talk later."

Everett nodded and without so much as a glance in Pearl's direction, he replied to his father. "Is there a hotel here?"

Hubert chuckled. "Hotel? Yes we have a hotel, but I'd rather hoped you'd want to stay with me." He extended his arm to Pearl, gesturing for her to join them.

"Um, Hubert?" Pearl reached out to touch his sleeve. "Excuse me for interrupting, but since it's only a little after eleven o'clock, you can't close the store right now. Why don't I take Everett to the boardinghouse? He can relax and refresh himself, and I can make sure he has a hearty lunch. After he rests, you can take him to your house."

A flash of something foreign darted through Hubert's eyes—an indescribable emotion she'd never seen on his face before. He appeared to hedge a moment, trying to form a response. Before he could reply to her offer, however, Everett spoke.

"Thank you, Mrs. Dunnigan. I'm sure you mean well, but I think it best if I remain with my father." He turned away from her, and she felt an air of dismissal. "Father, surely you have employees who can operate your enterprise in your absence."

Pearl's mouth dropped open at Everett's cold reaction to her invitation. Did Hubert notice his son's rudeness? To her surprise, Hubert hurriedly agreed with Everett.

"It's no problem to close the store for the remainder of the day."

"But Hubert, your customers—"

"Will simply have to come back tomorrow." He started up the boardwalk with Everett on one side of him and Pearl hastening her steps to keep up with him on the other. "This is a special occasion. My son has arrived for a visit."

They stopped at the mercantile so Hubert could hang the CLOSED sign and lock the doors. Pearl stood to one side, unsure if Hubert even remembered she was there. Determined not to dampen his joy over Everett's arrival, she waited quietly for him to share his plans.

Hubert dropped the store key in his pocket and turned a broad grin on his son. "Now, we have the rest of the day to spend catching up with each other."

When Hubert finally turned to her, the warmth had returned to his eyes. "Pearl, my dear, why don't you join us? We can have an early lunch at the hotel and then take Everett to my place."

At his mention of the hotel, her spirits dipped a bit. Hubert always loved her thick roast beef sandwiches and potato salad, and she'd made an applesauce cake just that morning.

"I'd still like to make lunch for both of you at the boardinghouse." She slid her gaze between father and son. "But you are entirely correct, Hubert. This is a special occasion. Whatever you want to do is fine with me."

Everett's frown made her feel like an intruder. Was she being presumptuous?

Of course he probably wanted his father to himself, at least for the first day of his visit. She could understand that. But before she could voice her thoughts, Hubert took her hand and tucked it within the crook of his arm.

"Since I'm taking the day off, you should, too." His smile calmed her mounting apprehension. "Join us for lunch, then I'll get Everett settled at my house."

They crossed the street and entered the hotel dining room, but when Hubert held her chair as she was seated, Everett's glower caught her attention. Her smile fell from her face. She wasn't imagining it. Everett resented her presence.

"So Father, I'm a bit confused." Everett scooted his chair closer to the table. "You have no employees trustworthy enough to run your establishment while you're away? Closing the place doesn't seem prudent."

Hubert chuckled. "I am my only employee. I suppose at some point I should consider hiring someone to work part-time." He smiled across the table at Pearl. "Especially after the wedding."

Her stomach normally danced with delight at Hubert's references to their upcoming nuptials, but Everett's apparent displeasure cast a pall on her happiness. She couldn't help but wonder why he'd come. At first, she assumed his intention was to reunite with his father and share in the joy of the wedding. Now she wasn't so sure. What if she didn't pass muster as his father's future wife? Is that why he was here? To inspect the woman who was about to marry his father?

She silently admonished herself for her undisciplined imagination. *Don't be silly. After receiving the letter Hubert and I wrote together, telling him about our marriage plans, of course he'd want to come and celebrate with us. Hubert invited him to come. He's simply tired from his journey.* She returned her attention to the conversation between the two men, only to discover them both training expectant gazes upon her.

"Pearl?" Hubert's eyes studied her with concern.

Heat rose from her middle and filled her face. "I'm sorry. I wasn't paying attention. That was rude of me."

Everett cleared his throat and arched his eyebrows. "I asked you if you operate the town boardinghouse."

"Why, yes." She took a sip from her water glass. "I've been running the boardinghouse for many years, ever since my husband died."

"I see." Everett's chin rose slightly. "What kind of people stay at a boardinghouse?"

She wasn't sure she understood his question. What was Everett's point in asking? Did he think she operated a house of ill repute?

"Everett." Annoyance seeped through Hubert's voice at his son's inquiry. "Pearl runs a respectable establishment."

"Of course she does." There was no remorse in his tone, nor was an apology forthcoming. "I merely wondered if the clients she served are dependent upon her charity or if they contribute to society in any way."

Pearl couldn't have been more surprised if Everett had tossed the contents of his water glass in her face. There was no mistaking the disdain in the young man's voice. Whatever Hubert's answer was, it didn't register in her mind.

The waitress brought their food, and Hubert asked the blessing. Pearl picked at her plate, glancing up at Hubert from time to time. An uncomfortable lapse in conversation ensued, and Pearl got the distinct impression Everett had things he wished to discuss with Hubert, but not in her presence. By the time they finished their meal, Pearl couldn't remember what she ate. They rose to leave, and Hubert paid for their lunch.

Once outside on the boardwalk, he turned to Everett. "Will you excuse us a moment, son?"

Without waiting for Everett's reply, Hubert gently guided her a few steps away. "I'm so sorry, my dear. Once he is settled at the house, I intend to have a talk with him and let him know I didn't approve of the way he spoke to you." He gave her elbow a little squeeze. "For now, may I see you back to the boardinghouse on our way home?"

The warmth of Hubert's hand on her arm gave her spirit reassurance. "No, I still have a couple of errands to run." She risked a quick glance in Everett's direction and found him scowling. "I'd like for the two of you to come to dinner, if you have no other plans."

Hubert sucked in a breath. "I think it will probably be best if Everett and I spend the evening at my house. We have some things to discuss. May I stop by the boardinghouse in the morning on my way to the store?"

"Of course. I'll have fresh coffee ready."

He squeezed her fingers and said good-bye. Though her heart felt a certain amount of vindication that Hubert intended to confront Everett about the way the young man had behaved, she couldn't push away the distress. Nor could she forget the expression on Everett's face when Hubert introduced him to her. Her own words echoed in her mind as she made her way down the boardwalk.

You mustn't let anything stand in the way of reconciling with your son.
Hubert's response to her encouragement that initially prompted joy now resounded like a dirge. *"I don't intend to."*

Chapter 5

Hubert fought a tug-of-war with his emotions as he studied his cup of tea and waited for Everett to finish unpacking and join him. From their first embrace at the stage depot, Everett's demeanor had reminded him of the young man's grandmother—condescending and haughty. He hoped Everett's churlishness was simply due to travel fatigue. He shook his head. Why did his joy over being reunited with his son have to be dampened?

A discordant duet played in his mind. Everett's arrival was a surprise. It had pained Hubert to toss the last page of the letter he and Pearl had written together into the fire—grieved him to watch the flames destroy the invitation to the wedding. How could a man be so torn in such distinctly opposite directions? For years, his heart had longed for reconciliation with Everett. But Everett's knowledge of Hubert's past choices made him the one person Hubert didn't want to introduce to Pearl. He thought removing the invitation from the letter was enough.

But Everett chose to come. Judging by his son's attitude thus far, celebration didn't seem to be his purpose for traveling halfway across the country.

Hubert reprimanded his thoughts and sipped his tea. "Drop the investigator posture, Behr. You're not a Pinkerton any longer."

"Did you say something, Father?" Everett entered the room and sat in the leather chair across from Hubert.

Hubert forced a smile. "Just talking to myself. It's one of the hazards of living alone."

Everett's fingers curled around the arms of the chair as he sent a slow, surveying scan around the room. Even though Hubert had indulged in several luxuries when he'd built the house, no doubt Everett considered it rustic. Why, surely the spacious front sitting room with its river rock fireplace and colorful woven rugs could never be deemed a proper parlor by Everett's standards. After living in affluence for so many years, would his son consider the house inferior? But Everett's opinion of the house

171

wasn't what burdened Hubert.

Hubert gestured to the teapot and extra cup sitting on the low table between them. "Would you like some tea? It's Earl Grey."

His son raised one eyebrow. "So you do enjoy a few genteel things out here in this. . .wilderness."

Hubert's heart pinched. His detective skills were still as sharp as ever. His son indeed viewed the town with contempt. A breath of defensiveness rose in his chest, but he pushed it back.

"It's hardly a wilderness. I've found I rather enjoy the quiet life here in Willow Creek. There is a serenity in the surroundings one can't experience in the noise of the city."

Everett snorted as he poured himself a cup of tea. "There's a great many things one can't experience in a backwoods hamlet that the city affords. Culture, society, conveniences, sophistication. . ." He stirred a spoonful of sugar into his cup and took a tentative sip.

Debating the advantages of the city with those of rural Iowa wasn't what Hubert wished to discuss. "I know your grandparents provided you a higher standard of living than that to which the good people of Willow Creek are accustomed. However, I would ask that you demonstrate a bit more graciousness. It so happens that I love this little town and its residents."

Everett's expression darkened, and he set his cup on his saucer. "My apologies, Father. Reverend Werner suggested I try to employ more understanding and compassion of others."

"Reverend Werner?"

"Yes, he was the minister who came regularly to see Grandfather. I believe he pastored a small church on the other side of town." Everett set his cup and saucer on the table. "At first I was a bit taken aback. The minister from the largest church in Baltimore where we attended for years never came to the house, even when Grandmother died. When Grandfather took ill, Reverend Werner started coming to visit. I never did learn how Grandfather met him."

Hubert ran his finger around the rim of his cup. "This Reverend Werner— did he come often?"

A shadow flicked over Everett's face, followed by a slight raise of his chin. "He came every week, mostly to talk with Grandfather, but whenever Grandfather was asleep, Reverend Werner would sit and talk to me. He spoke of Jesus like a best friend rather than a distant entity."

"Did this man preach your grandfather's funeral?"

"Yes." Everett sat forward and his expression took on a hint of animation. "He said Grandfather knew Jesus in a personal way. It was most comforting to hear him talk about heaven, and how those he called 'believers' could one day go there."

Hubert's heart leaped. "Did you make the decision to believe?"

Everett leaned back in the chair and hesitated for a minute. "You know, I kept telling myself it was nonsense—nothing more than a comforting story a minister might tell to a dying man. But I must admit the different passages Reverend Werner suggested I study raised some questions in my mind."

Joy filled Hubert's soul, but before he could inquire further about his son's possible faith, Everett abruptly changed the subject.

"So tell me, Father, when did you first meet Mrs. Dunnigan?"

Once again caught off guard, Hubert covered his hesitation by taking another sip of his barely warm tea. He'd wait for God to supply another opportunity to talk to Everett about his faith.

After briefly filling Everett in on the details of his last Pinkerton case that brought him to Willow Creek three years earlier, he leveled his gaze at his son. "I realized several months ago that I was falling in love with Pearl. That might sound strange coming from someone my age, but I am quite certain God brought me to Willow Creek for the purpose of meeting the woman I would eventually marry."

Cynicism crept into Everett's expression. "Really, Father. The woman runs a boardinghouse."

Hubert bristled, but he held himself in restraint. Nothing would be gained by allowing his passion to take control of the situation. Instead, he purposely modulated his voice. "There is certainly nothing wrong with running a boardinghouse. But since you brought it up, I must say I didn't appreciate the tone you took with Pearl at lunch or the attitude you displayed when you posed your questions to her. Pearl Dunnigan is a fine, hardworking Christian woman, and the boardinghouse she runs has an excellent reputation."

Almost a full minute of silence passed while Everett turned his gaze toward the window. When he returned his vision to Hubert, scorn twisted his lips. "Father, I happen to know the Pinkerton Detective Agency pays its investigators quite well. You even mentioned in one of your letters that your retirement bonus was a rather tidy sum."

Hubert wasn't sure he followed Everett's line of reasoning. What did his Pinkerton salary or his retirement bonus have to do with Pearl's boardinghouse? His confusion must have shown on his face because Everett arched one eyebrow and tipped his head toward the window that overlooked the edge of town.

"I suspect this woman is—"

"Her name is Pearl." The muscles in Hubert's neck tensed, but he forced his tone to remain even. "When you speak to her or refer to her, please do so respectfully."

Everett's eyes narrowed but he didn't retort. Instead, he appeared to take a deep breath—whether to sigh in resignation or calm himself, Hubert couldn't tell.

"All right, I will be respectful. But Father, I can't help but feel you are marrying beneath you. Mrs. Dunnigan likely doesn't make a great deal of money running a boardinghouse for people who can't afford a home of their own." He paused before making his point. "Have you considered that she might be seeking a marriage of comfort and position?"

The tightness in Hubert's neck extended to his jaw muscles. He clenched and unclenched his fingers. Allowing his temper to erupt would not only destroy the fragile relationship between him and Everett, it would also negate any chance to speak of his faith with his son. He certainly didn't want to start out by setting parameters, but he couldn't allow Everett to voice such speculations about Pearl. Distress burned in his chest. Unless Everett changed his attitude, the possibility loomed of having to make a choice between his son and the woman he loved.

He pulled in a deep breath and gentled his response. "Everett, I can't describe how happy I am that you have come to visit." It wasn't a lie. He was both overjoyed and alarmed. "I've prayed for years that the wrongs of the past could be made right between us, that you might forgive me for the mistakes I made when you were a child, and we might begin to enjoy being father and son." He nailed Everett with an unblinking stare. "But this you must understand: I love Pearl, and she loves me. What we share is a gift given by God. We both feel God is blessing our plans for marriage." He took another steadying breath as the knot in his stomach tightened. "Son, I cannot tolerate derogatory statements about Pearl's character. She is going to be my wife."

Thick uneasiness pervaded the space between them, and for a minute Hubert was afraid Everett might go and purchase a ticket for the next eastbound stage.

Finally, Everett gave a slight nod. "As you wish, Father. I was merely wondering if Mrs. Dunnigan was an appropriate match for my father, but it seems you have already made up your mind. As I recall, once you set yourself to do something, there is nothing that can sway you."

Hubert realized Everett's statement had little to do with his plans to marry Pearl. He dropped his gaze to his teacup. The remaining beverage in the cup was now cold, much like Everett's words.

"Son, if I could live my life over, there are a lot of things I'd do differently." He shifted his jaw back and forth, despising the admission of guilt he knew he needed to offer to Everett, and asking God for the grace to do so. "In hindsight, I can now see that taking cases that kept me on the road for weeks, and sometimes months, was not the choice I should have made. My place was at home with you and your mother. Perhaps. . .perhaps if I'd allowed God's wisdom instead of my ambition to drive me, you might not have grown up without your parents."

Silence as oppressive as the July heat filled the room and hung there like an impenetrable fog. Voicing the admission of guilt put him in a vulnerable position. He wasn't saying anything Everett didn't already know, but the words had to pass between them before a bridge could be built. He blew out a pent-up breath and continued.

"Your grandparents were good people and even though they gave you a fine home, I regret leaving you there for them to raise. I should have been the one to influence and teach you as you grew. I'm asking you to forgive me for not being the father I should have been."

Everett's gaze remained lowered, but he blinked several times. "We both have regrets, Father. Mine is that I allowed Grandmother to poison my mind against you."

Hubert shook his head. "You were only a child. If I'd been a better husband and father, you wouldn't have grown up in your grandparents' house." There were other regrets, but none that he felt comfortable sharing with his son, especially not on the first day of his visit.

Everett stifled a yawn behind his hand. "I'm rather tired. If it's all right with you, I think I'll lie down for a while." He rose and went to his room, leaving Hubert alone with his tangled thoughts. Ironic how he was able to give voice to the remorse he felt over his past mistakes, but he couldn't bring himself to sit down with Pearl and tell her the same thing. So many what-ifs and if onlys.

"If only. . ." He closed his eyes and rested his head against the leather back of the chair. The fact that Everett hadn't responded to his plea for forgiveness wasn't lost on Hubert. How strange that God was so quick to forgive him, but his son withheld that which God gave freely. He gave a huff of resignation. He couldn't condemn Everett for his lack of forgiveness. After all, despite God's outpouring of pardon the moment he'd asked, he had yet to forgive himself.

&

"I'd never forgive myself if I came between Hubert and his son." Pearl punched her fist into the soft blob of bread dough on the kitchen worktable.

Tessa set her coffee mug down with a thunk. "That's ridiculous. Why would you think something like that?"

Pearl's shoulders drooped with a sigh. "It's clear Everett doesn't like me. I felt like an interloper sitting at lunch with them. If I could have thought of a clever way to excuse myself, I'd have left them alone, but I suppose I was just so stunned. . ." She left the thought unfinished and returned her energy to kneading the dough.

"Stunned?" Tessa dipped her head and tilted it at an angle so Pearl couldn't help catching her wide-eyed look.

She wished she could simply shrug off the angst that sent a chill through her every time the expression on Everett's face came to mind. The memory of his disdain sent darts of foreboding through her.

"I suppose I don't measure up to Everett's expectations." She separated the dough into four equal portions and placed each one in a pan. After lining the pans up on the warming shelf above the stove, she turned and wiped her hands on her apron. "I don't think Everett approves of his father marrying me."

A frown pinched Tessa's brow. "Why not?"

Pearl sat opposite her friend. With her elbows on the table, she clasped her hands and rested her chin on her closed fingers. "I'm not sure, but I think he feels I'm not good enough for Hubert."

An explosion of air sputtered from Tessa's lips. "He obviously doesn't know you. You and Hubert are a perfect match. Neither one of you would be complete without the other." The young woman pressed her palms down on the table. "What did Hubert tell him?"

Pearl forced a tight smile and shrugged. "Hubert stopped by this morning for coffee on his way to the mercantile, like he always does. He told me that he and Everett talked some yesterday afternoon." She rose and checked the heat in the oven. "He seems to think Everett will come around." She added a couple more pieces of split stove wood to the firebox.

"Meanwhile. . ." Pearl placed her hands on her hips as she turned back to Tessa. "I suppose I'll just see what God has in store. I don't know what else to do." She returned to her chair and reached across the table to wrap her fingers around those of the young woman who was as dear to her as a daughter. "Mercy sakes, I don't know what to do, Tessa. What if Everett is so set against me being his father's wife that he talks Hubert into breaking our engagement?" Tightness in her throat caused her words to come out in a croak.

Moisture glinted in Tessa's eyes, and she covered Pearl's hands with hers. "I seem to remember a time when I asked you questions along the same line. I was so confused about my feelings for Gideon. The idea of being in love with a man scared me to death. So I came and talked it over with the wisest woman I know." She gave Pearl's fingers a tug. "And you know what she told me?"

Pearl blinked a tear away. "Now I suppose you're going to feed me my own words?"

A grin tipped Tessa's lips. "The advice you gave me was to seek God and ask Him to guide me."

Pearl pulled back one hand and rubbed her forehead. "Tessa, I feel like I'm riding both sides of the seesaw in the schoolyard. Not only am I afraid Everett might insist his father break the engagement, there is another side to this." Needle pricks of agitation stung the back of her neck, and she couldn't remain seated. Leaving her chair, she paced to the window and stared out through the red gingham-checked curtains to the hollyhocks in the backyard.

She swallowed hard. "Of course I'll seek God's guidance. But I can't come between Hubert and his son. I can't. Hubert has prayed for this reunion for so long."

Behind her, she heard chair legs scrape the floor and Tessa's soft footsteps closing the distance between them. Her friend's arms slipped around her shoulders, and her soft voice nudged Pearl to face the question she'd been avoiding.

"What does your heart tell you?"

Chapter 6

So I got to thinking..." Pearl tilted her head to one side, seeking Hubert's approval of her plan. "Perhaps if the two of you came to the boarding-house for dinner tomorrow night, we could get better acquainted."

After turning the situation over in her mind for three days, Pearl had risen much earlier than normal and spent time asking God to reveal His will to her. By the time she'd put breakfast on the table for her boarders, the Old Testament scripture in Isaiah echoed through her mind: "*Come now, and let us reason together....*" Sitting down together over dinner simply made sense. She'd spent many years serving people at her table and found most folks more amiable after a satisfying meal. She'd impatiently watched for Hubert to stick his head in the back door, as was his habit every morning.

Now her heart fluttered as a tender expression softened Hubert's eyes and a smile creased his face. "Ah, Pearl my love, you always know the right thing to do. That's a splendid idea."

Pearl glanced beyond his shoulder to see if any of the boarders heard his expression of endearment.

He drained his coffee cup and carried it to the dishpan, then paused, a twinkle in his eye. "Might I talk you into making your special pot roast?"

Delight skittered up Pearl's spine. "Pot roast it is." Hope swelled in her chest. "Do you really think Everett will be receptive to the idea?"

Hubert retrieved his hat from the peg by the door. "I'll talk to him about it when I see him this evening." He caught her hand and brushed a soft kiss across her fingers. "Once he gets to know you, I'm sure he'll understand why I fell in love with you. Dining together is a perfect way to start."

She gave Hubert's fingers a gentle tug. "Hubert, I'm so happy that he has come all this way to attend the wedding."

A brief shadow flicked across Hubert's face. Everett's arrival revealed a strain she'd not seen before in Hubert's eyes. No doubt he couldn't help but be anxious over their reunion. She prayed her dinner plans would help ease the tension.

"I'm happy he's here as well." A tiny twitch of the space between his brows, however, pricked Pearl with wonder. She wasn't accustomed to seeing him nervous about anything. His uneasiness underscored how important this reconciliation was to him. Her determination to see Hubert happy doubled.

Hubert departed for the mercantile and Pearl began cleaning the kitchen, but her mind wasn't on her task. Everything about this dinner had to be perfect, from the main course to the dessert. But one thing niggled at her. How could Everett and Hubert feel relaxed and converse freely with four boarders sitting at the table scrutinizing them?

"That will never do," she muttered to herself as she plunged dishes into the hot soapy water and pondered how to create a comfortable atmosphere. Vexation rubbed a raw spot on her heart, and she remembered Tessa's encouragement to seek God. "Father, I know this idea came from You. So You're going to have to help me with the planning."

The menu was easy; she'd make all Hubert's favorites, starting with the pot roast.

When she turned to wipe the worn kitchen worktable, she halted. Glancing around the cheerful kitchen, an idea began to take shape.

꙳

Pearl smoothed her best tablecloth over the kitchen worktable, concealing the scarred surface. A bouquet of summer flowers in a glass vase adorned the center of the table while the tantalizing aroma of roasting beef and vegetables filled the room. Two plump, golden-crusted apple pies sat on the warming shelf of the stove. She was grateful her understanding boarders didn't mind her not sitting with them in the dining room tonight, and she'd spent the day fussing to make the intimate confines of the kitchen as festive and inviting as possible.

She tapped her chin with one finger as she studied the table. Would candles be too formal? The kerosene lamp that hung over the table, along with the two wall lamps, would afford enough light, but candles might lend an air of graciousness. She scurried to the breakfront in the dining room to fetch the candlesticks that had belonged to her mother.

After polishing the candlesticks to make them sparkle, she arranged them on the table and stepped back to inspect the finished layout. She was pleased with the result of her efforts, but hers wasn't the opinion that counted. Another prayer winged heavenward from her lips for a successful evening.

She glanced at the clock and hurried to her room to change her dress.

Hubert and Everett were due to arrive in a half hour, and she wanted to serve her boarders first so she'd be free to sit and enjoy the evening. A pinch of apprehension caused her heart to skip.

Her hands shook as she unpinned and rearranged her hair. "Oh, mercy sakes, Pearl, stop behaving like a silly goose." She berated her image in the oval mirror. The memory of getting ready for her first dinner with Hubert tiptoed through her mind, and she smiled at the fond recollection. The upturn of her lips faded into a rueful grimace as a thought settled into the pit of her stomach. This was different. Her anticipation of the coming evening wasn't filled with schoolgirl flutters but rather a sense of foreboding.

She scurried to put the boarders' dinner on the dining room table. Pearl left them to ask the blessing and pass the food around while she returned to the kitchen to recheck every detail.

The roast was ready, and butter swam in the indentations of the potatoes mounded in Pearl's favorite china bowl. Glazed carrots and fresh green beans sat on the warming shelf above the stove. She peeked into the oven at the rolls. A rap at the front door made her catch her breath. She smoothed her skirt and touched her hair as she bustled to open the door.

"Good evening, Hubert, Everett. Please come in." She stepped aside to allow the two men to enter. Hubert gave her a stealthy wink and she smiled in return. But when she turned to welcome Everett and take his hat, his contemptuous frown seared her tattered shreds of hope.

"I–I'm so g–glad you could come, Everett."

"The pleasure's all mine, I'm sure." Everett's sweeping gaze took in the entry hall and the doorway that led to the dining room where the voices of the boarders and clinking of silverware on china indicated dinner was already underway. He took a step in that direction, but Pearl spoke up quickly.

"Hubert, I thought it would be nice if we'd have this time to ourselves." She sent him a pleading look to beg for his support. "So I set up the kitchen table for us. We can have our dinner and talk in privacy there."

Hubert slipped her arm through the crook of his elbow. "A fine idea, my dear. And dinner smells wonderful, doesn't it, son?"

Pearl nearly wilted in relief at Hubert's encouraging agreement, but when Everett stopped and turned to look over his shoulder at her, his scathing glare left no doubt as to his opinion, even before he opened his mouth.

"We're eating in the kitchen?" The young man pulled his stare away from Pearl and flung it at his father.

Pearl's feet felt nailed to the floor, but thankfully Hubert didn't miss a beat. "The kitchen is fine, and I've brought my appetite. Is that your special pot roast I smell?" He started down the hall toward the kitchen with Pearl on his arm, bypassing the dining room.

She almost reminded him that he'd requested pot roast, but realized he was covering her nervousness by making the observation. "Yes, I knew it was your favorite. Just let me take the rolls out of the oven and we can sit down." She busied herself setting brimming bowls and the meat platter on the table, along with the rolls, browned to perfection.

"Why, it looks like a banquet hall in here," Hubert said as he held her chair. She placed a small bowl of butter next to the basket of rolls and sat across the table from Everett, thanking Hubert for his gentlemanly gesture. Too late, she realized her position would require her to look directly at Everett throughout the meal.

Hubert sat and offered the prayer while Pearl squeezed her hands together in her lap. She could feel Everett's cold stare, even with her head bowed. When Hubert said amen, she passed the sliced roast to him and the rolls to Everett.

"This looks magnificent, my dear." Hubert forked a generous portion of tender beef onto his plate and passed the platter to his son. "Everett, tell us about the new piers and shipping interests being built along the Patapsco River and Baltimore Harbor. Some of these enterprises will greatly boost the economy. Isn't that what you said, son?"

Pearl passed the bowl of carrots to Everett, who ignored the offering. When Everett didn't reply to his father, she glanced at Hubert, while still holding the bowl in limbo. The young man's demeanor didn't seem any friendlier this evening, and he couldn't use travel fatigue as an excuse. She set the carrots down.

"Sounds fascinating." She lied, desperate to encourage conversation on any topic.

An indifferent sniff came from Everett's side of the table. "Really, Father, I doubt Mrs. Dunnigan would care about Baltimore's commerce." A disdainful frown punctuated his features.

Hubert and Pearl exchanged glances. The evening had started out badly and was going downhill. Hubert mentioned a few new items he'd ordered for the mercantile—idle chat designed, Pearl suspected, to fill the cold silence.

Pearl's gaze slid in Everett's direction, and she found him scowling at his plate from which he'd barely eaten a bite. Perhaps preparing all Hubert's favorites had been a mistake. Should she have inquired as to Everett's preferences?

Finally, just as she was about to bring the apple pie and coffee to the table, Everett abruptly scraped his chair across the wooden plank floor and stood. "If you will excuse me. . ." He tossed his napkin on his plate and exited the kitchen.

Pearl started to rise. "But Everett—"

Hubert reached over and caught her arm. With a sigh, he closed his eyes. "Let him go, Pearl."

Pearl could barely keep her voice steady. "But I made apple pie for dessert." Her throat tightened. "Hubert, what did I do wrong?"

"You did nothing wrong." Hubert shook his head. "This is between Everett and me; things we still need to discuss to. . .clear the air."

They both rose and Hubert took her hand. "I'm sorry, my dear. You worked hard to make this evening special, and everything was lovely." He pulled her into a gentle hug and the comfort of his embrace eased the sting of Everett's rebuff.

Hubert cupped her chin. "I'm going to go talk to him, and then I'll be back. You keep a piece of that pie warm for me, all right?"

Tears burned the back of her eyes and a vise gripped her middle. All she could do was nod before Hubert let himself out the back door.

⁂

"Doesn't she know that servants eat in the kitchen?" Everett's arrogance rang in Hubert's ears. "I was insulted, as you should have been."

By the time Hubert caught up with Everett, his son had already crossed the threshold of Hubert's house. He clamped his teeth down on the anger he wanted to lash at his son. Instead, he pointed to a chair. "Sit down, son. There are some things we need to discuss."

Instead, Everett tromped across the room, then spun to face his father. "You know I'm right. Mrs. Dunnigan is hardly the type of woman you should be considering for a wife. I doubt there is anyone in this town suitable—"

"You're wrong, son. There is one person and I am engaged to her." Anger warred with compunction in his breast. "Your behavior tonight was completely unacceptable. I asked you before, now I'm telling you—you will treat Pearl with respect."

He rubbed his hand over his mouth and chin, shoved the other hand in his pocket, and took three steps toward the window. He could see the rooftop of the boardinghouse from his front window. Pearl must be distraught. She'd worked so hard on the preparations for the dinner, and it turned into a disaster.

An insolent huff sounded across the room as Everett continued pacing back and forth. "This isn't really about your engagement, is it, Father? This is about you doing whatever you want to do, no matter what anyone else thinks."

Hubert turned to face his son and saw contempt on Everett's face. "Son, there is no way I can turn the clock back and make the wrongs right again. I've told you how sorry I am, how much I regret the choices I made twenty years ago."

Everett turned his back on his father, not saying a word for a full minute. His shoulders rose and fell as if a great battle were taking place within. "How was I supposed to understand, Father? I was eight years old." When he turned, Hubert saw the sheen of tears in his son's eyes despite the shadows in the room. "I couldn't understand why my father was always gone, or why my mother left me at my grandparents' house and never came back. It was your fault Mother left, because you didn't care about anybody but yourself."

The words stung, but Hubert did nothing to stop the torrent. He pulled off his jacket and sat in one of the chairs facing the cold fireplace. This was the real reason Everett came. After so many years of bitterness building up in him, he wanted—no, he needed to spew it all out at his father. Hubert sat quietly and let his son rant.

When Everett finally ran out of accusations, he slumped in the chair across from his father. Hubert leaned forward. "Son, I'm sorry. I wish I could undo my past choices, but I can't. All I can do is love you right now, and pray you will one day find it in your heart to forgive me."

Everett raised his head, looking drained of the anger that initiated the tirade. The rage that burned in his eyes minutes before now smoldered into resignation. "In spite of everything, I finally realized that I love you, too. But knowing that just seemed to make me angrier." He pulled his tie off and loosened the top button of his shirt. "There are a lot of things I still don't understand, Father."

Hubert nodded. "My engagement to Pearl is one of those things, isn't it?"

"Yes." Everett lifted his chin and pointed a recriminating look at Hubert. "I know you don't want me speaking ill of her, but I still feel this engagement is wrong."

"Why?" Bewilderment dug a hole into Hubert's chest. "Is it because she doesn't have the social standing you and your grandparents were accustomed to? Because if that's your only objection to her, I can counter by describing her standing in this community."

Scorn lifted one corner of Everett's mouth, and before he could reply, Hubert went on. "Pearl Dunnigan is a fine Christian woman, loved by just about everyone in this town. No, Willow Creek isn't much compared to Baltimore, and we may not have a social register, but we have something better. We have a fellowship, a family of faith. Wealth, influence, and prestige aren't the means by which we measure a person's worth. We look at their character, integrity, compassion, the way they love others and serve God. Those are the qualities that make Pearl the woman I love. That, and the way she loves me."

Hubert sat back, waiting for Everett's retort, but it never came. Instead, his son pulled himself to his feet. "I apologize for ruining the evening. If it's all right with you, I believe I'll retire. Good night."

"Good night."

Hubert let his head fall back against the leather-covered upholstery and heaved a sigh. The bitterness Everett had carried for so many years was like an infection that needed to be lanced and drained. He could only pray that when the surgery was over, their relationship would be healed.

He picked up his jacket and started toward his room, only to stop short. He'd told Pearl he would be back. She'd be wondering where he was. He pulled out his pocket watch and squinted at the hands. It was past ten o'clock. He couldn't risk Pearl's reputation by knocking on her door at such a late hour.

"In the morning," he muttered to himself. "I'll stop by first thing and explain why I didn't go back." He shuffled to his bedroom. "Lord, please comfort Pearl tonight."

Chapter 7

Dawn stained the eastern sky pink and gold as Hubert climbed the back porch steps of the boardinghouse. He tapped on the kitchen door before poking his head inside.

"May I come in, or are you angry that I didn't come back last night?"

Pearl closed the oven door and straightened. Her face reflected a combination of relief and anxiety. "Come in, Hubert. I'm not angry, but I was worried." She wiped her hands on her apron and poured him a cup of coffee. "Did you and Everett argue?" Lines creased her brow.

Hubert accepted the steaming brew and took a tentative sip. "I'm not sure one could call it an argument." He sat on the same chair he'd occupied hours before at dinner. "There are many issues Everett and I need to work through. The letter writing has opened the door, but painful things from the past still need to be addressed."

Pearl paused in the middle of cracking eggs into a bowl. "I don't understand. What does any of that have to do with me? It's as if he dislikes me for something I've done. . .or not done." She resumed cracking and beating the eggs. "What is it about me—"

"Nothing." Hubert quickly rose to close the space between them. "His behavior has nothing to do with you." He filled his lungs slowly and blew the air out. Was it a lie to tell Pearl that Everett carried no grudge against her? Regardless, Hubert refused to allow Pearl to blame herself for Everett's arrogance.

He took her hand and turned her to face him. Silver strands of hair hugged her ears, begging his fingers to trace their path. Instead, he tipped her chin up and gently stroked her jawline with his thumb. "Pearl, please don't fret about this. Everett did a lot of talking last night, and I did a lot of listening. His anger and bitterness go back several years, long before I met you." He hoped his tone sounded reassuring.

Pearl's eyebrows dipped and her lips formed a tight, thin line. She shrugged and turned back to the stove. "It's not any of my business, but why is Everett so angry? You never really told me what happened between you that caused the rift." She glanced over her shoulder at him. "If you don't want to talk about it, I understand. I just thought you might find it easier to get it off your chest to me, since I'm not the one who's angry."

Her offer of a listening ear, however innocent, hit him like a fist in the gut. He owed her his honesty, but once she knew all the details of his failed marriage, she could very well rethink accepting his proposal. Not telling her the whole truth wasn't an option. At some point he'd have to sit down with Pearl, reveal his selfish past, and leave the outcome up to God. He returned to sit at the table and finish his coffee.

"Perhaps you're right, my dear. If the weather cooperates, maybe we could take a stroll down by the creek this Sunday afternoon. It will give us time to talk."

"That sounds lovely." She bent and pulled a pan of fat biscuits from the oven.

Hubert cleared his throat and steered the conversation in a different direction. "Last night wasn't all hopeless. Everett said he realized that he loves me."

Her eyes brightened along with her beaming smile. "Well, that's certainly something to praise God for."

"Indeed." Remembering Everett's words filled him with swirling emotions. Although gratifying to hear, they were followed by Everett's insistent objection to Hubert's engagement. No use troubling Pearl with that revelation.

"Will Everett be joining us Sunday for church?"

"I haven't mentioned it yet." Hubert turned in his chair, the recollection of a smidgen of conversation with Everett tapping him on the shoulder. "He said something a few days ago about a minister back in Baltimore who came to visit his grandfather. Apparently this man spent some time talking with Everett as well. I didn't have the opportunity to ask him about it at any length, but I intend to."

He imagined the three of them sitting in service together. What would Everett think of the little Willow Creek community church? Wood floors instead of marble, no cushions on the pews, no fancy stained glass windows, not even enough hymnbooks to go around. But the Spirit of God was evident in the way the believers worshipped, and Pastor Witherspoon preached God's Word with fervor. Hubert prayed Everett might attend with an open mind and heart.

He drained the last swallow of coffee and stood. "I'd best be going or folks will think I've taken the day off."

Pearl reached into the pantry and handed him a plate covered with a blue-checked napkin. "I wrapped up a piece of pie for you. You can have it at lunchtime."

He grinned and leaned to brush a quick kiss on her cheek. "I love you, Pearl Dunnigan, and not just for your apple pie."

She shook her head. "How can a girl resist a line like that?"

❧

Pearl hummed as she ran her dustcloth over the mantel in the parlor. Since today was Saturday, it was doubtful she'd see Hubert unless she went to the mercantile. Many farm folks came into town on Saturdays, and he would be busy the entire day, but she looked forward to spending a leisurely afternoon with him tomorrow.

She moved from the parlor to her bedroom and dusted the dresser and washstand. When she came to the bedside table, she paused to pick up the silver music box and rub it until its brilliance resembled a mirror. Taking a moment, she turned the key on the side and opened the lid. Strains of Strauss's "Love Serenade" caressed her very soul, and she swayed gently back and forth, a soft smile of remembrance tickling her heart. She closed her eyes and invited the sweet memory to accompany her again.

"Yes, Hubert. I would be honored to marry you," she whispered.

A loud rapping on the front door intruded into her woolgathering.

"I'm coming," she called out, scurrying down the short hallway to the foyer. When she opened the door, she blinked in surprise.

"Everett." She stopped herself before blurting out "What are you doing here?" But the question stood front and center in her mind. "Please come in." She stepped aside to allow the young man to enter.

"Mrs. Dunnigan." He handed her his hat. "Since my father is quite busy today, I thought we might take this time to talk."

"Why of course." She hung the hat on the hall tree and gestured toward the parlor. A rueful pinch in her stomach told her Everett wouldn't appreciate being invited to sit in the kitchen for a cup of coffee. "Please sit down. May I fix you some tea?"

"No thank you." He sat in the maroon wingback chair closest to the door. Pearl speculated that he looked as if he wanted an unobstructed exit in the event he felt the need to escape. But an awareness pressed in on her that perhaps she might be the one wishing to escape by the end of this conversation.

She schooled her expression and pasted on a warm smile.

"I'm so glad you stopped by. I've been hoping we could have an opportunity to get to know each other better." The last time the young man graced her with his presence wasn't the happiest of memories. Hopefully they could start out fresh this afternoon.

"I, too, have desired the chance to talk to you." Everett propped his elbows on the arms of the chair and interlaced his fingers. "There are some things I'd like to clarify, and I feel the only way to do that is to meet the issues head-on."

Pearl nodded and took a seat across from him. The thought winged through her mind that she was glad she'd just finished cleaning this room. "I like straightforwardness as well. There's nothing to be gained by beating around the bush."

Everett raised one eyebrow in a speculative arch. "That's an interesting choice of words, Mrs. Dunnigan, because I've been wondering the same thing."

His meaning was lost on Pearl. "What is it that has you wondering?"

He sent her a skeptical look as if he doubted the validity of her question. "I don't presume to know the depth of your motives, but I can surmise."

He glanced about the room, and for the first time, Pearl felt embarrassed by the simple furnishings. But that was silly. Why should she be ashamed of the blessings God had given her? She shook off the thought and directed her mind to focus on Everett's puzzling statement.

"I'm sorry, Everett. Since we've agreed to speak plainly, perhaps you should come to the point and state the purpose for your visit."

Everett pressed his fingertips together and looked straight at her without blinking. "I am wondering about your motives, Mrs. Dunnigan. What exactly do you hope to gain by marrying my father?"

The question stole Pearl's breath. Was he implying what she thought he was implying? "Gain?" She paused to regulate her breathing. "I hope to gain a husband who loves me as much as I love him."

A sardonic twitch lifted the corner of his mouth. "Mrs. Dunnigan, let's not pretend we don't understand each other. I'm sure you're tired of working so hard here." He waved his open hand in a sweeping gesture of the room. "My father was well paid by the Pinkerton National Detective Agency, which included a substantial retirement bonus." He leaned his head slightly forward. "Of course, you already knew that. Why else would you pursue a man whose class is far above your own?"

Pearl couldn't have been more shocked if Everett had slapped her. "Wh–what?" A tremor jolted through her and nausea stirred in her stomach. "What are you saying?"

Everett sat back in the chair, his chin raised, eyes narrowed. "I think you want to marry my father so you can live a life of ease. Marrying a man of substance would elevate your position in the community and afford you comforts you don't currently enjoy."

She sat, dumbstruck and paralyzed. Her mouth moved but nothing came out. The words stuck in her throat along with her breath. Even the muscles required to shake her head refused to work.

"Not that I blame you, you understand." His condescending tone poured buckets of humiliation over her. "Running a boardinghouse must be drudgery. You certainly wouldn't be the first woman who tried to improve her situation by marrying into money." He lifted his gaze, as though a list of offending women was written in the air. "Those gold-digging creatures who prey upon wealthy, lonely men are rather pathetic in their own conniving way."

Pearl's protest froze within her. How was she to respond to such outrageous charges? Would Everett even allow her a defense? Did he truly believe she didn't love Hubert, but rather sought to marry him for whatever material benefits might come her way? Before words could form logically in her mind, Everett rose.

"I would ask that you ponder the ramifications of your intentions. You understand, of course, that if you go through with the marriage, you will effectively drive a wedge between me and my father. Now that you know I am aware of your purpose, perhaps you'll rethink your unseemly plan." He stepped into the hallway and retrieved his hat. "Good afternoon, Mrs. Dunnigan."

Long after the door closed behind him, Pearl sat unmoving on the settee, the words she couldn't speak locked in her heart.

ﺽ

Pearl clasped her hands in her lap trying to keep them from trembling. During the hymn singing, she'd moved her lips in a vain attempt to add her voice to the worship, but no music rang in her heart and the ache in her throat hindered words from escaping. Her Bible now lay open in her lap, but the numbness in her mind prevented comprehension of the minister's words when he announced his text. She could feel Hubert's disconcertment as he sat next to her on the pew. She dared not look at him. One glance at his tender gray eyes would be her undoing, and she must not turn back now. The pressure in her chest built with every passing minute.

Everett's presence on the other side of his father had an unsettling effect as well, and it sent shards of guilt through her. She should rejoice that Hubert's son came to church with them, but his close proximity only caused her sore heart more torment.

She hadn't closed her eyes all night, except in prayer. By dawn, she still had no peace about her decision, no clear leading from God, but she had no other choice. She knew what she had to do, and that knowledge was eating a hole through her from the inside.

People stood and moved about, and Pearl realized the service was over. She'd not heard a word of the sermon. Hubert's hand touched hers and she startled, pulling back like she'd been stung by a bee.

"Pearl, are you all right? You've been acting rather peculiar this morning." Hubert put a hand on her back and gently guided her ahead of Everett toward the door.

The trio stepped out the front door of the church and shook hands with the pastor. Since the summer day was clear and relatively mild for mid-July, Hubert had suggested they walk to church instead of riding in the buggy. The boardinghouse was a mere two blocks away, but Pearl felt as if she were walking to the gallows.

When they arrived at her gate, Everett remained by the street. She could feel his cold eyes on her while Hubert walked her to the door. It was now or never. She still couldn't bear to look directly at him, so she studied the tips of her shoes peeking out from beneath the hem of her dress. She took a deep breath. It hurt.

"Hubert, I can't go walking with you this afternoon."

"I knew something was wrong. Are you not feeling well?" Concern resonated in his voice.

"I'm fine," she lied. "Hubert, I. . .I've changed my mind. I don't think the marriage is a good idea. We simply aren't suited to each other."

Several moments of silence ticked by. Finally Hubert reached to grasp her hand, but she folded them tightly together and tucked them close to her waist.

"Pearl, what's this about? Are you nervous about the wedding? I'm told it's not uncommon for a bride to feel uneasy. Perhaps you can talk with Tessa and she can—"

"I'm not nervous about the wedding."

"What can I do to—"

"There isn't going to be a wedding." Her throat constricted and she couldn't swallow.

Hubert took hold of her upper arms. "Pearl, what's wrong? Why are you doing this?" A level of panic she'd never heard in Hubert's voice before threaded his words. "There is nothing we can't talk over, nothing we can't pray about together."

His plea for prayer almost did her in. She'd prayed—all night she'd begged God to tell her what to do. But His sovereign voice remained silent. She took a step backward away from Hubert's reach and dared to raise her eyes as far as his beard. "Hubert, please try to understand, and don't make this any more difficult than it already is. I cannot go through with this. I'm sorry." Her throat closed the rest of the way, cutting off her words as well as her air. She snatched the doorknob and pushed it, slipping inside and hastily closing the door before Hubert could say anything else.

She was surprised to feel her heart hammering against her rib cage. She'd expected it to stop altogether.

☙

As soon as she set Sunday dinner on the table for her boarders, she mumbled an excuse and slipped into her bedroom. How she wished she could latch the door and never emerge from this room again. If she did that, however, she'd lock herself in with nothing but her heartache for a companion. It was all she had.

She sank down on the bed. Her eyes instinctively moved to the silver music box on the bedside table. Picking up the treasure, she set it in her lap and raised the lid. The once angelic music now sounded like striated dissonance, haranguing against the shattered pieces of her heart. The tinkling notes mocked her. They'd become a requiem, harsh accompaniment for her own words. *You mustn't allow anything to stand in the way of reconciling with your son.* She closed the lid and warm tears dripped onto the polished silver.

Chapter 8

Pearl hung her damp dish towel on the wooden rod beside the stove and looked around the spotless kitchen. Her aching arms and shoulders and raw knees testified to the hours she'd spent scrubbing the place for the past several days. There wasn't a square inch of floor that hadn't seen her scrub brush or a window that didn't sparkle. Every curtain had been washed, starched, and ironed, every rug hung out and beaten. Scouring the baseboards wasn't her favorite activity, but being on her knees lent itself to communing with the Father, and her boarders couldn't tell if she was wiping away sweat or tears. But keeping her hands occupied didn't quell her pining for Hubert, nor did the activity so wear her out that she didn't see his face in her dreams at night.

A knock sounded at the door, setting Pearl's senses on alert. Hubert had already come by three times trying to persuade her to talk. Her heart was too shredded to endure another encounter with him. The knock sounded again.

With one finger, she moved the curtain on the parlor window just enough to see the person standing at the front door. A gentleman stood with his back to her. He appeared to be examining the front porch. Even though she couldn't see his face, she could tell by his stature that he wasn't Hubert.

She opened the door and the man turned around. When he grinned and swept his hat from his head, she sucked in a sharp breath. His auburn hair was a little thinner than she remembered and was now peppered with streaks of gray, but the green eyes were the same.

"Pearl Dunnigan, you are a sight for sore eyes." He took a step toward her, and for a moment she thought he was going to take her in his arms.

She stepped backward, and he must have interpreted the movement as an invitation to enter. He picked up a carpetbag and crossed the threshold. Proper manners dictated that she greet him. "Mercy sakes! M–Mr. Cain, I'm surprised to see you."

He released a merry laugh. "Mr. Cain? That's rather formal, isn't it, Pearl?" He set his bag down and reached toward her. "It's good to see you, Pearl.

Been way too long."

She sidestepped away from his reach. The sound of his chuckle brought back memories, and she suppressed a grimace.

She allowed a small smile. "It's. . .nice to see you, too. . .Silas. Please come in and sit down."

Silas sat in the same chair Everett occupied over a week ago. He looked around the room. "The old place hasn't changed much. Of course, neither has the town. After spending the last seven years in St. Louis and Chicago, Willow Creek is a nice break from all the noise."

Pearl flipped back the pages of her memory to the last time she'd seen Silas Cain, recalling the less than pleasant circumstances. She couldn't help wondering what he was doing here. Alone.

"How is your wife, Silas? Rebecca, wasn't that her name?"

A ripple of stiffness squirmed through him, and the smile on his face turned wooden. "Now Pearl, I tried to tell you seven years ago that was all a misunderstanding. Rebecca and I were never married. She—how shall I put this charitably? She was anxious to find a man to marry, due to her. . .um, delicate condition."

Heat flushed into Pearl's face at his words and her eyebrows rose. "That's not what she told me."

Silas uncrossed and recrossed his legs. "Of course she wouldn't admit something like that to a respectable lady like you." He shook his head, an expression of pity filling his face. "I actually felt sorry for her despite her fabrications. That's why I had given her some money when I first met her in Dubuque. She was in trouble and I wanted to help her. After all, I'm old enough to be her father. I never dreamed she would follow me, claiming to be my wife." He shook his head again. "Quite sad, really."

Since there was no way to confirm or deny Silas's explanation, Pearl couldn't very well argue, and she quite honestly didn't care. Even though Silas had tried to court her seven years ago, going so far as asking her to marry him, Pearl had no inclination to entertain him as a suitor then or now.

As if reading her thoughts, Silas's expression turned solemn. "You know you broke my heart, don't you, Pearl? After you turned down my marriage proposal, I wasn't certain what to do. I just knew I couldn't stay on here and see you every day, knowing you didn't return my love. So I tried to move ahead with my life." He sighed. "For the past seven years, I've been working with an investment firm out of St. Louis. I've done rather well, if I do say so myself."

Pearl had no desire to discuss the past with him. His dramatic explanation of the reason he'd left town almost made her roll her eyes.

Another question posed itself. "So what are you doing here, Silas? Surely cities like St. Louis and Chicago have much more to offer than our little town."

Silas cleared his throat. "Yes, well, it so happens I was glancing through the *Chicago Daily Tribune* last week and came across this." He pulled a scrap of paper from his suit pocket and held it out to her.

She took it and the words on the torn-out newspaper ad sent another slice of pain through her. *"For sale—well-established business in Willow Creek, Iowa. Seven-room, fully furnished boardinghouse. Contact P. Dunnigan in care of Willow Creek post office."* She swallowed hard and handed it back to him.

"When I read it, I knew it was your place. After all, how many boardinghouses are there in Willow Creek?" He chuckled like his reference to the town was a joke. "This is just the type of investment that interests my business associates." Silas tucked the scrap into his pocket and took another sweeping assessment of the room. "Could use a bit of fixing up, but if the price is right, I'm sure we can do business."

Pearl ordered the lump in her throat back down where it belonged. "I'm sorry you came all this way for nothing, Silas. The place is no longer for sale."

Disappointment flickered across his face. "You've already sold it?"

The muscles in her neck tightened with her effort to show no emotion. "No, I've decided not to sell." She fixed her eyes on the newly laundered curtains.

Silas harrumphed. "Well, I can be pretty convincing. Perhaps I can change your mind."

"No, I don't believe you can, Silas." She raised her chin and straightened her shoulders.

He sat forward. "You do still run this place as a boardinghouse, don't you?"

Her aching hands and sore knees affirmed his inquiry. "Yes."

He grinned. "Well, I hope you have a vacancy because I'd like to rent a room."

The truth was she had three rooms available and renting one of them would certainly help with her finances. There were a number of things that needed to be fixed or replaced, and having one more boarder might enable her to pay for those repairs. But a warning sounded in her head. She wasn't sure having Silas Cain under her roof again was a good idea. What would the town gossipers say when they found out Silas Cain was back in town? She shook off the thought. She was in the business of renting rooms and Silas was offering to rent one.

Something didn't make sense. "If you are doing so well with this investment company, why aren't you staying in the hotel? The rooms there are much nicer than mine."

He raised one finger in the air to make his point. "Ah, but the hotel is lacking in one very special area." His eyes took on a mischievous look. "They don't have Pearl Dunnigan. So—" He rubbed his hands together. "Do you have a room available?"

She still hesitated, wishing she could tell him no. But the need to rent the room was greater than her desire to send him away. "Yes, I do have a room." No sense in admitting to him she had three empty rooms. If he thought she was desperate, he might use that to his advantage. "It's not my best room, and it's rather small. There's only one window and it has a northern exposure, and the bed is—"

Silas's booming laugh interrupted her litany. "Pearl, my dear, you are the world's worst businesswoman. You're supposed to tell me how nice the room is so I'll have to pay a higher rent, not tell me everything that's wrong with it."

"My dear." She wished he had used any other term but that one. The only man she wished to call her *dear* was Hubert. Another painful dart stabbed her, but she stood and pulled in a breath. "The room is upstairs, the last door on the left. May I assume you will be taking breakfast and supper here as well?"

Silas stood and picked up his bag. "You may. If your cooking is still as good as I remember, that's another reason for staying here instead of the hotel." He pulled out his wallet, extracted several bills, and handed them to her. "Will that cover the first week, plus meals?"

Pearl's eyes widened as she looked at the money in her hand. "This will cover three weeks, Silas. You know my rates aren't this high."

He grinned and started toward the stairs. "Consider me paid up for three weeks."

She watched as her newest boarder climbed the stairs and turned the corner. Silas Cain—she'd all but forgotten he ever existed. Had she just made a mistake?

Hubert glanced out the storefront window, looking for a wagon or some other conveyance that might belong to his customer. The rather sizable pile of goods and clothing stacked on the counter would make an unwieldy load were the gentleman to carry it.

Before Hubert could ask, the man set a pair of boots on the counter beside the other items. "Add these as well."

"Yes sir." Hubert jotted down the price of the boots. "Are you going to be settling into our community?"

The gentleman glanced up. "Why do you ask?"

Hubert studied his customer with quiet perception. "You're obviously a chap from the city. Looks like you're outfitting yourself to accommodate our more rural way of life."

The man gave a curt nod. "I didn't have time to pack much before I left Chicago. Do you deliver?"

"Yes sir. I can deliver these things this afternoon as long as it's in town." He added up the grand total. "That all comes to fourteen dollars and twenty cents, Mr. . . ."

"Cain. Silas Cain." Mr. Cain counted out the money and laid it on the counter. "Can you deliver it to Pearl Dunnigan's boardinghouse?"

Hubert almost choked on his own breath. "Uh, yes. I can. . .have it delivered there."

"You know where the boardinghouse is?" Mr. Cain pointed down the street.

"Yes sir, I know where it is." Hearing Pearl's name caused his stomach to roll and pitch like waves on the ocean. "I'll see to it right away."

Mr. Cain bid him good day and left just as Hubert's friend Gideon Maxwell came in.

"Good morning, Gideon."

Gideon glanced over his shoulder at the departing customer. "That guy looks familiar. . . . Cain, isn't it?"

Hubert came out from behind the counter and nodded. "Yes. He said his name is Silas Cain. Do you know him?"

Gideon nudged his hat back and scratched the top of his head before tugging the hat back into place. "I sorta know him. He lived here for a short while some years back. I was only in my teens, but I remember. . ." He paused, his finger tapping his chin, and then turned back to Hubert. "It was back when my father still owned the mercantile. I remember Cain coming in the store from time to time. He stayed at Miss Pearl's place, and as I recall, he was pretty sweet on Miss Pearl."

Hubert's insides jerked into a knot. He shot a glance in the direction Cain had taken, but the man was out of sight. Had Pearl taken up with an old beau?

"Look, Hubert. . ." Gideon shuffled a booted foot. "Tessa told me what happened between you and Miss Pearl. I'm really sorry. I wish there was something we could do to change her mind."

Hubert shook his head and walked back behind the counter. "She won't talk to me. I've tried to see her, but she told me not to come back. All she said was she thought the marriage wasn't a good idea and we weren't right for each other." He pounded a fist on the counter in a rare display of frustration. "Did you ever hear such nonsense? Not right for each other. There isn't a woman on the face of the earth who is more right for me than Pearl Dunnigan." He took a slow, steadying breath. "She won't give me a real explanation."

Gideon stuffed his hands in his pockets. "Tessa told me that Miss Pearl wouldn't talk about it—just kept saying it was something she had to do. Is there any way I can help?"

Hubert gave a huff and tipped his head at the stack of goods still sitting on the counter. "There is. Can you deliver these things to Mr. Cain at the boardinghouse when I get them wrapped up?"

Gideon frowned at the items and then glanced out the door again. "This is Cain's stuff? He's staying at the boardinghouse?"

Hubert pulled out a length of store paper and began wrapping the pants and shirts. "That's what he said."

Gideon gave a low whistle. "Yeah, I'll take them by there. I have to stop at the Feed and Seed, but I'll come back here in about a half hour." He started toward the door. "Oh!" He stopped and pulled a piece of paper from his vest pocket. "Here's Tessa's list. She'd be mighty put out if I came home without these things." He handed the list to Hubert. "Don't bother wrapping any of it. I have a couple of empty crates in the back of the wagon."

Just as he reached the door, Gideon stopped again. "You know, I seem to remember. . ."

Hubert looked up from pulling a length of string around the package. "Yes?"

Gideon put his hands on his hips. "Now I remember why Silas Cain left town all those years ago." He walked back to the counter. "Cain had asked

Miss Pearl to marry him. It was all over town."

The string slipped from Hubert's fingers and fell to the floor. "Are you sure?"

Gideon frowned as if pulling the recollection from the back of his brain. "Yeah, I think I was sixteen or seventeen at the time. My dad was running the mercantile, and I helped out in here. Cain had run up a bill." Gideon rubbed his forehead as though the motion might free up the long-buried memory. He yanked his head up. "I remember now. Cain had charged a lot of stuff, and every time he came in, he told my father he was expecting a bank draft any day. His bill was almost forty dollars, as I recall. He asked Miss Pearl to marry him, and then he left town without ever paying his bill. If you look through the old record books, you'll find it. It was at least six or seven years ago."

Hubert's hands hung motionless at his sides. "He asked Pearl to marry him?" He stared at the string lying on the floor. "Why didn't he marry her?" He pulled his gaze up to meet Gideon's wry, sympathetic smile.

"She turned him down."

As he left, Gideon called back over his shoulder that he'd be back after a while to pick up his own supplies as well as Cain's, but Hubert barely heard him. Was Cain the reason Pearl broke their engagement? Hubert couldn't remember seeing Cain in town until today, but that didn't mean he hadn't been corresponding with Pearl. She could have known Cain was coming back to town.

Hubert shook his head. For that scenario to have any validity, Pearl would have to be deceptive, and the very word didn't even fit her pinkie finger. Nevertheless, her former suitor was residing under her roof again. An unfamiliar tightness growled in his chest when he wondered if Pearl's head had been turned. An acid taste filled his mouth.

Gideon's recollection of Cain running up an unpaid bill set Hubert's detective instincts in motion. The man had paid for the merchandise he purchased today, but if he had a history of not paying his bills, it was possible he might try to swindle Pearl out of the rent money. Despite the broken engagement, Hubert couldn't stand by and watch anyone take advantage of Pearl. He'd have to devise a way to find out if he'd paid Pearl for his room. Easier said than done since she wouldn't talk to him. Perhaps Tessa could ask some discreet questions.

By the time he finished wrapping Cain's purchases, Hubert's resentment of the man nearly strangled him. Every part of him wanted to confront Cain and run him out of town. But prior experience taught him to remain calm, even friendly, around the man, if he wanted to discover Cain's intentions. And if those intentions harmed Pearl in any way, Hubert meant to see the man stopped.

He hung the BACK IN TEN MINUTES sign on the front door and locked it behind him on his way out. He strode down the street to the building that served as both the telegraph office and the stage depot.

The gray-headed telegrapher greeted him. "Howdy, Hubert. Nice day, ain't it?"

Truthfully, Hubert hadn't noticed what kind of day it was. His heart was crushed and now this interloper had returned to Willow Creek to—he wasn't certain yet what Cain's purpose was, but he intended to find out.

"Sam, I need to send a telegram." He took the pencil and paper Sam handed him and began to write.

To ZACK PETERSON, PINKERTON NATIONAL DETECTIVE AGENCY, CHICAGO. NEED INFORMATION. *Stop.* PRIOR RECORD AND ARREST WARRANTS FOR SILAS CAIN. *Stop.* ANY INFORMATION HELPFUL. *Stop.* LETTER TO FOLLOW. *Stop.* HUBERT BEHR.

Hubert pushed the paper across the desk along with a few coins to pay for the telegram, adding an extra silver dollar. "Confidential, Sam."

Sam showed a gap-toothed smile. "You betcha."

Chapter 9

Pearl studied the back of Hubert's head from her vantage point four rows back. She'd tried to focus her attention on Pastor Witherspoon's sermon, but the distraction of having Hubert in front of her was too great. Perhaps next Sunday she should sit on the front row.

Everett sat beside his father, his back as straight as a board. Pearl battled feelings of resentment toward the young man. *If it weren't for Everett. . .* No, she'd not think that way. Everett's presence brought joy to Hubert. Wasn't that the whole point of her stepping aside, so she wouldn't hinder the strengthening bond between them? Once more she prayed that God would remove the seeds of animosity from her heart. She'd had a choice. She could have kept Hubert selfishly to herself and watched his heart break when Everett severed relations with him. But she loved Hubert too much to come between him and his son, or to ask him to choose between them.

The pastor closed his Bible and exhorted the congregation to seek the Lord in their everyday lives, quoting from the book of Acts. " 'In Him we live, and move, and have our being.' " A few announcements followed, but Pearl paid little attention. Her mind was fixed on slipping out before Hubert could catch up to her.

As soon as the "amen" to the final prayer was spoken, Pearl stepped from her seat and hurried toward the door. Her plan fell apart, however, when Pastor Witherspoon stopped her as she shook his hand.

"Miss Pearl, I was very sorry to hear that I won't be performing your wedding ceremony after all." His white eyebrows puckered in dismay, and he lowered his voice. "If there is anything I can do to help you and Hubert resolve your differences, please call on me. Sometimes issues arise, and they seem much larger than they really are. Often a third party, a mediator of sorts, can help a couple to see those issues from the other's viewpoint."

She heard Hubert's voice directly behind her. "You go ahead, son. I won't be long."

Pastor Witherspoon still held her hand, and it would be rude to jerk it away. The kindly minister smiled. "Prayerful consideration is always the best resolution to these disagreements. There's nothing that can't be worked out when God is in the midst." He patted her hand before releasing it.

She forced a tight smile and hurried to put distance between herself and Hubert, but in her haste she set her foot down on the edge of the step and pitched forward. When she thrust her hand out to seize the railing, her arm was captured in a strong, steadying grasp.

"Pearl, are you all right?" Hubert's voice, deep and husky, sounded next to her ear.

His grip on her arm and hand on her back felt like a safe sanctuary, but it was a place she couldn't stay, safe or not. She reluctantly pulled her arm free and smoothed her skirt, but the sensation of Hubert's touch lingered. Desiring to memorize the moment his hand came in contact with her, she slid her eyes closed for a split second.

"I'm fine, thank you." Her mumbled reply was so soft she barely heard it herself. Dare she raise her eyes to meet his? If she looked into his face at such a cozy juxtaposition, her resolve might crumble into dust. Before she could discipline her traitorous gaze, her chin tipped upward, and Hubert's dear image came into view.

Heat rose from her midsection to flood her face. His eyes spoke what his lips didn't, and she could not remain in his proximity.

"Excuse me. . ."

"Pearl, might we speak privately?"

She halted. Other people were emerging from the church, and she had no wish to be on display or become a topic of tomorrow's gossip. Praying for steel in her spine, she turned halfway. Hubert stepped beside her.

"Please, Pearl—"

"I'm sorry, Hubert." She restrained her feet from running but held her pace to a ladylike walk, grateful that she didn't hear Hubert's footsteps following her. Watching carefully where she placed her feet, she nearly collided with a man standing at the far edge of the churchyard.

"Oh!" She jerked her gaze up and encountered Everett, watching her. His cynical expression chilled her.

"Are you quite all right, Mrs. Dunnigan?" She didn't miss the acerbity in his tone.

"Yes, thank you." She sent him a polite nod, and he touched the brim of his hat in return.

Never before had the desire to get home driven her with such urgency. She walked briskly along the boardwalk, trying to forget the events from the churchyard. Despite the initial desire to indelibly etch Hubert's touch into her memory, now she thought better of it. No good would come of filling her mind and thoughts with longings she could never realize.

She turned the corner and caught sight of Silas walking toward her. The same wariness that caused her to hesitate about renting him a room filled her again.

"Good morning, Pearl. Isn't it a lovely day?"

"I thought you had a headache. Isn't that why you said you couldn't attend church?"

Silas fell into step beside her. "Ah, the cup of tea you gave me must have been a magical elixir because the headache melted away."

Pearl cut her gaze sideways to take in his profile. "I'm glad it helped. Dinner will be ready soon."

They came to the white picket gate that led to the boardinghouse porch, and Silas held it open for her in gallant fashion. "You know, it's too bad you have to hurry home to so many duties. I should think you'd hire a cook and a maid to perform the chores for you."

Pearl stopped on the porch steps and turned to aim an incredulous stare his way. "Hire a cook and a maid? Mercy sakes, I'd have to double everyone's rent to afford that. Besides, you said my cooking was the reason you preferred to stay here instead of the hotel." She continued across the porch and Silas hastened to hold the door open.

"One of the reasons, Pearl."

She chose not to explore further possibilities but rather hurried to the kitchen. Silas followed her and leaned against the worktable.

"You know, I have a very promising enterprise in the planning stages."

Pearl tied her apron on and flicked a glance his way. Why he thought she would be interested in his business deals, she had no idea, but she wished he'd leave her kitchen.

"If things work out the way I foresee, I'll be in a very good position." He inspected his fingernails and buffed them on his lapel. "I could help you in a lot of ways, Pearl."

She waggled her fingers in a gesture for him to move out of her way so she could mix the biscuit dough. "What makes you think I need help?"

He moved around the opposite side of the table and faced her. "Pearl, look at how hard you work. If you'll allow me, I could make it so you'll never have to work like this again."

Pearl's hands halted midmotion. Whatever in the world was he talking about? "Silas, I'm sure you mean well, but I don't need any help. Now if you'll excuse me, I need to get these biscuits in the oven."

"Perhaps later, when you aren't so. . .distracted, we can talk in more detail." Silas excused himself and left the room.

Pearl continued scurrying about the kitchen, but she couldn't help wondering what initiated Silas's speculation. Once more, she questioned her decision to rent him a room.

ૐ

Pearl sat alone on an old quilt between two cedars in a corner of the churchyard. Silas decided at the last minute to accompany Pearl to church and attend the picnic afterward, but he'd struck up a conversation with one of the local businessmen, leaving Pearl to herself. Taking advantage of her solitude and the privacy afforded by the cedar boughs, Pearl had a clear view of Hubert spreading his blanket under the cedars across the yard. She knew she shouldn't allow her musings to include Hubert, but her thoughts often took on a will of their own, and like it or not, he remained first and foremost in her dreams—both night and day.

Had circumstances been different, she and Hubert might be married by now and sharing the shady spot. Now she wished she'd told Tessa no when her friend had urged her to come to the church picnic.

"Mind if we share this quiet spot with you, Grandma Pearl?" Tessa slipped down onto Pearl's quilt, holding a very cranky toddler by the hand. "I think she might nap if she's away from all the activity."

Pearl smiled and pulled Susan into a hug. "Just the company I needed." She laid the child in the middle of the quilt and gently rubbed her back until Susan's eyes closed.

"I thought you looked a little lonely." Tessa gave Pearl an understanding smile. "After all the coaxing I had to do, I'm surprised you came by yourself."

A sigh escaped, but Pearl didn't try to hold it in. The longing in her heart heightened when she looked across the yard at Hubert, sitting alone and picking at the food on his plate.

Tessa reached across the quilt and squeezed Pearl's shoulder. "Why don't you go talk to him and clear up whatever it is that has come between you. Look at the two of you. You're both miserable."

Pearl slipped her hand up to cover Tessa's. "I appreciate your concern, honey, really I do. But it's not that simple. Besides, I didn't come by myself."

Tessa's eyes widened. "You didn't? Who did you come with?"

Not wanting Tessa to get the wrong idea, Pearl flapped her hand and shook her head. "It's not what you think. One of my boarders decided to come to church today, and when I told him there was going to be a picnic afterward, he asked if he could accompany me. That's all."

Tessa leaned forward. "Is it that new man, Mr. Cain?"

Now it was Pearl's turn for surprise. "How did you know that?"

Tessa shrugged. "I suppose I heard someone talking about it."

Pearl groaned. "Who was talking? What were they saying?"

A sheepish grimace stretched across Tessa's face, and she lifted her shoulders. "Gideon said Mr. Cain used to live here some years ago. Then he heard a man in the post office the other day saying Mr. Cain was back in town and he was probably here to see you." She tipped her head close to Pearl's shoulder and lowered her voice. "Two ladies in the butcher shop yesterday said Mr. Cain proposed to you some years ago." Tessa's gaze shifted left and right. "Is that true? Did Mr. Cain ask you to marry him?"

Pearl covered her eyes with her hand and shook her head in trepidation. "Yes, it's true. Mr. Cain tried to court me, but that was seven years ago. I suppose rumors are flying all over town."

Tessa leaned back and brushed a lock of downy hair from her sleeping child's face. "I don't know about all over town. I think people are just curious. Most folks know you and Hubert were engaged."

Pearl let out a huff. "Silas Cain is one of my boarders. Nothing more." She stretched her arms, then propped them behind her, leaning back slightly and taking in a slow, deep breath. "I can't change what folks want to believe."

She let her gaze wander across the yard again. Hubert was no longer sitting on the blanket by the cedars, but Everett was there with a young lady. Pearl squinted her eyes and put a hand up to shade them against the sun's glare. Everett's companion appeared to be Tillie O'Dell, a girl Tessa had worked with at the hotel a few of years back.

"Is that Tillie sitting with Everett?"

Tessa craned her neck. "I believe it is. Tillie is such a sweet girl."

While Tessa continued to chatter, Pearl sent a searching sweep across the expanse of the wide yard. Hubert was nowhere in sight, but Silas was heading in her direction, apparently to claim her attention for the remainder of the afternoon. The day's end couldn't come soon enough as far as Pearl was concerned.

&

The tension in Pearl's neck and shoulders had crept up into the back of her head, and all she wished to do was disengage herself from Silas's company. After enduring the walk back to the boardinghouse, listening to his prattle about his successful business ventures, she finally excused herself and closed her bedroom door. She slipped into her nightgown and folded the bedcovers back. Lowering herself slowly to her knees, she leaned forward on the bed and clasped her hands. "Dear Lord, it's been quite a day. I don't have to tell You about this pain in my heart that won't leave me alone. But I don't know how to make it stop other than asking You to take it away.

"Lord, folks are talking, as folks are prone to do, but I'm not used to being the topic of conversation. It doesn't seem like there's anything I can do about that either, so I'll leave the gossipers to You.

"I'm not sure what to make of Silas being here. He says he has business here, and I'm asking You to help him finish whatever his business is so he can leave." Pearl sighed and shook her head. "I don't mean to tell you what to do, Lord. I'm sure You have a plan for Silas being here. You are a God of second chances and maybe that's what You're asking me to do where Silas is concerned. But I have no feelings for Silas. Never did. How can I do that when Hubert occupies my heart?" She felt an immediate check in her spirit. Was the Lord cautioning her about Silas's intentions or allowing Hubert to remain steadfastly in her heart?

She ended her prayer and slipped into bed, but despite her weariness, sleep remained elusive. Questions still tarried on her mind and images of Hubert lingered in her very soul.

&

"I wish you hadn't left the picnic, Father. People were asking me where you were." The look Everett sent across the room at Hubert was bereft of any real annoyance but rather edged with concern.

Hubert gazed at the ebbing flames in the fireplace and took another sip of his favorite tea. He cared little what people thought, unless the one asking was Pearl. Despite the spread of delectable treats brought by the ladies of the congregation, every bite he'd eaten was tasteless.

"I'm afraid I wasn't very good company today, and I didn't wish to spoil the fellowship." He angled a look at Everett. "Besides, I noticed you were keeping company with Miss Tillie, and I presumed you'd rather be alone."

A slight blush crept into Everett's cheeks. "She's a delightful young woman, easy to talk to, and not flighty and giggly like some I've known. All in all, the afternoon was quite enjoyable."

Hubert nodded. "I agree she's a lovely girl." He wondered if Everett knew her father was a farmer and Tillie herself worked in the hotel dining room. "She comes from a fine Christian family."

Everett pulled his eyebrows into a thoughtful frown and set his teacup down. "I've noticed you often refer to a person being a Christian like it's something special and unique. You sound very much like the minister back in Baltimore who came to visit Grandfather."

A surge of hope filled Hubert's chest. "You must understand, son, being a Christian isn't something you inherit. You told me that you are waiting to hear from your grandfather's attorney regarding your inheritance. You also mentioned that this minister said your grandfather *knew* Jesus." He paused a moment to let Everett respond, but his son remained silent and simply nodded as though mulling over his father's words. So Hubert continued.

"You might inherit money or property from your grandfather's estate, but you cannot inherit the relationship he had with Jesus Christ. When you acknowledge the sinfulness of your heart—and all of us have sinned—and desire to accept the payment of Christ's death as atonement for that sin, you inherit eternal life. But you don't inherit it from your grandfather, you inherit it from God. You become His child. It's a decision you must make on your own."

Hubert's heart thumped in hopeful anticipation. He'd prayed for the opportunity to share his faith with Everett. Gratefulness flooded his soul, especially when Everett didn't respond with indignation as Hubert feared he might.

Everett sat quietly for several minutes staring at the dying fire. Finally he rose. "I think I understand what you're saying, Father. Reverend Werner explained it much the same way. You've given me quite a lot to think about." He started toward his bedroom but stopped and turned back to Hubert. "You say Tillie and her family believe this way also?"

Hubert clasped his fingers together. "Not being able to examine their hearts the way God can, I can't say for certain. But when a person becomes a child of God, it's usually evidenced in their life. That being the case, I think I can be relatively sure that Tillie and her family are Christians because of the testimony they live. When Jesus is in residence, a change occurs in the person's life that's hard to hide."

Everett nodded. "Hmm. Well, good night, Father."

"Good night."

After Everett's door closed, Hubert sat watching the glowing embers in the fireplace fade. He whispered a prayer of thanksgiving for Everett's willingness to listen, and once again asked God to send the power of the Holy Spirit to deal with Everett's heart. Only one thing squeezed him with regret. He wished he could share this answer to prayer with Pearl.

Chapter 10

Pearl glanced through her mail as she exited the post office. Even the envelope with her favorite niece's return address on it failed to stir her excitement. She glanced down the street where the mercantile doors stood open. Oh how she longed to march straight inside and tell Hubert she'd marry him no matter what Everett thought, but she'd already made her choice. There was no going back.

She crossed the street and headed toward the Feed and Seed. In order to keep the residents of the boardinghouse in fresh vegetables all season, as well as have enough to can for the winter, she needed to plant more peas, carrots, cabbage, and parsnips in her garden. The tedious work hoeing the ground in preparation for the late summer and early autumn vegetables would be a welcome diversion. Anything that kept her hands busy and her mind occupied helped to head off the melancholy moods that haunted her.

"Mrs. Dunnigan."

Pearl looked up to see Everett coming toward her. She hesitated. Given their last conversation, the young man must have already fired every poison dart in his arsenal at her. She certainly hoped he wasn't planning on further accusing her of any more ulterior motives. She set her lips in a tight line and waited for him to approach.

"Mrs. Dunnigan, forgive me for interrupting your day." He glanced around. Was he afraid someone might see him speaking to her? "I wonder if you would agree to accompany me somewhere we might talk privately."

She bit her lip to keep from blurting out what she truly wanted to say. Instead, she raised her eyes to meet his in an unblinking stare. There was little Hubert's son could say or do at this point to inflict any more pain than he'd already done.

"I can't imagine there being anything else you need to say to me, Everett. I fulfilled your wishes, only because I care so much for your father." Was it her imagination or did she see a grimace flit across Everett's features? "I will not stand in the way of you and your father growing closer. I believe I've proven that. Now if you'll excuse me. . ."

She started to step around him, but his hand on her arm stopped her in her tracks.

"Please, Mrs. Dunnigan."

The arrogance that had laced his tone three weeks ago was absent. Curious, but wary, she nodded. "All right." Common sense told her to employ caution. Like one who learned by touching a hot stove, she wouldn't be burned again. "Can't you say whatever is on your mind right here?" There weren't many people coming and going on the boardwalk in front of the Feed and Seed, but the noise of horses and wagons driving by necessitated the raising of voices.

"I stopped by the boardinghouse, but you were out." Everett glanced up at the sky and shaded his eyes. "Why don't we go someplace where we can get out of the sun? The hotel dining room, perhaps."

Pearl wasn't sure why she agreed, but she gave him a single nod and walked along beside him. Had he, by chance, had a change of heart? If he started accusing her again of improprieties, she would simply walk away and not dignify his outrageous claims with a reply.

He held the hotel door open and escorted her to the dining room. Too late for breakfast and too early for lunch, the dining room was nearly deserted. Everett led her to a table close to the entry but tucked into a nook. Three months earlier she and Hubert had sat at this very table the first evening he had taken her to dinner. Pearl swallowed back the tightness in her throat.

He held her chair before seating himself. She waited for him to speak.

"Mrs. Dunnigan, this is rather awkward, but I feel I must ask something of you."

Pearl had no intention of indicating her agreement with his request until he'd spoken his mind. "You may ask, and I may refuse, depending on what it is. But I will hear you out."

A fleeting glimpse of relief softened his eyes for a moment. He folded his hands in front of him and studied them before raising his gaze to her again. "First of all, thank you for agreeing to listen. You are under no constraint to heed anything I say."

They agreed on that much.

He cleared his throat. "I am quite concerned about my father."

Pearl's defensive posture fell away and instantly her senses were piqued. Her first instinct was to immediately see to Hubert's welfare, but she'd seen him earlier that very morning sweeping the boardwalk in front of the store, so she knew he wasn't ill. Or was he?

"What's wrong? Hubert isn't sick, is he?" She tried but couldn't modulate her voice, and concern for Hubert's health and well-being wove its way into her inquiry.

"No, at least not physically sick." Slight lines appeared between Everett's brows. "That is, not yet. These past few weeks, my father seems to have fallen into a state of depression. He doesn't eat except a bite or two. He sleeps poorly. I hear him up at night, pacing. He has dark circles under his eyes and his complexion is pale. He seems quite listless. Often his thoughts are distracted, and he is unable to carry on a conversation without asking me to repeat something I just said."

Pearl lowered her gaze to her hands. Everett had just described her own habits for the past weeks. Her heart longed to go to Hubert, but she could not. Everett's candid remarks revealed a transparent side of the young man she'd not seen before. If Everett was thinking of someone besides himself, perhaps he wasn't the self-serving individual she thought him to be. Quite frankly, she didn't understand why he was telling her these things. How did he think she could help if he'd demanded she break the engagement?

"There is talk. . ." Everett shifted his gaze aside. "Your new boarder, a Mr. Cain, if I am not mistaken, was once a suitor of yours."

Heat ignited in Pearl's middle and rose to her face. Was everyone in town gossiping about her? She clamped her teeth tightly and waited for Everett to continue.

"Mrs. Dunnigan, I don't mean to be impertinent, but I wondered if you and Mr. Cain have renewed your courtship."

Impertinent didn't begin to describe her opinion of his question, but she held her temper. No good would come of a display of anger, but she became aware that if pushed far enough, her self-control might give way. She took a deep breath.

"Mr. Cain expressed his wish to court me seven years ago, which I refused. He is a paying customer at the boardinghouse, nothing more." She narrowed her eyes at Everett. "Not that it is any of your business. I can't help wondering why you are asking such a personal question, and what does it have to do with Hubert not eating or sleeping well?"

A flush crept up his neck. At least he had the grace to appear uncomfortable. "Mrs. Dunnigan, despite what you may think, I care very much about my father. I am distressed to see him making himself sick. I thought perhaps, if you and Mr. Cain announced your intentions, my father could free himself of any lingering thoughts of his courtship with you being revived, thus allowing him to move past his melancholy moods."

Outrage rushed into her chest and threatened to explode. How dare he make such a suggestion! Before she could express her offense, the waitress came to take their order.

"Hello, Miss Pearl."

Pearl glanced up to see Tillie O'Dell's pretty face. The girl sent Everett a shy smile and lowered her dark lashes in a demure fashion.

"Hello, Everett. It's nice to see you again."

Everett cast a puzzled glance toward Tillie. Pearl watched the scope of his gaze take in her apron and the tray in her hands.

"What may I bring you?" Tillie pulled a pad and pencil from her apron pocket.

The expression on Everett's face changed from confusion to disbelief, and then to disdain. If Pearl's vexation over his shocking and insulting suggestion wasn't so great, she might have found his disconcertment comical.

He looked away from Tillie and cleared his throat. "Tea, please. Cream and sugar. Mrs. Dunnigan?" His abruptness took Pearl aback. This certainly wasn't the attitude he'd displayed last Sunday at the church picnic. Quite the contrary, he and Tillie had seemed to enjoy each other's company. So why was he now acting like he didn't know her?

"Uh, nothing, thank you, Tillie." She looked into Tillie's face and saw bewilderment, even though the girl's focus was on Everett.

Tillie bit her lower lip for a moment. "Everett, I wanted to tell you again what a nice time I had at the picnic."

A momentary flinch raced across Everett's face, and he slid a glance around the room. "Just the tea, please."

Tillie blinked and took a backward step. If Everett's demeaning suggestion to take up with Silas Cain incensed Pearl, his blatant condescending attitude toward Tillie magnified her anger even further. As soon as Tillie hurried away, Pearl stood and picked up her reticule. Every nerve ending in her body wanted to shout her indignation at Hubert's son, but to do so would only further alienate him. However, regardless of his treatment of her, she refused to stand by and watch a sweet girl like Tillie get hurt.

She sucked in a steadying breath and rose from her chair. "Everett, I'm going to forget this meeting took place, except for one thing." Pearl lifted her chin and straightened her shoulders. "Tillie O'Dell is a lovely, sweet Christian girl, and for you to snub her the way you just did is simply. . .mean and hateful."

She didn't bother to wish him a good day as she turned and marched resolutely out the door.

ﻬ

Hubert ran his hand over a bolt of new material he'd just pulled from the crate and placed on the shelf. Blue, Pearl's favorite color. The fabric with its tiny forget-me-not pattern sprinkled over it was the same shade as Pearl's eyes. Maybe when she came into the mercantile, he'd just give her a dress length. *If* she came in. She'd not set foot in the store in over three weeks. He suspected that she'd coaxed Tessa to pick up supplies for the boardinghouse.

He'd caught glimpses of Pearl at church or as she walked down the boardwalk. His heart wanted to call out to her, but he couldn't embarrass her that way. The day he'd caught her when she tripped on the church steps, she'd made it clear that she considered a public confrontation inappropriate. He'd considered writing a letter, but he could only imagine the postmaster's amusement when Hubert spent two cents to mail a letter he could walk down the block and deliver in person for free.

He glanced toward the door, like he did a hundred times a day, hoping to see Pearl entering. Instead, a young lad with unruly brown hair and too many freckles to count stepped through the door. With only a cursory peek at the candy jars lined up on the counter, the youth marched up to Hubert.

"Hullo, Mr. Behr. Fine day, ain't it?"

The boy's precociousness pulled Hubert's mouth into a smile. "Hello there, young fellow. I believe I've seen you at church, haven't I?"

"Yessir. I'm Grady O'Dell."

"How nice that you've come to visit, Mr. O'Dell."

A few of Grady's freckles went into hiding when the boy grinned. "I ain't here to visit. I'm workin'."

Hubert chuckled. "Is that so? Well then, how may I assist you today, sir?"

Grady dug into his pocket, the tip of his tongue stuck out in concentration. He extracted a wrinkled scrap of paper, which he held out to Hubert. "This here's the list. I'm gettin' paid a nickel to take these things to—" He clapped his hand over his mouth, eyes wide.

Hubert took the paper and ruffled the boy's hair. "Don't you worry, Grady. I won't tell anyone about your good fortune." He unfolded the paper. "Now, let's have a look at your employer's list and—"

The handwriting on the paper was as familiar as his own. *Pearl.* Realization sent a stab of remorse through him. Pearl apparently wanted to separate herself from him and was paying Grady to pick up and deliver her groceries.

"Got my cart out on the boardwalk," Grady declared. "I'm a lot stronger than I look, so I can load it myself. Oh, and I got the money right here." He pulled a wadded-up hanky from his other pocket. When he set it on the counter, coins clinked inside its folds.

Hubert rubbed his hand over his bearded chin. So that's the way it was. His heart grappled with his common sense. Why couldn't he simply take the supplies to Pearl himself?

"Well now, there's no need for you to tote all these things." Hubert flapped Pearl's list. "I can deliver them to Miss Pearl this afternoon."

Grady's eyes bugged out. "How didja know they was for Miss Pearl? I wasn't s'posed to tell."

Hubert patted the boy's shoulder. "It doesn't matter. But I'd be more than happy to deliver these items to her personally."

Grady's bottom lip stuck out in a pout. "But then I can't earn my nickel. I was gonna buy some peppermint sticks for my sister Tillie's birthday."

Hubert bent at the waist and put his hands on his knees. "Tell you what. I'll give you the peppermint sticks. How's that?"

A frown tainted Grady's countenance and he shook his head vehemently. "Uh-uh! My pa says a man should do a day's work for a day's pay. I want to do what Miss Pearl's payin' me to do."

How was Hubert supposed to refute that? He straightened and heaved a sigh. "All right, son. It'll take me a few minutes to get everything on this list together. Why don't you go look at the peppermint sticks."

Grady's frown dissipated, and he stuck his hand out to Hubert. "Yessir."

Hubert shook the boy's hand and began making Pearl's selections. After he wrapped up each item, and while Grady was still distracted, he quickly measured out a dress length of the blue forget-me-not material and added a yard of lace trim. Discreetly folding store paper around the yard goods, he tucked the package between Pearl's other supplies.

"Here you go, Grady. Everything is ready." Hubert counted out the money from Grady's hanky while the boy loaded the packaged items into the handcart.

All smiles, Grady waved good-bye to Hubert and turned the cart toward the boardinghouse. Hubert waved back, the pain in his heart so sharp he thought it might draw blood.

How he wished he could deliver those goods into Pearl's hands himself, but he had a terrible feeling she would close the door in his face. She'd never given him a reason for breaking their engagement, and when she'd told him not to come back, he'd abided by her wishes. For the hundredth time, he questioned his judgment.

If her decision not to marry him had anything to do with Silas Cain, why was he standing by allowing it to happen? What kind of man was he that he'd let the woman he loved walk away without fighting for her? No, he couldn't go on like this any longer. Somehow he had to make her listen. He must think of a way to catch her alone so he could talk to her without Cain's interference. In the meantime, he intended to grab hold of God's throne and beg Him for favor.

Chapter 11

Hubert poured two cups of coffee and carried them to the table, setting one in front of Everett before returning to his own chair. Neither of them had done justice to their supper plates. Hubert's appetite had abandoned him a few weeks ago, but Everett pushed his food around on his plate, ate little, and spoke even less.

"Is everything all right, son?"

Everett jerked his head up. "I beg your pardon?"

Hubert studied his son a moment. The air of pomposity that usually accompanied Everett's tone and manner was noticeably absent, but a frown of contemplation had carved creases in his brow for the past two days.

"Care to talk about it?" Hubert sipped his coffee.

Everett pushed his plate away and leaned back in his chair. "Father, why didn't you tell me Tillie worked in the hotel dining room?"

Hubert gave a shrug. "I don't know. . .why? Is it important?"

"Important!" Everett nearly spewed the word. "She's a waitress, a servant. Do you realize how foolish I felt?" He leaned forward and jabbed his finger into the air in Hubert's direction. "Father, she stood there in her apron waiting to take our order, telling me what a good time she had at the picnic."

Hubert folded his arms across his chest. "Frankly, I don't see the problem. If you liked Tillie at the picnic, why wouldn't you like her now that you know she works at the hotel?" His deliberately calm demeanor seemed to irritate Everett further, but Hubert went on before Everett had the chance to retort. "I tried to explain to you—the people of Willow Creek are fine, hardworking folks, and they aren't judged by their wealth or lack thereof. This isn't Baltimore. Social registers mean nothing here. You aren't any better than Tillie O'Dell because you were raised in affluence and she wasn't."

Everett opened his mouth, but Hubert held up his hand. "What makes a person worthy of your respect? Position? Status? Power? If that's the case, you must not hold me in very high esteem. I'm simply a storekeeper."

"That's different," Everett countered. "You chose to be a storekeeper. You just wanted something to do when you retired."

Hubert nodded. "Yes, that's so. But nevertheless, I wear an apron and I serve the people who come into the mercantile, the same as Tillie wears an apron and served you in the hotel dining room. She is still the same person she was at the picnic."

Everett turned and stared out the window, frustration edging his expression. "My upbringing isn't something I can casually toss away."

"I'm not asking you to do any such thing." Hubert rose from his chair. "Your grandparents were fine people." He picked up his coffee mug and carried it to the sitting area, gesturing for Everett to join him. "Are you telling me your grandparents would approve of you holding someone in contempt because they didn't have as much as you?"

The hard edges of Everett's indignation softened as he sank into the overstuffed chair by the fireplace. Hubert could see him thoughtfully weighing the question.

Finally Everett answered. "Grandfather wouldn't." His fingers curled around the ends of the armrests. "Grandfather treated everyone the same regardless of their position. Grandmother was the one who insisted on observing proper social protocol." After a minute, he looked across at Hubert, a tiny smirk tweaking the corner of his mouth. "Grandmother would have been appalled at me attending a church picnic and sitting on a blanket on the ground. She would have needed her smelling salts had she known I'd spent the afternoon with a young woman who worked as a waitress."

Hubert pressed the tips of his fingers together and allowed Everett time to contemplate the difference between the values taught by his grandparents. "So is Tillie your picnic companion different from Tillie the waitress?"

Everett didn't reply immediately. He drew in a deep breath and let it out slowly, dragging his hand through his hair. "That's something I'm going to have to think about." His expression took on a faraway look, and he spoke more to himself than to Hubert. "When she came to take our order, she smiled the same way she did at the picnic."

"Our order?"

"Mrs. Dunnigan and myself."

Hubert sat forward so abruptly his coffee sloshed over the rim of his mug. "You and Pearl were at the hotel dining room together? When was this?"

Everett jolted out of his reverie. Telltale redness crept into his complexion. "Uh, a couple of days ago."

"Why didn't you mention this to me?" Every nerve ending in Hubert's body stood at attention.

Discomfort etched a frown into Everett's brow again. "I simply ran into her in town."

"You ran into Pearl in the hotel dining room?"

"Well no, not exactly." Everett shifted his position and examined his fingernails. "I invited her to have a cup of tea."

Hubert sat, stunned. Was his son having a change of heart about Pearl? He'd love to prod Everett into disclosing what they'd talked about, but his son's countenance had closed up tighter than shutters over a window before a storm. Was a cup of tea all it took to persuade Pearl to engage in conversation?

"Perhaps I'll do the same."

Everett's quizzical look begged an explanation.

Hubert pulled himself out of his chair and stood. "I had planned to go over to the boardinghouse this evening and try to convince Pearl to talk to me. Perhaps a cup of tea will help smooth the way."

"What?" Everett stood and faced his father. "She broke off the engagement. There's no need—"

"No need to what, son?" Hubert stared at him. "You sound like you know why she broke the engagement."

The red in Everett's face deepened. "All I know is she made her choice. Why do you insist on talking to her now that her attention is elsewhere?"

Hubert nailed Everett in place with a steel gaze. "You seem to know an awful lot about this." He took a deep breath, glanced down, and released the air on a restrained sigh. "Ever since you and I began corresponding a year ago, I prayed that we could someday be reconciled. Your being here is the answer to that prayer."

Hubert crossed the room to stand in front of the window. He stared across the expanse of the hillside that separated his house from the edge of town. Just past the treetops, the peak of the boardinghouse roof pointed skyward. The lengthening shadows and the golden hues of the descending sun winked together against the wood-shingled rooftop. Under that roof resided the woman he felt God had chosen for him.

"Everett, I don't know if you had anything to do with Pearl's decision. I don't know if her new boarder, that Cain fellow, had anything to do with it. But I know this." He turned, wanting Everett to see the determination in his expression. "I will not let her go without a fight." The waning light revealed disconcertment on his son's face. "I love Pearl. And as happy as I am that you have come to Willow Creek, I cannot let you or anyone else stand in the way of Pearl and me being together."

Everett skewed his lips into a sneer. "I can't believe this. Twenty years ago you chose your job over your family." He thrust a hand out toward Hubert. "You *say* you're glad we've reconciled. You *say* my being here is an answer to your prayers." Sarcasm threaded his tone.

Hubert took a step forward. "I *am* glad, son. You must know that. But you must also know you cannot dictate to me how to live."

Dead silence reigned for the space of a few seconds while Everett narrowed his eyes into a reproachful glare. "Where were your prayers when I was a child, Father? Did God tell you to turn your back on your family? Was the lure of adventure what kept you away for weeks and months at a time while my mother spent her days and nights in fear, wondering where you were and if you were coming back? What was I supposed to think back then? Both my parents deserted me, my father in favor of his job and my mother for another man. Where was God then? Or was ambition your god?"

The same accusations Hubert had hurled at himself repeatedly over the years now flowed unchecked from his son's lips. The bitter remorse he thought he'd finally put behind him reemerged as needle pricks to his soul. God may have forgiven him, but until he forgave himself, guilt would continue to haunt him.

But apparently Everett wasn't finished. "Now, just when you have finally begun to act like a father, you're making the same choice you made twenty years ago. Except this time it's not your job, it's a woman."

The way Everett said *woman* sounded so disparaging Hubert almost drew his fist back. Only the knowledge that he deserved his son's scorn kept him from doing so. He turned back to the window. Was the acid anger in his chest aimed at Everett or himself?

"Well, Father? Isn't it true?"

Hubert waited until his breathing slowed before answering. "Everett, I admit I was wrong all those years ago. I was so enamored with my job, everything else paled in significance. I chose to take the cases that kept me on the trail for a long time. Deep inside, I knew it was wrong to leave you and your mother alone. I should have left those cases to the unmarried men. But all I focused on was solving the toughest cases so I could gain recognition and status."

He turned to look at Everett. As painful as he knew it would be, he had to look his son in the eye when the words he had to speak crossed his lips. "Don't you see? I was guilty of putting prestige at a higher level of importance than anything else, including my family. . .and God." He swallowed hard. "I allowed ambition and success to blind me. I disobeyed God. I chose to do what I wanted instead of what God was telling me."

The lump in his throat restricted his air, but he had to make Everett understand his remorse. "The day I learned your mother had left, I came face-to-face with my own sinful selfishness. I haven't lived a single day since without regret."

Moisture glinted in Everett's eyes and Hubert crossed to him, taking hold of his son's shoulders. "Everett, you're my son and I love you. It is still my deep desire for us to be close. If I had the opportunity to rethink my choices, I'd do things differently." His fingers squeezed into Everett's shoulders. A quiver passed through his son's stiffened muscles. "I'd give anything to reclaim the time I lost being your father, but I can't."

He dropped his hands. A mixture of sorrow, relief, and hope stirred within him. A surprising lightness eased the pressure in his chest, confession releasing the burden of guilt he'd carried for so long. There would always be consequences and regrets connected with his past disobedience, and he still didn't know if he'd ever feel the right to forgive himself, but one thing was certain. God's forgiveness was absolute.

"I believe God has given me a second chance to be the kind of husband He meant for me to be twenty years ago. And that's why I'm going to go talk to Pearl. If she won't listen tonight, I'll go again tomorrow, and the day after that, and the day after that, until she believes how much I love her. I only pray I'm not too late."

Everett's posture sagged, as though drained of energy to fight. "All right, Father, if that's your decision, I won't argue and I won't try to stop you." Grief darkened Everett's eyes. His voice lacked all hint of animosity or arrogance. "Tomorrow I'll inquire about stage connections to Dubuque and train schedules east. I'll be leaving at the end of the week."

Hubert's stomach muscles tightened. Saying good-bye to Everett would break his heart. He wished his son knew the power of God's forgiveness. Perhaps if he did, he'd be able to find it in his heart to extend forgiveness to his father.

Pearl was up to her elbows in dishwater when she heard the knock at the back door. She frowned and glanced through the red gingham-curtained window. "It's almost dark outside. Who is stopping by at this time of the evening?"

She grabbed a dish towel and wiped her hands on the way to the door. The moment she cracked the door open, her breath caught in her throat.

"Hubert." His name came out in a hoarse whisper.

He stood before her, holding a blue-and-white china teapot and a box of her favorite chamomile and ginger tea. "Hello, Pearl. Please don't close the door. I just want to talk, and thought perhaps we could share a cup of tea."

Pearl couldn't find her voice. She knew she should tell him to go away, but her heart refused to allow her tongue to work. She tried to shake her head but found herself nodding instead. Why was she opening the door wider?

"Thank you." Hubert stepped across the threshold into the kitchen. "I'll even put the water on to boil and brew the tea if you'd like."

She flapped her fingers and took the box of tea from him. "The kettle is still warm from supper." She pushed it over the hottest part of the stove. "Hubert, you shouldn't be here."

"Why?" He set the china teapot on the table. "You know I still love you, Pearl. Nothing has changed for me except the fact that you've broken our engagement. And you won't even give me a good reason for doing so."

Her heart kicked against her ribs. She couldn't answer him. How could she tell him Everett was the cause? She sidestepped the issue. "Grady O'Dell made a mistake the other day when he delivered my supplies. There was a piece of yard goods that I didn't order. I'll go and get it for you."

She started to go to her bedroom to fetch the material, but Hubert's gentle hand on her elbow held her in place. "Pearl, there was no mistake. I knew it was your list. I recognized your handwriting. I know you so well, I even know how you cross your *T*s. The cloth was a gift. It matches your eyes."

The simmering kettle covered the sound of the breath that caught in her throat. Her hands shook as she measured the tea into the china pot and poured in the scalding water.

"Hubert, that was thoughtful, but I can't accept a gift from you." Immediately her mind was stricken. Hubert's silver music box sat on her nightstand. Anguish twisted her stomach when she knew she must return the music box that she loved. Perhaps it was better if she did give it back. Every time she looked at it, tears burned her eyes. When she lifted the lid and listened to the tinkling notes, the love she kept locked away in her heart begged for release.

"I want you to have it, Pearl."

She winced. How could simple words cut so deeply? Even if Hubert referred to the blue material, how she wished she felt free to keep the music box. Hubert went to the breakfront and retrieved two teacups while she stood, fighting with her emotions. If he didn't leave soon, she'd lose her resolve.

Hubert set the cups on the table and pulled out Pearl's chair and held it for her. But she didn't sit. Instead, she balled up one corner of her apron and clenched it in her fingers.

"Hubert, I can't do this. Please go."

In one stride he was beside her and grasped her trembling hands. "Why, Pearl? Just tell me why."

She shook her head and closed her eyes. "It's not right."

Hubert gripped her shoulders and gave her a little shake. "Not right? Being apart isn't right." He cupped her chin. "Pearl, look at me. Look me in the eye and tell me you don't love me. Tell me, Pearl."

She tried to force her eyes to connect with Hubert's, but her heart couldn't comply with his demand. She turned away to stare into nothingness. "I can't marry you, Hubert."

Hubert's head dipped and angled to force her to look at him. "Pearl, my dear, being a Pinkerton detective for almost thirty years, I learned to read people's faces to see if they were telling the truth." He gently placed two fingers under her chin and tipped her head to face him. "Your eyes don't match your words."

Tightness in her throat prevented her from insisting he was wrong. Truth be told, he wasn't wrong, and she teetered on the brink of admitting as much. Just as her resolve began to topple, the kitchen door swung open and Silas Cain stood in the doorway.

"Say, what's going on in here?"

She never resented an intrusion more than she did at that very moment.

Chapter 12

Nothing is going on, Silas." Pearl's eyes lingered on Hubert as she spoke. She'd never seen him with such an angry glare as the one he threw in her boarder's direction. The steely determination in his eyes made her catch her breath, and she forced herself to turn and look at the man standing in the kitchen doorway.

Silas took two steps forward. "Is this man bothering you?"

"Now, see here, Cain. . ." Icicles hung on Hubert's tone, and Pearl felt his hand tense on her arm. Surely they wouldn't come to blows!

"Gentlemen." Pearl stepped away from Hubert and held up both hands, a palm in each of their directions. "It's been a long day. I'm tired, and I must ask both of you to—" She glanced toward Hubert. The words *leave me alone* refused to cross her lips, so she turned back to her boarder. "Silas, please go back to the parlor. Everything here is fine."

Silas scowled at Hubert and grumbled under his breath but turned on his heel and strode out of the kitchen.

As soon as she looked fully at Hubert, she knew it was a mistake. His image so impacted her, she felt as though his arms encircled her, gently holding her close, even though he stood three paces away. "Good night, Hubert."

"Pearl, I'm not going to give up. I intend to keep coming back until you understand how much I love you, and nothing, I mean absolutely nothing, is going to change that."

She couldn't look at him any longer. Her heartbeat thrummed in her ears, and her chest ached to tell him she loved him. Instead, she fixed her gaze on the worn worktable and dropped her voice to a whisper. "Please, Hubert. Don't make this any harder."

"Good night, Pearl. I'll be back."

The soft click of the door closing behind him as he exited sent a pang of grief through Pearl's heart. If only Hubert would treat her with contempt or respond in anger to her repeated insistence that she would not marry him, forgetting about him might be easier. But every time she saw him she noticed he looked pale and drawn with dark circles under his eyes, and pain filled his expression. She wasn't sure how much longer her resolve would remain intact, especially if Hubert fulfilled his promise to return.

Fickle emotions warred within her as she poured out the lukewarm tea. Her fingers traced the blue flowers on the teapot Hubert had brought. How like him to do something like that. As adamant as she was about her decision, deep inside she wanted Hubert to come back, and she knew her heart wasn't ready to let go. A groan escaped.

"I can't keep doing this." She covered her face with her hands. "God, please help me put my feelings for Hubert aside and remember why I made this choice in the first place."

"What choice is that, Pearl?"

She startled and yanked her hands away from her face. Silas once again stood in the kitchen doorway. Ire bristled in her middle.

"Silas, must you sneak into my kitchen that way?"

A smooth, self-confident smile slid into place on his countenance. "I wasn't sneaking, Pearl. I was merely checking to make sure you were all right." He tossed a casual glance toward the back door. "Wasn't that the fellow who works in the mercantile?"

Pearl narrowed her eyes at her boarder. "Silas, is there something you need, or are you just trying to irritate me?"

He held one hand over his heart, and his disbelieving expression mocked her. "Why Pearl, I'm hurt. Here I come to check on your safety and well-being, and you accuse me of an ulterior motive."

If her emotions weren't already so ragged, she might have snorted at his ridiculous statement. The only part of her in danger in Hubert's presence was her heart, but she had no intention of discussing Hubert with Silas.

She pulled her shoulders back and picked up her dish towel. "As you can see, I'm just fine. Now please excuse me so I can finish up my chores. I'd like to turn in early."

"Pearl. . ." Silas closed the space between them and took the towel out of her hands. "May we talk?"

Was he *trying* to provoke her? "Can't it wait? I still have much to do to finish my work."

He laid the dish towel on the worktable. "I apologize, Pearl, but I truly cannot wait another minute. I must speak with you."

She tried unsuccessfully to stifle a sigh. "All right. What is so important that it can't wait until morning?"

Silas gestured toward one of the kitchen chairs. If weariness wasn't climbing her frame she might have chosen to stand just to be contrary. Immediately she chided herself. Whatever was on his mind was important to him, and God didn't want her behaving in such a petulant manner. Besides, the sooner he spoke his piece, the sooner he would leave her alone with her thoughts. She crossed to the chair and sat, clasping her hands in her lap. Raising a questioning look, she waited for him to speak.

He cleared his throat. "Pearl, as you know, I am a successful entrepreneur, working with an investment company out of St. Louis and Chicago."

He'd already told her as much the day he showed up on her doorstep. She supposed his point in repeating the declaration was to impress her. But she wasn't impressed. "I believe you've mentioned that."

Silas tugged at his brocade vest. "I am in the process of acquiring certain properties that, once in my hands, will become growing enterprises with the potential to. . .well, let's just say I will have the ability to live *very* comfortably."

She frankly didn't care a fig about Silas's investments and couldn't understand why he felt the need to share the information with her. If all he wanted was to brag to her about his soon-coming wealth, she wasn't waiting to hear any more. She started to rise.

"Silas, I—"

"Wait Pearl, please." He took a long stride, his polished boots stopping inches from her own scuffed but sturdy button shoes. She plopped back onto the chair. Before she could draw another breath, he lowered himself to one knee and enfolded her hands between his.

"Pearl, it grieves me to see you work yourself into exhaustion day after day. I can see to it that you won't ever have to work another day in your life. Marry me, Pearl."

꙳

Pearl picked up the silver music box and sat on the edge of her bed. As promised, Hubert had come by each evening, patiently but persistently trying to persuade her to tell him the reason she'd broken their engagement and assuring her of his love. With each visit, she felt her resolve weaken. She'd forced the words, telling him not to come back, but he'd just kept repeating that her eyes didn't agree with what she was saying. How could she continue to send him away when her heart throbbed in anticipation of seeing him?

She gently turned the key on the side of the music box two full revolutions, and she lifted the lid. The sweet, plaintive notes of Strauss's haunting melody engraved their print on her soul. Last night she thought if she returned the music box to Hubert he would accept that as her final word. But he refused to take it, and now relief pushed anxiety out of the way. Only God knew how much she treasured Hubert's engagement gift. She closed her eyes and invited the memory of Hubert's proposal—a foolish use of her time since it only intensified her anguish. But instead of Hubert's face, the unexpected recollection of Silas getting down on one knee imposed itself in her mind. She frowned and shook her head.

For the past three days, Silas had watched her expectantly. She could feel his eyes following her as she moved about the dining room serving meals or clearing the table. Every time he poked his head into the kitchen she'd made certain her hands were busy. Thankfully, he left the boardinghouse each morning after breakfast to conduct his business—whatever it was. She closed the lid on the music box and returned the treasure to her bedside table, unwilling to allow the memory of Silas's proposal to be accompanied by Hubert's music.

She'd tried to tell him her answer while he was still on his knee, but he'd laid his finger over her lips and told her to think about it. She could still picture the way his eyebrows dipped, as though he were admonishing a child, when he told her not to keep him waiting too long for her answer.

"Think about it! *Pfft*. There's nothing to think about. I tried to tell him, and he wouldn't let me."

She stood and straightened her shoulders, determination pressing her lips together. She had work to do. Gathering her mop and dustcloth, she headed upstairs to clean the boarders' rooms.

A prick on her conscience snagged her attention. After Everett had come to the boardinghouse to see her, she'd spent nearly the entire night in prayer. She'd begged God to direct her. But she had to admit, to herself and to God, that she'd not had peace about her decision to end her engagement to Hubert. She'd reached the conclusion on her own and did not wait for assurance from God. "What other choice did I have? How could I be content with Hubert knowing I'd contributed to his unhappiness, coming between him and his son?"

She reached the first bedroom at the top of the stairs and began running her dust cloth over the furniture. Her tasks were so routine she could perform them without thought. She pushed her mop back and forth across the floor, straightening items as she went. Moving to the next room—Silas's room—she blew out a stiff breath of annoyance and plunged into her chore.

A messy array of papers cluttered the top of the bureau. She picked them up to dust and one fell to the floor. She put the rest into a tidy stack and bent to retrieve the one that had fallen. As she laid it with the others, however, her eye caught her own name written toward the bottom. She hesitated a moment. Reading the paper would be an invasion of Silas's privacy, wouldn't it? But if her name was on this paper, didn't she have the right to know why?

Her gaze scanned the paper. It was a letter to a man named Wendall. Judging by the tone of the letter, Pearl assumed he was one of the business associates Silas was always talking about. As she read further, she gasped.

As far as Pearl Dunnigan goes, I'm wearing her down. She has been rather stubborn, but it shouldn't take too much longer until her property is in my possession. I will employ whatever means are necessary in order to. . .

She heard the front door open and close.

"Pearl?"

Silas. What was he doing here in the middle of the day? She folded the paper and jammed it into her apron pocket, clenched her teeth, and exited the room. With each footfall on the stairs her indignation grew, but she mustn't allow Silas to know she had read the letter. Not yet.

"Silas, I'm surprised to see you in the middle of the day. I thought your business kept you occupied."

A glib smile creased his face. "There you are." He met her at the bottom of the stairs with a bouquet of wildflowers in his hand, but she ignored him and the flowers and immediately turned toward the kitchen. As she assumed he would, Silas followed her. She took a wooden bowl from the shelf, then walked purposefully to the pantry to fetch a crock of lard and an assortment of spices. "What are you doing here, Silas?" She set the items on the worktable and returned to the pantry for a basket of apples.

"Well Pearl, that's rather insensitive. . ." He stepped out of her way as she pushed the basket onto the table. "Seeing as how I've given you three whole days. . ."

She reached in a drawer and drew out a large knife. Silas backed up and moved to the other side of the table.

"Pearl, I simply cannot wait any longer. You've kept me in suspense long enough. I must know your answer."

Pearl picked up an apple, quartered it, and began peeling the sections without looking at him. The oversize blade made the chore a bit awkward, but she didn't bother trading the knife for a smaller, less intimidating one. "Silas, if you recall, I tried to give you my answer the other night, but you wouldn't let me."

"W–well, I know that. . .ladies. . .need time to think things over."

She selected another apple from the basket and paused, her knife poised. "I didn't need time to think it over at all." She pushed the blade through the fruit and split it into halves and then into quarters. "But now I am actually glad I had time to consider the whole matter, because a new issue has come to light." Slivers of red peelings dropped into the wooden bowl. "My answer to your proposal shouldn't surprise you. It was *no* seven years ago, it was *no* three nights ago, and it's still *no*." She sliced the apple into thin pieces.

"But Pearl, how can you cast aside such an opportunity? Think of what it would mean for us, for you. This house—"

Pearl jerked her head up and shot a pointed look at him. "You were saying something about *my* house?"

He blinked and hesitated, as though rearranging his words. "Well yes, of course it's your house. That's beside the point." He came around the side of the table, eyeing her knife as he did so. "You can't continue to operate this house, this business, alone. Just think of how hard you work every day, the arduous duties, the drudgery. You shouldn't have to do this. Marry me, Pearl."

She sucked in a deep breath. "Silas, I've already given you my answer, and I don't plan to change it. But there is still one other matter to address." Before he could argue further, she pulled the letter from her apron pocket.

Silas's face turned purple and the veins popped out on his neck. He reached for the paper, but Pearl yanked it back out of his reach.

"That's my personal business. You have no right to—"

"I was cleaning your room and this fell on the floor. You should really be more careful what you leave lying around, Silas."

His icy glare and twitching jaw defined his anger, but Pearl refused to be intimidated.

"It appears the only reason you wanted me to marry you was so you could"—she unfolded the letter and glanced at it—"'take possession of my property.'"

A sound akin to a growl emanated from Silas's throat. "It's against the law to read other people's mail."

"It's also against the law to defraud someone of their property." She tucked the letter back into her pocket. "And this wasn't in the mail yet. It was a paper in a room in *my house* that I was cleaning."

She picked up another apple and sliced it in half. "You have five minutes to pack your things and leave this house. Otherwise, I'm going to the sheriff."

It felt good to state emphatically what she felt, but judging by the thunderclouds forming in his eyes and the sneer on his lips, Silas wasn't finished. "You'll be sorry you did this, Pearl. I'm used to getting what I want."

Chapter 13

S treaks of pink and gold painted the eastern sky, but Hubert had been up
for hours. Sipping his third cup of coffee, he stood at his front window
and watched the morning yawn and stretch its arms over the treetops
that hugged the outline of the boardinghouse. He'd not told Pearl about
Everett's decision to go back East. If their relationship was to be renewed, it
had to be because Pearl loved him, not because Everett was leaving, if that
was the reason she'd broken the engagement in the first place. He shrugged.
She'd learn about Everett's departure eventually. Besides, if the news Silas
Cain had told him yesterday in the store was true, she might not care anyway.

"Lord, I've made so many wrong decisions over the years, but I still feel
Pearl is the woman You have chosen for me. If that's true, won't You please
change her mind?"

He heard Everett stirring in his room. Probably packing his bag before
coming out for breakfast. How Hubert wished he could convince his son to
stay in Willow Creek. Having spent the predawn hours in prayer, Hubert
rested in the assurance that God would work out every detail according to
His pleasure. A smile lifted one corner of his lips. There was comfort in
knowing the outcome wasn't up to him.

"Lord, You are worthy of my trust. You've proven Yourself faithful so many
times, even when I didn't deserve Your mercy. Instead of telling You what I
want, I'd rather just remain close to You and see what Your will has in store
for me and Pearl. . .and Everett."

The door to Everett's room opened. Hubert turned with his coffee mug in
hand. Everett was dressed in his traveling clothes, and a valise of fine, tooled
leather dangled from his hand. Disappointment pierced Hubert's heart once
more, and he sent a quick prayer heavenward, asking for the fortitude to bid
his son good-bye.

"Good morning, son. Would you like eggs for breakfast?"

Everett set the bag down and crossed to the kitchen. "No thank you. Just
coffee."

229

"Let me make a fresh pot." Hubert wrapped a kitchen towel around the handle of the coffeepot and dumped the grounds into the bucket by the dry sink.

"I don't want you to go to any trouble." Resignation replaced the haughtiness that had laced Everett's voice a few weeks ago.

How could he make Everett understand that doing little things for him was a pleasure, not an imposition? "It's no trouble, son." Hubert rinsed out the pot and then pumped fresh water into it, adding the freshly ground coffee. There was plenty of time. The stage wasn't due for another three hours.

While the coffee's aroma wafted through the room, Everett withdrew his watch and checked it, then tucked it back into his vest pocket.

Hubert studied his son "You know it's not too late to change your mind."

Everett pulled out a chair and sat at the table. "I spent the night listening to you pace out here." He shifted in his chair. "I couldn't sleep either."

"I'm sorry if I kept you awake."

Everett shook his head. "You didn't. I had so many things on my mind, it was hard to close my eyes." He looked at Hubert. "It doesn't seem that we've been able to resolve our differences, but perhaps it's not as much your fault as I once thought."

If Everett was willing to initiate further discussion on the matter, Hubert was ready to listen. "Did you come to any conclusions?"

His son rose and walked to the front window where Hubert had stood watching the sunrise a few minutes earlier. "I'm not sure." Hubert heard him sigh. "But I wasn't sure when I came to Willow Creek either. I thought I knew what my purpose in coming was, but now. . ."

Hubert checked the coffeepot and returned to sit at the table. "You know I want you to stay, but it's your choice. Do you have plans?"

Everett blew out a breath and turned away from the window. He extracted an envelope from his inside coat pocket. "I received this letter from Grandfather's attorney last week." He stared at the envelope, a scowl marring his features. "I was unaware of the unpaid debts and liens against Grandfather's business."

Surprise at Everett's statement raised Hubert's eyebrows. Everett had told him he stood to inherit a great deal of money and planned to take over his grandfather's business, but it sounded as though bad news from the attorney might change his son's future.

Everett unfolded the missive and studied it silently. Judging from his son's slumped shoulders, Hubert suspected he'd already read it several times.

Everett held the letter up, waving it slightly. "At first I didn't plan to share this information with you. I didn't want you to know."

Hubert frowned, not in anger but in puzzlement.

Everett shuffled over and sat at the table again, laying the letter in front of him. "But there is something here you *should* know."

Hubert cut his gaze to the letter. Several pages lay on the table, so whatever explanation it contained was lengthy.

"This lawyer, Mr. Goss, was originally my grandmother's attorney. She hired him to handle some legal affairs involving my mother. After Grandmother died, Mr. Goss contacted my grandfather, who retained him at that point. He says that he was under obligation to my grandfather to keep this information confidential until now." Everett stared at the letter with doleful eyes. "It seems we were wrong about not knowing where my mother went."

Hubert blinked and raised his eyebrows. "But we *didn't* know."

"Grandmother did." He looked across the table at his father. "And on more than one occasion, she wired money to my mother—large amounts of money." He turned the pages over. "By the time we got word of Mother's death, Grandmother had sent almost a hundred thousand dollars to her. Mr. Goss says the bank drafts were sent to various places and cashed at different banks, and he suspects the man with whom Mother ran away may have been blackmailing her." His fingers curled up the corners of the pages and his eyes remained riveted to the paper.

Hubert tried to digest the staggering information. "You mean. . ."

"Mother's leaving wasn't entirely your fault." Everett leaned his head back and blew out his breath through pursed lips. "I wanted to keep on blaming you. Grandmother always told me you weren't a good man; you weren't good enough for my mother." He thumped his open palm down onto the letter. "But I blamed you based on her word, without knowing the facts."

Hubert shook his head. "It sounds like none of us knew the facts."

A grim line defined Everett's lips. "Except Grandmother. After she died, Mr. Goss had to tell Grandfather about the missing money as well as several large bills my grandmother ran up without his knowledge. At some point, and the letter isn't completely clear on this, Grandfather signed over 51 percent ownership of the business to Grandmother. She apparently used Grandfather's business as collateral for loans, sending the money to my mother. Mr. Goss is in the process of sorting out the details of settling the estate, but the house and furnishings may have to be sold to pay off the creditors. Grandfather's business is in receivership."

Hubert stood to retrieve the coffeepot that had begun to boil. "Since you may not have a house to go back to, why don't you stay here?"

Another sigh hung on the air as Everett refolded the letter and tucked it back into his coat pocket. "You've made a life for yourself in this place, but Iowa isn't where I belong."

"It could be." Hubert poured two cups of coffee and set one before Everett. "I have a comfortable home and the mercantile. I know it's not the life to which you are accustomed, but—"

Everett waved his hand and took a sip of coffee. "Mr. Goss indicates he will have some papers for me to sign and there should be a small inheritance after all the creditors are paid. I'm afraid it will be a fraction of what I was expecting, but at least it's something. Once I return to Baltimore, I'll weigh my options."

"Couldn't Willow Creek be one of your options?"

Everett hesitated before answering. "No, Father. I have no future here. I hope you can find happiness in Willow Creek, but I think it's best if I leave."

૨૭

Since Everett needed the wagon to carry his trunk and his valise, Hubert had taken his time walking to the mercantile. The normal sounds of Willow Creek's commerce that usually brought a smile to his lips failed to cheer him this morning. The sun hid behind gloomy gray clouds that matched Hubert's melancholy mood. He puttered around the store, waited on a half dozen customers, and opened a crate of merchandise. When the clock on the shelf behind the counter chimed, Hubert pulled out his watch, thinking the clock must surely be running fast. But the hands of his watch confirmed it was nearly time to bid Everett good-bye.

He hung the CLOSED sign on the mercantile door and walked down the street to meet Everett at the depot before the stage arrived. As painful as it was, he'd not let his son leave without telling him one more time that he loved him and wanted him to stay.

Everett stood beside his valise and trunk on the boardwalk in front of the depot. There wasn't much left to say, other than repeating what had already been spoken. Hubert opened his mouth to entreat his son one last time to stay in Willow Creek when he heard a shout from down the street. He'd hoped on this day the stage might arrive late, thus giving him extra time with Everett.

But instead, the conveyance must be pulling into town early. They both looked in the direction of the noise.

Within moments, more people added their voices to the shouting, and Hubert realized it wasn't the stage's arrival. Some kind of commotion drew the attention of nearly everyone on the street. Several folks ran toward the clamor. Just as he turned to see what was happening, he saw billows of smoke rising above the trees, and one of the men yelled over his shoulder as he ran.

"The boardinghouse is on fire!"

Horror gripped Hubert by the throat. He forced his brain to function and his feet to move. Down the alley was a shorter route. With his heart pounding in his ears and his chest constricting, he ran toward Pearl's place.

"God, let her get out of there. Please let her be safe."

He was vaguely aware of footsteps hammering out a rhythm behind him in step with his own.

"Father!"

When he reached the yard of the boardinghouse, men were already manning the pump, working the handle up and down with ferocity. Others carried buckets and burlap sacks.

But where was Pearl? His eyes darted from one side of the yard to the other. "Pearl!"

He raced to the front of the house. No Pearl, but the curtains at the parlor window were already in flames. Yelling Pearl's name at the top of his lungs, he elbowed past the lilac bushes. There was no answer. His frantic search brought him back where he'd started. Pearl was nowhere outside.

As he pushed past the men who had formed a line, slinging water buckets, the crackle of the fire reached his ears. Dense smoke nearly blotted out the location of the back door.

"Pearl!"

Without hesitation, Hubert lunged toward the door. Several hands grabbed at him, and a conglomeration of voices accosted his senses—urgent entreaties for him to not enter the burning house.

"Stay back! Don't go in there!"

"Are you crazy, man? You won't come out of there alive."

He yanked his arms free of the restraining grips and pushed forward. Another voice pierced through the commotion.

"No, Father! Stop!"

But he couldn't stop. His feet, propelled by a force he didn't see, carried him past the porch steps. A degree of strength he'd never known before sent jolts of energy through him.

"Pearl!"

A roiling wall of black smoke met him when he flung the door open. He raised his arm, waving the deadly veil away, and covered his face in the crook of his elbow. "Pearl! . . .Pearl!"

He plunged into the kitchen. The smoke drove him to his knees. It unfurled against him from every side, and he couldn't determine the direction from which the fire came. The thick vapor was denser near the ceiling, but lower down he could make out the forms of the kitchen table and chairs, the legs of the cast-iron stove, the bottom edge of the pantry door. He tried to scream out Pearl's name again, but black fog that tasted like tar burned his throat. If he'd taken a moment to wet a cloth and tie it over the lower half of his face, he might be able to breathe easier, but the action would have taken several precious seconds, and he didn't know how many seconds he had to find Pearl. He pulled his shirt up to cover his nose and mouth, and continued crawling through the kitchen, but Pearl wasn't there.

"P–P. . .earl." Spasms of coughing choked him. The sound of the crackling grew louder and something crashed behind him. "P–P—" Impenetrable smoke wrapped virulent fingers around his throat. He could no longer push Pearl's name past his lips, but his heart continued to scream. Only God could hear him. Heat intensified moment by moment, but awareness of time began to slip away. Coughs tore at his windpipe and wracked his chest.

Pearl, my love, where are you? God, please show me where she is. Lead me to her.

His shoulder came in contact with something solid, and it fell over with a thud that joined with the growing cacophony of the fire. He crawled blindly, unable to open his eyes to the searing heat and smoke. Something scraped and toppled behind him. From the same direction he'd come? He couldn't tell. Another thump and a knocking sound reached him. Somewhere a window shattered and an ominous cracking and splintering of wood meant the beams would soon collapse.

Please, Father, lead me to Pearl.

With his hand he groped to the right of him and encountered a wall, then an opening. A doorway. He stretched his arm and probed farther through the recess. His fingers floundered in the space and collided with warm softness lying on the floor just inside the door.

His lips formed the word *Pearl*, even though he couldn't force out any sound. He'd found her, but darkness entombed him and his sense of where he was in the house began to slip away. Locking his hand around her limp arm, he tried to drag her. A sensation of lightness overpowered him and took possession of his ability to think. The urgency that drove him into the house faded as oppressive heat enveloped him. His last shred of strength withered and died. The demon smoke was swallowing them, and they were falling. . . falling. . .

Chapter 14

Hubert fought to breathe through a snarled labyrinth of cobwebs, seeking an escape from the burning in his throat. Muffled voices called his name and encouraged him to open his eyes. Part of him desired to push his way through the fog and another part simply wanted to sleep. Could he find the strength to open his mouth and tell whoever was repeating his name to go away? A searing pain knifed his throat when he swallowed. He turned his head to one side and met gentle fingers touching his cheek and blotting his face with something blessedly cool.

"Mr. Behr, can you hear me?"

The voice sounded familiar, but he couldn't connect a name or face to it. If responding to the entreaty intensified the pounding in his head, perhaps lying perfectly still was his best option. His lips refused to cooperate when he tried to form the question *Where am I?*

"Don't try to talk. Just open your mouth and take a sip of water."

Water. The very word sounded heavenly. He parted his lips, and his bottom lip cracked painfully. He pulled his eyebrows in as a wince filled his whole being. But an instant later, cool water dripped into his mouth and quenched some of the pain. His tongue, thick and swollen, detached itself from the roof of his mouth and relished the wetness. Gradual awareness seeped into his brain. Whoever held the cup to his lips poured a tiny bit more water into his mouth, and Hubert let the precious moisture roll over his tongue. Since his first attempt to swallow was so painful, he wasn't eager to repeat the experience. He mentally braced himself and allowed his swallow reflex to work. As expected, it felt like pouring kerosene on an open wound.

"I know your throat hurts, but the doctor said you must try to take some water."

Understanding finally broke through. The voice belonged to Hannah Vogel, the doctor's wife. Most people just called her Mrs. Doc. Along with the realization of who ministered to him came the horrific memory of

236

crawling through the burning boardinghouse. Shred by shred, the picture came together.

Footsteps scurried away from where he lay, and he heard Mrs. Doc's voice again. "Mr. Behr is awake." Heavier footsteps accompanied those of the town doctor's diminutive wife.

"Hubert? It's Doc Vogel. Can you hear me?"

Hubert fought past the pain and tried to force his lips to work. Was there enough air in his lungs to push a single word out? "P. . .P. . ." He reached deep within himself for the determination to speak. The word came out as a hoarse whisper. "Pearl."

The doctor's fingers forced one of Hubert's eyes open, then the other. The air stung his eyes and they watered, blurring the image of the doctor. "Let's take a listen." Doc laid an instrument on Hubert's chest and moved it around several times before he seemed satisfied.

"Mm-hm. Mm-hm." Doc thumped his fingertips on Hubert's chest. "Has he coughed yet?"

Mrs. Doc answered in the negative. "But he has swallowed a few sips of water."

"Good. Let's sit him up." The two pairs of hands grasped his arms and shoulders and pulled him forward. His head swam, and the cot on which he lay floated like a leaf on an air current. Hubert opened his eyes again, tiny slits, enough to see Doc and Mrs. Doc standing on either side of him. Mrs. Doc moved to stuff pillows behind him. Then they leaned him back on the pillows and after several moments, the room stopped swaying like a runaway stagecoach.

"Pearl." It hurt to even whisper, but his concern for Pearl outdistanced his own discomfort.

"Hubert, I want you to try and cough. It's going to hurt, but you need to expel that bad air in your lungs. We don't want you developing pneumonia."

Why wouldn't Doc tell him about Pearl?

Hubert commanded his eyes to open as wide as he could make them. He wrapped his fingers around Doc's wrist. "Pearl."

Doc's grave expression sent shards of fear through him. "She's in the next room. She hasn't awakened yet. I'm afraid she took in quite a bit of smoke, and she has a few burns on her arm and hand."

Hubert tightened his grip involuntarily, and the doctor's expression softened. "If she wakes up in the next few hours, and if we can get her to sit up and cough like we are trying to do with you, I'll have a better idea of her prognosis. But right now, the best one I can give you is *guarded*."

Hubert gave the doctor a nod. Even the muscles in his neck and shoulders ached. A cough climbed up his tortured windpipe. He tried to hold it back, but it burst forth with lancing pain. Once he started coughing, he couldn't stop and the spasms wracked his chest. Perspiration collected on his face. Mrs. Doc continued to blot the damp cloth over his brow until the throes of coughing subsided. Exhausted, he leaned back against the pillows.

Doc Vogel listened to Hubert's chest again. "I know it hurts, but you need to cough." He pulled up a chair and sat next to Hubert's cot. "You probably have some questions, and since speaking is difficult, I'm going to guess what those questions are and answer them the best I can."

Hubert locked eyes with the doctor, hoping to communicate his concern over Pearl. He remembered finding her but not pulling her out of the house. How had they gotten out? "Nobody knows yet how the fire started, but the sheriff is still poking around over there. You and Mrs. Dunnigan were both unconscious when you were pulled out. The flames broke through the wall, and the place was starting to collapse." Doc leaned forward and put his hand on Hubert's shoulder. "If it wasn't for your son pulling both of you out of there when he did, we'd be burying you today. He pulled you out first, then went back in for Miss Pearl. He even had the presence of mind to roll her in a rug. Otherwise, her burns would have been much worse."

Everett pulled Pearl and me out? I didn't even realize he'd followed me into the house. With the memory of the harrowing trek through the smoke-filled boardinghouse, more pieces fell into place. He recalled hearing something thump behind him. Was that Everett?

The idea of Everett saving not only his life but Pearl's as well, sank in. With the realization came fear for his son's condition. "Ever–ett." He pushed out the hoarse croak.

Doc Vogel's brow knitted into furrows. "He has some pretty nasty burns. Before the laudanum took effect, he kept asking if he had gotten to you and Mrs. Dunnigan in time."

More coughing seized Hubert, and he fought his way through the spasm. "How bad. . .Everett?"

Doc shook his head. "Well, he didn't swallow too much smoke because he'd tied a wet rag over his mouth and nose. Unfortunately, parts of his clothing caught fire when the ceiling caved in. I'm not going to lie to you, some of his burns are serious. But if we can keep infection from setting in, he has a good chance."

Hubert slumped back onto the pillows. Everett saved his and Pearl's lives at the risk of his own. It was a staggering revelation. But Doc continued to fill in the blanks.

"One of the men who helped fight the fire said Mrs. Dunnigan had come out, but then she ran back in before anyone could stop her. When your son pulled her out of the house, she had a silver music box in her hands. I had to pry her fingers away from it."

~

Her head throbbed and wracking pain filled her chest and throat, but Pearl opened her eyes to find a small mountain of pillows behind her back and shoulders, and Hannah Vogel bathing her face. As soon as the doctor's wife realized Pearl was awake, a huge smile split her face. "Oh, thank the good Lord. We've been praying for you for two days." The woman hurried to the doorway and called her husband, then returned to Pearl's bedside.

Doc Vogel's smile matched his wife's when he saw Pearl. "You certainly gave us a scare, young lady." He immediately poked the ends of his stethoscope into his ears and listened to her chest.

Young lady? Mercy sakes, who did he think he was talking to? She started to open her mouth, but the doctor stopped her.

"No, no. Don't try to speak." He flipped the stethoscope around his neck. "You suffered some burns in your throat from breathing in the hot air. The smoke caused some damage, too. You've already coughed up some blood. That's why we have you propped up like this."

He motioned for his wife to bring a lamp closer, and he stuck a piece of flat wood in her mouth. The doctor frowned and made some grunting sounds as he peered inside. "Well, your throat is still swollen, but it's showing signs of healing. Until it heals completely, I don't want you to talk at all. Drink sips of water, as much as you can, and Hannah will help you gargle with some salt water later." He patted her shoulder.

When she tried to raise her arm, a sharp pain jolted her, and she noticed the bandages on her left hand and arm. Doc Vogel partially unwrapped one of the bandages and peered beneath it. "The burns aren't too serious. In a few days you won't need the bandages any longer. I'm more concerned with the burns in your throat." He gently replaced the swathing around her hand.

Pearl tried to mouth words, but the doctor kept admonishing her to keep silent. She held up her hands, palms facing each other, a few inches apart, and Hannah brightened.

"I think I know what she wants." The woman went to a small bureau and opened the top drawer. When she turned, she had Pearl's music box in her hands. "Is this it?"

Relief filled her. The box looked a bit tarnished but otherwise unscathed. She reached out for the cherished treasure.

"You have a couple of visitors. Mr. Behr has been in the next room asking about you ever since he regained consciousness yesterday."

The peculiar statement took Pearl aback. Hubert regained consciousness? Puzzlement must have shown on her face because Mrs. Doc hurriedly explained that Hubert was pulled out of the burning boardinghouse along with her. It still didn't make sense.

Doc Vogel instructed his wife to give Pearl sips of water, as much as she would take. Then he turned back to Pearl. "The sheriff has been waiting to talk to you. He can tell you everything that happened, at least what he knows so far. Do you feel up to a visit with him?"

Confusion boggled her mind. She vaguely remembered the fire but didn't recall Hubert being there. Why were they telling her Hubert had been pulled from the burning house? Was he all right? And why did the sheriff want to speak with her?

Doc Vogel went to the door and motioned with his hand. Sheriff Webster stepped into the room and removed his hat. He was a pleasant sort, and although he'd only been in Willow Creek for a little over a year, she knew Hubert liked him.

"Ma'am. I'm sure pleased to see you doin' better, and I apologize for intrudin' like this while you're recoverin'."

The doctor brought a chair for the sheriff to sit next to Pearl's cot and waggled a warning finger at the lawman. "I don't want you upsetting her or tiring her out. She is not allowed to speak. If you have a question that she can't answer by nodding or shaking her head, it'll have to wait."

"Is she allowed to write?"

Doc scowled. "If it's absolutely necessary." He told his wife to find a tablet and pencil, then turned back to the sheriff. "My wife is going to stay in here, and if she thinks Miss Pearl needs to rest, your visit is over."

Sheriff Webster agreed. "This shouldn't take too long. Mrs. Dunnigan, I do have a few questions."

Frustration seethed inside her. She had some questions, too, and as soon as Hannah Vogel put paper and pencil in her hands, she intended to ask them.

"First of all, do you have any idea how the fire started?" Pearl shook her head.

"Were you inside the house when you realized it was on fire?"

She nodded. Hannah finally reentered the room with paper and pencil, and handed them to Pearl.

"Did you notice anyone hangin' around the boardinghouse?"

Pearl started writing, but her pencil scrawls had nothing to do with the sheriff's question. *"Why was Hubert unconscious? What was he doing there?"* She handed the tablet to the sheriff.

"Well, he went into the house after you. He was hollerin' your name." The sheriff gave her a tiny half smile. "Only a crazy man would run into a burnin' house, unless he's lookin' for someone. In that case, I reckon he's in love."

She reached for the tablet and scribbled another question. *"Is he all right?"* When she shoved the paper back at the sheriff, he nodded and widened his smile.

"I reckon so. I was just talkin' to him a little bit ago. Funny, he keeps askin' the same question about you."

Relief washed over her. Her Hubert had risked his life trying to save her. Thank God he was all right.

"Ma'am? Do you mind if I ask some of my questions now, 'fore Doc comes back in here and throws me out?"

Hannah snickered over in the corner as she poured fresh water into a cup. Pearl nodded at the sheriff, blinking back grateful tears.

"Ma'am, did you happen to notice Everett Behr anywhere around the boardinghouse that morning?"

She nodded.

The lawman frowned. "You did. Do you know what he was doin'?"

She nodded again and picked up the pencil. *"Came to see me."*

A peculiar expression fell across Sheriff Webster's face. "Did he threaten you in any way?"

Pearl shook her head. What was this about? Everett might not like her, but she was fairly certain he'd never physically harm her.

"When he came to see you, what did he want?"

She set the pencil in motion again. *"Apologized and said good-bye."*

The sheriff rubbed his bristly chin and chewed on his lip for a moment.

Before he could ask Pearl to expound on her statement, she scratched out another note. *"Find Silas Cain."* She nudged the note toward the sheriff and Hannah gently suggested that Pearl needed to rest and he could come back tomorrow. She shooed him out the door. After the woman gave Pearl a few sips of water, she told her to rest and slipped out, leaving the door ajar. The voices of Sheriff Webster and Doc Vogel drifted into the room from the hallway.

"How much do you know about Everett Behr?"

Doc harrumphed. "He's Hubert's son. Lived back East, Baltimore, I think. He's been in town for about a month or so. Why?"

"What else do you know about him? Did he have any disagreements with anyone?"

Pearl heard Doc snort. "Only if you count Hubert and Pearl. I don't think he knew any other folks hereabouts. But some say he came to Willow Creek to stop the wedding between his father and Miss Pearl."

"That a fact?"

"Fact? I can't attest to any gossip I hear being fact. But there is one thing I know for sure: Shortly after Everett Behr arrived in town, Pearl and Hubert stopped seeing each other."

Pearl wished she could see the men's faces. What was the sheriff getting at? As if he could read her thoughts through the wall that separated them, Sheriff Webster spoke again.

"There's rumors afoot that maybe Everett Behr set the fire. I talked with a few folks who gave me statements that the young fella didn't especially like Mrs. Dunnigan. Some say he was the reason she and Hubert Behr cancelled their weddin'. What I can't figure out is why."

"Why indeed? Pearl Dunnigan is a fine lady. Just about everyone in town loves her."

A few moments of silence were followed by the sheriff's voice. "You know anything about Silas Cain?"

"Not much, other than the fact that he lived here years ago. As I recall, he wanted to court Miss Pearl back then, but I don't think she wanted any part of that."

Pearl squirmed against her pillows, listening to the exchange.

Doc Vogel continued. "I remember Cain up and left town real sudden. Most folks thought it was kind of strange, seeing as how Cain had asked Miss Pearl to marry him, but one day he was here and the next day he was gone."

Chapter 15

"When can I see my son?"

Though still raspy, Hubert's throat was better. Doc Vogel attributed the improvement to the fact that Hubert had pulled his shirt up over his face to block some of the smoke as he crawled through the burning house.

The doctor's thick brows bunched together into a shaggy caterpillar hovering over his eyes. "Hubert, I'm glad you're feeling better, but I let you go home yesterday thinking you could rest better in your own bed. Why aren't you home in bed?" He held up his hand. "Never mind. I already know the answer. My wife told me she had to shoo you away from Miss Pearl's door earlier." He beckoned Hubert toward his office. "Come and let me explain some things."

Grumbling to himself about simply wanting some answers, Hubert followed Doc to the cramped nook in the corner of what should have been the front parlor in the doctor's house. Medical books lined the shelf above the desk and neat stacks of papers sat ready for the doctor's attention. Doc pointed to the chair beside the desk, and Hubert took the cue and sat.

"Doc, all I want is to know how Pearl is doing. When will she wake up? How is Everett? Is there any infection? Is he still—"

"All right, I get the idea." Doc leaned back in his chair and crossed one leg over the other. He pulled off his spectacles and pinched the area between his eyes. "First of all, Miss Pearl is doing as well as can be expected. She has already awakened a few times since yesterday, but she is under strict orders not to speak. Her throat and lungs sustained more damage than yours because she was exposed to the smoke and heat longer, but her breathing is somewhat better today. And like I told you yesterday, she has a few minor burns."

Relief washed over Hubert at the doctor's assessment of Pearl's recovery. He closed his eyes and whispered a prayer of gratitude.

Doc added his "amen" to Hubert's. "We've been keeping your son as comfortable as possible with laudanum, which not only takes the edge off his pain but also lets him sleep." He rubbed a hand across his gray whiskers. "Burns can be pretty difficult to treat. The burned skin must be cleaned off, which is a very painful process."

Hubert winced involuntarily, empathy cramping his gut at the thought of what his son was enduring. Guilt gnawed at him as he pictured Everett following him into the burning house.

The doctor continued. "There are some who advocate treating burns by holding the burned area as close as possible to the fire until it blisters, then draining the fluid from the blisters to promote healing." He harrumphed. "I've always disagreed with that approach. Besides, most of Everett's burns were beyond the blister stage anyway."

Tears stung Hubert's eyes and his irritated throat constricted. "How long until you know when he will recover?"

Doc Vogel turned compassionate eyes on Hubert, his tone as gentle as a doctor's could be when delivering words a loved one didn't want to hear. "*If* he will recover, Hubert. He still must fight off infection. Without skin covering these large wounds, infection can set in very easily. Daily cleaning and removal of burned flesh, along with applying a carbolic acid salve, will give him the best chance. But it's going to take a miracle for him to pull through this without infection."

The weight of Doc's words slammed into Hubert, stealing his breath. *Father in heaven, please don't ask me to say good-bye to my son this way.*

"Can I see him? Sit with him?"

The doctor shook his head. "I'm sorry, Hubert. Since we're trying to prevent infection, it would be best if as few people as possible go near him just now."

A tap on the door drew their attention, and Mrs. Doc poked her head in. "Sorry to interrupt, but the sheriff is here looking for Mr. Behr."

Hubert nodded and as he rose, Doc stopped him. "Hubert, in another day or two, I'll let you go in and see your son—when he's a little more stable."

Hubert clasped Doc's hand. "You said we need a miracle. That's just what we'll pray for." He followed Hannah Vogel out to the front porch where he found Sheriff Webster leaning against the porch railing. The two men greeted each other.

The lawman took his hat off and ran a hand through his hair. "Mrs. Doc tells me that Miss Pearl is doin' some better today."

Hubert nodded. "I've only gotten to see her once for a few minutes, but she was asleep." The sooner he found out what the sheriff wanted, the sooner he could go sit with Pearl again. "What can I do for you, Sheriff?"

Webster hooked his thumbs in his belt and studied Hubert. "I need to know if you can vouch for your son's whereabouts before the fire broke out."

Hubert raised his eyebrows. "We had breakfast together, then I left the house to go open the mercantile. He still had to pack a few more things. I told him to use the wagon to take his trunk and bag to the depot. The stage wasn't due in until ten o'clock."

The sheriff's poker face revealed nothing, but past experience being on the other side of the investigation process told Hubert there was more to the man's question.

He coughed and cleared his throat. "What's this about, Sheriff?"

The man pulled a bandana from his back pocket and wiped the inside band of his hat. "Well Hubert, it's no secret that your son doesn't like Miss Pearl. I'm tryin' to determine just how much he doesn't like her. There's been some talk. . .purely speculation, mind you, but I'm obliged to follow up on it."

Hubert pulled on his most professional investigator air. "Gossip is never a reliable source, as you well know. Investigations are based on facts. So let me remind you of a few facts." He raised his pointer finger. "Fact number one: Everett was at the depot when the fire started."

"Nope." Webster shook his head. "He was at the depot when the fire was *discovered*. We don't know how long it had been burning."

Hubert nodded. "All right, but let me remind you of fact number two: He was just as shocked as I was when people started yelling that the boarding-house was on fire. Thirdly, he ran into that burning house, and finally, he not only pulled me out, he pulled Pearl out as well. Doc Vogel said he rolled her in a rug. Otherwise she would have been burned much worse. Does that sound like the actions of an arsonist?"

Webster nodded. "Yep, I'm takin' all that into consideration. But it's also a fact that shortly after Everett came to town, you and Miss Pearl broke off your engagement."

Nobody needed to remind Hubert of the painful truth, but he kept his stoneface intact. "If you're insinuating that Everett caused the cancellation of the wedding, why would that make him a suspect in the fire?" The exchange was edging too close for Hubert to maintain his cool poise, and the tension made him cough. "What you're suggesting is preposterous. He saved Pearl's life, and mine, and was burned in the process." He gritted his teeth and fought to control the anger and anxiety colliding in his chest.

Webster scratched his head and slapped his hat in place. "For what it's worth, I tend to agree with you. Was Everett's purpose in comin' to Willow Creek to stop the weddin'? If so, then why would he try to hurt Miss Pearl if the engagement was off?" He stuffed the bandana back in his pocket. "Makes no sense, but I have to ask, especially since Pearl herself told me that Everett was at the boardinghouse about an hour before the fire."

"What?" Hubert struggled through another coughing spasm. "When did she tell you this?" He tossed his professional posture to the wind.

"Yesterday." The sheriff pulled a folded paper from his shirt pocket. "When I asked her why he was there, she wrote this." He held out the missive.

Hubert unfolded the paper and scanned it. " 'Came to see me. Apologized and said good-bye.' " As he stared at Pearl's handwriting, it blurred and he sucked in a breath. "He went to apologize to Pearl?" He allowed his gaze to wander toward the door that led to where Everett lay unconscious. "What was he apologizing for?"

"The lady didn't say." He tucked the folded paper back into his shirt pocket. "Just so you know, I wanted to question Silas Cain, too."

Hubert yanked his attention back to the lawman. "So did you?"

"Would have." Webster pushed away from the porch railing. "He left on the westbound stage the day of the fire."

"He left?" Hands on hips, Hubert weighed this bit of information against another piece of news, unsure of whether to share it with the sheriff. Discomfort made him shuffle his feet. "I don't know if you're aware, but Cain came into the mercantile a few days ago. He told me he'd asked Pearl to marry him."

Webster's eyebrows rose. "Is that so?"

"That's what he said. I had gone to see Pearl one evening last week, and while she and I were talking in the kitchen, Cain came out and asked if I was bothering her." Hubert rolled the entire scenario over in his mind. "Then the day before the fire, Cain came into the store and told me he'd proposed to her. As I recall, he didn't come in to buy anything. It was as if his mission was to inform me that he had a claim on Pearl."

He and Webster stared at each other. "Doesn't it seem odd to you that Cain would leave town without coming to see Pearl or even attempting to find out how the woman he planned to marry is doing?"

A vague awareness of not being alone stirred Pearl's consciousness. Did she hear a voice?

"Pearl, my love, I'm here. I will always be here. Nothing can keep me away."

She tried to swallow, but the pain in her throat reminded her where she was, and why. Sunlight from the nearby window coaxed her eyes open. The first image that captured her vision was Hubert, sitting by her cot with his knees pressed as close as he could get to the side of the bed. A smile lifted the corners of his mustache, and she realized her hand was enfolded within his. Sweet warmth washed over her, and she had no desire to pull her hand away.

"Ah, my Pearl. You've been such a sleepyhead." His fingers squeezed hers.

Hannah Vogel stood behind Hubert's shoulder. "This man of yours simply will not take no for an answer. I got tired of chasing him out of here, so I brought him a chair. Would you like a few sips of water, dear?"

Hannah's description of Hubert danced in her mind. *"This man of yours. . ."* She wanted to hear it again. Instead, she nodded at Hannah's offer of water.

With an air of efficiency, Hannah moved to retrieve the water pitcher and fill a cup.

"Can I do that for her?" Hubert held out his hand for the cup.

"Humph! As if a man can do such a thing without making a mess."

Pearl could hear a hint of humor in Hannah's voice. She wished she could laugh but held her amusement inside. To her delight, Hannah passed the cup to Hubert.

"I'll be right outside the door if you need anything." Hannah tugged Pearl's covers up to her chin, then cocked an eyebrow at Hubert. "Don't you upset her now." She exited, leaving the door standing open.

"I don't think Mrs. Doc approves of me acting as your nurse." Hubert slipped his hand behind her head and helped her lean forward. Pearl started to reach for the cup, but Hubert held it gently to her lips. When he tipped the vessel, the cool water sloshed over the rim, dribbling down one cheek to her neck and wetting the neckline of her gown as well as the edge of the sheet.

"Oops!" Hubert scowled. "Sorry, my dear. Clumsy of me."

"Told you so." Hannah's voice drifted in from the hallway.

He pulled his handkerchief from his pocket and blotted her face and neck, ignoring the teasing from the doctor's wife. "Let's try this again."

Endeared by Hubert's efforts, she didn't bother to show him she was perfectly able to give herself a drink. This time he held his handkerchief under the cup. His second attempt was more successful, and Pearl swallowed, albeit painfully, several sips of water.

"There now," he said, triumph defining the timbre of his voice. He set the cup down on the bedside table, returned to his chair, and reclaimed her hand. "Doc tells me you aren't allowed to talk for another day or two, so if you want more water, just point, all right?"

She nodded. How good his hand felt around hers. She never wanted him to let go.

"Has anyone told you anything about the fire?"

She shrugged one shoulder and held her thumb and forefinger close together.

"A little bit?" His gray eyes darkened, reflecting the distress he obviously felt over the incident. Small wonder since he was pulled from the house after having gone inside to find her. How could she express to him her gratitude for saving her life?

"Well, maybe I can fill in some of the blanks." He coughed a bit, then began telling her of the progression of events.

She made a motion with her hand, indicating she wanted to write. Hubert picked up the pad and pencil from the bedside table and handed it to her. Her position propped up in the bed made it awkward, but she scrawled on the paper, *"You saved my life,"* and handed it to him.

"No, love. It wasn't me, though I tried. I searched all around the outside of the house, but I couldn't find you. I went in through the back door thinking you might be in the kitchen. The smoke was so thick I couldn't see a thing, so I crawled through the kitchen and into the hallway. I'm afraid I did a mighty poor job of rescuing you. Sheriff Webster tells me you had escaped from the house, but you ran back inside." He squeezed her hand. "That was foolish, my dear."

She shook her head and touched the music box that lay beside her on the blanket.

"We could get you another music box." The tenderness in his expression and tone communicated to her he wasn't really scolding. "I'm just grateful to God, and to Everett, that you're going to be all right."

Everett? What was he talking about? If she'd been surprised to learn of Hubert's presence in the burning house, his last statement completely took her aback. She sent him a quizzical look.

Tears formed in Hubert's eyes. "It was Everett. He followed me into the house and pulled both of us out."

She stared at him, wide-eyed, too stunned to respond.

"Sheriff told me Everett came by to see you that morning. I'm glad he came to apologize for his attitude."

She started to form words but stopped when her raw throat constricted painfully. A coughing spasm gripped her, but she shook her head and picked up the pencil again. *"Apologized for insisting I break the engagement. Said he knew he was wrong."*

Pearl's coughing brought Hannah back into the room. The woman shook her finger at Hubert. "What did I tell you about upsetting her?" Hannah scurried to the bed and fussed over Pearl, giving her a sip of water.

When the spasm eased, Pearl watched as Hubert read the note she'd scrawled. A look of astonishment filled his face.

"He insisted. . . When was this?"

But Hannah pointed at Hubert like a strict schoolmarm. "You're going to have to leave now. Pearl needs to rest."

Pearl grabbed Hannah's arm and pleaded silently with a slight shake of her head and reached for Hubert's hand.

Hannah gave them both a stern look but acquiesced. "All right." She turned to Hubert. "But it's up to you to see to it that she doesn't exert. The doctor wants her to stay quiet."

Hubert patted Pearl's hand. "I promise." To underscore his vow, he reached for the music box, turned the key, and lifted the lid. The sweet notes brought a smile to her heart as well as her lips. As soon as Hannah left, she reached for the paper and pencil again.

"Please don't go."

Seeing the smile that creased Hubert's face and crinkled his eyes was worth risking Hannah's ire.

Chapter 16

Pearl smiled as the doctor's wife repeated her admonishment not to speak more than necessary. Hannah was worse than a mother hen. Doc had given his permission that morning for Pearl to sit out on the sunny back porch of the doctor's residence. Hubert sat beside her on the porch swing.

Hannah draped a shawl around Pearl and warned her not to get chilled, then bustled back into the house. Hubert caught Pearl's eye, and they shared a chuckle. Since it was August, a chill was unlikely, but Hannah meant well.

"I'm so glad you're feeling better, my dear." Hubert's voice was still slightly raspy.

"It feels good to be outside." Her croaky whisper resembled that of a frog with the croup. "Who is running the store while you're here?"

Hubert raised a cautionary pointer finger and waggled it at her. "I love hearing your voice, but you'd best follow the doctor's orders."

Mercy sakes, she'd be glad when she could be up and about, doing the things she loved, instead of sitting here like a useless, voiceless sluggard. Impatience nipped at her, but then she remembered once again God's goodness in getting her out of the fire alive. Still in awe over Hubert's revelation of Everett's role in rescuing both of them, she sent another silent prayer to the throne room of heaven, asking God to heal Everett.

Hubert stood and crossed the porch where Hannah had left a tray with a pitcher of water and cups. He poured a cupful of water and brought it to Pearl, then reclaimed his seat beside her. "To answer your question, I hired young Phillip O'Dell to come work in the store part-time." Hubert grinned. "I'm not sure how many O'Dells there are. Phillip is a few years younger than Tillie, but he's her oldest brother. He's a bright youngster and a hard worker, and having him there frees me up to come and be with you and Everett."

The warm sun on her shoulders offered a cheery welcome to her first venture outdoors, and she drew in a cautious breath as deeply as she could. The fresh essence of the morning air was tainted by the stale scent of smoke that still lingered, a sinister reminder of the flames that nearly took Hubert's life and her own. And Everett's.

At some point, she knew she'd have to view the destruction and see what she could salvage. Her heart wept for the residents who had called the boardinghouse home for several years. Sheriff Webster hadn't elaborated on the degree of loss for her or her boarders. He'd only stated he thought the fire may have been purposely set. The very thought sent a sickening shiver through her.

Hubert tugged the shawl a little higher around her neck. "Are you cold?"

She shook her head. "Just thinking of the fire," she whispered.

He slipped an arm around her and patted her shoulder, as though reading her thoughts. "If you will allow me, I'd like to help you sift through the rubble when you feel up to it. No need to think of that today though."

"What will my boarders do now?"

Hubert patted her hand. "Praise God none of them were there when the fire started. Mr. Hogan was on one of his sales trips. He said there is a rooming house in Clermont where he can stay. Miss Frick was at her dressmaker shop. Since she and Mrs. Pettigrew are such good friends, she has moved in with her. Mr. Gallimore was at the newspaper office of course. Apparently there is a small room in the back of the office and he plans to stay there for now. Mrs. Russell's nephew came yesterday and has taken her home to live with his family. When the school opens again next month, Miss Pendergrass will have to find a place to stay when she comes back. I heard the school board was looking into that."

Pearl nodded as Hubert addressed the situation of each of her former boarders, grieved that they lost whatever possessions they had, but grateful they were unharmed and had a place to stay.

Hubert shifted around, facing her more fully. "There is something else we need to talk about, or rather something I need to tell you."

She turned her eyes to him and saw his gaze leave her and slide downward, as if studying his boots suddenly became important.

"Hubert?"

He lifted his head back to face her, but the smile that forced the upturn of his lips didn't reach his eyes. The love she'd seen there for weeks was replaced by misgiving, and unease deepened the lines in his brow.

"Pearl, there are some things in my past that you need to know. I promised God I would be completely honest with you, but I wanted to wait until you were feeling better." He paused, his steady gaze holding hers. For a moment he inclined his head toward her like he was about to kiss her, but he halted and glanced right and left. Apparently rethinking his action, he leaned back against the swing's cushions.

"You already know that my first wife left me for another man, but you don't know why."

"Hubert—"

He held up his hand. "No, Pearl. Let me say this. The doctor doesn't want you to talk, so please don't try. It's important that I confess everything to you."

Something akin to fear sent a slight jolt through her, but she nodded and folded her hands in her lap. Whatever was on his heart had carved obvious furrows of heartache through him, and she wasn't at all sure she wanted to hear it. She'd not yet told him she wished to renew their engagement. What if his disclosure changed the course of their relationship forever?

Hesitation edged his bearing. He pulled in an unsteady breath. "I went to work for the Pinkerton Detective Agency the same year Everett was born. From the start, I knew it was the career I wanted, and I was determined not to allow anything to interfere with my success." A scowl marred his features, and Pearl fought to stay her hand from smoothing out the crease between his eyes.

"Normally, the married men handled the investigations close to home and the single fellows were the ones who received the accolades for their daring exploits chasing down criminals." He shook his head. "I knew the more complicated cases would require me being away from home for long periods of time, but I began to push my superiors to assign those cases to me."

He closed his eyes and drew in his brows, his face a reflection of the painful memory. She wished she could tell him nothing from his past mattered. Her heart grieved to see his whole demeanor slumped as though he carried a heavy load.

"There were times I was away from home for two or three months at a time. I'd come home long enough to be congratulated for my good work, receive a citation or two in my personnel file, and I'd take another case even more difficult than the last."

He turned sorrow-filled eyes on her. "Pearl, I knew God was speaking to my heart, telling me I should be home with my family, but I pushed everything aside—my family and my God—and allowed ambition to drive me. Prestige became my god." He rose from the swing and paced several steps away before turning and plodding back again. "Lucinda, my wife, began demanding that I resign from the Pinkertons. The more she demanded, the more determined I was to be the best agent in the country. About a week before Everett's eighth birthday, she told me she was planning a party and all Everett had requested was for his father to be there."

He turned and pressed his hands on the porch railing, his head hung like the demons of remembrance pushed his posture into submission. "The following day my superior received a wire about a notorious bank robber and murderer. Every time this man committed a crime, the story made the headlines. I knew if I was the one to bring him in, it would mean not only the esteem of my peers, but also the promotion in rank I sought." Derision laced his voice. "I talked my boss into letting me take the case, went home, and packed a bag. Lucinda railed at me and accused me of being married to my job. Everett cried and begged me to stay for his birthday party. I knew God was telling me to go back to the office and tell my boss I'd changed my mind. But I didn't. I left that afternoon."

Hubert's chin almost touched his chest. Pearl longed to reach out and take his hand and tell him not to say any more, but she couldn't. She sat suspended in time. How could the man she loved and respected be the same one he was describing?

"It took me almost four months, but I captured the man I was after. I turned my prisoner over to the US marshal and stopped at the nearest telegraph office to send a wire to Lucinda, telling her I was coming home. I had no way of knowing it couldn't be delivered."

Pearl watched the raw memory batter the man she loved.

He cleared his throat repeatedly and continued. "I stopped on the way home and bought Everett an Orvis fishing rod and a brass reel with silk line. Thought he'd forgive me for missing his birthday if I brought him the best fishing rod money could buy." Hubert's voice cracked and he started coughing, whether from speaking too much or from emotion, Pearl couldn't tell.

He poured a bit of water into a cup and took several sips. His coughing subsided, but he remained several steps away from the swing, as though purposely holding himself apart from her. Didn't he know she longed to wrap her arms around his neck and whisper to him that he didn't need to say any more?

"When I discovered Lucinda and Everett were gone, I went directly to her parents. Everett was there, but I was told he didn't want to see me—that he hated me." He heaved a sigh. "They wouldn't tell me where Lucinda was. Her mother said I didn't deserve her daughter, that I didn't know how to be a good husband or father. A few days later I learned Lucinda left Baltimore with another man."

Weariness etched its signature all over Hubert. He turned slowly to face Pearl and raised his eyes to meet hers. "I hurt my family by letting success and my thirst for importance direct me, and I hurt myself by disobeying God. I've lived with the regret for more than twenty years." He held his hands out, away from his sides, palms up. "You had to know, Pearl. I couldn't ask you to spend the rest of your life with me, not knowing the truth. Now that you are aware of the kind of man I was, if you wish to terminate our relationship, I'll understand, and I won't persist in pressing you to change your mind."

He dropped his hands to his sides and moved toward her, his hesitant step uncharacteristic of his usual confidence. "You need to rest now, Pearl. But there is just one question I must ask you." A flush filled his cheeks behind his beard. "Did Silas Cain really ask you to marry him?"

She glanced down at her folded hands on her lap and gave a small nod. "Yes."

Several moments of silence hung between them and Pearl lifted her eyes to light softly on the man standing before her. Dear Hubert—how she loved him.

She reached her hand out to him. "Come sit with me."

Hubert settled into the swing beside her and enclosed her hand between both of his. The warmth of his nearness gave her the courage to be as honest with him as he'd been with her.

"There is something I must tell you as well," she whispered. Hubert appeared about to protest, but she shook her head. "I must."

She took a few sips of water. "I don't know how much you've heard about Silas. He first came to Willow Creek seven years ago. He stayed at the boardinghouse, and it wasn't long before he began asking if he could court me. I told him I had no desire to be courted, but that didn't seem to stop him." She took another sip of water.

"After a few weeks, everyone in town knew Silas wanted to court me. It didn't seem to matter that I'd said no. Then one evening, Silas asked if he could speak to me out on the porch. He made a big show of getting down on his knee and asking me to marry him."

She began coughing, and Hubert nudged the cup of water. "Please, my dear, you don't need to say any more."

Pearl shook her head again. "Yes, I do." She sipped more water and set the cup aside. "The following day, everyone in town was congratulating me on my engagement. I tried to tell them there was no engagement because I'd refused Silas's proposal." She dipped her head. "Imagine my shock when a woman knocked on my door a few days later and told me she was looking for her husband, Silas Cain. My other boarders weren't home yet, but Silas was always the first one home in the afternoon, so I asked the woman to wait. When Silas came in, there was a confrontation. Silas and his wife went for a walk, but he came back without her."

She paused to cool her throat with more water. Hubert seemed to understand her need to tell him about the past chapter of her life, and he didn't insist she stop. After a minute, she went on, her voice not much more than a croaky whisper.

"Silas left very early the next morning. I don't know where his wife was; I didn't see her again. I assumed she went with him." She bowed her head. "Hubert, I felt so dirty. That poor woman! I know none of the blame was mine, but what if the news of Silas having a wife had gotten out? I could only imagine what that would do to my reputation. Why, it would make me look like a Jezebel. I kept the story to myself and prayed no one would ever find out. I've never told this to anyone until now."

Hubert squeezed her hand. "That's enough talking now. The sheriff has already told me what you wrote out concerning Cain's intentions and how he threatened you." He slid his arm around her shoulders. "It's behind you now. God has a future for us to look forward to."

❧

Hubert sat forward in his chair beside Everett's bed, grateful for the doctor's permission to sit with his son. But he hadn't been prepared for the swathe of bandages or the swelling of Everett's face. Part of the burned area on one arm was exposed, and the sight of the angry, red flesh made Hubert's gut twist. He could only imagine what lay beneath the bandages.

"He's so still. I can barely see him breathing." Hubert sent a worried glance to the doctor on the other side of the bed.

Doc Vogel stuck the ends of his stethoscope into his ears and pressed the apparatus to Everett's chest. "He's breathing just fine."

"There's a rather pungent odor in here."

The doctor nodded and hung his stethoscope around his neck. "Part of the smell is the carbolic acid salve we're using on the burns. We're making a liniment with linseed oil and limewater to blot on the less serious burned area. But there is also some dead flesh that we're still cleaning off."

An involuntary shudder shook Hubert. "There's no more risk of infection?"

"I didn't say that." Doc gingerly pulled back part of the bandage on Everett's neck and the lower part of his face. "We're keeping the wounds clean and removing bits of burned skin and flesh as we are able. Until new skin grows to cover the burned areas, the risk of infection will exist, but he's showing some encouraging signs of healing."

Hubert peered at the grisly red, purple, and blackened wounds along Everett's jawline. An ache of commiseration surged through him, and he clenched his teeth to hold back a groan of sympathy.

Doc replaced the bandages and straightened. "I'm afraid he's going to have some rather ugly scars."

Hubert fixed his gaze on the part of Everett's face not covered by the clean, white bindings. The thought of the once-handsome features being disfigured by lasting effects of the fire spurred grief, and condemnation strangled him. If only Everett hadn't followed him into the burning house. Had circumstances taken a different turn, however, he and Pearl would both rest in the town cemetery now. He longed to hold Everett's hand but was fearful that any touch could bring pain. He wished he could take some of that pain and bear it for his son.

Everett stirred.

Hubert leaned forward and gently touched a finger to Everett's unscathed left hand. "I'm here, son."

A faint groan sounded from Everett's lips, and he moved his head slightly, a wince defining his forehead.

Doc Vogel glanced at his watch. "He's not due for another dose of laudanum for two hours. We'll wait to clean off any more dead skin and tissue until we can give him more pain medication."

"Father?"

Unspeakable joy filled Hubert at the sound of Everett's voice, however weak. "Yes, son, I'm here."

"The quieter he stays the less pain he'll have," Doc Vogel advised. "I'll let you have a little time together, then he needs to rest."

Everett blinked. "Father, you're all right. Doctor Vogel told me you were, but I had to see for myself."

"Yes, I'm fine, son. Pearl is going to be all right as well, thanks to you. We both owe you our lives."

A slight shake of Everett's head accompanied the tiny dip of his eyebrows. "It wasn't me."

Hubert frowned, thinking surely he'd heard Everett's words incorrectly. Of course it had been Everett who'd dragged him and Pearl from the inferno. Sheriff Webster said so. Perhaps Everett was delusional from the medication.

"You don't have to talk, son. Just lie quiet." Hubert hoped his voice communicated soothing reassurance.

But Everett seemed insistent. "You don't understand, Father. It wasn't me. The smoke was so thick I was completely blinded. The fire was all around—all sides. Windows were breaking—"

"Shh, it's all right, son. Just be quiet now." But the more Hubert coaxed him to be quiet, the more determined Everett grew.

His fingers caught Hubert's and curled around them, as though driven by an urgency to make Hubert understand. "I knew I couldn't find you by myself. I needed help. I cried out to God—begged Him to help me find you."

Hubert froze. Could it be? Had God answered his petition he'd prayed more times than he could count? Tears slipped down Hubert's cheeks and a shout of praise began to gather within his chest, rising into his throat.

"I was lost in that smoke. . .had no hope of finding you or Mrs. Dunnigan. The walls were caving in. . .roof was next. No way out. God was the only one who could find you. I pleaded with Him to keep you safe and lead me to you. God found you, Father, not me." Serenity erased the anguish in Everett's eyes as he relaxed against the pillow. "And I found God."

Chapter 17

Hubert stood outside the post office and broke the seal on the envelope from Zack Peterson, his old friend from the Pinkerton Agency. It had taken longer than he'd anticipated to hear back from Zack. Since Silas Cain had already left town, whatever information Zack was able to find on Cain would be of little use to Hubert now. But curiosity drove him to open the letter to see if any of his suspicions were confirmed.

He quickly scanned the pages, taking in the list of charges and arrest warrants. Cain was wanted in four different states on eleven warrants, and had left behind a trail of jilted women he'd defrauded of money and property. A few he'd married without mentioning he already had a wife. . .or two. Hubert snorted with disgust.

The last page described Cain's associations with known criminals and the seedy underworld of corruption, and included a list of several aliases Cain used. "Fletcher Cain, Silas Fletcher, Silas Riley, Terrance Smith."

Anger surged through Hubert. Pearl was just another woman on Cain's list. Hubert clenched his teeth and stifled a growl. How he wished he could slap the handcuffs on Cain himself.

He strode across the street to the mercantile to check with young Phillip O'Dell, his part-time clerk. Satisfied that Phillip had everything under control, Hubert headed down the boardwalk toward the sheriff's office. On the way, he stopped by the stage depot to speak with Sam, the ticket agent.

Sam's drooping suspenders hung off his shoulders as he peered out from the depot window and nodded his head with such vigor, his spectacles slid down his nose. "Yeah, Sheriff was already here askin' the same questions. I'll tell you the same thing as I told him." He pushed his lopsided spectacles back into place with two fingers. "That Cain fella was standin' here waitin' for me to open up the mornin' Miss Pearl's place burned." Sam stroked his chin. "First, he said he wanted to buy a ticket to Cedar Rapids. Then he asked how many stopovers there was between here and there." The agent pursed his lips and pulled his pencil from behind his ear. "Thought it kinda strange, but it weren't none of my business."

Hubert fixed his eyes on the agent. "What was strange?"

Sam shrugged. "When I told him the southbound stage wasn't due in until late afternoon, he changed his mind 'bout where he was headed. Asked what stage was due in first. I says the westbound. But as soon as I told him that stage stopped at Fort Dodge, he asked what was the last stop *before* Fort Dodge. I told him Otter Springs and don'tcha know, he bought a ticket to Otter Springs." The man shook his head like the information he'd just given made no sense.

"What's in Otter Springs?"

"That's just it. There ain't nothin' in Otter Springs 'cept a way station."

Why would Cain buy a ticket to the middle of nowhere? "Is there a telegraph in Otter Springs?"

Sam leaned his elbow on the edge of the counter and sniffed. "Sometimes. Lines are down more than they're workin'. But as I recall, I got a wire from there about a month ago. Maybe the lines are still up."

Hubert rolled the information over in his mind. "Can Cain buy another ticket in Otter Springs, maybe heading in another direction?"

"Sure. He could pick up the southbound to Des Moines. 'Course there's a few places in between where he could board a train, too."

"Thanks, Sam." Hubert continued on to the sheriff's office, armed with the letter from Zack Peterson.

Sheriff Webster was pouring himself a cup of coffee when Hubert entered the office. "Mornin', Mr. Behr."

"Good morning, sir." Hubert pulled Zack's letter from his pocket and held it out to the lawman. "I thought perhaps you'd be interested in this."

Webster arched his eyebrows and took the letter. He scanned it quickly and grunted. "Accordin' to what Miss Pearl's already told me, looks like he was plannin' on makin' her one of his victims."

Hubert set his jaw and nodded. "Based on the information in that letter and Pearl's statement, seems like you have enough for a conviction once Cain is apprehended."

"Don't make much sense, him settin' the fire, but I reckon it ain't the first time revenge was the motive for a crime." The sheriff scowled at the papers and wanted posters cluttering his desk. "I don't have anything on Cain here. I already checked. But I'll go through this pile again and look for those other names he used."

"I stopped by the depot this morning and talked to Sam."

Webster nodded. "I sent a wire to Otter Springs. I'll let you know if I find out anything and you can wire your Pinkerton friend. I notified the federal marshal at Fort Dodge, too. Maybe we'll get lucky."

The men shook hands and parted company. Hubert's desire to return to the doctor's place and speak with Pearl widened his anxious strides. He'd spent most of the night in prayer, partly for Everett's recovery and partly for Pearl. He'd waited as long as he could bear. If he didn't ask her today, his heart would burst.

❧

Tears gathered in the corners of Pearl's eyes as she listened to Tessa and Hannah outline their plans. The three women sat together in the morning sun on the back porch of the doctor's residence.

"I must have the sweetest friends on the face of the earth." Pearl's raspy voice and sore throat improved daily. She leaned forward to wrap one arm around Tessa and the other around Hannah. "Mercy sakes, I don't know what to say."

"You don't have to say anything." Tessa laughed. "Just let us show you how much you're loved."

Hannah patted Pearl's back and offered her the hanky she pulled from her apron pocket. While Pearl blotted her eyes, Hannah scooted her chair closer. "Two of the women in the ladies sewing circle have sewing machines now. Johannah Fredricksen's husband gave her one last Christmas." The doctor's wife rattled off her efficiently coordinated plans. "Ivy Swenson and Johannah will bring their machines. Hilda Stone, Florence Hoffner, and Vera Owens are going to do the cutting, and there will be four or five other women there as well, in addition to Tessa and me."

Tessa reached over and squeezed Pearl's hand. "Please let us do this for you."

"Do what?"

All three women turned. Hubert climbed the back porch steps.

"Oh Hubert, these ladies want to have a sewing bee for me tomorrow at the church. They're going to—"

"All Pearl's clothes got burned up in the fire."

"We're going to sew some dresses, skirts, nighties, and under—" Tessa clapped her hand over her mouth and her cheeks glowed bright pink.

Hannah flapped her hands. "She needs everything, so the ladies are going to make a day of it and sew her a new wardrobe."

Pearl blinked back tears as she watched the reaction on Hubert's face. The smile that creased his face pulled his mustache into a crescent.

"That's a fine idea, ladies, and so gracious of you." Hubert crossed the porch and pulled one of the wicker chairs over next to Pearl's rocker. "I'd be happy to supply the yard goods."

Pearl started to protest, but he turned his soft gray eyes on her. The twinkle she saw there was more than she could resist.

"Please?" He wiggled his eyebrows.

She ducked her head so he wouldn't see her blush. "I don't know what I'm going to do with you!" Her attempt to sound exasperated failed miserably. Hubert's grin tingled her toes.

The wicker chair squeaked as Hubert lowered himself into it. "I spoke with Doc a few minutes ago, and he tells me you're doing fine. So why don't you and Tessa come over to the mercantile and pick out whatever you want."

Doing fine. Reality gnawed at her. She had no place to go, and she couldn't stay with the Vogels forever. If the doctor felt she was well enough to walk to the mercantile, she was well enough to find some place to stay. She couldn't impose on Tessa and her little family. They had no extra room. She supposed the hotel was her only option, albeit an expensive one. Her savings was small and wouldn't pay for a hotel room for very long without a means of income.

"Pearl?"

She snapped her attention back to the conversation. "You all are so generous. How is a body to say thank you?"

Hubert picked up her hand and drew it to his lips, placing a chaste kiss on her fingers. "Then I'll be expecting you and Tessa this afternoon."

Pearl's heart fluttered, and she tucked the moment away in her memory to enjoy later.

Hubert cleared his throat. "I have something else I'd like to discuss with you, but I must beg the indulgence of these lovely ladies." He sent Tessa and Hannah an apologetic look. In unison, the pair rose and excused themselves, knowing smiles on both their faces.

As soon as they were alone on the porch, Hubert's expression turned serious. "I've done plenty of talking in the past few days, telling you those things I felt God prompting me to share with you." He ran his thumb up and down the underside of her fingers and fidgeted in his chair, causing a symphony of squeaks from the wicker.

She lifted her free hand and touched one side of Hubert's peppery beard.

She knew this man as well as anyone could know another person, and everything about him stirred her. She held her breath as she waited for him to say what was on his mind. Surely he must be able to hear her pounding heart.

"The past several weeks have been sorely painful for me. When you broke our engagement, I didn't understand. I was so sure that you loved me." A wince flickered over his features. "I now know that Everett had something to do with your decision, and that he has since asked your forgiveness."

Pearl lowered her eyes for a moment. The events of the past week had changed everything, including the way she viewed Hubert and Everett's relationship. Did it even matter why she broke the engagement? Yes, Hubert had been completely honest with her. It was time for her to reciprocate. She owed him that much.

"Hubert, first of all, I want to say that my reasons for ending the engagement have changed. But I still think I should explain."

He gave a slight nod but didn't interrupt.

"When Everett came to see me at the boardinghouse several weeks ago, he told me that reconciliation between the two of you would be impossible if we married. I couldn't do that to you. I couldn't come between you and Everett knowing how important your son is to you." Her throat tightened, and she swallowed several times trying to keep the tears at bay. "But the morning of the fire he came and apologized and told me he was wrong. He wanted your happiness and he said if marrying me made you happy, then he'd give his blessing."

Hubert's fingers squeezed hers, and she couldn't stop a tear from meandering down her cheek. Hubert gently wiped it away.

He pulled in a slow, measured breath. "When I was searching for you through the smoke, I was afraid I'd lost you forever. All I wanted was one more opportunity to tell you that I love you, and I don't want to live a single day without you. I never want us to be separated again this side of heaven." Still holding her hand, he slipped from the chair to one knee in front of her. "Will you, once more, agree to be my bride?"

Unchecked tears filled her eyes and overflowed. Oh, how she loved this man.

❧

Pearl clung to Hubert's hand as they sat at Everett's bedside telling him of their renewed plans to marry. The sight of the young man's bandages made her cringe, especially since he'd suffered the burns rescuing her and Hubert. There were no words to thank him for what he'd done.

"And so, son. . ." Hubert paused to glance at her, and the look he gave her made her catch her breath. He returned his gaze to Everett. "We've decided to postpone the wedding until you are able to be there with us. It's what we both want."

A shadow of a smile touched Everett's face, and he lifted his left hand toward his father who clasped it. "I'm pleased. . .that you're going to be happy." He looked at Pearl with genuine contrition in his eyes. "I hope you can forgive me."

She caught a glimpse of Hubert in Everett's features. He was part of the man she loved. "Of course, Everett. I'm praying for your recovery."

He frowned a bit, and she thought perhaps he was in pain. "The boardinghouse?"

Hubert shook his head. "It's a total loss. Pearl and I talked a little while ago. Since I moved into my house last year, the living quarters above the mercantile are empty. Pearl is going to stay there for a few weeks until the wedding."

Everett nodded his affirmation and a blush warmed Pearl's face. She dipped her head. . . .*until the wedding.* Her pulse picked up speed, and she silently chided herself. *Mercy sakes, folks are going to think we're behaving like a couple of moonstruck youngsters.*

"Hubert, I think we should let Everett rest now." They rose and told Everett they'd return to visit with him later.

Once they stepped back out onto the back porch, Hubert tucked Pearl's arm in his and tugged her toward the steps. "Let's go for a walk."

She hesitated. "Shouldn't we ask Doc first?"

"Why? He's not invited." Hubert's mustache twitched with amusement.

She flapped her hand at him and made a clucking sound with her tongue. "Hubert! You're incorrigible."

The smile that stretched across his face made the years fall away. He caught her hand as they strolled through the doctor's backyard, past the edge of town, across an expanse of meadow, toward a grove of willow trees that lined the meandering creek.

"Let's sit for a while." Hubert steered her to the creek bank. "I don't want you to get tired out."

A sweet memory tickled Pearl's mind. "Should I have brought a picnic? The last time we came to this place, we had a picnic." But it wasn't the picnic that made the recollection so sweet.

With his hand supporting her elbow, Hubert helped her sit on a thick bed of grass. He bent to pluck some of the daisies and cornflowers scattered along the creek's edge, adding a few sprigs of purple clover. He handed her the flowers and sat beside her, reaching out to touch the side of her face. She sighed and pressed her cheek into the warmth of his hand.

"My Pearl." His tender eyes searched her face. "God is so good to give me another chance to be the kind of husband He wants me to be." His steady gaze fixed on her eyes and a tremble danced through her. "In a few weeks, as soon as Everett is better, we'll take our vows before our friends and neighbors at the church. But I wanted to give you and God a holy promise today, that I pledge my whole heart to our marriage. I offer my covenant to you that, with God's help, I'll seek His wisdom and leading for us, and I will love you with everything within me until my last breath."

With that pronouncement, he inclined his head toward hers and placed the gentlest of kisses on her lips.

Epilogue

N ervous?"

Pearl glanced at her groom and caught the wink he sent her. "Mercy sakes, no. Why should I be nervous?"

Hubert chuckled. "Most brides are."

She couldn't seem to stop smiling, and her eyes locked on to his. "But we aren't like most brides and grooms, are we?"

Hubert appeared to contemplate her question. "I don't suppose we are. We have a few extra years and some strands of silver hair, but that doesn't change how much we love each other."

"Nor does it change the way God has blessed us."

Pastor Witherspoon would call for the wedding to start in a matter of minutes, but Pearl wanted to capture this moment and etch it into her memory where nothing and no one could steal it. Their friends milled around, lingering after the Sunday morning service to witness the nuptials. Happy anticipation of the celebration to follow buzzed through the congregation, but Pearl blocked out everything but Hubert.

She leaned close to his ear. "I'm so grateful God gave us another chance."

Hubert's smile stole her breath. "I'm grateful you said yes."

"All right now, folks." Pastor Witherspoon beckoned to the congregation. "Let's take our places. Hubert, you and Pearl stand right here."

Pearl smoothed the bodice of the soft blue brocade dress the ladies had helped her sew for her wedding. Tessa handed her a bouquet of black-eyed Susans and purple coneflowers and stepped over to stand on Pearl's left side. Everett, bandages still binding one hand and arm and swathing one side of his face and neck, stood to the right of Hubert.

The pastor cleared his throat. "We almost didn't get to see this wedding happen. If it hadn't been for Everett here and the way God used him, Hubert and Pearl might not have been here for this day. So we first want to lift our praise and thanks to God for allowing this union to take place."

Hubert squeezed her hand, and she caught a glimpse of Everett from the corner of her eye. He was smiling.

Pastor Witherspoon continued. "So friends, we are gathered here in the presence of God and this company to witness the joining of this man and this woman in holy matrimony."

The words of the traditional vows as the pastor spoke them and Hubert echoed them fell sweetly on Pearl's heart. When it came time for her to repeat her promise to love, honor, cherish, and obey, the precious vows spilled from her lips without any prompting.

Hubert took her left hand and slid a gold band onto her fourth finger. The pastor was speaking, but Pearl's senses were fixed on the gift God had given her, the man standing before her, holding her hand. Their love, forged and strengthened by God, had been tried, refined, and revealed by fire and had emerged as pure gold.

"You may kiss your bride now, Hubert." The pastor's words broke through her consciousness.

Her groom cupped her face gently in his hands. Pearl's eyes closed, a prayer of gratitude forming in her heart as a benediction on their first kiss as husband and wife.

Scars of MERCY

Dedication

To Suze:
Thanks for being there when I needed you.

Chapter 1

Everett Behr shot a scowl of self-loathing at his reflection in the hand mirror. If it weren't for having to shave, he might well refuse to own a mirror. With cautious, deliberate strokes, he drew the razor around the scars along his jawline on the right side of his face. He'd hoped a thick crop of whiskers would hide the scars. He couldn't abide the stares, however sympathetic. They only served to remind him that the price of his arrogance would be forever branded across his face. Much to his frustration, his beard grew in patches, refusing to sprout in the scarred areas he most wanted to hide. The fragments of whiskers popping out in an irregular, crazy quilt pattern surrounded the scars instead of covering them, as if framing the ugliness for display.

He wiped the last of the shaving soap from his face just as the bell on the little church at the end of the street began calling the people of Willow Creek to worship. Everett didn't hurry. Attending church services meant doing so on his terms. Accepting his scars was one thing, and he wanted to know more about the God who'd allowed them. He just didn't relish mingling with people before or after the service.

He turned the mirror glass-side down on the washstand and released an involuntary huff. With practiced fingers, he tied his cravat and combed his hair—grateful he could perform those duties by feel rather than by sight.

By the time the church bell stopped clanging, Everett knew most of the congregation had entered the building and taken their seats. With curious eyes now safely confined within the walls of the church, Everett picked up his Bible and prepared to walk to the church and slip in unnoticed.

He descended the recently completed back steps that afforded him a private entrance to the living quarters over the mercantile his father owned. In the past several months he'd memorized every alley and wooded path so he could avoid walking down the town boardwalk whenever possible.

A squirrel chattered from a nearby tree, scolding Everett for disturbing his breakfast. Digging into his pocket, Everett withdrew a few peanuts and held them aloft. "Here's your treat, little buddy." He tossed the peanuts at the base of the tree from which the squirrel regarded him, now with less animosity. But the little creature switched his bushy tail back and forth like the lash of a buggy whip and refused to come closer until Everett backed off.

"All right, I don't blame you. Nobody else wants to come near me either." A twinge of guilt over his self-pity pricked him. He should be grateful to be alive. Everett turned and proceeded toward the church. By the time he reached the edge of the churchyard, the sounds of the hymn singing beckoned him to draw near the little house of worship. He hoped he'd find a seat at the back near the door.

The congregation's enthusiastic praise rang within the walls of the church as he opened the door just enough to step inside. It didn't seem to matter to these people that their church had no stained glass windows, thick carpeting, or ornately carved pews. They raised their voices to God as though they stood in a magnificent cathedral.

"How firm a foundation, ye saints of the Lord, is laid for your faith in His excellent Word." Everett's heart started singing along with the congregation in praise to his newfound Lord.

He closed the door silently and took his place on the bench against the back wall. No heads turned, no pitiful or repulsed looks greeted him. Everett relaxed. The hymn ended, and the congregation sat. Everett opened his Bible, being careful to turn the pages quietly.

Looking over the backs of the heads in front of him, he located Father with his new bride. Hubert and Pearl Behr sat in the second row near the aisle. When Pearl leaned closer to his father as they shared one Bible, Everett berated himself again for his past misguided efforts to separate the two. Pearl was a good woman, and she made his father happy.

Across the aisle from Father and Pearl, Tillie O'Dell sat with her family. Her dark blond hair, pinned up and secured with a green ribbon, gleamed in the morning sun streaming through the window. A memory teased his subconscious. The afternoon he'd spent with Tillie last year at a church picnic wafted across his mind like a gentle breeze. He shook himself and pushed the picture away. That was a lifetime ago—before the fire that left his face and hands mottled with ugly scars. No sense in entertaining thoughts now far beyond the reach of reality. Even if his face, neck, and hands weren't scarred, the disdain with which he'd treated Tillie a week after the picnic when he learned she worked in the hotel dining room ensured she'd want nothing to do with him.

Everett pulled his attention back to the sermon. Deep in his heart he wanted to know how God could use him. Could God take a broken and marred vessel like him and remake it into something good? Doubts pricked him, but he listened intently anyway, hoping to grab on to some fleeting comment from the pastor—anything to give him a glimmer of worthiness.

He followed along as the pastor read the scripture and made a notation in the margin of his Bible in preparation to return to the passage later and study it in depth. But his attention kept drifting to the back of Tillie's head. Something within him kept tugging at his mind, a futile wish to turn back the calendar and recant his arrogance. He supposed nobody lived without some regrets of one type or another, but his behavior had hurt people he cared about.

The singing of the congregation startled him. He'd been so lost in his own brooding, he'd missed the rest of the sermon. Heat crept into his face, even though he was relatively sure his presence at the back of the room had gone unnoticed. He stood and slipped out the door, hurrying down the steps before the people began spilling out of the church.

Halfway across the churchyard, he heard a familiar voice call out his name.

"Everett! Wait, son."

He welcomed the pleasure of his father's company, but he'd rather choose a less public place. Stepping into the shadow of the thick cedar trees that lined the churchyard and casting self-conscious glances around him, he waited for his father and Pearl to approach.

"We weren't sure you were coming to church this morning, son." His father extended his hand and clasped Everett's.

Pearl reached out and touched his arm. "We'd be pleased if you'd join us for Sunday dinner." Her blue eyes twinkled. "I suspect that you're partial to my chicken and dumplings, since you asked for seconds the last time I made them."

Everett's mouth watered. He'd never tasted anything quite as good as the simple, hearty dishes Pearl served at her table. Even the fancy beef roasts and lobster on which he'd dined while growing up in his grandparents' home couldn't compare to Pearl's chicken and dumplings.

271

The rest of the congregation milled about the churchyard, shaking hands with the pastor and visiting with each other. If he wished to escape their scrutinizing stares, he needed to give Pearl an answer.

"I would enjoy that. Thank you for the invitation."

"This way, son. Our wagon is over by those cottonwoods." Father placed a tender hand on Pearl's back and led the way to the conveyance. Just as Everett started after them, another voice hailed him.

"Everett? Everett Behr."

His feet froze momentarily. The unmistakable lilt identified the voice as belonging to Tillie O'Dell. Two other times in recent weeks she'd called out to him in the churchyard, but he'd pretended not to hear. No longer the same man with whom she'd spent a carefree afternoon almost a year ago, he couldn't face her. Even if he wanted to apologize for snubbing her, the finger-print left by the flames on his face and hands made him wish he could duck into a cave somewhere and never emerge again. He forced his feet to move rapidly toward his father's market wagon.

ॐ

Tillie O'Dell plunked her hands on her hips and heaved an exasperated sigh as she watched Everett hasten away. Goodness, that man was as elusive as a will-o'-the-wisp. She hurried to help Ma gather her younger siblings into their family's farm wagon and then turned toward her father, who was checking a hoof on one of the horses.

"Da?"

He dropped the hoof and straightened. The moment he fixed his gaze on her, merriment danced in his eyes. "Lass, you look like a cat preying on a sparrow."

She pressed her lips together. No use trying to fool Da. His sage insight pierced right through her. "Would it be all right if I go talk to Everett Behr?"

Da glanced across the churchyard, where Everett was climbing into the back of the wagon his father used to make deliveries from the mercantile. A wistful expression came over her father's face as he ran one finger over the scar that carved a ragged furrow from the bridge of his nose to his ear—an unconscious gesture she'd seen her father do from time to time, usually when he was contemplating something. If he had any misgivings about her spending time with Everett, he'd say so. Instead, he gave her a nod, and she could have sworn she caught a glimpse of a smile.

"Thanks, Da. Don't bother waiting for me. It's a delightful day for a walk."

With lifted chin, she scurried across the yard before the Behrs' wagon left.

As she approached, she caught Pearl Behr's eye. The sweet, gray-haired woman sent her a warm smile and then flicked her gaze over her shoulder where Everett settled himself behind the bench seat. Taking the welcoming smile as encouragement, Tillie walked up to the wagon and drew in a deep breath.

"Hello, Miss Pearl, Mr. Behr. . .Everett. How are all of you this morning?"

"Hello, Miss Tillie." Hubert Behr's mustache always jiggled when he smiled and spoke at the same time. "Fine Lord's morning, isn't it?"

From the corner of her eye, she saw Everett hunch his shoulders and pull his collar up despite the warm sunshine. His left hand slid toward his face, and he turned away from her. A pang of sadness twisted within her, and she wished Everett weren't so self-conscious of the scars he had sustained in the fire.

"Yes, it's a lovely day. Don't you think so, Everett?" She'd use whatever means at hand to engage Everett in conversation, even a trivial discussion of the day's weather. To her dismay, Everett merely shrugged a noncommittal response and tugged his broad-brimmed hat a bit lower. Clearly she needed to come to the point. She sucked in another deep breath to fortify her waning courage and plunged ahead.

"Everett, I've been trying to speak with you for weeks now, but every time I see you, you hurry away. Is there some reason you don't wish to talk to me?" She waited to see if her boldness might loosen his tongue.

"I apologize, Miss Tillie. I didn't mean to be rude. . . ." Everett's mumbled reply from behind his hand barely reached her ears.

"Tillie, won't you join us for Sunday dinner?" Miss Pearl's graciousness made Tillie's heart speed up and her cheeks grow warm. She hadn't been fishing for an invitation to dinner, but if it meant spending the afternoon with Everett, the prospect sent a tingle all the way to her toes.

"Why, that's so kind of you, Miss Pearl. I'd love to."

Everett jerked his head toward his stepmother. The expression on his face—either anger or panic, she couldn't tell which—pulled his mouth into a frown. For a split second, she thought maybe Miss Pearl might rescind the invitation, but she didn't, and Tillie's acceptance put a smile on the woman's face, if not on Everett's.

Since Everett made no move to help her climb into the wagon, Tillie turned with her back to the wagon and placed both palms on the edge of the tailgate, hoisting herself up. She tucked her feet beneath her to steady herself and scooted back farther into the wagon bed. Not a very ladylike maneuver, to be sure, but since Everett chose to leave her to her own devices, she scrambled aboard the best she could. Once seated across from him, she primly arranged her skirt to cover her ankles. With teeth clamped together, she forced a smile and willed herself not to make mention of Everett's lack of gallantry.

"Everybody set? Let's go. I can smell the chicken and dumplings from here." Mr. Behr released the brake and slapped the reins on the horse's back. The lurching motion of the wagon caught Tillie off balance, and she careened into Everett's shoulder. His hand flew out to catch her, but he immediately snatched it back.

"Oh, I'm sorry." Telltale heat climbed up her neck, and her mind raced to remember which of Everett's arms was burned. "Did I hurt you?"

Everett glared at her from under the brim of his hat. "No harm done," he mumbled, and shifted his position until she could barely see even the unblemished half of his face.

Tillie brushed an errant strand of hair from her face. "I missed seeing you in church. I was hoping I could speak with you before the service."

A soft huff defined Everett's opinion of her attempt at conversation. "I arrived late."

"Oh." She waited to see if he would elaborate. He didn't. "You know, my Ma and I made a huge batch of Irish soda bread yesterday. I just love it with fresh currant jelly. I should have brought you some. Perhaps Miss Pearl and Mr. Hubert might enjoy some as well. As soon as the currants are ripe for picking, I'll bring you a jar of jelly. With six brothers and sisters, we certainly go through a lot of jam and jelly at our house. My brother Phillip can eat almost a whole loaf of bread by himself if he has a jar of jelly at hand. Ma and I just finished putting up a double batch of strawberry jam, and the blackberries should be ready in a few weeks. Do you—"

Everett cleared his throat. "That's fine, Miss Tillie. I'm sure Father and Pearl would appreciate it."

Too late she remembered her Da's twinkling eyes when he teased her. *"Don't know of another female who can outchatter a magpie like our Matilda."* Clearly Everett wasn't inclined to engage in small talk. Either she could carry the conversation, or they could sit in uncomfortable silence.

Perhaps silence wasn't uncomfortable to Everett. Growing up in a houseful of noisy children, with a blarney-filled father and a mother who liked to sing while she worked, the O'Dell house was never quiet. She didn't even know if Everett had siblings.

They rode the rest of the way to the Behr house without any further attempts on her part to coax Everett into talking. Tillie studied his profile—what she could see of it. His hat brim shadowed his brow and eyes, but the corner of his mouth bore a distinct downturn, evidence that he wasn't happy being stuck with her company. If he remained in such a sullen mood, a very long afternoon threatened to stretch out before her.

Chapter 2

Tillie set a china bowl of green beans on the linen-covered table and sneaked a glance from the dining room into the living area. Everett and his father sat across from each other in large leather chairs in front of the fireplace. She'd caught the grimace in Everett's expression when they stepped into the Behrs' house and he had to remove his hat. He'd seemed relieved when she offered to help in the kitchen. Pearl set the tureen of chicken and dumplings on the table and called to the men. Everett hesitated, and Tillie could only guess by his reticence that he was trying to think of a way to excuse himself and leave.

Instead he walked into the dining room and held Tillie's chair for her before seating himself to her right. She thanked him, her face warming at his polite gesture. As soon as they were all seated, Hubert held out his hands, one to Pearl and one to Everett.

"Let's join hands and pray."

Join hands? Well, of course they held hands at home when Da offered the blessing at mealtime. He always teased that it was to keep the boys from snitching his portion of the food while his head was bowed. But now, Hubert and Pearl were waiting for Everett to take Tillie's hand. She could feel his reluctance hanging like a thick fog in the space between them.

After several seconds, Everett extended his hand. The moment their fingers touched, her breath caught in her throat. How to describe such magic? Is this what a dove felt when it took flight? Did a butterfly know this exhilaration after it struggled free of its cocoon and spread its wings for the first time?

Guilt pricked her as her attention fled from Hubert's prayer. Could Everett hear her heart pounding? When Hubert's rumbling voice pronounced the amen, Everett instantly dropped her hand. But the magic remained, and she had to remind herself to breathe normally.

It occurred to her that from this angle, she couldn't tell the flames ever touched him unless he turned his head toward her, which he didn't. Perhaps that was why he'd held her chair—to ensure she wouldn't be able to see his scars from where she sat. A pang arrowed through her, and she searched for a definition. It wasn't pity. . . . No, it was more like sorrow that Everett felt he had to go to such lengths to hide his scars.

"Everett, would you like a roll?" Pearl picked up the bread basket and held it out to him.

He started to accept the basket with his right hand but quickly switched. "Thank you." He set the basket down, took a roll, and deposited it on his plate; then he picked up the basket with his left hand again and passed it to her. Watching Everett maneuver reminded Tillie of attempting to cross a swiftly running stream, jumping from rock to rock, trying not to get wet. She suddenly realized his tactics were because of her presence. Surely he wasn't this self-conscious around Hubert and Pearl. Perhaps it was time for some maneuvering of her own.

"Everything is so delicious, Miss Pearl." Tillie scooped a small second helping of chicken and dumplings from the tureen onto her plate. "These dumplings are as light as an angel's wing."

"Why, thank you, Tillie. For compliments like that, I'll just have to invite you to dinner more often." Pearl chuckled and passed the butter to Hubert.

"And how would you know how much an angel's wing weighs?"

Everett's question took her so by surprise she assumed he was teasing, and she laughed with delight at the thought of him joking with her. But Everett didn't laugh. Tillie swallowed back the giggle and coughed to cover the sound.

"I must admit I don't have any idea how much an angel's wing weighs. It's just an expression my Da uses."

Hubert chuckled. "I've heard some of Timothy O'Dell's Irish expressions. That man could charm a smile from the grumpiest person in town." He blotted his mouth with his napkin. "Timothy came in the store the other day and asked if I sold slippers for wee folk. I thought he was talking about one of his little girls, that cute little one. . .the one with the freckles and pigtails. What is her name?"

Tillie laughed. "That would be Brenna, but Brenna is not wee folk."

Hubert shook his head and laughed again. "That father of yours sure had me going. He kept showing me, like so"—he held his thumb and forefinger two inches apart—"how small the slippers needed to be, and he was quite adamant they had to be green. I was checking the catalog to see if I could order slippers that tiny. He finally told me that *wee folk* are—"

"Leprechauns." Tillie grinned. "Da loves to tease."

Hubert and Pearl both enjoyed the amusing story, and Tillie watched Everett for some indication of a smile, but there was none. She reflected back to the afternoon she'd spent with Everett at the church picnic a year ago, before he was burned, and pictured his warm, engaging smile. She wished to see it again.

"I suppose"—she glanced at Everett and winced inwardly to see the frown still in place—"I should yield to Everett's challenge and admit I was stretching my description of your dumplings, Miss Pearl, since no one can measure the lightness of an angel's wing."

Everett shrugged. "I didn't mean to insult." A barely audible huff blew past his lips, and he pushed his plate away.

Tillie forced a small laugh. "No offense taken." How hard must one work at being so surly? While it sorrowed her heart to think of the drastic change the fire had caused in Everett's personality, a part of her bristled. She felt like shaking the young man and informing him that he wasn't the only person who'd ever experienced pain or adversity. She nibbled on a few more bites of dumpling. God didn't make mistakes, and she was quite certain she'd felt His nudge, but this man was mighty pigheaded.

A three-way conversation continued over the meal. Everett's lack of participation rang hollow in Tillie's ears. Within her spirit, she conceded to her disappointed anticipation. After enough time elapsed that the remainder of food on his plate must have surely grown cold, Everett pushed back his chair and stood. "Forgive me, I'm afraid I'm not very good company."

"Oh Everett, you can't go yet," Pearl declared. "I've made a gingerbread cake for dessert."

Hubert flapped his hand, motioning for Everett to sit. "Please stay, son."

Tillie rose. "Yes, Everett, please stay." She glanced at Hubert and Pearl for support. "Why don't I help you clear the table, Miss Pearl, and let these two catch up on their man-talk." She began picking up plates and flatware to carry to the kitchen.

"You don't have to do that, Miss O'Dell." Everett's tone sounded brittle. "This isn't the hotel dining room."

Tillie froze in her tracks with a stack of dishes in her hands. Was this the same arrogance and disdain he'd extended to her the day he discovered she worked as a waitress at the hotel? Her Irish temper flared in her chest, but she immediately suppressed it.

"Everett." Hubert stood and cast an apologetic look at Tillie. "Don't be boorish."

Tillie willed her hands not to tremble. "It's all right." Her voice was so hushed she almost couldn't hear it herself. Her father's favorite verse and gentle admonition ran through her head. *"Be ye kind one to another, tender-hearted, forgiving one another. . . ."* It wasn't Everett's fault. They'd practically forced him into spending the afternoon with her. He wasn't used to being around people since the fire. She'd grown up watching people react to her father's scars—the looks of pity, horror, and repulsion.

"I apologize, Everett, if I've offended you in any way. Please forgive me." She hurried to the kitchen with the stack of dishes.

Before she could deposit the china on the work counter, Everett followed her. "Miss O'Dell. . .Tillie, I'm sorry. I didn't mean that the way it sounded. I just meant that you're a guest, and you shouldn't have to do those things."

As soon as she turned to face him, he averted his gaze and drew his left hand up, his fingers covering his right jawline. Da always said a person's eyes and expression could be read like a book to see what was going on in their heart. But Everett's expression was unreadable, especially when he kept turning away from her.

She returned her attention to scraping the dishes. "I don't mind helping. It makes me feel useful. Being a guest is too stiff and formal for me." She paused, her back still to him. "Everett, I'm sorry, too. I didn't stop to think that being with people might be uncomfortable for you."

She heard him sigh. "I suppose I'll have to get used to it."

Tillie started to turn, and Everett slipped his hand back up to his face. "Everett, a man is made up of what's on the inside."

"Yes, well, that's easy for you to say. You're—"

When she turned to see why he didn't finish his sentence, Everett spun on his heel and strode out of the kitchen.

"I'm what?" She pondered the question. Curiosity pricked her to hear him finish his thought, but underlying misgiving prevented her from following after him to ask what it was he had been about to say.

❧

Everett laid down his fork. Half of his dessert sat untouched on his plate. Normally he devoured Pearl's gingerbread cake, but today it went down like sawdust. He took a swallow of coffee.

Hubert cleared his throat. "The crops look good this year. If the weather holds, there will be plenty to celebrate come harvesttime."

Tillie nodded. "Da says he expects a bumper crop of corn and beans. Even Ma's kitchen garden is keeping her busy with canning. Has there been any discussion of the annual harvest picnic? I realize it's early yet—harvest won't take place for another three months, so there is ample time to plan."

Everett's senses went on alert at Tillie's question. Apparently the picnic was some sort of tradition every autumn. While Tillie and Pearl chatted about the possibilities of having a pie-eating contest and apple bobbing at this year's event, Everett wished he could think of a way to excuse himself and hurry back to his living quarters over the mercantile. He didn't intend to participate in the celebration, even if it was still three months away. His devised method of slipping into church unnoticed after the service began and leaving ahead of the rest of the congregation allowed him to attend worship in relative comfort. Lingering after the services to fellowship with folks didn't appeal to him in the least. He had no intention of giving people the opportunity to gawk.

"What do you think, Everett?" Tillie's soft voice tickled his ears, and he almost turned his head in her direction.

"About what?"

Tillie shook her head. "Pfft! Just like a man. Cogitating on things instead of paying attention to what my Da calls 'women's frivolities.' But he just says that to agitate Ma. He has more fun at the picnics than the children do."

Tilting his head just enough to see her from the corner of his eye was a mistake. Her smile lit up the room. Why did she have to smile like that? Just when he'd settled into his grumpy disposition, wishing she would mind her own business and leave him alone, the sound of her laughter and her sparkling green eyes chipped away at his defenses.

The heat that rose from his belly and upward into his face tingled the scars along his jawline. He gritted his teeth and stiffened his spine. "Why should I pay attention to a discussion that doesn't concern me?"

Tillie's face reddened. "I just thought. . .that is, I hoped. . ." Everett watched her slide her gaze to Pearl, and she appeared to be silently asking for help. Guilt smote Everett. He'd been asking God to help him break down his arrogant demeanor and replace it with kindness. Clearly he still needed more work.

Hubert broke in. "The harvest picnic is something the whole town looks forward to. It's a time when we all come together as a big family and celebrate the way God has blessed us. Why don't you ladies speak to Pastor and Mrs. Witherspoon about it?" He patted his stomach. "Pearl, my love, you've done it again. I'm so full I can hardly move." He rose and pushed his chair back. "I'm going to see if I can walk off some of this dinner. Everett, come and keep me company."

Everett rose and readily joined his father. At least it would get him out of the house and away from Tillie. Dodging her attempts at conversation as well as maneuvering so she couldn't stare at him wore him out. "Yes, I believe I will. Thank you for dinner, Pearl. It was delicious. If you will excuse us." He sent a curt nod in Tillie's direction. He didn't wish to be rude, especially since she was only trying to be nice. But he didn't need anyone going out of their way to demonstrate pity.

He followed his father out to the front porch and down the steps. Pearl had planted a variety of colorful flowers along the front of the house. He had to admit that between the flower beds outside and the curtains and cushions inside, the place did look more inviting. His father's house had been the grateful recipient of a woman's touch.

A woman's touch. The very idea seared his heart much like the flames had tracked their fingerprints across his face. No woman would want to make a life with him. Not even Tillie. Why did she keep trying to pull him into a conversation?

He sucked in a breath of fresh air, free of the encumbrances of trying to hide his scars. His father turned wisdom-filled eyes on him.

"You looked like you needed an escape."

Mottled skin pulled when he smiled. "You're very insightful. Tillie is a nice girl, but having people stare at me is quite uncomfortable."

"Tillie wasn't staring at you."

Everett snorted. "Only because I stayed in constant motion trying to out-maneuver her. I'm exhausted."

Even without looking at his father, Everett could hear the smile in his voice. "Maybe you should stop running and let her catch you."

Surely Father was joking. He didn't plan to dignify the jest with an answer. Instead he changed the subject.

"I finally received a letter last Friday from Grandfather's lawyer." He sighed. "If you'll recall, last year Grandfather's business went into receivership. Thankfully, all the creditors have now been paid."

Father walked silently beside him as they headed toward a stand of poplars. He'd have to break the news eventually. Might as well be now when there was nobody else around to overhear.

"The money that was left is a small fraction of what I'd expected." He adjusted his lapels and the silk cravat at his throat. "I'd hoped to start an import business back in Baltimore, but I won't have enough capital."

"Son, I have some money saved. I can—"

"No!" Everett immediately softened his expression. "I mean, no thank you, Father. I know you mean well, but I have to stand on my own two feet. Whatever business venture I invest in, it will be with my own assets."

His father stopped in the shade of the poplars and rubbed his gray whiskers. "I don't want to pry, son, but if you don't mind me asking, how much money was left after the estate was liquidated?"

Everett hesitated and examined his feelings. He no longer resented his father, nor blamed him for the estrangement between them for so many years. In fact, he found that he truly wanted his father's advice—a discovery that filled him with warmth.

"A little over two thousand. Certainly not the figure I thought I would inherit." He reached up and plucked a leaf from a poplar tree, twirling the stem between his thumb and forefinger.

Father slipped his hands behind his back and clasped them together. "Well, I agree with you that an import business would require more capital than two thousand." He pursed his lips and frowned, and Everett could see the thoughts turning over in his father's head. Finally, the older man spoke again.

"Willow Creek has been in need of a freighting company for quite a while. Every time I place an order for merchandise, I have to wait until one of the freighters from Dubuque or Manchester can schedule a run north. Sometimes my goods sit in their freight office for two or three weeks before they can get them here." He stared in the direction of town and rubbed his mustache with one finger. "Old Cully at the livery has complained about how long it takes to get harness parts, and Jake Peabody had to shut down the mill last year for more than two months because he was waiting for a new gear to be delivered."

His father turned a thoughtful gaze upon Everett and tipped his head. "Son, you have a business background already, so establishing such a venture shouldn't be too difficult for you."

Everett wasn't sure what running a freight operation entailed, but if his father's assessment was an indication, the town definitely had a need for the enterprise. "This is interesting, but I don't want to leap into a business about which I know nothing. Would you have time later to talk this out and help me put some plans on paper?"

Father grinned. "Of course. We can talk about it now if you like. I have the rest of the afternoon and evening."

His emotions were already dueling where Tillie was concerned, and he didn't wish to discuss his financial future in her presence. He glanced toward the house through the low-hanging branches of the poplar trees. Pearl stood on the porch, and Tillie walked away from the house in the direction of town, pausing to turn and wave back at Pearl. He and his father could discuss the business possibility in private after all, but a twinge of guilt assailed him at the thought of Tillie walking home alone. Perhaps he should have offered. . . No, he shouldn't.

Chapter 3

Tillie peeked in Everett's direction from the corner of her eye but couldn't find him without turning her head. Her father, seated beside her in the pew, raised one eyebrow at her. She could almost hear his unspoken admonition and returned her attention to the man in the pulpit at the front of the room.

Pastor Witherspoon closed his Bible and made some closing comments, exhorting the worshippers to take the morning's message with them and apply it in their lives. *"Bear ye one another's burdens."* How might she go about helping Everett carry the burden of disfigurement? Her Da never seemed to be bothered by the scars *he* bore, and likewise she and her mother and siblings were so accustomed to Da's appearance, they barely took notice of the gash that trailed across his cheek and the bridge of his nose. Were Everett's scars still too fresh? Or perhaps they ran deeper than one could see on the outside.

Tillie heard the church door creak, and a slice of sunlight fell across the floorboards next to her. She risked a surreptitious glance and caught a glimpse of Everett just as he slipped out. If she waited for the preacher's closing prayer, she might miss him. She caught her bottom lip in her teeth and chafed, her feet itching to follow Everett. Finally, the pastor raised his hands for the benediction. Tillie tip-toed to the door and prayed Pastor Witherspoon's voice would cover the squeaky hinge. She stepped out and quickly scanned the churchyard. She located Everett closing the distance to the parked wagons and buggies with his long strides. The low-hanging branches of the cedars and the few white pines appeared to be his destination.

As soon as her feet hit the dirt at the bottom of the steps, she broke into a trot, but she didn't call out Everett's name until she was well away from the church.

"Everett, wait."

He slowed his forward progress and cast a brief glance over his shoulder, annoyance outlining his posture. He took a few more steps, as if he pretended not to hear her. For a moment she wondered if he would ignore her altogether. When he reached the deepest shadows of the trees, he stopped. His shoulders heaved with a great sigh.

"Everett." Tillie panted with exertion. Everett's reclusive tendencies frustrated her, but Da's repeated admonitions for compassion echoed in her memory. She stopped a few feet from where Everett stood cloaked in shadows. "I'm sorry to hold you up. I've wanted to tell you something for a while, but—" She planted one hand on her hip. "You're a hard person to nail down."

Everett turned, presenting his left side to her. It was nearly impossible to see his facial expression as he stood in the shadows and she in the bright sunlight.

"What was it you needed to tell me?" Impatience threaded his tone.

A sudden burst of unaccustomed shyness overtook her tongue, and she fidgeted with her hands. "I've pondered for months how to say this." She hooked her fingers together to stop their nervous twitching and raised her eyes to the silhouette of his profile. Her heart performed a curious flutter, and the words she wanted to say tangled in her throat. She covered her mouth and coughed.

Everett turned and cast a glance toward the church, where the door remained closed, the congregation still inside. His chest rose and fell, as if he was trying to fend off anxiousness. She only had a moment to say what was on her mind and heart because she knew folks would come spilling out into the churchyard any moment. She drew in a breath.

"Everett, it takes an extraordinary man to put aside his own safety and demonstrate the kind of compassion you showed last year. Had it not been for your bravery and mercy, Miss Pearl and your father would surely have died in that fire. I just wanted you to know that I think you are a man of great courage and character." She glanced over her shoulder at the church, where the pastor had stepped out and stood by the door to greet the worshippers as they departed.

"Thank you," Everett mumbled. "If you'll excuse me. . ."

"Everett, wait."

He halted but a stiff sigh blew past his lips.

She took a step closer, and the patchwork of sunlight and shadows played across her eyes. "My da is an amazing man. He has such a tender, giving heart. I've never known another man who expressed his love for his family in the way he sees to their needs like Da. Your act of self-sacrifice reminds me of him."

Apparently forgetting to hide his scars, Everett widened his eyes and turned to fully face her. She waited for him to respond, but no reply was forthcoming.

Tillie dropped her gaze and stared at her clasped fingers. "Well, that's all I wanted to say. I—I guess I should let you go now."

Everett didn't seize the opportunity to escape the way he normally did. She glanced up in time to see him toss a glance at the parishioners who were gathering in the churchyard, and then he turned his attention back to Tillie.

"That's a very kind thing for you to say." He cleared his throat, and his hand trailed up to his face, even though the shadows concealed the scars he tried to hide. "I can see you are very close to your father, so for you to make such a comparison is very generous. Thank you, Tillie."

A smile unfurled from deep within her and found its way to her face. For a brief moment, she basked in the pure pleasure Everett's reply birthed in her heart. But the glow was short-lived. As quickly as Everett's guard had fallen away, he snatched it back into place. He tugged the brim of his hat down.

"Please excuse me." He turned abruptly and strode beyond the shade of the thick trees and down the boardwalk, disappearing around a corner into an alley.

Frustration niggled at her. Every time Everett raised his hand to hide his face, she longed to grasp that hand and pull it away. She wished she could make him understand his scars made no difference to her. She pondered the thought. Was that really true? Maybe his scars did make a difference, but not in the way he thought. She found his scars noble, even virtuous. They stood for something that proved the character of the man. If only she could help him see his scars the way she saw them.

Pastor Witherspoon's message about listening to God's voice and heeding His nudges to help carry the burdens of others echoed in her mind and heart. But what if God seemed to be nudging her in the direction of a stone wall?

ଈ

Everett looked out the dusty window of the empty building. Roland Sewell, the bank's rotund president, stood outside on the boardwalk, fanning himself with his hat and mopping his forehead with a handkerchief. Everett suspected the portly gentleman with thinning gray hair felt uncomfortable in his presence. Why else would the man elect to remain outside in the hot sun while Everett looked over the building he was considering leasing?

The location at the edge of town, directly across the street from the livery, was perfect for a freight operation. There was a good view of the main street and plenty of room for wagons to pull up and unload. Everett looked through the door that separated the larger front portion of the building from a small, private area in the rear and scrutinized the space. The back room would suffice as an office, while the front could serve as an adequate work and storage area.

Everett tugged his cravat a bit higher around his neck and stepped to the open doorway. "Mr. Sewell, the building has possibilities, but since there is no corral or other accommodation for livestock, I'll have to check with Mr. Cully at the livery to see if arrangements can be made to house the horses I'm planning on purchasing."

The man's gaze flitted over Everett. A wince of pity and revulsion flickered across his expression, neither of which Everett could abide. He turned away from the banker with the pretense of studying the framing around the door. "If the terms of the lease are still what we discussed earlier, I'd like to proceed."

"Very well, Mr. Behr. I can have the lease ready for your signature in a few days." Sewell slapped his hat back on his head and stepped off the boardwalk. "Good day."

"Good day," Everett mumbled, certain the retreating man couldn't hear him. He pushed back encroaching resentment and sighed. Roland Sewell was one person. Willow Creek was full of people who surely viewed Everett with repugnance. He might as well accept it. He pulled his hat lower to shade his face more fully and headed across the street to talk to the owner of the livery.

Poking his head in the stable door, he didn't see anyone about. "Mr. Cully?"

A thumping sound drew his attention to the rear stalls, where a grizzled, bent man stomped his feet on the packed dirt floor, apparently trying to dislodge a foreign substance from his boots.

"Mr. Cully?"

"Hold your britches on. I'm comin'." The livery owner sounded like he'd been chewing on gravel.

"Might I have a few minutes of your time, sir?"

The liveryman snorted. "Sir? Just who do you think you're talkin' to, sonny?"

"I beg your pardon, Mr. Cully."

"Ain't no need to be beggin', and my name ain't *mister*. It's just plain Cully. I don't answer to nothin' else." He dusted his grimy hands on his equally grimy pants. "A man who lives, eats, and cleans up after horses don't need no mister in front of his name." He plopped his hands on his hips. "Well? Speak your piece. I ain't got all day."

Everett cleared his throat. "I've come to discuss a business proposition, that is, if you have the time."

"Got more time than money, young fella. What's on your mind?" He clomped over to a large bin, apparently expecting Everett to follow him, and scooped grain into two wood buckets.

The dimly lit interior of the stable lent a shroud of comfortable darkness. "Well, mister. . .I mean, Cully, I'm Everett Behr, and—"

"I know who you are. You're Hubert's boy." He set the buckets down and mopped his brow.

Everett blinked in surprise. "Yes, Hubert Behr is my father." He couldn't decide if he should be put off or amused by Cully's manners, so he decided to come right to the point. "I'm planning on renting the building across the street—"

"I seen you and old man Sewell jawin' over yonder."

It was all Everett could do to hold back a snort of laughter. Cully appeared to have quite a few years on Roland Sewell, so to hear the livery owner refer to the banker as an old man threatened to undo Everett's quiet dignity.

"Um, yes, I'll be leasing the building from Mr. Sewell for the purpose of starting a freighting operation based here in Willow Creek. I'd like to contract with you to stable my horses."

Cully's thick eyebrows sprang up into his hairline. "You don't say! That's some of the most welcome news I've heard in a while. A freightin' business, right here in Willow Creek?" Cully slapped Everett on the back. "Young fella, you bring your horses here whenever you're ready. I'll give you a fair deal."

❧

Gideon Maxwell led a glossy black Belgian gelding around the yard for Everett's appraisal. "He's only four years old, but he's gentle and steady. Since he and the other three were broke to harness and trained together, they're well matched. They'll pull in pairs or in a four up."

Everett surveyed the four horses before him. "Magnificent animals. It's hard to believe a horse as big and muscular as this can be so gentle."

Gideon patted the black's neck. "That's one of the reasons I chose to breed Belgians. They're strong and have great endurance, and they also have a wonderful temperament, which makes them trustworthy with families."

The big gelding snorted and turned to look in Everett's direction, as if investigating his prospective new owner. Everett rubbed the horse's velvety nose. "I'm quite impressed. I believe these four horses will serve me well." He gave the black a pat on the neck. "What are their names?"

"I reserve the privilege of naming the horses for the buyers." Gideon grinned at him. "You get to think of four names. So when do you think you'll be ready to start your freighting operation?"

"I sent a telegram yesterday to Julien House Hardware Company in Dubuque. They've recently become a supplier of Springfield wagons." Everett stood aside while Gideon led the big gelding back to the corral. "I hope to send a man to Dubuque later this week to pick up the wagon."

"This town sure can use a freighting company. Let's go into the house and draw up the papers."

Everett pulled off his coat and hat and crossed the yard to lay them on the seat of the buggy he'd borrowed from Cully's livery. He'd been so engrossed in watching the splendid draft horses go through their paces, he'd forgotten about concealing his scars, but Gideon didn't seem to notice. As Everett followed his host to the two-story whitewashed house, Gideon's wife, Tessa, stepped out the front door with a young child on her hip. Tillie O'Dell followed on Tessa's heels. Everett instinctively ducked his head and tugged his cravat up higher around his neck till it hid his lower jawline. He glanced over his shoulder where his hat lay atop his coat on the buggy seat.

Tessa stopped on the top step of the porch. "Gideon, Tillie and I have been working on some quilt patterns together, and I was planning to take her home, but Susan is a little feverish." She brushed her hand over the child's forehead. "I'm afraid she might be coming down with something."

Before Gideon could reply, Tillie stepped forward and joined her friend on the step. "Tessa, I told you I could walk. It's only about four miles."

A feeling of tightness that had nothing to do with his collar or cravat crept around Everett's throat. The very sound of Tillie's voice rained like soft mercy-drops on his ears. He'd never known such a feeling before, and it surely bewildered him now. The breeze caught her honey-blond hair and wisped it across her face. The curve of her cheek was interrupted by a tiny dimple that accented her smile. She might not possess the ravishing beauty of some of the socialites back east, but her gentle manner and soft smile arrested him, and her Irish green eyes held him captive.

Heat climbed Everett's neck and made the scars along his jawline sting. Sorrow pricked him. Why did God taunt him with the illusion of being attracted to a young lady like Tillie?

What a joke. It wasn't as if he was Tillie's beau. She was a mere acquaintance and could never be anything more.

"Is that all right with you, Everett?"

He startled at the sound of his name. Gideon stood looking at him with expectation and a hint of amusement.

"Um. . .I'm sorry, is what all right?"

Gideon grinned, deepening Everett's level of discomfort. "This paperwork will only take a few minutes. Would you mind driving Tillie home in your buggy?"

His gaze shot to the porch, where Tillie stood wide-eyed and blushing. Drive her home? Refusing would be rude and ungallant, but the very thought of sitting in such close proximity to her for four miles tied his tongue into knots and made it hard to breathe. A sense of motion jarred him, and he realized he'd nodded his head.

Gideon motioned him inside, and they made short work of the bill of sale for four horses. As Everett counted out the purchase price, his hands shook in anticipation of having Tillie for a traveling companion.

Outside in the yard, Gideon helped Tillie into the buggy, and Everett breathed a sigh of relief that she'd be sitting to his left, where she couldn't view the scarred side of his face. His heart galloped as he climbed into the buggy seat beside Tillie, and he had an urgent need for a drink of water, but there was no turning back now. He released the brake and slapped the reins gently on the horse's rump.

Tillie waved at her friends as the buggy pulled away from the house. "I hope Susan feels better soon," she called to Tessa.

She turned and settled back into the seat beside him. "Thank you for the ride, Everett. I know it's out of your way, and I apologize for the inconvenience. If you like, you can just drop me off in town, and I can walk the rest of the way. It's not terribly far."

Her tone held no pretense. All the young women back in Baltimore were consumed with obligatory society protocol. Tillie's lack of social status would have made his grandmother swoon, but as his father had pointed out on a few occasions, Willow Creek wasn't Baltimore.

He swallowed hard a few times to push down the boulder that had taken up residence in his throat and sucked in a deep breath. "Nonsense. Of course I'll drive you home."

Tillie squirmed a bit in the seat, giving him the impression of discomfort. Was she embarrassed to be seen with him? She'd made a point of speaking with him in the churchyard, but perhaps riding with him in a buggy indicated more than friendship—something she didn't want misunderstood by anyone who might see them together.

The next mile passed in awkward silence. Sweat popped out on his brow, and he ignored his proper upbringing and dragged his shirtsleeve across his face.

"Oh Everett, look." He jumped when Tillie clutched his arm and pointed. He followed the direction she indicated and noticed nothing but a few clumps of small purple flowers.

"Would you mind stopping for a minute so I can pick some of those violets? They're my favorite."

He pulled the mare to a stop and watched as Tillie hopped down and ran across the rutted road. She fell to her knees and began picking the purple blossoms and gathering them into a bouquet. As she held them to her face and closed her eyes, Everett's breath caught. What a picture she made. His heart picked up speed and thrummed double time. He stepped down and offered her a hand up when she returned to the buggy with her nosegay of violets. Was it his self-consciousness or Tillie's nearness that caused his heart to resemble Cully's hammer at the forge?

Chapter 4

Everett checked another item off the bill of lading on his clipboard. A year ago, he'd never have believed he'd find enjoyment in earning a living by the sweat of his brow. Though not familiar with physical labor, he discovered it suited him. Most of the time he worked alone, content to shut himself off from the rest of the townsfolk, toiling over tally sheets, invoices, and inventories in the back office or building sturdy shelves in the front room. He'd even learned to harness the teams and hitch them to the wagon. When he fell into bed at the end of an exhausting day, he felt a satisfaction he'd never known before. The local merchants and business owners were quick to contract his services, giving him cause to wonder if he'd need to purchase a second wagon and another team by next year.

"Good morning, son."

Everett glanced up to see his father coming in his direction. He set down the clipboard he was holding and pulled a handkerchief from his pocket to wipe his perspiring forehead. "Good morning." He jerked his thumb in the direction of the crates and barrels in the back of the sturdy Springfield wagon. "Most of this load is the goods you ordered three weeks ago. As soon as I get everything inventoried and checked off the bill of lading, I'll have the fellow I hired bring them over to the mercantile."

A grin tweaked his father's mustache. "It used to take at least six weeks to get merchandise, and even then sometimes I had to send someone to take a wagon to Waterloo, Manchester, or Dubuque to pick up goods from the freight depots there."

Gratification seeped into Everett's breast. Since the fire, he'd struggled to feel useful. Since he now provided the community with a needed service, perhaps he wasn't a throwback after all. He cautioned himself, however. Just because the community appreciated having a freight company in town didn't mean they could look at him without shuddering.

"Your business seems to be growing, even in the short time since you've

292

opened your operation." His father rubbed his chin. "What's it been. . .three, four weeks?"

Everett's smile tugged on the scarred tissue along his jaw. "It's been a little over a month since I opened, and I already have enough work to keep me busy."

"You say you've hired a man?"

"Yes, only two or three days a week right now, but if business continues the way it has, I might ask him if he'd like to work every day." Everett reclaimed the clipboard and pulled his pencil from behind his ear. "You probably know him. His name is Ben Kiefer."

"Oh sure, I know Ben. He's a nice young man." His father stuck his thumbs in his belt. "What does his job entail?"

Everett counted spools of wire and checked them off the invoice on the clipboard. "Mostly he drives the runs to and from the other towns around here, since he's more familiar with the area. He helps load and unload, and he learned pretty quickly how to inventory the goods." He paused and then added, "And when he's here, he'll be handling most of the face-to-face transactions."

A slight flinch of sorrow shadowed his father's face, but thankfully he didn't argue the point. Instead he tugged his watch from his pocket and flipped open the cover. "It's time I open the mercantile door for business before folks think I've closed down and retired. I'll be waiting for Ben to bring the supplies around." He snapped the watch closed and tucked it back into his pocket, clapped Everett on the shoulder, and set off toward the center of town.

Everett checked the bill of lading once more before starting to unload the items slated to go to recipients other than the mercantile. With a grunt of effort, he dragged a crate marked FRAGILE—CHINAWARE addressed to the hotel and hoisted it off the tailgate to the boardwalk. Just as he set it down gingerly, something warm and furry brushed his arm. Startled, he released the crate and yanked his arm back, nearly falling over a skinny gray cat who regarded him with great yellow eyes.

"Watch out, you mangy cat." He scowled at the animal, who took a dignified seat with its tail curled over its front paws. "Where did you come from anyway?"

The cat continued to stare as though it expected Everett to bow in obeisance. One of the cat's ears bore a ragged edge, no doubt the result of one too many skirmishes, and its gray fur was dirty and dull.

"Go on, shoo." Everett waved his hand at the cat, who proceeded to stand and stretch, and then pad through the door of the freight depot like it owned the place. "Where do you think you're going? Come out of there." He followed the animal inside just in time to see it meander into his office and leap gracefully onto the desk. The cat settled down with its white paws tucked under its body.

"Well, just make yourself at home," Everett declared with his hands on his hips. He blew out a stiff breath. "You'd better be gone by the time I get back, because I'm going to need that desk."

The cat merely blinked in reply. Everett shook his head and returned to the wagon to finish sorting the crates. He climbed up into the wagon bed and bent to haul a crate to the edge of the tailgate when a hard object hit him sharply on his backside. He jerked upright and was met with hoots of glee. Three boys, ranging in age from around eight years to perhaps ten or eleven, pointed fingers at him and laughed uproariously.

"See? I told you he was just like a freak in a circus." The tallest boy elbowed the lad who held the slingshot. "Hey mister, we need a scarecrow out in our cornfield. You want the job?" The trio continued to jeer, and Everett stood, stiffened with anger and embarrassment. They were only children, but their mocking filled him with humiliation. Fire rushed up his neck and into his face, searing his ears. How many people on the street heard their insulting taunts? The boy in the middle poked another stone into the slingshot and prepared to launch it in Everett's direction.

"Johnny Frasier, Billy Snipes, and William Curtis, you boys stop that this instant!"

Everett spun in the direction of the reprimanding voice. Tillie stood a few yards away, a basket over one arm and the other hand on her hip. Mortification strangled him when he realized she'd witnessed the whole thing.

Tillie took several steps toward the boys, who glanced back and forth for a way of escape. "I have a good mind to take a switch to all three of you, but I'm sure your parents can do a better job than I can." She narrowed her eyes at the trio. "Don't you know who this man is? He's a hero. He saved two people from certain death last year when the boardinghouse caught fire and was burned in the process. You all ought to be ashamed of yourselves. Now, go on home, all of you. And you'd better tell your parents what happened here today, or I will."

The boys raced off, and Tillie turned apologetic eyes on Everett. But he was in no mood for her pity. He snatched his clipboard, jumped down off the wagon, and stalked toward the depot door.

"Everett, wait."

He didn't stop. Instead he pushed a crate aside and sought refuge in the back office. He sucked in a noisy breath through clenched teeth. The words *Just go away and mind your own business* stung the tip of his tongue, but he bit down and held them at bay. His face still flamed, and he kept his back to her.

"Everett, I'm so sorry."

"Why?"

He heard her sigh. "Those boys need to learn some manners."

He turned just enough to see Tillie standing in the doorway between the front room and his office. "They're children. They don't know any better. Some people go through their entire lives without any heed to the rudeness of their words."

He heard her soft footsteps on the wooden floor behind him. When she touched his elbow, he flinched as though she'd poked him with a sewing needle.

"I'm sure their parents will have them apologize."

He almost swung around to confront her but halted and reversed his motion, facing away from her once again. "I would rather you'd just stay out of it. I don't want them to apologize. I don't want their parents to know what happened. I just want to be left alone."

ॐ

Everett's terse tone nailed Tillie in her tracks. Was he implying *she* needed to learn manners? The boys' cruel taunting had stirred her ire, perhaps because for more years than she cared to count, she'd heard similar unkind remarks aimed at her own father. As a young girl, she'd retaliated in angry defense of her Da, but she remembered his tender admonition for her to " *'be ye kind one to another, tenderhearted, forgiving. . . .'* " Learning to forgive those who said hurtful things to someone she cared about was still a struggle for her, but intentional meanness was something she couldn't abide.

She bit her lip. Judging by Everett's insistence that she stay out of it, she'd overstepped the bounds of propriety, and he'd considered her admonition of the boys rude. Vexation chafed at her, and she huffed, mentally counting to ten before her temper got the better of her. Squashing the retort that perched on her tongue, she drew in a slower, quieter breath and set her basket on the desk beside a skinny gray cat. A quick prayer for a gentle spirit winged its way heavenward, and she lowered the volume of her voice almost to a whisper.

"I apologize if I was out of line. Perhaps you're right. Since you were the one the boys insulted, I should have let you handle it. I'm sorry."

As she hoped, Everett turned halfway toward her, presenting his left side as always, and leaned closer. "I beg your pardon?"

She repeated her apology, watching Everett tip his head in her direction as she did so. Her quiet response to his sharpness produced the desired effect, as the stiffness in Everett's shoulders visibly relaxed, and he set his clipboard aside. "It's not your fault. I need to get used to things like that and learn to ignore it."

The resignation in his voice pricked her. As time went by, maybe God would show him what his scars symbolized to her. Meanwhile, all she could do was be a friend. How did one go about extending the hand of friendship to someone who continually hid himself away?

She kept her voice soft and gentle. "Everett, you are a fine, unselfish, courageous man. I pray that you can one day see that for yourself."

He gave a snort. "I see myself every day when I have to look in the mirror. Everything those boys said is true. One can hardly fault them for stating the truth."

Mild surprise raised her eyebrows, and she tilted her head to one side. "I never would have taken you for one to wallow in self-pity."

Apparently forgetting his abhorrence for letting people view his scars, he spun to face her, storm clouds gathering in his eyes. "When you're disfigured for the rest of your life, then you can pass judgment on me. Until then, I must ask you to leave now. I'm busy."

She stood her ground. "Poor Everett. He's the only person in the world who ever had to deal with difficult circumstances. It strikes me as odd, though, how a man can willingly perform such a selfless act and then feel so sorry for himself afterward. Didn't you think before you ran into that burning boardinghouse?" She lifted her gaze toward the ceiling and tapped her chin with one finger. "Hmm, perhaps entering a burning house isn't a good idea. I might be injured, or perhaps even killed. No, I think it's more prudent to let my father and Miss Pearl get out on their own."

Everett's face flooded red, and he clenched his fists. He opened his mouth but instantly clamped it shut again. Rage narrowed his eyes into slits, and his chest rose and fell as though he'd just finished a footrace. "Are you quite finished?"

She ignored the wrath that sharpened the lines of his face and dipped his eyebrows into a deep valley. Instead she extended her hands, palms turned up in entreaty. "Don't you see? That's exactly what you *didn't* do. Without any thought to your own safety and regardless of the possible consequences, you acted in pure selflessness. What you did is the noblest thing a man can do."

She lowered her hands and took a half step toward him. Predictably, he lifted one hand to cover his scars. Her impulse was to pull that hand away, but she resisted the urge and dipped her head in a demure fashion, eyes closed and prayer winging from her heart. One day she hoped to help him forget about hiding, but that would have to wait until another day. First things first. "May I ask you a question?"

He snorted again. "Do I have a choice?"

She bit the inside of her lip to keep from smiling. "No, you don't."

The gray cat on the desk poked its inquisitive head into her basket, investigating the contents. She absently ran her fingers over its head, and the animal leaned into her touch.

"Everett, obviously the only thing on your mind when you ran into the burning house was finding your father and Miss Pearl and getting them out. You didn't think of anything else. But if you had, would you have stopped? Would you have stood out in the yard and waited for your father and Miss Pearl to come out? How would you have felt after the fire was out and you found their bodies in the burned rubble?"

Everett's shoulders rose and fell as he blew out a sigh. "That's more than one question."

This time she didn't try to conceal her smile. "I see the flames didn't completely destroy your sense of humor; they only singed it a mite." She waited for him to react to her flippant reference to his ordeal. He sent her a long, menacing glower, and she wondered if he planned to throw her out. Finally, he shook his head and looked away.

He reached out to stroke the cat, who immediately transferred its attention to Everett with a rumbling purr. A full minute went by before he answered. "I have to admit, during all those days I was lying in bed over at the doctor's house, I did think about my father and Pearl and how glad I was they were alive and safe. The pain was so intense at times, I wished I would die and be done with it. I didn't understand why God let me live. I still don't."

Grief over his statement turned her heart over. She'd never experienced anything close to what he'd been through. She started to touch his sleeve but drew her hand back, fearful that her touch might cause him to recoil. Instead she added her fingers to stroking the cat under its chin.

"You're right, I don't understand either." She tipped her head and sighed. "God brought you through the fire and let you live because it was His will. I don't think we have to understand. All He expects us to do is trust Him."

Everett jerked his head up as though her words startled him, then turned from the desk to stare out the window. His tone lost its hard edge. "Trusting is something that doesn't come easily for me. I've been learning to trust God more, but I suppose I'm not very good at it yet."

A smile, born of hope, found its way to Tillie's lips. "Just look at this dirty, half-starved creature. Why does God let it live?"

Everett turned back to look at the bedraggled cat. He shrugged and shook his head. "He just showed up this morning and acted like he owned the place."

Countless times, Tillie remembered Da instructing her or one of her siblings to perform a kind deed for someone else to take their mind off their own troubles. By focusing on another's needs, she forgot about whatever it was that caused her displeasure. Even if she couldn't understand the purpose for a hard lesson at the time, more often than not, Da's wisdom drew a lasting picture, indelibly etched in her heart. She hoped her words wouldn't anger Everett.

"Living or dying isn't up to us." She stroked the cat's ears. "God put all of us here for a purpose. Sometimes that purpose might be to save the life of another person. But such a deed can take on several forms, and we are sometimes used by God in ways we'd never expect. I think this poor cat found its way here because you need him."

A muffled sound that might have been a laugh emerged from Everett. "I think you've misplaced your good sense. Why would I need a mangy cat?"

The cat closed his eyes in obvious bliss at the attention he was receiving. She suspected Everett might catch the lesson better from God's whisper than from her lips, so she merely smiled and retrieved her basket. "I have errands to run, and I'd best get to them. Take care of that mangy cat."

Chapter 5

Everett shifted in the wooden desk chair and finished adding a column of figures in the ledger. He squinched his eyes closed and rubbed the tight muscles in the back of his neck. It had been a good day, business-wise, with the addition of two more local accounts. He stepped to the window and adjusted the shade to allow the waning afternoon light to fall across his desk. He preferred keeping the shade drawn during the day, allowing only the slender shafts of sunlight that sneaked around the edges of the shade to illumine his desk. The murky shadows suited him much the way a nocturnal animal shunned the daylight.

Ben Kiefer poked his head into the office door. His straw-colored hair, dampened by perspiration, stuck out like a signpost pointing in a dozen directions. His flushed face evidenced how hard he'd been working. A faded blue chambray shirt hung loosely from his lanky frame. It came as somewhat of a surprise to Everett that he liked Ben. The young man, though a bit unpolished, might be considered a rustic bumpkin by Baltimore's society standards, but he gave Everett an honest day's work for a day's pay. And he didn't stare at Everett's scars or look away as if repulsed by them.

"Mr. Behr, I finished loading the wagon for tomorrow's run to Clermont."

"That's fine, Ben. Did you lash down the canvas? Those clouds to the west look like it might rain overnight."

Ben nodded. "Yes sir." The young man dragged a sleeve across his face. "I'll stop by the livery on my way home and tell Cully I'll need Joshua and Jericho first thing in the morning."

The two big black geldings Ben mentioned were steady and strong, and an asset to his growing business. He recalled Ben's amusement when Everett introduced the young man to the four sturdy draft horses, all with biblical names. "You don't think you'll need the team of four?"

Ben shook his head. "No. This load isn't that heavy, and the load I'm picking up isn't a full load. Besides, I think Elijah and Solomon need an extra day of rest. If it's all right with you, I'd like to have Cully take a look at Elijah's right front shoe. I had to pry a stone out of it, and I think the shoe is a little loose."

Everett nodded his approval. "Thanks for seeing to that. Oh, wait a minute." He reached into the bottom desk drawer. "Here's your pay." He pushed an envelope across the desk. "I put a little extra in there. You drove two runs already this week, and the run tomorrow is keeping you busier than we expected. When you get back, we need to talk about you coming on full-time."

The smile on Ben's face indicated his pleasure at the unexpected bonus. "Thanks." He picked up the envelope and shoved it into his back pocket. "I plan to be on the road by daybreak." He plunked his hat in place as he headed for the door.

"Good night, Ben." Everett listened to the young man's departing footsteps across the front room followed by the opening and closing of the outside door.

The gray cat jumped from the windowsill to the desk and squeaked a meow at him as if expecting Everett to answer.

"Hello, Gray. I suppose you think it's suppertime?" He rubbed the cat's head. "Sorry, but you'll have to wait a little longer. Pearl sent over a fine stew, and I promise I'll save you some." The feline produced another kitten-like chirp in response. Everett pulled his face into a grin. "You know that pitiful sound you call a meow doesn't sound very masculine. I thought male cats were supposed to yowl." He ran his hand down Gray's back and noticed he could barely feel the cat's ribs now that his new friend benefited from regular meals. Gray arched his back and leaned against Everett's stroking, a rumbling purr communicating pleasure. Everett chuckled at the cat's response to the gesture of affection. "One of these days, I'll have to try my hand at fishing the creeks around here and see if I can catch you a fresh trout. Would you like that?"

Everett scratched the cat's ears and stood, glancing out the window at the position of the sinking sun. God's paintbrush had begun to sweep the twilight sky with shades of lavender and orange edged with deeper purple. Ever since he'd established a close relationship with God, he never ceased to be amazed at the works of God's hand—things he never took the time to appreciate before.

Hunger made his stomach rumble, but when he stepped out and turned to lock the door, the nearly empty street caused him to pause and savor the freedom of not having to duck his head or tug his hat down to hide his face. Supper could wait.

He stepped off the boardwalk and crossed the street. A few people came and went from the hotel, but they paid him no attention. He strolled past the mill and admired the willows dangling their delicate tendrils along the ground near the creek bank. The breeze teased them into waving an invitation to him.

The sun hugged the horizon to his right, indicating perhaps thirty more minutes of daylight, and he intended to take advantage of the solitude. He headed toward the shadows among the willows lining the creek. A sweet calmness fell over him. Here, in the refuge offered by the sweeping willow trees and the gathering dusk, he felt no need to hide himself. He pulled in a deep breath and released it slowly. A few night birds had already begun tuning up for their evening serenade, and fireflies played tag in and out of the willows' curtains. An easy smile slipped across his face as he immersed himself in the pleasant sanctuary. A song deep within him rose to his throat, and he began humming "O for a Thousand Tongues," one of the hymns sung at last week's church service.

"The glories of my God and King. . ." "Thank You, Lord, for this place and this beauty." He gazed through the crisscrossed branches at the ever-changing colors in the sunset sky.

"Breathtaking, isn't it?"

Everett spun to see who was intruding on his seclusion. Tillie stood a few feet away, outside the willows' fringe. He instinctively took a step backward into the deepening shadows and shrugged. "Yes, it is."

"I'm sorry if I startled you." Tillie pulled her shawl around her shoulders. "I was on my way home and saw you walking this way. It's lovely this time of the evening when stillness covers the town. I love listening for the whip-poorwills and watching the fireflies come out."

He couldn't blame her. The very things that had coaxed him to take an evening walk along the creek bank were the same things she mentioned enjoying.

"Yes, I love the—" He started to say *privacy*. "The quiet." He sent her a short nod and briefly touched the brim of his hat before stepping away and continuing farther down the creek bank. A flat rock offered a place to sit and enjoy the solace. To his consternation, Tillie followed and took a seat on the grass a few feet away. His initial inclination—resentment—melted before it grabbed hold of him. Instead curiosity niggled. He bent and picked up a few pebbles and tossed them into the gurgling water.

Tillie said nothing, and Everett was glad, if not surprised. He recalled the Sunday Pearl invited Tillie to dinner. Her endless chatter in the wagon on the way home that day nearly drove him to jump out and walk. At least this evening she didn't feel the need to fill every moment with conversation. She leaned forward and plucked a few clover stems, setting them into the water and watching as the gentle current wound around a few rocks and carried them downstream. He studied her out of the corner of his eye but found it unnecessary to hide his observation, since she leaned her head back and closed her eyes as she took in a deep breath. A small smile tipped the corners of her lips.

After a few minutes she glanced sideways at him, a playful look in her eye. "Would you think me scandalous and unladylike if I took off my shoes and stockings and dipped my feet in the creek?"

Everett almost chuckled out loud. "Not at all. I was just thinking of doing the same thing."

They both removed their shoes and let the cool water run over their toes. Everett couldn't remember ever doing something so undignified, even as a child. What other simple pleasures had he missed because he'd been reared by a grandmother who put more stock in social standing than enjoying the gifts God gave His children?

Tillie sighed. "Ahh, that feels so good."

Everett took in her profile, and her expression was pure bliss. Of course her feet must be tired. He presumed she didn't have much opportunity to sit down during the day, working in the hotel dining room. Less than a year ago, he'd held Tillie in disdain for her menial job. Odd, how the thought of Tillie's occupation no longer filled him with scorn. On the contrary, he felt a new respect for her, working as hard as she did. No one could accuse her of being lazy.

"Won't your family wonder where you are?" Everett almost bit his tongue the moment the inquiry slipped out. He didn't mean for it to sound as though he was anxious for her to leave. But she didn't seem to take offense.

"No. Sometimes when I work the supper shift, I don't get home until after dark." She flicked a mosquito from her arm. "When I have to work late, my brother and sister do some of my chores."

Everett raised his eyebrows. On top of working at the hotel, she had household chores to perform. "Doesn't your brother work at the mercantile for my father?"

She splashed her foot in the creek. "My brother Phillip. Regan and Grady help with my chores when I get home late. Grady's only ten, but he likes to think he can do the work of a grown-up."

"And who is Regan?"

Tillie placed her hands on the grass behind her and leaned back. "My oldest sister. Well, I mean, I'm the oldest, and Phillip is the next oldest at fifteen, but Regan is the sister closest to me in age at fourteen. Then comes Fiona—she's twelve. Then Grady. Brenna is my youngest sister—she's six. And the baby is Cory—he's four."

"Such a large family," Everett mused. "It must be noisy at mealtimes. I never had any siblings."

Tillie's laugh blended with the sound the water made as it danced over the rocks. Together the harmony played on Everett's ear like a gentle interlude.

"The only time it's not noisy around our house is when Da reads the Bible and prays with all of us before bedtime. Even Cory has learned to be quiet and listen." She grinned. "But you're right. Such blarney around the breakfast table every morning. And supper time. *Whist!* What a chatter. Da claims he can't even hear himself ask for seconds."

Everett tipped his head back and laughed. "All of a sudden I feel my meals are very lonely. It's just me and the cat."

Tillie shifted around and began drying her feet on the grass. "So you decided to keep that mangy cat, did you?"

"He's not so mangy anymore." Everett followed Tillie's example and twisted around to set his dripping feet on the rock beside him. "He's getting sleek and fat. I think he's adopted me."

Her musical laughter gifted his ears once more. "Have you given this fat cat a name?"

"Gray."

"Gray what?"

"The cat's name. I just started calling him Gray. He doesn't seem to care. He doesn't come when I call him anyway, unless I have food in my hands."

Tillie's hands halted in their task of pulling on her shoes. "Gray? What an unimaginative name. I think I would have named him. . .Sir Lancelot or Solomon."

"That's the name of one of my horses."

"You named your horse Sir Lancelot, but you named the cat Gray?"

"No, Solomon. I bought four horses from Gideon Maxwell, and I gave them all biblical names."

Tillie cocked her head to one side as if weighing his choice of names for his livestock as he described each animal. They continued for a few more minutes, laughing as he relayed an amusing story of Gray bringing a mouse to him, only the mouse was still alive. Tillie responded with an account of one of her brothers sneaking a squirrel into the house that he intended to keep as a pet until it got loose from its box and led the entire family on a merry chase. Everett couldn't remember a time when he'd laughed so much, or enjoyed a conversation with such a lovely young woman.

Realization hit Everett that they'd spent a half hour in each other's company and he felt completely at ease, unlike the Sunday afternoon he'd worked so hard to distance himself from her. The gathering darkness surely had something to do with it, but at some point he became aware that while she looked him directly in the eye, she hadn't once stared at him. He detected neither pity nor repulsion in her expression or tone. Being in Tillie's company as dusk settled in around them was more pleasant that he could have imagined.

She finished tying her shoes and tugged the hem of her skirt down to cover her shoelaces as she stood. The murmuring water provided background music. Shadows blended with the encroaching night, and Everett rose and faced her fully.

Tillie bent to retrieve her reticule. "Do you go walking in the evening often?"

"Not really, but it is quite pleasant this time of day, isn't it?" A flicker of hope tickled his stomach.

She dipped her head, and in the retreating streaks of the sunset, Everett saw a demure smile grace her lips. "Perhaps. . .I might see you again out walking some evening."

The pinpoint of hope became a glimmer. "Perhaps." In unison they stepped away from the grassy creek bank and walked toward the edge of town, Everett measuring his strides to match hers.

Their easy conversation continued, and before he realized what was happening, he'd walked with her nearly all the way to her family's farm a mile past town. He hadn't intended to walk her home, but the relaxed manner Everett discovered in the twilight made being with her so pleasant that his self-consciousness faded like the daylight. To his surprise, they now stood at the edge of her father's cornfield. The small farmhouse, silhouetted against the darkening sky, didn't look large enough to hold the number of family members Tillie had told him about, but the welcoming lamplight that spilled from its windows opened its arms in a warm greeting. He wondered what it might be like to step through the door of one's home and embrace loved ones. A momentary picture flitted through his mind. What if Tillie were the one greeting him at the door with her gentle ways and ready smile? The image stole quietly into his mind and lingered.

"I'd best go in now. Da and Ma will be wondering about me."

Tillie's soft voice jolted him out of his reverie. "Oh—uh, yes, of course. Well, good night, Tillie." His hands seemed to not have an occupation, for they fidgeted between clasping together and seeking refuge in his pockets.

"Thank you for walking me home, Everett. It was very kind of you."

He couldn't be sure in the darkness, but her voice sounded like she was smiling.

૪

All the way home, Everett chided himself for his foolish thoughts. Tillie was merely being polite and charitable. She might concede to sit with him in the shadow of the willows or walk with him at nightfall when nobody could see them, or even speak to him in the churchyard after hearing a sermon on compassion. But no respectable young woman would care to be seen in public with the likes of him. The garish light of day would always reveal the ugliness he would never be able to hide.

He clenched his fist and punched the side of his leg as he strode toward town. "I suppose, Lord, that I should get used to the idea that I'll live out the rest of my days alone." He shook his head. "I accept the blame, Lord. The way I tried to separate my father and Pearl last year, the arrogance that drove me to be so hateful and manipulating—Lord, I know I have no right to think I could find happiness with anyone. You've forgiven me, and I'm grateful. I just have to learn to live with. . .with a face that offends people."

He slowed his steps as he passed the grove of cedars that edged the churchyard. Their pungent scent wafted on the night air. "I know I shouldn't allow myself to think about how things might be with Tillie. Because they can never be." He crossed the street to the mercantile, cut through the alley, and climbed the stairs at the back of the building.

Gray greeted him, having found his way between the freight depot and Everett's living quarters over the mercantile. Everett absently rubbed the cat's head. Gray didn't mind his scars. Neither did God. He might never experience the intimate communion a husband and wife shared, but God's all-consuming love would be enough. After all, God saved him from the fire. Surely there must be something more God intended for him other than running a freight company.

"God, it isn't that I doubt Your sovereignty. I just can't imagine how You can use somebody like me—somebody who looks like me." He crossed the room and opened the window, pushing the curtain aside and taking a lungful of scented night air. The tree frogs and cicadas were in full voice, and the whippoorwills answered in harmony. It seemed every creature had a purpose—everyone but him.

Chapter 6

Familiar chatter greeted Tillie like a welcoming hug the moment she opened the front door. Her sisters Regan and Fiona giggled while Phillip teased Grady about the frog the lad had carried home in his pocket. Ma sat in the rocker brushing Brenna's hair, admonishing Grady to take the frog outside and threatening to take a switch to Phillip if he didn't stop his endless teasing. Little Cory clamored for his share of attention while Da leaned back in his threadbare, overstuffed chair by the fireplace.

"Ah, and here's our lovely Matilda, come to join the family chorus of all this heavenly music." Da sent her a lopsided grin.

"Pfft! Music, he says." Ma waved the hairbrush, gesturing to her noisy offspring. "The song of the angels in heaven surely must fall on the ears sweeter than this commotion." She set the brush aside and nudged Brenna toward the ladder that led to the loft. "Off with you now. Go and put on your night-dress. Scoot." She rose and pointed to Grady. "Take your little brother and help him wash his face and put on his nightshirt. Girls, stop that giggling, and finish up the dishes. Phillip, did you fill the woodbox?"

Phillip traded playful punches with Grady. "Yes'm."

Tillie smiled at what Da deemed heavenly music and gave her mother a peck on the cheek. "Glad I wasn't too late to take part in the concert."

"Humph. The hen has ruffled feathers until her flock is grown." Ma slid a sideways look in her direction. "I wish you didn't have to work so late. You know I don't like you walking home alone in the dark." Without waiting for a reply, her mother shooed young Cory up the ladder to comply with her instructions and hurried Regan and Fiona through their task.

Tillie fetched the plate Ma always left in the warming oven for her and sniffed appreciatively at the rabbit stew. "I wasn't alone. Everett Behr walked me home."

The confusion of herding the youngsters to prepare for bed seemed to occupy her mother's attention, but a swift glance at Da told her that he might have a few questions later about her escort. Her father's deep green eyes

307

fastened a silent inquiry on her as she ate her supper. A measure of comfort made her heart smile. Da's protective watch-care over his brood was a sweet assurance she'd treasured from childhood.

The younger siblings, clad in nightclothes, descended the loft ladder and assembled on the floor around Da's chair, tumbling over each other like tussling puppies. He opened the worn pages of the Bible and hooked his wire spectacles over his ears. Once the round lenses perched on his nose, he cleared his throat and began to read, capturing each child's attention. Even little Cory, snuggled on Ma's lap, hushed while Da read. Tillie memorized the picture, hoping to re-create the scene for herself one day.

Scriptures read and prayers said, Ma hustled the young ones up to the loft to tuck them in and distribute good-night kisses. Tillie slipped over and sat on the floor in front of her father, smiling at his upraised eyebrows. "What is it you want to know, Da?"

He blew out a breath through pursed lips. "Well now, girl, how is it you think I'm wantin' to know somethin'?"

She couldn't stop the smile from spreading across her face. "You're wondering about Everett walking me home."

Da lifted one shoulder in a noncommittal shrug, but the twinkle in his eyes gave him away. "I might be wonderin' just a wee bit." He cocked his head toward her and peered over the top of his spectacles. "Don't mean to be stirrin' the pot here, but is this the same Everett Behr who looked down his nose at you last year when he found out you worked in the hotel dinin' room?"

Tillie watched the flames lick the logs in the fireplace, considering her answer. "No, Da, he's not the same. I believe God has used the events of the past several months to change him. He has a humility he didn't have before. But more than that, he reminds me of someone I admire and respect more than anyone on this earth."

Da removed his spectacles and tucked them into his shirt pocket. "Respect isn't somethin' you want to give away freely, daughter. It has to be earned. You'd best be makin' sure o' that."

Pride swelled in her chest. "Da, the person I admire and respect the most in this world is you. The way you love your family and work hard, your integrity and faith, are the things I love most about you. I hope to one day marry a man just like you."

A tiny frown pinched Da's brows as he looked away and sniffed. Raising his arm, he blotted his face on his sleeve before returning his gaze to his eldest.

"Girl, you've kissed the blarney stone for certain." He leaned close and whispered, "But sure and you know how to get to your old da's heart." He patted her hand. "So you're sweet on this fellow, are you now?"

Tillie wrapped her arms around her knees and released a soft sigh. "I'm not quite sure yet if I'd call it that. When he first came to town last year, he was so handsome—I was just as smitten as every other girl in town. But now. . ."

"Now?" Da left the obvious unspoken. Everett was no longer handsome, at least in the eyes of some people.

She brushed a wisp of hair from her face. "I'm drawn for a different reason. A man who puts aside his own well-being and faces danger to save the lives of two people is a man with a depth of character that sets him apart. Handsomeness doesn't seem so important anymore." She paused, more to consider her own words than her father's reaction. "It's what's inside that makes a man, and I want to get to know the man Everett Behr. I want to learn what kind of character moves a man to suffer what he did on behalf of someone else."

She raised her eyes to the ceiling and listened to the soft murmur of good nights being exchanged overhead in the loft. "This evening as I was leaving work, I saw him walking alone. He always ducks his head, or turns away, or lifts his hand to cover his face when people are near. But as the sun set and the darkness came on, it seemed he didn't feel the need to hide."

Her father nodded. "I understand a wee bit about wantin' to hide from the world."

Gratified by her father's insight, she went on. "I walked over and spoke to him, and it was as if he felt free to carry on a conversation, like the sun dropping below the horizon rendered him safe." She shook her head slightly. "I wish he understood that his scars don't matter to me."

Da absently ran one finger along the jagged scar across his face. "You grew up lookin' at my scar, daughter, so it's normal for you. It's not for Everett." He rubbed his chin. "You know that story in Jeremiah where the prophet goes to the potter's house and watches a clay pot bein' formed on the wheel? There was somethin' amiss in the clay, and the pot couldn't be useful the way it was. So the potter made it over again. That's what happened to me. I had somethin' amiss in my life, and I broke. God had to reshape me. The scar is just a reminder that I never want to go back to that place o' sin again. I'm thinkin' maybe God has made Everett over again as well." He reached out and cupped Tillie's chin, his thumb caressing her cheek. "But give him time to settle into the new vessel God's creatin' of him.

"I'm thinkin', too, that Everett wasn't the only one refined by the fire. Seems I've seen a bit of a change in you, too, my darlin'. 'Tis difficult to put a wise head on young shoulders, but I'm noticin' you've learned a deeper level o' compassion. Instead of shuttin' out the person who hurt you in the past, you've opened your heart, lettin' God show His love and carin' through you. It's proud I am of you, girl."

Tillie felt a blush rise at her father's praise. "Everett said he liked walking in the evening, and when I mentioned maybe we'd see each other again out walking, he seemed pleased." She leaned forward and looked fully into her father's face. "Da, if it's all right with you, I'd like to walk with Everett again some evening after work. He was so relaxed as we talked tonight, and I think it was because he didn't feel like he had to hide his face."

Da frowned, and at first Tillie thought he was going to forbid her to see Everett under the cloak of darkness. His eyes searched her face, and finally he laid his hand on her head. "Appearances are important, child. You must mind yourself that you don't allow people to draw the wrong conclusion." He studied her for a full minute before continuing. "I'm trustin' the way I raised you, daughter. You've heard me say such before, and there's no sense in boilin' the cabbage twice. You use good sense, and guard your reputation." A tiny smile tweaked his lips. "And whilst you're at it, guard your heart as well. Your da doesn't want to see you get hurt again." He leaned forward and placed a kiss on her forehead.

≈

Everett gave Gray a few strokes and a scratch behind the ear when the cat rubbed against his leg. "I know, old man—it's almost time to close up and go home." He glanced out the window of his office. The sun hung low in the western sky, almost touching the horizon. Perhaps another half hour until the shadows stretched into wide, sweeping cloaks. Anticipation tickled his stomach, and he purposefully disciplined his mind, returning his attention to the invoices on his desk. He flipped through a few of the papers and realized he had no idea what he'd just read.

Don't be ridiculous! Just because he happened to run into Tillie three times last week and twice already this week didn't mean she'd be waiting for him at the creek this evening. Each time they'd strolled among the thickening shadows, their conversation flowed more freely. Talking to Tillie felt. . .right. Was it so wrong to look forward to being with her, talking with her? Was he foolish for harboring memories of each evening they'd walked together, like a schoolboy carving initials into a tree trunk?

He recalled the sound of her laughter, and he pushed away from the desk. Leaning back with his hands tucked behind his head, he closed his eyes and gave himself permission to dream. A smile twitched his lips as memories of his evening walks with Tillie traced soft images across his mind. He'd had friends in Baltimore, and he'd seen a few young ladies socially. But he couldn't remember ever having a friend like Tillie. He had to admit she was more than just a friend. Sunset strolls with her at the end of the day eased his anxiety and melted away the apprehension he normally experienced with others. Tillie demonstrated no insincerity or charade, nor did she present any expectations. She encouraged him to speak his mind or sit by the creek in silence, to contemplate the intricacies of a clover blossom or count fireflies, to discuss last Sunday's sermon or regale her with Gray's hunting exploits.

The tiresome events among Baltimore's society had demanded he always present himself with proper poise and dignity. Twilight conversation with Tillie often found them dangling bare feet in the creek. Why, just a few evenings ago, they'd sat at the water's edge pitching pebbles into the current and singing "Rock of Ages," laughing as they improvised the harmony. Wouldn't the debutantes in Baltimore titter behind their hands at such a sight?

For all the pleasantness of being in her company, however, there remained the hard truth. Tillie might be a wonderful friend, but that was all she could ever be. If he were to be honest with himself, he'd have to acknowledge that he wished he and Tillie could be more. Much more. A lonely ache defined a desire for a deeper bond, but even as the idea flitted through his mind, he knew such closeness could never be realized.

He shook his head and pulled himself up to the desk. Pursuing a romantic relationship would only result in heartache for him and embarrassment for Tillie. It was her kindheartedness and generous nature that induced her to offer friendship. To expect anything more was selfish, and he'd not put her in the awkward position of having to refuse his request for courtship.

Another glance out the window told him the sun was almost gone. Gray followed Everett out the door of the depot but seemed to understand the honor of his presence was not requested as a chaperone. The feline sat and groomed himself on the boardwalk as Everett locked the door.

"I'll see you later at home." He bent to rub Gray's head and headed off toward the creek, lending his voice to a hymn sung at last Sunday's service.

"Be Thou my vision, O Lord of my heart, naught be all else to me, save that

Thou art." Not remembering the rest of the words, he continued humming as he strode along. When he turned the corner at the mill, the creek came into view. The breeze swayed the willow branches, allowing him a glimpse of Tillie's blond hair catching the ebbing sunlight.

The hymn remained on his lips as he approached. He knew the moment she heard him humming, for she turned her head toward him and joined her pure soprano voice with his.

"Waking or sleeping, Thy presence my light."

He stepped over to where she sat beside the creek. She'd already shed her shoes, and her toes played in the water. Out of habit, he took a position to her right, keeping his left profile toward her.

"That's one my Da's favorites. It's an Irish hymn from the eighth century." She twirled a buttercup between her thumb and forefinger. "It's a lovely evening for hymn singing."

"Yes, it is." He removed his shoes and let his feet dangle in the creek. "But I'm quite sure any attempt on my part to sing harmony would be an affront to the composer," he added with a chuckle. "I'm afraid I scared off all the fireflies the other night when I tried to sing with you."

Her soft giggle rained like dewdrops. "My Da can stampede cattle, but that doesn't stop him from singing. Haven't you ever seen him walking down the boardwalk in town singing?"

He'd seen her parents at church, but only the backs of their heads or from a distance across the yard. He noted she had the same color hair as her father and wondered from which parent she inherited her clear green eyes. Her question prompted a recollection. Less than a week ago he saw a man, a farmer judging by his dress, entering the mercantile singing at the top of his lungs, drawing amused looks from the townsfolk. While he didn't think it too strange for the man to be singing, he was astounded that the fellow didn't mind drawing attention to himself. Even from several paces away, the jagged scar that stretched from the man's cheekbone to the bridge of his nose was clearly visible.

"I think I may have seen him." Everett rubbed his chin. "Green bandana and singing an Irish folk song?"

Tillie laughed again and nodded. "That'd be Da."

The shadows played around them, and their growing friendship coaxed him into asking a question of a more personal nature. "What happened, Tillie?" He almost snatched the inquiry back and apologized, but Tillie's eyes held no defensiveness. "What happened to your father to leave him with such an ugly scar?"

She tilted her head to one side, a tiny, sad smile tugging at her mouth. "Da used to frequent the saloons—before he became a child of God. Sometimes he'd drink so much he couldn't find his way home."

Everett heard the wistfulness in her voice. She leaned forward and dipped her fingers in the clear running water. The obviously painful memory cut a furrow into her brow, and he started to tell her she didn't need to say any more, but she spoke again.

"I remember Ma crying in the night when Da didn't come home. I was about Brenna's age when Da got into a barroom fight. One of the men he was fighting slashed Da across the face, chest, and arm with a broken whiskey bottle." Her voice caught and softened into a hush. "He was hurt very badly. By the time a few of his friends carried him to the doctor, he'd lost a lot of blood. The doctor couldn't say for sure if he would live." Everett couldn't imagine how frightening it must have been for her as a little girl to see her father so terribly injured.

"After a while he began to heal, and Ma talked him into going to church with us. There was a visiting preacher, and for the first time in his life, Da *listened*. He decided he never wanted to cause his family so much grief again, and he asked God to forgive him and make him into a new man."

In the cloak of shadows, he heard her sigh—a soft sound full of reflection. "Da gave his heart and his life to God that day, and he says every morning when he looks in the mirror and sees the scars, he remembers how far God has brought him."

She sat back and turned to face him. "You know, it's never occurred to me to think of Da's scars as ugly. To me, they're beautiful, because they represent that precious time when God gave me back my Da."

Chapter 7

Everett polished off his wedge of apple pie and wiped his mouth on his napkin. "Delicious, Pearl. But I feel guilty for accepting so many invitations to dinner when I haven't extended any." He grinned. "Not that you'd want to eat my cooking."

Father laughed out loud. "Pearl cooked for a crowd at the boardinghouse for so many years that she's had a hard time learning how to cook just for the two of us. If you didn't come to dinner and take some of this food home with you, we'd be eating it for a week."

Pearl flapped a hand at her husband. "He's right. One of these days I'll figure out how to make a casserole that feeds two instead of twelve." She rose and began clearing the dishes. "You two go on in the living room. I'll bring the coffee in later."

Everett pushed away from the table and headed for the large leather chairs in front of the fireplace. The delectable meal and pleasant conversation made for a relaxing end to the day, but his mind wandered to the shadowy creek bank and Tillie's special company. He wondered if Tillie had walked by the creek this evening on her way home. It wasn't as if they made plans to meet. He'd never actually asked her to join him for a walk. They always left it to chance.

His father sat opposite him. "I noticed you've been seeing Tillie O'Dell."

Everett jerked his head up. How did Father know about that? Could he read his son's mind?

The twinkle in Hubert's gray eyes indicated approval. "I've seen the two of you walking together a few times as I'm closing up the mercantile. Most recently, I saw you one evening last week. I had a late delivery to make. On my way back, I went by Pastor Witherspoon's house. While he and I sat on his front porch, we saw you and Tillie off in the distance, down by the creek." He rubbed his mustache and smiled. "Tillie is a very nice young lady. I'm happy you two are getting to know each other."

Not wishing his father or Pearl to misunderstand, he cleared his throat and shook his head. "Tillie *is* a nice girl, but she's just being kind. She's nothing more than a friend." He gave a dismissive shrug and hoped his father would change the subject.

Father's bushy eyebrows came together. "Why couldn't she be more than a friend? You won't find a sweeter girl in the whole county." He uncrossed his legs and leaned forward. "Son, if you intend to pursue her, you'd best make your intentions known. I've seen how the other young fellows buzz around her. It won't be long and one of them will be asking her father for courting privileges."

A knot formed and twisted in Everett's stomach at the idea of another man courting Tillie. He'd tried having a stern conversation with his heart, pointing out the obvious disadvantages of continuing to meet Tillie for their evening strolls. It simply wouldn't do for him to lose his heart to her, especially when reciprocation was impossible. Certainly Tillie's whole purpose in forming a friendship with him was purely charitable. There was no sense in envisioning anything more. He slammed his mind's door on the scenario.

"If Tillie wants to see other fellows, that's entirely up to her. I certainly have no claim on her." He brushed an imaginary piece of lint from his cuff. When he glanced up again, the elder Behr was studying him with an unreadable expression. Everett continued, anxious not to give the wrong impression.

"Father, Tillie has been very kind to go walking with me, and I suspect she is doing so as a demonstration of compassion and mercy like Pastor Witherspoon talks about on Sundays." He absently ran his fingertips over the ridges and valleys of the mottled skin along his right jawline. "Tillie should see other fellows. I'm grateful for her benevolence, but I must find some way to tell her that she needs to accept the attention of some of these other gentlemen." He tucked his chin and frowned. "They *are* gentlemen, aren't they?"

A quiet smile spread across Father's face, stretching his salt-and-pepper beard. "Timothy O'Dell wouldn't allow anything less." He took his whiskers between his thumb and forefinger and tugged absently. "That young fellow who works for you—"

"Ben Kiefer?"

"Mm." His father's gaze wandered toward the window. "I've noticed him waiting on Sunday mornings out in the churchyard. When the O'Dells' wagon pulls up, he is usually the first one to step over and help Tillie down from the wagon."

The knot that took up residence in Everett's stomach earlier rolled over, and he clamped his teeth together. By arriving to church late every week, he didn't get to see who Tillie's admirers were. For some reason he couldn't explain, it bothered him to know Ben Kiefer was among them.

"How do you feel about that?"

Everett shook himself and focused his attention back on his father. "About what?"

Hubert smiled again. "Son, I've seen you and Tillie out walking several times. Why would you go for evening strolls together if you didn't have some feelings for her? Knowing other young men are coming around and paying attention to her must generate something inside you."

There was no point in trying to fool his father. Everett sucked in a breath and let it out slowly. "Father, you must understand that I'm not in the position to make any offers to Tillie." He slid his gaze to the window and swallowed. "All we do is go for walks in the evening when there's nobody around to see us together."

"I've seen you together." Father leaned back in his chair. "So has Pastor Witherspoon and his wife. It's not like you're hiding. You walk in plain sight of the town."

Everett dipped his head. Did he have to spell it out? A sigh stretched from his heart to his lips just as Pearl entered the living room with the coffee tray. "In the evening, it's growing dark enough so most people can't see who she's walking with. I won't embarrass Tillie by asking her. . .to accompany me in broad daylight, or allow me to escort her someplace where people will stare at the two of us. She's probably too kindhearted to turn me down, but I won't put her in that position."

Pearl set the tray down on the low table between Everett and his father. She flicked a glance in Everett's direction and poured a cup of coffee, setting it in front of him. "Everett, that's nonsense. You have so many fine qualities—I can't list them all. Any girl would consider herself lucky for such a beau." She poured two more cups of coffee and slid one toward her husband before glancing back at Everett. "I know you aren't my son, but over the past year I've grown to love you. If I could choose the best young lady this side of the Mississippi for you, I couldn't find one sweeter than Tillie."

He stirred a spoonful of sugar into his coffee and took a tentative sip of the steaming brew. "I appreciate your concern, both of you. Believe me, you don't have to tell me about Tillie's sweetness." He wished he could dismiss it from his mind. He caught Pearl from the corner of his eye giving Father a tiny shake of her head. Her message was clear. *Leave him alone—don't push.* Everett released a relieved sigh.

Pearl lit the oil lamp on the mantel. Everett eyed the glow inside the glass globe, and his heart seized the way it always did when he looked at a flame. He pulled his gaze away and concentrated on the mug in his hands. They sipped their coffee in silence, listening to the cicadas and tree frogs singing their shrill chorus, interrupted occasionally by the call of a whippoorwill—a concert he wished he was enjoying in Tillie's company.

Everett finally set his empty cup on the tray and rose. "It's time for me to go. Gray gets crabby if he has to wait for his supper."

Pearl bustled to the kitchen and returned with a basket covered with a blue-checked napkin. "I put the rest of the apple pie in here along with the chicken casserole. Now don't give it all to the cat." She patted his hand. "You remember what I said, all right?"

A tiny smile tilted his lips. "I will, and thank you. Good night, Father, Pearl."

The walk home stretched just long enough for him to do some thinking. Perhaps he should reassess this friendship with Tillie. A closer relationship could only end painfully, since it would hold no future for either of them.

"I need to put a little distance between us. Maybe I should encourage her to see other men before this goes too far." He cut down the alley and climbed the stairs to his apartment.

Gray sat patiently waiting on the landing and welcomed Everett with a squeaky *meow*. The cat wound himself around Everett's ankles, waiting for him to scoop out a cat-sized portion of Pearl's chicken casserole on a small plate. As Gray enjoyed his supper, Everett recalled his father's comment about Ben Kiefer. He swallowed back the knot in his throat and ignored the tightening in his chest. Ben was a good employee and a hard worker, and Everett liked him. At least up until now.

"Don't be ridiculous." He pushed the budding resentment aside. "Ben's interest in Tillie doesn't change the kind of employee he is." He plopped down in a chair and pulled off his boots. "So what if Ben is interested in her. He's a nice guy, and she's a nice girl." Unease pierced its way into his gut.

Gray looked up from his supper plate and licked his whiskers, showing minimal interest in Everett's solo conversation.

"I suppose you think I'm being foolish."

The cat blinked and returned to his food.

"Humph. Big help you are." He lit the lamp in the sitting room and opened a book, but try as he might to concentrate, thoughts of Tillie continued to spiral in his mind.

Tillie pulled her shawl up around her shoulders and sent Everett a shy smile. "It's getting a little too cool for dipping our toes in the creek. And it's beginning to get dark earlier as well." The sun had already disappeared, and the lingering light was fading fast.

A mild scowl interrupted Everett's features. For all the pleasant conversations they'd enjoyed during the summer evenings, now that August was coming to a close, he'd been mighty quiet. She'd had to remind herself not to chatter like a magpie. But if he didn't talk to her, how could she know what he was brooding about?

"How are things going with your business?"

Everett shuffled the toe of his boot in the dirt. "Good."

"Da said he ordered a new blade for the plow and it got here in only two weeks."

Everett didn't look at her but kept his gaze fixed on the worn path that traced the meandering creek. "Good."

"Mr. Kyle, the owner of the hotel, was delighted that the new fixtures he ordered for the dining room arrived so quickly."

"Hmm."

Tillie raised her eyebrows and cocked her head to one side. "And wasn't it fun watching the circus elephants parade down the middle of the street this morning?"

"Mm-hmm."

She halted in her tracks and shook her head. "Everett Behr, have you heard a word I've said?"

He jerked his head up with a look of surprise. "I beg your pardon?"

Exasperation nipped at her. Since early summer they'd shared all sorts of things with each other. But lately Everett had reverted back to the sullen moodiness he'd displayed a few months ago. What had happened to make him so aloof and preoccupied? Had she said something to offend him?

"Is something wrong?"

That tiny frown pinched Everett's brows again, and his hand slid up to cover the right side of his face. "Nothing important."

As much as she wished to prod an answer out of him, she held her tongue and pursed her lips. His distraction likely had to do with business, and she wouldn't intrude. She expelled a soft sigh as she fell back into step with him. Perhaps a change of subject might coax a smile into his eyes.

"The harvest picnic and barn dance are coming up next month, as soon as everyone has their crops in. Miss Pearl and Mrs. Witherspoon have been planning it. They've asked Dan and Sarah Miller if we can use their barn for the dance. It's scheduled for Saturday, the twenty-sixth of September."

Everett gave a soft grunt. "I heard. Ben mentioned it the other day."

"I love autumn." She schooled her voice to sound carefree. It had been a long time since she'd had to work so hard at a conversation between them. "It's a little sad to see summer go, but I love the cooler temperatures and watching the trees turn color. The harvest picnic is Willow Creek's way of saying farewell to summer and welcoming autumn."

She hesitated, hoping that bringing up the topic might plant the idea in his head, and maybe—just maybe—he'd get up the nerve to ask to escort her to the picnic and dance.

To her disappointment, he steered the conversation in another direction. "You know, Ben Kiefer's a very nice fellow. I was noticing a few days ago what a good job he's been doing. He's very diligent. I never have to tell him to do anything twice. And he's well mannered, too. And generous. You know I saw him helping that older lady—Mrs. Wagner, I think is her name. Ben carried a crate of supplies to her buggy the other day. Yes, Ben is a fine fellow."

Tillie slowed her steps and slid a sideways look at him. What did the change of seasons have to do with Ben Kiefer? "Yes," she said slowly. "I agree. Ben is a nice fellow and certainly not lazy." Was Everett trying to make a point, showering his employee with accolades?

"Yes, Ben was telling me all about that picnic and how he's looking forward to it. He said he loves the barn dances, especially if he has a good partner." His tone seemed artificially cheerful. "I sure hope he isn't disappointed."

Tillie drove her eyebrows downward into a V. "At the risk of seeming a bit foolish, what exactly is your meaning?"

He gave a noncommittal shrug. "Nothing, except that Ben Kiefer has been paying attention to you, and maybe. . ."

Her feet came to a halt so quickly she almost stumbled. Planting her hands on her hips, she challenged him to finish his sentence. "Maybe, what?"

He stopped and pulled a few yellowing leaves from the dangling willows. "Maybe you should. . .pay attention back, is all I'm saying."

"Everett Behr, are you trying to aggravate me?"

He turned toward her but stopped halfway so all she could see in the shadows was his profile. "No, of course not. I'm merely suggesting that Ben might be a good candidate for an escort. That is, if you planned to attend the picnic and barn dance."

Most of the time Tillie felt proud of her Irish heritage. Other times, like now, having Irish blood coursing through her veins could be a pure trial. She sucked in a deep breath and mutely counted to ten, hoping it might tamp down her temper.

"And when exactly did God put you in charge of selecting my escort to the picnic and barn dance?"

She heard him whoosh out a breath with what sounded like frustration. He took a step closer and turned to face her fully. His eyes met hers for only a moment before he lowered his head and raised his hand up to his face. In that brief heartbeat, she read something—something forbidden to her for months because he wouldn't look straight at her. But for one instant she caught a glimpse of the agony of loneliness. When he spoke again, belligerence colored his voice.

"I'm not implying any such thing, and why are you being so stubborn?"

She bit her lip and swallowed back the retort that rose up in her throat. His purpose for pushing her in Ben's direction wasn't lost on her. That fleeting blink of insight painted the real picture of Everett's turmoil, and a keen ache skewered her heart as she realized his intention. He viewed his scars as a stone wall too high to climb and too wide to circumvent, the result of which was permanent isolation. Well, she disagreed. The question now was how to get Everett to see things from her perspective. A shouting match didn't seem prudent. Da always said the best way to avoid an argument was to refuse to argue and lower your voice. She removed her hands from her hips and adopted a more sedate posture, hoping to disarm him.

Instead of giving Everett the chance to turn away as he normally did, she turned and ran her hand through the dangling willow branches. She pulled three of them toward her and began twisting them into a braid like she did with Brenna's flaxen hair. The activity served its purpose. The fire of aggravation that had kindled a minute ago fizzled.

Only then did she trust herself to open her mouth and speak gentleness to Everett's heart. "I'm not trying to be stubborn." She continued braiding and listened for his response. A defused sigh reached her ears, and she was grateful for the darkness so Everett couldn't see her smile.

She released the willow withes and watched them untangle. "I agree with you that Ben is a fine fellow. But it would be difficult to attend the picnic and dance with him."

This time when Everett spoke, all she could hear was resignation. "I don't see what you're waiting for."

She looked at him over her shoulder. "He hasn't asked me." She returned her attention to the mangled willow curtain. "And a certain fellow I'd like to go with hasn't asked me either."

Chapter 8

Everett took the last sip of his cooling tea and rose to set his cup in the dry sink. Gray looked up at him expectantly and produced a squeaky *meow.*

"You've already had your supper," Everett said, holding the door open. "Go catch a mouse."

Gray ambled out, brushing Everett's leg as he passed. Everett stood in the open doorway for a few minutes, gazing at the stars flung across the inky sky. What was the verse that Pastor Witherspoon had used the previous Sunday? Everett scrunched his eyes shut in his effort to recall the scripture. It was somewhere in Isaiah—chapter 40, he thought. He closed the door and went to take up his Bible and see if he could find the words the preacher had used. Pulling up a chair, he leaned closer to the lamplight and leafed through the pages. He wished he were more familiar with the scriptures—something he meant to remedy. His finger slid down the page and across the verses until he found it.

"Isaiah 40:26. 'Lift up your eyes on high, and behold who hath created these things, that bringeth out their host by number: he calleth them all by names by the greatness of his might, for that he is strong in power; not one faileth.'"

He leaned against the back of the chair and let his gaze travel to the window. Beyond the pane, the starry host winked against the black backdrop in silent testimony of God's faithfulness. The very thought of being kept by a God who knew the precise location of each star and knew every one by name washed over him with soothing comfort. Those who put their trust in God were more important to Him than the stars. So if God cared enough to know the name of each star and secure it in place so that not a single star was missing, then surely God cared about him.

Everett propped an elbow on the arm of the chair and leaned his head into his palm. "God, I'm grateful for Your love. I just wish I understood why You've allowed the circumstances in my life to be what they are. How do I fit into Your plan? Can You use someone who looks like me?"

The book in his lap coaxed his attention. His father had encouraged him to read through Proverbs. He found the place he'd left his bookmark in chapter 4. A frown tugged his brows together. So many of the verses talked about getting wisdom and understanding, but for the life of him, he couldn't understand why God wanted him to live with scars. Maybe if he just read on, the understanding would come later. He turned the page and hadn't read a half dozen verses when he backed up and reread a verse.

" 'My son, attend to my words; incline thine ear unto my sayings.' " He tipped his head back and stared at the ceiling. It wasn't hard to understand the first part. God instructed him to pay attention to His Word. The second half of the verse, however, gave him pause. " 'Incline thine ear.' " He mulled over the words. "How does one incline the ear?' "

Puzzling over God's choice of words, he rose and carried the lamp into the bedroom to prepare for bed. Tired as he was, his tumbling thoughts dogged him as he lay down on the feather tick. Despite shifting positions and determinedly keeping his eyes closed, he found that sleep eluded him. The clock on the bureau ticked away too many minutes to count as he lay awake. Surrendering, he opened his eyes and tucked his hands behind his head with a sigh.

A thin shaft of moonlight filtered through the curtain and fell across the darkness of the room like an invitation from God, assuring Everett He was listening. Staring at the ceiling, he allowed his thoughts to wander. Not surprisingly, Tillie's image crept into his mind.

Father and Pearl seemed to think he should pursue a deeper relationship with Tillie. In order to do so, he'd have to put himself in a position of vulnerability. He doubted that he'd fooled either of them into believing he didn't care for Tillie. Here in the dark solitude of his bedroom, he admitted concern for her was only part of the reason he felt the need to put distance between them. Of course he didn't wish to hurt her, but if he were to be completely honest, he'd have to admit being vulnerable scared him.

He rolled over and studied the pale sliver of moonlight dimly illuminating the room. "God, I thought if I could live the life of a hermit and limit my contact with other people, I could create some kind of a private cocoon for myself—a niche in this world where people couldn't point and stare and laugh." An ache began to swell in his chest. "But it's lonely here. God, You know the smallest detail of my heart. Down deep, I really want to court

Tillie. Sometimes I lay here in the dark and think of how it might be to watch her walk down the aisle to me and put her hand in mine. I can hide here where nobody knows my thoughts except You, and imagine how it might feel to kiss her."

Shoving back the covers, he sat up and swung his legs over the side of the bed. Elbows on knees, he ran both hands through his hair. "When it's daylight, I think how foolish it is to dream about such things. I can't lie to You. You know I'm not being noble by saying I don't want Tillie to be embarrassed or hurt, because that's only half the truth. I'm a coward, Lord. I'm afraid of the reactions of other people if I dared to behave as a normal man and ask a lovely young woman like Tillie if I could court her."

He stood and crossed the room, pushing the filmy curtain aside to look once again up at the stars that all had names. "God, help me grow my faith. You care for me like You care for the stars. I'm tired of being isolated and smothered. Give me the courage to step out and ask Tillie to accompany me to the harvest picnic." A warm breath of comfort caressed the side of his face—the side he continually tried to hide.

瑶

Everett didn't see Tillie for three whole days. Whether she left work earlier than usual or he closed the depot late, he wasn't sure. He'd rather have taken advantage of the privacy of their evening walks to ask if he could escort her to the picnic and barn dance. Perhaps this was part of God's answer to his prayer—nudging him to step away from his private cocoon.

Sunday morning dawned gray and gloomy with the scent of rain in the air. Everett paced the kitchen with a cup of coffee in hand, waiting to hear the church bell ring. He'd rehearsed what he planned to say a hundred times. Now he couldn't remember a single word. What if he tripped over his tongue and stammered? What if someone else overheard? He came to an abrupt halt. "What if she says no?"

The tolling of the church bell reached his ears. Before the final clang died away, Everett was down the back stairs and cutting through the alley. When he rounded the cedars at the edge of the churchyard, a few stragglers were still entering the church. Everett lingered behind the screen provided by the thick evergreens. There were no shadows, the sun remaining hidden behind a bank of heavy gray clouds.

The sound of hymn singing floated on the air. Despite the gloomy day, hearts and voices were raised in worship. The thought bolstered his courage, and he straightened his shoulders, lifted his chin, and strode toward the church.

He slipped in during the last verse of "Come, Thou Fount of Every Blessing." *"Here's my heart, Lord; take and seal it. Seal it for Thy courts above."* The praise ringing within the walls of the church covered the sound of the door closing. He took his usual place at the back.

The hymn ended, and the congregation was seated—all except one small boy on the second pew from the rear who seemed determined to stand up on the bench despite his mother's efforts to tug him down on the seat. Finally the lad gave in to her admonitions and plopped down on the pew.

Pastor Witherspoon stepped into the pulpit. "Let's open our Bibles this morning and look at Paul's letter to the Colossians, chapter 3." The rustle of pages whispered across the room as folks found the text and settled in to listen to the preaching.

Before the pastor could begin reading, however, the little boy near the back stood up once again on the pew and turned, making faces at the people behind him. When the child's eyes locked with Everett's, the boy's stare widened. He pointed at Everett and yelled, "Mama! Look at that man! What's wrong with him?"

Nearly every head in the room turned, and all eyes followed the direction the lad pointed. Nausea twisted in Everett's gut, and his face flamed. Jerking his left hand up to cover his face, he ducked his head and leaped to his feet, his Bible falling on the floor. Two long strides took him from the bench to the door, where he yanked on the door handle and fled, leaving the gawkers behind.

꙳

The ache in Tillie's chest prevented her from hearing most of what Pastor Witherspoon preached. Her heart ricocheted back and forth between anger at the child and at his mother for not keeping him under control, and grief for Everett. What kind of humiliation tormented him? Of course children said unkind things. She'd witnessed that earlier in the summer when the three youngsters from town mocked Everett in front of the freight depot. Oh, how she wished she could make him understand his scars didn't determine what kind of man he was, nor did they dampen her admiration of him.

She tried to discipline her mind to focus attention on the preacher but continually had to pull her thoughts back to the sermon. Finally, she gave up and closed her eyes, asking God what He might have her do. Should she go and find Everett and try to comfort him? That might make him assume that she pitied him. She'd seen firsthand how destructive pity could be, and she didn't wish that on Everett. No, her goal, with God's help, was to break down the wall he'd erected around himself and encourage him to seek God's will for his life. She spent the remainder of the service in prayer.

The last hymn was sung, the final prayer offered, and the service dismissed. As Tillie fell into line with her family, filing toward the door, she caught sight of Everett's Bible. Someone had picked it up and laid it on the bench. Her hand hesitated only a moment before reaching for the book and tucking it into her shawl.

As she stepped to the open doorway, she scanned the churchyard even before she shook hands with the preacher. No sign of Everett. He might have simply gone home. Hubert and Pearl Behr stood in the middle of the yard, their searching eyes covering a wide circle. Tillie imagined they, too, hurt for Everett.

Da and Ma herded her siblings toward their wagon as a soft rumble of distant thunder rolled across the hills. She hurried to close the distance between her father and herself. When he turned to look at her, she saw the same anguish in his eyes that she felt in her heart. He seemed to read her mind.

" 'Twas a hard thing for young Behr. But daughter, he's goin' to hear such for the rest of his life. Either he learns to push it aside, or it'll do him in."

Tillie gave a slow nod. If anyone understood, Da did. "I don't pity him, Da, if that's what you're thinking. He must allow God to help him overcome the feelings of shame and embarrassment. I just want to let him know I still think he's a fine man."

Da's eyebrows arched, and he tilted his head up to look at the thick clouds roiling in the sky. Another gentle rumble of thunder sounded as if to punctuate his point. "And you feel the need to let him know that today, do you now?"

She saw him peek at her from the corner of his eye. He winked, and she threw her arms around his neck. "Yes, Da, I do. I don't know for certain where he is, but I suspect he might have gone down to the creek."

Da helped little Cory into the back of the wagon and latched the tailgate before turning back to Tillie. "And how do you plan to stay dry?"

She looked down at her shoe tips and gave a slight shake of her head before raising her head to give him a beseeching look. "Dry doesn't seem very important right now, Da."

He rolled his eyes heavenward. "I must be daft. I wonder if the good Lord gave my portion of common sense to somebody else. Go ahead. Find your young man."

Tillie didn't wait for him to change his mind, or for Ma to protest. She pulled her shawl snugly around her shoulders and scurried in the direction of the creek. Most of the other wagons had already departed, no doubt trying to beat the rain.

In the minute it took for her to run down the well-worn path to the willow trees lining the creek, a few sprinkles began to fall. Puffing from exertion, Tillie pushed the willow withes aside, her eyes searching through the gloomy shadows for Everett's familiar silhouette. Perhaps he had more good sense than she and had headed for home.

She hiked up the creek bank, retracing her steps. Did she dare go knock on his door? That would certainly set the town tongues to wagging, and Da had admonished her about protecting her reputation. She blew out a huff through pursed lips. Just as she reached the edge of the churchyard once again, she caught a glimpse of movement beyond the cedar trees.

It's Everett.

Not knowing why, she stepped back, letting the cedar boughs conceal her as she watched to see where he'd go. He looked from left to right, apparently to satisfy himself that he was alone, and reentered the church. Indecision anchored Tillie in place. She longed to speak with him, but judging by his furtive glancing around the yard, he preferred solitude. An argument ensued within her. Should she leave him be or go reassure him? She didn't want him to feel abandoned, but she didn't want to intrude either.

"If I go in and sit with him, even if I don't say a word, at least he'll know I care."

Another rumble of thunder, this one a bit louder and longer, growled across the clouds. A soft, steady rain began, and she hastened her steps across the yard. The thought occurred to her that perhaps he merely came back for his Bible. Glancing to make certain the book was protected from the rain by her shawl, she climbed the stairs and slipped in the door as the patter of rain increased.

There, at the front of the little sanctuary, Everett knelt. Her eyes traced the back of his head, bowed in prayer. How silly of her to think he'd feel abandoned. *He isn't alone. A child of God is never alone.* As she stood there, the words of his prayer reached her ears, and she felt like an interloper.

"I don't understand why You allowed me to live through that fire, God.

Sometimes I think I'd rather be dead than look like this."

Tillie's throat tightened, and she put her hand over her mouth.

"But I know You don't make mistakes, so You must have a reason for these scars. I just wish I knew what that reason was."

Tillie laid his Bible on the back bench and started to leave, but the moment she shifted her weight, the floorboard under her foot gave a tiny squeak. She froze. If she moved, he'd know she'd been standing there eavesdropping. Holding her breath lest he hear that, too, she waited for the next roll of thunder and winced under an onslaught of guilt for listening to Everett pray.

"God, I'm tired of running and hiding, but the ugliness won't let me rest. I want to do something—be something—for You, but how can You use a broken vessel like me? Nobody wants to look at a man with a deformed face."

Tillie heard his voice grow tighter and more intense with each word.

"I keep telling myself it doesn't matter what other people think. It doesn't matter to You, God, but it does to me. I know it shouldn't, but it does. God, please—please make something beautiful of my life."

Everett's prayer stole Tillie's breath. She tightened her hand covering her mouth in an effort to prevent a sob from escaping. Even the years of watching people act repelled by her father's scars didn't prepare her for such a heartrending entreaty. Her eyes burned with unshed tears.

A flash of lightning lit the darkened interior of the church, followed seconds later by a booming crash of thunder. The noise echoed long enough for her to exit without being heard.

"Something beautiful." His plea blew softly across her heart, mournful yet hopeful. She pulled her shawl up over her head and ran down the road, releasing the tears she'd held in check until now. When she passed the bend in the road and was quite sure Everett couldn't see her, she slowed her pace and plodded through the rain. Everett's heart-wrenching words echoed through her mind.

"I don't understand why You allowed me to live through that fire, God. Sometimes I think I'd rather be dead than look like this."

An unseen hand squeezed her heart. Tears continued to burn her eyes. "Please, God, let Everett hear Your voice. Fill him with an awareness of Your presence so he understands that his usefulness to You depends on his heart, not his appearance."

Tangled emotions stirred her stomach into turmoil as the rain dripped off the ends of her shawl, and the leaden sky wept in one accord with her.

Chapter 9

Tillie asked the two other women in the hotel kitchen to cover for her while she ran an errand. A twinge of guilt poked her as she scurried down the street toward the freight depot. It wasn't truly an errand, but her mission held an urgency that had kept her tossing and turning for the past three nights. If she hoped to get any sleep tonight, she'd best meet the situation head-on. Both determination and trepidation roiled in her stomach as she forced her feet to slow and walk sedately.

She paused a moment in front of the newspaper office, glancing at her reflection in the window. A few stray strands of hair had escaped their pins, and she tucked them back into place. With a rush of heat to her face, she hoped no one inside the office was watching her primp. Her gaze darted back and forth, and relief filled her when she saw the office seemed to be empty.

Just inside the window, a large calendar hung on the wall. Big black *X*s marked the passing of the days. Today's date, Thursday, the seventeenth of September, had yet to be marked off. Tillie took that as an encouragement—there was still time today to accomplish something significant. A tremor ran through her stomach as she considered her errand. She could still change her mind and return to the hotel. Momentary indecision held her in place.

Everett wasn't a coward—his heroic actions the day of the boardinghouse fire already proved that. Asking her if he could escort her to the harvest picnic and barn dance would take courage—he'd have to put aside his aversion to being seen in public. But how long should she wait for him to gather that courage?

She sucked in a fortifying breath. Her intentions might not be considered proper, especially back east where Everett came from, but if she let many more days pass without her planned discussion with him, her only opportunity might slip through her fingers. Resolve straightened her shoulders, and she continued down the boardwalk. The small sign on the door of the freight office declared the business open. She stepped inside, but instead of encountering Everett, Ben stood at the front counter. The moment he saw her, he swept his hat off.

"Miss Tillie." Ben's lopsided smile accentuated his deep brown eyes. He ran his hand over his head, smoothing out unruly hair the same color as a wheat field ripe for harvest. "It's sure nice to see you in the middle of the week instead of just on Sunday." He dusted off his shirt and wiped his hands on the seat of his pants.

A bit of the determination that had propelled her down the boardwalk seeped out of her. "H–hello, Ben."

Ben hung his hat on a nail stuck in the wall behind him. "It's been kind of hard to talk to you at church, Miss Tillie. You're always hurrying off some-where." He shuffled his boot against the corner of the counter. "I'd like to talk to you, if you have a minute."

Tillie clasped her hands tightly in front of her waist. She hated to admit it, but she hadn't given Ben much of a chance for fellowshipping either before or after church. He always seemed to be standing there in the churchyard, waiting to help her down from her family's wagon on Sunday mornings. In her haste today, she'd not stopped to think that she'd likely run into Ben at the depot. Now he stood before her waiting for a reply.

She gave him an apologetic smile. "I'm sorry, Ben. I didn't mean to be rude." She slid a surreptitious glance beyond Ben's shoulder toward the door to the rear office, wondering if Everett could hear their conversation. "The other ladies in the hotel kitchen are expecting me back in a few minutes, so I really can't linger."

Ben took a step forward. The hopeful expression on his face pricked her. She'd never noticed before the depth of his eyes. There was something warm and welcoming about them. She could well imagine some young lady falling beneath their spell and sighing with contentment in their captivity. The thought brought a tiny smile to her lips.

Ben's hands fumbled, and he stuck one hand in his pocket as if he didn't know what else to do with it. "This won't take long, Tillie. I—I was just wondering if you planned on going to the harvest picnic and the barn dance. I mean, I didn't know if "—he glanced toward Everett's office door— "anyone had asked you yet."

Tillie drew in a breath and held it. She didn't want to hurt Ben's feelings. She liked Ben. He was a pleasant fellow, honest, hardworking, and polite, but his invitation caught her off balance. Her purpose in taking time away from her lunch break had everything to do with the picnic and dance. In fact, her planned errand included something positively scandalous and bold. She intended to march straight into Everett's office and ask him herself. But she hadn't planned on running into Ben.

She could honestly say that she'd prayed about it. Most of the nighttime hours she'd spent tossing and turning had been filled with whispered prayers. In spite of her repeated petitions, she hadn't felt the affirmation she'd sought. Impatience chewed at her good sense. Waiting had always been difficult for her, but how long did God intend for her to wait on His answer? A flash of caution shook her. She truly didn't have peace over what she was about to do. Maybe encountering Ben was God's way of stopping her from making a huge mistake.

Apparently, her hesitation communicated indecision to Ben. "Well, you think on it a spell, Miss Tillie. Guess I don't need an answer right now. But since the picnic's just a little over a week away. . ." He didn't need to finish the sentence, and Tillie knew she wasn't being fair to make him wait for an answer. If Everett had asked her weeks ago when she'd first hinted about it, she wouldn't be in this predicament. Because of his reticence, she found herself putting Ben off.

She looked down at her entwined fingers. "Ben, I. . ."

Ben gave her another lopsided smile with a small sigh of resignation. His eyes traveled again to the door of the inner office and back to her, like he read her mind. "I know, Miss Tillie. I was just hoping is all. Maybe I'll see you there." He retrieved his hat and plopped it back on his head, tugging at the brim. "Good day, Miss Tillie." He stepped out the door, leaving it standing open, and ambled across the street.

Guilt skewered her as she watched Ben retreating toward the livery with shoulders slumped, and it was all Everett's fault. He'd had plenty of opportunity to ask her. She blew out a pent-up breath and raised her hand to knock on the office door, only to have the door open and her knuckles collide with the very man she came to see.

"Whoa." Everett caught her hand, his fingers wrapping around hers for the space of two heartbeats. A tingle shot up her arm and accelerated her pulse. He abruptly released her fingers and yanked his hand up to cover his face.

He took a step backward. "Are you all right?"

At the moment, she wasn't certain how to answer that question. Their impromptu meeting in the doorway had left her none the worse for wear on the outside, but a war was raging on the inside. She narrowed her eyes and plunked both hands on her hips.

"Everett Behr!"

An expression of expectation arched his eyebrows. "Yes?"

She marched past him into the office, vaguely aware of the dimmed light with the window shade partially pulled down. She sat on a chair only to bounce back up again an instant later and pace across the room. Exasperation curled her fingers into fists held tightly to her sides in an effort to keep them from reaching out and grabbing Everett's hand away from his face.

"Sometimes you make me so angry!"

Mild surprise flitted across his face, at least the part of his face she could see. "What have I done?"

Irritation climbed up her frame and spilled over. "Nothing. That's just the problem."

"Oh?" His mouth tipped into a half smile.

His quiet amusement rankled her even further. A fleeting nudge signaled her to hold her tongue and her temper, but she shoved it away and barged ahead. She thrust both hands out, palms up, fingers splayed. "Everett Behr, you've got to be the most aggravating, pigheaded, prickly man I've ever met!"

He tucked his chin back a bit and blinked. "I beg your pardon?"

"Argh!" She spun around and turned her back to him. *Count to ten before you say anything else.* "You—you—" she sputtered. *"Be ye kind one to another, tenderhearted. . . ."* She whirled back around. "You are a stubborn man."

"Mm. I've been called worse." He reclined against the edge of the desk, seemingly unperturbed by her outburst. "I'm having a little difficulty, however, understanding why you've taken the time to come all the way over here just to tell me I'm stubborn."

"And aggravating and pigheaded!"

He covered his mouth with his hand and muffled a cough. "And prickly." He folded his arms across his chest. "Would you mind telling me what this is all about?"

She could have sworn she heard a grin in his voice. Tears threatened to embarrass her, but she clamped her teeth together and swallowed hard. She took in his familiar form, swathed in shadows as always. How her heart longed to draw him out of those shadows.

"Everett, why can't you see yourself for the man you are? The man on the inside. Because that's the man I see."

His posture stiffened, and a hint of sarcasm threaded his tone. "You must not be looking hard enough."

"You won't let me." She thrust her hands in the air in frustration. "Every time I see you, you either turn away or cover your face. You hide in the shadows and refuse to let anyone come close. I thought we were friends, Everett. No, more than just friends. At least I'd hoped so. But if you keep hiding behind this wall you've erected around yourself, how will I ever know for sure?"

He unfolded his arms and braced his palms against the desk, lowering his chin and staring at the floor. "Tillie, open your eyes. You say you see me for what I am. Well, what I am is ugly. I can't be what you want me to be, and that's the reality of it." He turned and walked around the other side of the desk. "I happen to know Ben was planning on asking you to the picnic and barn dance."

The tears that tried to choke her earlier sneaked back into her throat. "He did."

"So are you going?"

"I don't know."

Everett blew out a breath, sounding as exasperated as she. "What do you mean you don't know? What are you waiting for?"

"I was waiting—hoping—that you. . ." Her original plan seemed to be crumbling at her feet.

"No, Tillie. I can't." His words sounded frozen.

She drew herself up and raised her chin. "Well, I came to tell you there isn't a man in this town who appeals to me as much as you do."

Everett shook his head. "Tillie, you aren't listening. You're being foolish, making Ben wait for an answer."

"So it's foolish I am, is it?" She plopped both fists on her hips. "I suppose I've been foolish to go walking with you in the evening. Have I been foolish to sit by the creek and share personal thoughts and cares?" Her voice rose in pitch as her throat began to tighten. "Are you telling me I've been foolish to pray for you?"

With every word she came closer until they were glaring at each other across the desk. She planted her palms on the desk and leaned in. "For your information, I do know my own mind and heart, but I'm beginning to doubt if you've ever listened to your heart. I think you've lied to yourself. You've talked yourself into believing you aren't good enough for polite company.

Well, let me tell you something, Mr. Everett Behr. You're wrong."

Characteristically, Everett turned away. With his back to her, he stepped to the window and tugged the shade, darkening the room a bit more. "Tillie, stop this. Go back to the hotel. We both have work to do."

His cool dismissal crippled her. She tried to draw in a deep breath, but her lungs rebelled. "So that's it? That's all you have to say?"

He opened a file drawer and pulled out some papers, flipping through them as though they were of great importance. "Go to the picnic with Ben."

His reply stung. This wasn't the same Everett with whom she'd spent leisurely evening hours, walking and sharing her thoughts. In fact, the man in front of her now seemed more like the old Everett, the one who didn't care who he hurt. The former arrogance was missing, but the same coldness she remembered cloaked him once more. She huffed out a stiff breath. "Maybe I will."

"Good," he said, his quiet voice taking on a cynical tone as he reached for another file. "It's about time you took my advice."

This wasn't turning out the way she'd planned at all, and it was her own fault. She'd allowed her temper to break its restraints and run amok, instead of letting compassion control her. The tears finally won the battle and slid silently down her cheeks.

≈

Everett's acerbic tone surprised even him. He didn't relish telling her to accept Ben's invitation. The very words carved another scar—this one across his heart. But what else could he do? Tillie had accused him of being pigheaded, but he suspected she could match him stubborn for stubborn. There was no other choice but to make her angry enough with him that she'd want to seek other companionship. Her kindness and compassion were so clearly etched into her words and actions that he'd seen the reason she had reached out to him from the very beginning. As much as he'd enjoyed her friendship, it was time for her to move on.

He listened for her stomping footsteps retreating, punctated by the slamming of the door, but he heard neither. When he turned, she was still standing there, but the picture she made wasn't at all what he anticipated. He expected her anger. He didn't expect her tears.

An unseen fist belted him in the stomach and sent a bitter lance careening through his chest, robbing his breath. His fingers curled tightly around the papers in his hand. This was wrong. He never intended for Tillie to be hurt by his tactics. She deserved to find a man who could love her and make her proud of him. A man with whom she could spend the rest of her life. Not someone like him.

God must have intended for him to live a solitary life. Why else would He allow the scars? If he could survive the pain of being burned, then surely he could survive the pain of being alone.

But Tillie. . .ah, sweet Tillie. *Girl, don't you know I'm doing this for you?* A raw ache twisted and seared his stomach at the thought of pushing her away. He'd carefully designed his words to make her just angry enough that she'd direct her affections elsewhere. Only knowing she would eventually find the man God intended for her enabled him to sever their friendship. A startled tremor rattled him. What he felt for Tillie wasn't friendship, and he could no longer remain in her presence and pretend that was all he wanted.

His gaze fastened on to the tear sliding down her cheek and dripping off her chin. This wasn't turning out the way he'd planned, and self-loathing filled him to think he'd made her cry. But if he relented now, the carefully laid groundwork would be destroyed.

"I'm sorry, Tillie, but it's best this way."

She remained motionless, as though her feet were nailed to the floor. The longer she stood there, the more difficult it was for him to draw breath. His arms ached to hold her close. He longed to apologize for causing her pain and whisper soothing words of comfort. But the words knotted together in his throat. What would it take to get her to leave? He stiffened his spine and sat at his desk, spreading papers in front of him and studying them with rapt attention. The words and figures blurred and ran together, but he kept his eyes fixed. *Please, God, just let her leave. I'm sorry I had to be mean to her, but she'll be happier in the days to come.*

Finally, a soft sigh reached his ears, but it hit like Cully's hammer.

"I'm sorry, too, Everett. I wanted to make you see. . . . But I realize now I was trying to do God's job for Him. He's trying to tell you something, Everett, and it's up to you whether or not you listen. I won't stop praying for you."

The sound he thought he'd wanted to hear, her footsteps exiting the office, echoed in his heart like a funeral dirge. It made little sense now to pray that what he'd done was right. It was done, and Tillie very likely would never be back.

He propped his elbows on the desk and lowered his head to his hands.

"God, please wrap her in Your comfort." He sat thus for a long time. When he finally raised his head and looked at the papers on the desk before him, he realized they were all upside down, a painfully familiar perspective.

Chapter 10

The pungent scent of autumn greeted Everett when he stepped out his door. He breathed deeply of the crisp air, more for fortification than enjoyment of the season. Instead of waiting until he heard the church bell ring this morning, a motivation he couldn't explain drove him to leave for church early. What was the point? It wasn't as if he planned to talk to anyone. A battle of inclinations fought a tug-of-war in his chest. He both relished and dreaded seeing Tillie.

Perturbed at his own fickleness, he proceeded down the back stairs and walked resolutely through the alley to the well-worn path leading to the thick cedars that surrounded the churchyard. He could see several wagons and buggies arriving, folks calling out greetings to each other, parents tugging at their children in a vain attempt to keep them clean. Their cheerfulness gnawed at him. Even the cornflower blue sky lent a sharp contrast to his mood. If he'd had the privilege of choosing the day's colors, a dark, gloomy sky layered with gray clouds matched his spirit better than the sunny morning with tinges of gold, russet, and red highlighting the trees.

Everett stepped closer but remained in the shelter of the cedars. Ben Kiefer arrived on foot and shook hands with a few of the other men. Ben attended church most Sundays, but today his employee sported a tie. And was that a new shirt? Ben rubbed the tops of his boots on the backs of his pant legs and stood, shifting his weight from one foot to the other, glancing repeatedly to the road coming into town. A growl rumbled in Everett's throat, but he pushed it down.

Another wagon pulled into the yard, this one carrying Everett's father and Pearl. His gaze lingered on the pair. Perhaps today wasn't a good time to contemplate the way God had blessed his father, leading him to find love again late in life. He didn't begrudge his father the happiness, but how he longed to know that kind of happiness for himself. A twinge of envy pinched Everett as he watched the solicitous manner in which the elder Behr aided his bride down from the wagon, holding her shawl for her and

337

offering his arm as they made their way toward the church. A fresh pang of loneliness sliced through him, and a bitter thought taunted him. God would have to send a blind woman for him to be so blessed.

"Halloo, Hubert and Pearl. A fine Lord's day to ye." The ringing voice yanked Everett's attention back to the churchyard activity. Timothy O'Dell waved from the wagon seat as he pulled his team to a stop and set the brake. Before Everett could blink, Ben Kiefer was beside the O'Dell wagon, reaching to take Tillie's hand and help her down.

Everett's jaw tightened. What was the strange sensation whirling in his stomach? If he had to put a title to it, might it be jealousy? That was ludicrous. Such an emotion served no purpose, save stirring a slightly nauseous wave rising within him.

Ben removed his hat and ran a hand over his head to smooth his already neatly combed hair. He nodded and spoke briefly to Tillie's parents. But as the rest of her family made their way into the church, Tillie remained beside the wagon with Ben. Everett turned his head to incline his ear toward the two, but between the breeze rustling the leaves, a nearby dog barking, and a flock of noisy crows squabbling over a few grains of corn next to the mill, he couldn't make out a word they said to each other. Judging by the red stain on Ben's face, they weren't discussing the weather.

The church bell began to ring, and the handful of people who lingered in the churchyard scurried toward the front door. Except Ben and Tillie. They remained in place, conversing about something. Tillie nodded her head, and a pleased smile stretched across Ben's face. Then he said something that made Tillie laugh. Everett's breath caught, and for a moment he feared he might give away his hiding place by coughing. But no cough could make it past the stranglehold in his throat when Ben offered his arm to Tillie and she slipped her arm through his—just like his father did with Pearl.

Whatever he'd eaten for breakfast that morning sat like lead in his stomach. An image formed in his mind and mocked him with the relentless persistence of a wood-boring insect. What if, from his usual seat against the back wall of the church, he had to look at Ben and Tillie sitting side by side in a pew ahead of him, sharing a hymnbook? At the moment, it mattered little how often he'd tried to encourage Tillie to welcome Ben's attention. The reality of it coming to fruition slammed into him like a locomotive.

He turned and strode away, no destination in mind. He simply knew he wasn't ready to watch his own plan unfold before him.

"I know it's for the best, Lord. I just wasn't prepared for the way it would make me feel."

A dozen contradictions collided in his head, good sense conflicting with paradox. He kept walking until he reached the familiar screen of willow branches, the same ones among which he and Tillie had strolled and talked. In this very spot he'd first realized how easy Tillie was to talk to. Sitting on this rock, the two of them had dangled their feet in the creek and tried to improvise a harmony to "Rock of Ages." They'd shared thoughts, stories, and laughter.

Everett sat down on the rock. It was too chilly to dip his feet in the creek, but he closed his eyes, and despite his glum mood, a smile found his lips when he remembered the twinkle in Tillie's eyes when she first suggested they do so. He picked up a round, flat stone and skipped it across the water. The memory of her laughter, sweeter than the most haunting concerto, accompanied the stone as it flirted with the water, only to be consumed by it.

Missing church saddened him. Learning scripture and listening to the pastor's practical lessons, the joy of growing stronger in his faith and closer to his Lord, had become a delight. More than that, his awareness of God's presence had begun to expand into an appetite he couldn't satisfy. He hungered to know more of his God, even if he couldn't always understand His ways. As he cast a slow scan around him, the trees and grasses waving in the breeze, the music of the water flowing over the rocks, even the dance of the butterflies, all lent themselves to an air of worship. He knew, in the coming weeks, he'd fortify himself and step into church again, even if it meant seeing Ben and Tillie together. Today he would praise God right here. The cathedral God Himself created would serve as his altar. He lifted his face and felt the warmth of the sun as he opened his mouth and sang.

"Rock of Ages, cleft for me; let me hide myself in Thee." He halted in the middle of the verse. He'd hidden in the shadows and behind his hand, pulled his hat down low on his face, turned away from staring eyes, and sequestered himself. He'd searched for every conceivable place to hide except in Christ.

"How could I not have seen it before, Lord? You are my Rock, and You can shelter me in Your hiding place better than any device on this earth. Let me hide myself in Thee." Letting God minister to him in solitude this day was exactly what his raw heart needed.

"God, I feel so hollow inside. As difficult as it is to accept, I know Tillie isn't the one to fill the emptiness. But if I can hide in You, then I know You can fill those barren places with Yourself."

He rose and began walking with no thought of direction, cresting hills and crossing meadows, climbing rocks and hiking up ridges. He continued until his legs begged for rest. Now surrounded by mostly wooded hills, he found a shady place near some rocks and stretched out in the grass.

≈

The moment the pastor pronounced the final amen, Tillie turned to look behind her. Of course Everett wasn't there. He always slipped out before the end of the service. But during the singing, she'd sneaked a few brief glances, and his usual spot remained vacant. She hoped he wasn't ill. Sorrow stung her. What if he'd chosen to stay out of church? She hadn't been able to get his plea for God to make something beautiful of his life out of her mind. That wasn't the only thing she couldn't forget. She could still hear his voice—like the sound the ice on the pond made in early winter when someone tried to step on it before it was strong enough. An ominous groan. *"I'm sorry, Tillie, but it's best this way."*

"Are you looking for something, Miss Tillie?" Ben's warm eyes glanced down at her and then followed the same path hers had just taken across the room.

She gulped and forced a smile. "I was hoping to see my friend Tessa Maxwell." It wasn't a lie. She did want to speak to Tessa. She needed her friend's sympathetic ear. She spotted Tessa across the crowded chapel as folks were moving toward the door. It didn't seem likely she'd get a chance for a private talk with Tessa today, but maybe they could plan to get together later in the week. Her heart was sore and full of regret. A chat with Tessa usually made her feel better, but this time she wasn't sure anything could soothe her.

They moved along with the exiting worshippers. Ahead of her, Da and Ma gathered the young ones before they had a chance to scatter. Ben shook hands with the preacher and then took her hand as she descended the stairs. Tillie sent another surreptitious glance, this time around the churchyard. Everett was nowhere to be seen, but she did catch a glimpse of Hubert helping Pearl into their wagon.

"Please excuse me, Ben. There's someone I need to catch before they leave."

Ben nodded and tipped his hat like a perfect gentleman, but she didn't wait for his reply. Dodging around some children playing tag, she hurried toward Hubert and Pearl's wagon.

"Pearl." She called out and waved a hand to stop them.

"Good morning, Tillie." Pearl smiled down from her perch on the wagon seat. "I wondered if we'd get a chance to speak."

Tillie wasn't unaware of the heads turning to take note of her sitting with Ben in church. No doubt the town gossipers would have them engaged by nightfall. Pearl didn't gossip, but Tillie was certain she wondered about Ben. She'd have time later to explain that Ben was nothing more than a friend. At the moment, she had a much more pressing question on her mind.

"I didn't see Everett this morning. Do you know why he's not here?"

Pearl turned to look at her husband and then back at Tillie. "We were hoping you would know."

Tillie shook her head. "I haven't seen him for a few days." She dropped her gaze to her fingers clutching the ends of her shawl. "We. . .had words. I went by the depot a few days ago, and we argued." She looked back at Pearl and Hubert. "I hope he hasn't stayed away from church because of me."

Pearl glanced at her husband, who gave Tillie a grandfatherly smile. "Everett is a big boy. He makes his own decisions. It's best we leave him alone for a while until he feels like talking."

They bid each other good-bye, and Tillie stepped back as the wagon rolled away. She scanned the yard again in search of Tessa and found her with Gideon and their little daughter talking to one of the area ranchers. A quick glance toward her family's wagon revealed Ben standing there talking to Da. A fleeting curiosity skittered through her as she speculated over the topic of their conversation. She dismissed it as inconsequential.

Hurrying across the yard, she touched Tessa's shoulder. Her friend greeted her with a smile and a hug.

"We went out to Fletcher Hamilton's ranch last week to deliver a horse, and Fletcher was trying to interest Gideon in the sheep. Susan was fascinated by the woolies." Tessa tilted her head toward her husband and the rancher. "Looks like the little imp is trying to talk her daddy into going back for another visit."

Despite her melancholy, Tillie couldn't help but smile at the tiny girl holding her father's hand. When she looked up, Tessa was studying her. "I see pain in those eyes. Is something wrong?"

Tessa's question nearly unleashed the tears she'd been holding at bay for days. "Oh Tessa, I think I've ruined everything. Everett and I argued, and it was my fault."

Her friend gave her a gentle smile. "It takes two people to argue."

Tillie shrugged. "Maybe. But what if he never wants to see me again? I don't know if I could stand that."

Tessa's eyebrows arched along with the intensity of her voice. "You're in love with him." She quickly slipped her hand over her mouth and glanced left and right, her gaze lingering past Tillie's shoulder.

Tillie followed Tessa's line of sight and turned to find Ben standing behind her, crushing the brim of his hat in his curled fist. The peculiar expression in his eyes indicated he'd heard Tessa's declaration, but to his credit, he didn't comment on it.

"Miss Tillie, would you do me the honor of allowing me to walk you home? I already asked your pa, and he said it was all right."

Tessa reached to lay a gloved hand on Tillie's arm. "Go ahead. We'll talk later. Can you come for tea this week?"

Tillie nodded numbly. Mortification shot up her spine at the thought of Ben overhearing her conversation with Tessa. She liked Ben—even believed him a suitable candidate as a beau. When Everett had told her it was time she took his advice and accepted Ben, maybe he'd given that advice in a big brotherly way. The thought wounded her. She already had brothers, and what she felt for Everett had nothing to do with sibling affection. But perhaps he was right. She peered up at Ben, searching for those qualities Everett had tried to point out.

"That's very kind of you, Ben."

He took her hand and tucked it in the crook of his elbow. "It's a beautiful day. Just right for taking a walk."

She forced a smile, and they set off down the road—the same road Everett had walked with her that first evening when the crickets and whippoorwills accompanied them.

❧

Everett opened his eyes, surrounded by the sweet scent of meadow grass and autumn leaves. When the breeze died momentarily, he heard a faint gurgling sound. Pushing himself up to a sitting position, he found a tiny trickle of water seeping from between the rocks a few feet away. A smile found his lips as he recalled the scripture he'd read from Proverbs about cold water to a thirsty soul. God found a way to minister to him even when he wasn't looking for it. He scooted over and cupped his hand, capturing the flow and lifting it to his mouth. As he expected, the water was pure and sweet.

Everett carried handfuls of water to his lips and satisfied his thirst, then wiped his sleeve across his face. Dabbling his fingers in the cold spring, his thoughts wandered to Tillie and the times they'd enjoyed the creek water flowing over their toes. This tiny rivulet meandered down the slope, where it fed into a small branch that ran alongside the base of the hill. Everett assumed the branch emptied into Willow Creek. He wondered if Tillie knew about this spring. A tempting thought to bring her to this place taunted him, but he shook his head at the foolishness of the idea.

Dropping to his knees in the thick grass beside the spring, he tilted his head back and groaned to his heavenly Father. "God, I know it can never be. Please take these feelings for Tillie away from me. You are the God of all comfort. Every need I have, You've supplied. Father, I beg You to fill the dry, empty places of my soul with Your presence. Teach me to hide in You. I know You'll take care of Tillie. Truly, my desire is for her to be happy, and that can't happen with me. So, Lord, bring her happiness in whatever way You think is best."

He rose and began walking down the slope in the direction of town. He might not have worshipped within the walls of the church this day, but he'd spent time at God's footstool and had drunk in His refreshing presence. Grateful for the way God ministered to his spirit, he was determined to exercise his faith and leave the outcome to the One who gave cold water to his thirsty soul.

The sun was high overhead as he cut through the thick woods and crossed over grassy hills. The earlier nip in the air gave way to the warming rays. Everett removed his coat and loosened his tie. During the many evening walks he'd taken with Tillie over the past few months, he'd discovered he loved walking. Of course, walking with Tillie was different. They'd shared so much as they strolled among the willows. But Everett found this day's solitude was not lonely. His walking partner today was God.

Refreshed by the communion he'd shared with his heavenly Father, he hiked up a rise and paused. Below, the road that led to town wove through cornfields and grazing pastures. A couple walked down the road. The young lady held a black book—a Bible?—snugly against her, and they appeared to be walking home from church. The lady's familiar honey-blond hair was pinned up and tied with a green ribbon. *Tillie and Ben.*

Ben stopped and bent to pick up a few colorful autumn leaves, and Tillie pointed across the meadow to a stand of maples aflame in seasonal dress. They appeared to be enjoying each other's company. Neither of them looked in Everett's direction.

The promise of God's comfort and hiding place washed over him once again. So this was His answer. An ache stole into the pit of his stomach, but he knew even then that God wouldn't leave him alone.

Chapter 11

Amusement teased the corners of Tillie's lips as she listened to Tessa patiently explain to her little daughter that they weren't going to see the lambs today. Little Susan's bottom lip pooched out, and her blue eyes filled. Tessa appeased her with a cookie.

"She sounds like Cory when he's got his mind made up about something." Tillie stroked the child's hair.

Tessa sighed. "Susan, take your dolly and put her down for a nap. If she doesn't go to sleep, you might have to lie down beside her until she does."

Susan cradled her rag doll in her arms and trotted off toward the bedroom, crooning to her baby. As soon as she was out of earshot, Tessa chuckled.

"Gideon's thinking about purchasing a half dozen head of sheep from Fletcher, but he hasn't had time to go back out to the Hamilton ranch. When we were there last week, Susan got a look at the new lambs, and that's all she's talked about ever since." Tessa shook her head and stirred a spoonful of sugar into her cup.

Tillie took a sip of tea and bit into a cookie. The little girl was so appealing that her parents surely must be hard-pressed to say no. A wistful pining squeezed her, and for the space of a heartbeat she experienced a tug of envy.

"But you didn't come over here to talk about Susan and the lambs."

Tillie ran her finger around the rim of her teacup and lifted her shoulders. "Truly? I'm not sure what I came to talk about." She didn't look at Tessa, but she knew her friend was smiling.

"Am I safe in assuming this is about Everett?"

Hearing his name spoken sent an arrow of regret through her breast. "Tessa, all I wanted was for God to use me. I'd hoped Everett would see himself the way God does. Just because he's scarred doesn't mean he has to spend the rest of his life hiding from people."

"That doesn't sound like a bad thing." Tessa's expression indicated she didn't understand Tillie's low spirits. "Why are you so melancholy? Won't Everett listen to you?"

Tillie rose from her chair and crossed the kitchen to look out the window. The trees had begun to give up their summer green in exchange for autumn yellows, russets, and oranges—changes ushered in by the season—a gift from God's own hand. Strange, how such woeful thoughts could dim the brilliance of the Lord's blessings.

"Everett and I, well. . .we were seeing each other. Going for walks and sitting by the creek in the evening after work." The sweetness of the memories they'd made together ached within her, especially since she feared those memories might turn bitter. She turned and walked back to the table where Tessa sat. "Everett seemed so much more relaxed in the evening—you know, as it was getting dark. We'd talk and laugh."

Tessa tipped her head to one side. "You *were* seeing each other?"

Tillie nodded, her fingers tracing the back of the chair. "Sometimes two or three times a week. I enjoyed our time together so much, and I thought Everett did, too. He told me funny stories about the stray cat he adopted, and I told him about my little brothers' adventures. We discussed Pastor Witherspoon's sermons, and sometimes we even sang whatever hymns came to mind. Being with him felt so right." She slid back down on the chair she had vacated. "Then he started acting. . .different."

"Different how?"

The words to describe the way Everett seemed to pull away failed her, and she wasn't certain she even wanted to give definition to the fracture. If she could put it into words, did that make it so? How could she and Everett rediscover the closeness they'd shared? Was she simply supposed to accept the distance between them as inevitable and move on? She shook her head, stubbornness stiffening her spine.

"It was because of his scars—I'm sure of it. You know how he always pulls his hat lower or brings his hand up to hide his face?" She raised her hand and covered the right side of her own face, imitating Everett's habit. "Every time he does that, it breaks my heart. Why can't he see that his scars aren't important? Not to God, and not to—"

One corner of Tessa's mouth tipped up. "Not to you? So was I right? Are you in love with him?"

Oh, how she wanted to shout yes—yes, she was in love with Everett. Instead she looked away. "It doesn't matter. I've ruined everything."

Tessa gave a soft snort. "How do you figure that?"

"Because I did the exact opposite of what I told Everett he should do." She tipped her head back and slid her eyes shut. "He and I talked about trust one evening, and I said how people should wait on God and let Him lead in situations that are too difficult to handle." She leaned forward and popped her eyes open again. "So what did I do? Things weren't going the way I wanted, so I barged ahead and took matters into my own hands."

She stood again and began to pace, spilling out the story of her visit to the freight office and her argument with Everett. "We haven't seen each other for more than a week. He's cut off our friendship. He doesn't want anything to do with me, and he thinks I'm foolish."

Tessa rose and crossed the room, slipping an arm around Tillie. "You still haven't answered my question. Are you in love with him?"

Her friend's tender prodding released her hold on her emotions, and the tears began to flow. She nodded. "But it doesn't matter what I feel. Everett has pushed me toward Ben and shut me out." She wiped the moisture from her face.

"Pushed you toward Ben? What do you mean?"

Tillie sighed. "Ben asked me to the picnic, and Everett kept telling me I should go with him. All I wanted to do was make Everett see that his scars don't change the man he is. But I've made such a mess of things. Why didn't I wait on God?"

ஜ

Everett handed his father the letter from Grandfather's attorney and watched as he read it. The empty mercantile gave them a private moment to discuss the surprise Everett had received in the mail. "The last thing I expected was an offer from one of Grandfather's former business constituents."

His father laid the missive on the counter and scrunched his thick eyebrows together. "After the estate was settled and the creditors paid off, I assumed you'd never hear from any of those people again." He played with one end of his mustache. "I'm guessing this man respected the way you handled the settlement, since he says he's"—Father glanced down at the paper and ran his finger across one of the inked lines—"'looking for a dependable man of integrity to manage his financial interests.'" He blew out a soft sigh. "Have you decided what you're going to do?"

Everett shook his head. "Grandfather's attorney is a very trustworthy man, so I don't doubt the validity of the offer." He ran his hand through his hair. "If I'd received this letter last year, I wouldn't have hesitated to respond in the affirmative."

Father pulled the pencil from behind his ear. "The salary this man is proposing would certainly allow you to live quite comfortably."

If Everett had learned anything over the past year, it was that money wasn't everything. "I agree the offer is rather lucrative, but the money isn't that important." He picked up the letter and reread the description of everything the job entailed: overseeing accounts and expenditures, and keeping precise records, much like a comptroller. "The thing that attracts me most is having little contact with people other than the owner of the company. This is a job I could do behind a closed door."

The furrow between his father's brows deepened. "Is that truly what you want?"

Everett hated the indecision that lifted his shoulders in an uncertain shrug. "In the past few months, I've established myself as a businessman, and people seem to appreciate the service I provide. But now. . ."

His father didn't press him to finish his thought. The elder Behr's insightful eyes fastened on him. The growing bond between them coaxed Everett to allow transparency.

"When I first arrived in Willow Creek, I couldn't imagine myself living here. But after the fire. . .and the scars. . .I couldn't imagine going back to live in Baltimore, looking the way I do. Life in Willow Creek is simple. I thought I no longer had the choice of hoping for anything more."

A hint of sorrow clouded his father's eyes. "I want to see you happy, son, but I'd be less than honest if I didn't express my desire for you to stay in Willow Creek." Father stroked his whiskered chin. "What about your business? Do you think you could find a buyer?"

Everett shrugged. "I might talk to Ben about it."

"Does Ben have the capital?"

"I doubt it, but we could draw up an agreement whereby he could send me payments." He steeled himself against the pain that clawed at him. If Ben bought the freight operation, he'd have the means to support Tillie comfortably.

His father cleared his throat. "Is there another reason you're considering this offer? Does this have anything to do with Tillie?"

Everett thought his friendship with Tillie a healthy thing until his feelings toward her changed. Now he knew better. Since Tillie had finally taken his advice and accepted Ben's attention, seeing the two of them together was far more painful than he'd anticipated. At least if he moved back to Baltimore, he wouldn't have to watch Tillie being courted by another man. His father had seen through the smoke and nailed the real reason the Baltimore offer was so tempting.

"I'd like your opinion, Father."

No smile tweaked his father's mustache. "Son, please don't make up your mind yet. Pray about this. God will never start something in your life that He doesn't intend to finish." He squeezed his son's shoulder. "You know I want you to stay, but *you* must weigh the reasons you're considering this move. My opinion isn't the one that counts."

Everett's fingers itched to take up paper and pen and reply to the attorney's letter, but Father's advice was wise. It had to be for the right reasons. He folded the letter and tucked it into his pocket. Before he could accept this offer, he needed to spend some time in serious thought. . .and prayer.

❧

Everett wrestled for three days trying to compose a reply to the letter, only to crumple countless pages of stationery. During his time of prayer, he only heard one word from God: *"Wait."*

With Ben out on a delivery, Everett had to keep the door to his inner office open so he'd hear if a customer came in. He bent his head over the invoices on his desk and tried to concentrate on the figures, but the letter in his desk drawer fought for his attention.

The outside door opened, and Everett glanced up. A gust of wind accompanied a gentleman into the outer office, and from his vantage point in the shadowed inner office, Everett recognized Tillie's father. He rose from behind his desk and stepped to the doorway, his hand jerking up and then hesitating. Would Mr. O'Dell find his maneuver to conceal his scars offensive? He dropped his hand to his side.

"Good afternoon, sir. You're Mr. O'Dell, are you not?"

The Irishman removed his hat and raised his chin a bit, exposing his own facial scar to the light pouring in from the open door. "That I am, young fella."

While Everett could detect a lilt in Tillie's speech from time to time, Mr. O'Dell's brogue was much more pronounced. He could see where Tillie got her green eyes. If he didn't miss his guess, he was about to find out where she got her stubbornness as well.

Everett stepped into the front portion of the office. "What can I do for you, Mr. O'Dell?"

The man leveled a look at Everett that he could have sworn went all the way through to his back collar button. "Thought I'd see if you had time for a wee chat." Without waiting for Everett's reply, O'Dell continued, "I suppose my Matilda has told you that I love tellin' stories. Well, Mr. Behr, I have a story I'd like to tell ye."

It sounded more like a command than an invitation, and Everett bristled slightly. He doubted telling Mr. O'Dell that he didn't have time for stories would win him any points from the man. He dragged his desk chair from the inner office and offered O'Dell the seat. Tillie's father tossed his hat on the work counter and sat.

"A long time ago, a wee lass was born to a wretched man and his dear wife. The rogue wasn't worthy of such a sweet, beautiful baby girl child, but God saw fit to bless him anyways. One day, God took hold of this scurvy rascal and shook him so that he could finally see what a heathen he was. He told God he wanted to change his despicable ways and not hurt those he loved anymore, and God changed him. From that day on, that sweet little girl became the pride and joy of the man's life." O'Dell paused for a moment to clear his throat.

Tillie had already told him about her father's past, so it wasn't hard to figure out O'Dell was talking about himself. But why did the man think it necessary to tell Everett?

O'Dell placed both hands on his knees and continued his story. "One day, this man—*whist*—he turned around, and his baby girl was grown. 'When did this happen?' says he. Ah, but the man knows because he's watched his girl growin' into a beautiful young woman."

Tillie's father didn't have to remind him what a beautiful young woman she was. He spent his days and most of his nights trying to forget that very fact.

Mr. O'Dell held his chin between his thumb and forefinger and looked off to the side as though Tillie were standing there. "He's watched her so closely, mind you, that he knows every little thing about her—her laughin' and her cares, her wishin' and her hopin'. And the man knows when she's glowin' inside with joy and when her heart is breakin'—even though, the girl, she tries so hard to hide her woeful face from her da. She takes long walks all alone so she can do her cryin' in secret. But her da knows." O'Dell leaned forward and narrowed his eyes at Everett. "And this da wants to know what you did to make his baby girl cry."

The man could not have inflicted more pain if he'd run Everett through with a blade. He dipped his head and closed his eyes for a moment, trying to erase the picture O'Dell's story had painted in his mind.

"Mr. O'Dell, I hope you can believe me when I tell you it was never my intention to hurt Tillie. On the contrary, I was trying to spare her." He shook his head and raised his hand to run his fingertips over his scars. How could he tell this man who bore scars himself the real reason why he decided to stop seeing his daughter? "Mr. O'Dell. . .I couldn't. . . Tillie deserves better than me."

O'Dell's eyebrows arched. "Does she now? She told you that, did she?"

"Well, no, she would never. . . That's why I knew it was up to me. She's too tenderhearted." He stared down at his shoes, his stomach twisting into a knot. "Doesn't it bother you when people stare or when you see pity or repulsion in their eyes?"

"Are ye tryin' to tell me my Matilda pities you?"

Everett jerked his head up to meet Mr. O'Dell's steely gaze. "No! No, she doesn't. But other people do, and I couldn't ask Tillie to endure a lifetime of that. I'm sorry if that offends you, Mr. O'Dell, but I love your daughter too much to put her through that."

The moment the words blurted from his lips, Everett couldn't believe he'd spoken them. Fire rose up from his belly, searing his face almost as hot as the flames that had scarred him. He clamped his teeth together to prevent any more words from escaping.

Mr. O'Dell crossed one leg over the other. "So that's the way of it." The man angled his head and fixed his eyes on the trail the flames had made across Everett's face and neck. "Mm-hmm."

Everett fought to keep the grimace off his face under the man's scrutiny. It seemed O'Dell's eyes combed over every inch of his face.

Once his inspection was complete, O'Dell leaned back in the chair again. "I'm havin' a hard time understandin' exactly what 'tis you don't want to put my Matilda through."

Every reason, every argument Everett could employ would be an insult to the man sitting before him. His mind fought to put words into a coherent defense. "It's different for me than it was for you. You were already married and had children. You didn't have a choice. I do, and I choose to not hurt Tillie."

"It's a wee bit late for that way o' thinkin'. My Matilda is already hurtin'."

Mr. O'Dell's expression softened. "Son, God won't never leave ye alone, in your joy nor in your troubles. That don't mean God will take your scars away, and I'm thinkin' the Almighty has a bit of work to do on you still. But don't be closin' the door on a blessin' He's tryin' to give ye."

Everett nodded mutely. He leaned his elbows on the work counter and rested his forehead in his hands. "A couple of weeks ago, I gave considerable thought to asking Tillie to the harvest picnic. I'd just about made up my mind, but. . ."

He could hear Mr. O'Dell shifting in the squeaky desk chair. "I'm put in mind of another story. There was these five frogs sittin' on a log. Four of 'em decided to jump off. So how many frogs was sittin' on the log?"

Everett had about had his fill of Irish stories, but respect dictated courtesy. "One?"

The man rose from the chair and clapped him on the back. "Why, there's still five frogs sittin' on the log. There's a difference between decidin' and doin'." O'Dell patted his shoulder. "Son, don't be runnin' from what God is tryin' to do in your life. The blessin's He gives us each day are the blessin's we need the most."

Chapter 12

"Why did I even come here today?"

Even as he muttered the question to himself, Everett knew there were two answers, and neither of them had anything to do with satisfying his appetite. A makeshift table, constructed of wide planks the men had laid across several sawhorses, contained a scrumptious array of food that would tempt any normal man. From the safety of the shadowy cedars, Everett watched the women of the congregation load the tables to groaning, but the turmoil in his stomach left little room for food.

He'd finally given in to his father and Pearl and agreed to attend with them so they would stop pestering him. Understanding their good intentions soothed his irritation somewhat, but it wouldn't make the day any easier. Thankfully, they'd chosen a spot under the wide cedar boughs at the far edge of the churchyard, where he could distance himself from the activity.

The other reason was harder to define but no less compelling. It made no sense. Part of him wanted to see Tillie, even if it was from a distance. He wanted to see her smile, hear her laugh, and know she was enjoying herself. Satisfying himself that she was happy compelled him to scan the gathering of people, but the prospect of seeing her with Ben stirred his stomach into a whirlpool. Dread ate a hole in his heart.

From his vantage point, he found the pair making their selections at the food table, Ben's heaping plate dwarfing Tillie's half-empty one. He escorted her to a blanket spread across the way, not far from the one where her parents sat. She wore her light green dress, the one that made her eyes look like pure green crystal, and something in his chest rolled over.

"This is the way it's supposed to be. She'll be happier with someone like Ben."

"Did you say something, son?" His father and Pearl returned to the blanket with quizzical expressions and three plates laden with all manner of delicacies.

"I was just talking to myself." He started to scoot farther back under the low-hanging cedar boughs, but Pearl passed a filled plate to him.

She gave him a motherly smile. "I hope you don't mind me bringing you a plate. I was afraid if I didn't, you wouldn't eat."

His father's wife was developing an uncanny insight into his thoughts and feelings, but he didn't resent it. Instead he found it comforting that she cared. He reached out to accept the plate and smiled his thanks to Pearl.

He took a few bites, forcing himself to swallow. The ladies of the church always brought their best culinary efforts to these affairs, but at the moment everything he put into his mouth tasted like sawdust. Only vaguely aware of the conversation between his father and Pearl, Everett kept his eyes trained on Tillie and Ben. Tillie smiled and nodded from time to time. Ben seemed to be doing most of the talking. Was it his imagination, or was Tillie looking out over the crowd of folks? Was she looking for him? He shifted his position, precariously balancing his plate, until he felt certain the shadow of the cedar boughs concealed him.

"How's business, son?"

Everett pulled his attention back to his father and stepmother. "Fine. We're staying busy." He managed a stiff smile and bit into a piece of fried chicken.

Pearl poured water from an earthenware jug into a tin cup and held it out to him. "Have you thought any more about the letter from the attorney?"

Everett nodded his thanks and accepted the cup. "I've done a lot of thinking."

Pearl's gaze lifted across the churchyard. Everett followed her line of sight, and his eyes landed on Tillie and Ben. What were they saying to each other? Tillie reached up and tucked a tendril of hair behind her ear, and angst lurched in Everett's stomach. He looked down at the drumstick in his hand, unsure of what he might do if Ben reached over to touch those honeyed strands.

Stop it. It's out of your hands. Let her go. Had he stayed long enough to appease his father and stepmother? If he got up to leave now, would people stare?

"Everett?"

He looked up from the partially eaten chicken leg he was studying. His father's expression indicated Everett had missed something. "Yes?"

Everett read compassion in the elder Behr's eyes. He suspected Father understood the turmoil swirling in his middle.

"I noticed you had a visitor the other day."

"I did?"

"Timothy O'Dell?"

"Oh." The Irishman's story of Tillie going off by herself to cry seared him again. "Yes, he stopped by."

When Everett didn't say more, and the silence was broken only by the hum of nearby voices and the laughter of playing children, Pearl rose from the blanket. "I think I'll go and cut some pieces of gingerbread cake for us."

Father gave her a soft smile and a nod, and another ache twisted in Everett's chest at the unspoken communication shared between their two hearts. There were times during his twilight walks with Tillie that even though the encroaching darkness prevented him from seeing her face clearly, he knew what she was thinking by the way she tipped her head or twirled a wildflower between her thumb and forefinger, or even by the way she stepped. What he had with her was something so special he couldn't put a name to it, and he was relinquishing it—just opening his hand and allowing it to fly away like a butterfly discovering it had wings.

His father cleared his throat. "This is none of my business, and you have every right to tell me to mind my own affairs, but I have a feeling Timothy didn't come calling with shipping freight in mind." The look he gave Everett was one of speculation.

"No." Everett blew out a pent-up breath through pursed lips. "He didn't." With one finger he traced the edge of the scar along his face. "He wanted to know what I did to make his daughter cry."

"Ah." His father lifted his bushy eyebrows but didn't ask his son to elaborate.

"Father, you must understand, I'm doing this *for* Tillie. She deserves someone better than me." He leaned back on his elbows and closed his eyes. "I'm not the one for her."

A snort came from his father's direction. "How did you come to that conclusion?"

He willed himself not to shoot back an angry retort. Taking in a calming breath, he pushed himself upright again. "Father, I will not subject Tillie to the humiliation of being seen with me. Why do you think we met and walked together in the evening? Nobody is standing around gawking at that time of night. What would people think if they saw her with me?"

Father stroked his mustache with his finger and shook his head. "I must say, son, I never thought I'd hear you insult Tillie like that."

Everett jerked forward. "Insult her? What are you talking about? I'd never insult Tillie."

His father shrugged. "That's what it sounded like to me. You're certainly not giving her much credit. Tillie O'Dell isn't a shallow person, nor is she hypocritical. If she extended friendship and affection to you, you can rest assured it came from her heart. Don't you think you owe it to her to let her make up her own mind on the matter?"

Everett started to shake his head at his father's statement, but at that moment a commotion arose across the yard. He craned his neck to see around the cedar boughs. Tessa and Gideon Maxwell ran from one family's blanket to the next, calling their daughter's name.

"Susan! *Susan!*"

Several others joined the worried parents in searching around the immediate area and asking their children if they'd seen the little girl. They looked under the food table and the dessert table, and one of the women went to check the outhouse. Within a few minutes, every person was on their feet looking over the churchyard, calling the child's name.

Everett stood, his gaze fixed on Tillie as she crossed the yard to her friend. She took Tessa in her arms and held her tight, murmuring something into Tessa's ear. Tessa nodded and closed her eyes, her chest rising and falling with a deep breath.

Putting his abhorrence of being seen in public aside, Everett strode over to Gideon, who gathered Tessa in his arms. Tillie looked up as Everett approached. He locked eyes with her for a moment before turning to Gideon and waving Pastor Witherspoon over.

"Pastor, can you gather everyone together?"

The preacher nodded and hastily climbed the church steps and clanged the church bell. Everett grabbed Gideon's arm.

"She can't have gone far. We'll find her." He took the church steps two at a time to stand beside the preacher on the top step. Hiding his face didn't seem important with a child in danger.

"Folks, let's pair up and go in different directions. Some of you search in and around the church building. Others go over the yard again, and don't forget to check around the back. Still others spread out a little. A couple of teams should go down toward the creek. Don't leave a square foot unsearched. Pull back any low-hanging branches, and look in the bushes and underbrush. She might think she's playing hide-and-seek. Since she's so small—she's only

. . .three?"—he looked to Gideon for confirmation—"she can fit into places we can't. When Susan is found, the church bell will be rung."

As people teamed up and set off in specific directions, Tillie gave Tessa another hug. "We'll find her. You need to stay right here, because the first person she's going to want is you. Whoever finds her will bring her here."

Indecision tore through Tessa's eyes. Tillie knew she wanted to be out searching for her daughter but also saw the wisdom of the admonition. Tessa nodded, tears slipping down her face.

Tillie poured her friend a cup of coffee and guided her to the church steps to sit. She looked over her shoulder for Ben and found him approaching. She gave him a timorous smile. "Why don't we look over by the mill."

Ben reached out and took Tillie's hand. "Why don't you and Everett pair up and look around the mill? I'll go check the brush behind the church."

Tillie blinked in surprise, and Ben released a small chuckle. "It's all right, Tillie. I can see in the way you look at him there's something special there. I'd sure like it if you looked at me that way, but I don't reckon that will happen as long as Everett is around." He squeezed her hand before releasing it. "You won't find a finer man than Everett Behr."

Hearing such praise coming from Everett's employee made her heart skip. "I hope I didn't—"

"You didn't. I knew all along he had your heart in his pocket."

Yes, he did, but what did it matter now? Everett had made it clear he had no intention of continuing their friendship. She gave Ben a parting smile and set off toward the mill. *"Why don't you and Everett pair up?"* She sighed and set her mind to finding little Susan.

Paying particular attention to the thick reeds and cattails along the side of the mill, Tillie pulled back every bit of growth at the edge of the stream that fed the mill's waterwheel. Susan's name echoed through the trees as the other searchers covered the area.

"Please, Lord, help us find her. Set your angels around her, keep her safe, and lead one of us to her."

"Amen."

Startled, she turned abruptly to find Everett behind her. Her breath caught in her throat, and she bit down on her lip. Everett had already distanced himself from her because she hadn't controlled her tongue.

"I've been saying the same prayer." He glanced over his shoulder at the teams of other folks looking for the child. "If she isn't found in a little while, we'll have to organize a more widespread search."

Tillie nodded mutely. She didn't want to think about the possibility of Susan not being found. She couldn't imagine the distress poor Tessa was experiencing.

She stood there, silently gazing at Everett, wanting her feet to move and return to searching, but unable to force them into motion. Finally, she found her voice, even if it did come out as a whisper. "Thank you for helping."

He lifted one shoulder and gave a slight nod, his lips pressed together. "Look, maybe you should go and stay with Tessa," he said, gesturing toward the church. "Gideon is out looking, and I think Tessa's by herself. She might need a friend."

Tillie's heart agonized, as much for Everett as for Tessa. "We all need a friend, Everett." She fixed her eyes on his face, and he didn't turn away. Did he understand the depth of her statement? Could she communicate with a look what she longed to tell him?

He held out his hand, and she transferred her gaze from his face to his fingertips. She slowly lifted her hand and placed it in his. The magic of his touch sent shivers through her.

He closed his hand around hers and steadied her as she stepped up the short embankment. When her feet were on level ground again, he dropped her hand, and she felt a pang of loneliness. She held back the sigh that wanted to escape.

"I haven't checked the other side of the mill yet."

Everett nodded. "I'll look there. Are you going to stay with Tessa?"

She glanced in the direction of the church and shook her head. "Miss Pearl is keeping Tessa busy while the rest of us search, so she's not alone." She started toward the little footbridge that led to the opposite bank of the stream and the stairs to the millhouse. "I'm going to keep searching."

Everett fell into step beside her, turning his head from side to side, leaning down to part the cattails. "Do you know what Susan was doing before Tessa discovered she was missing?"

Tillie stopped. "Tessa said she'd laid Susan down on their blanket for a nap and thought she was asleep."

A puzzled look crossed his face. "She could sleep with all the talking and laughing, and with the other kids playing and shouting?"

Tillie smiled at his lack of knowledge of children. "Most little ones can sleep through just about anything if they're tired enough." She sobered. "Tessa would never leave her alone if she thought Susan might wander off. She said she had only stepped away from their blanket for a few minutes to speak with Mrs. Witherspoon. When she went back to check on Susan, she was gone."

Everett's brows lowered into a frown. "Come on. Let's keep looking." He climbed the millhouse stairs while Tillie covered every foot of space under the stairs and behind the mill.

"Susan!" *Oh Lord, please help us. Where is that child?*

❧

Despite the crisp autumn day, sweat collected on Tillie's forehead and trickled down her back after an hour of searching every conceivable place within a few hundred yards of the church. Her throat was growing hoarse from calling Susan's name.

The church bell clanged twice, and her heart leaped. *Oh praise God, she's been found!*

She picked up her skirts and ran but stopped short in the churchyard when she caught sight of a distraught Tessa standing by the steps with her arms wrapped around herself. Pastor Witherspoon motioned with his hand and called out for everyone to gather round.

"Folks, here's what we're going to do. The women will continue searching here in town, and the men are going to spread out and cover the hills and the woods. When Susan is found, either ring the church bell, or you men fire three shots. Let's step over to the table here and map out where all you fellows will go."

The women had cleaned off a section of the food table, and the makeshift structure now held a large coffeepot, cups, and the picnic leftovers, as if preparations for a long ordeal were being made. The ominous implication made Tillie shudder.

Pastor Witherspoon climbed down the stairs and paused just long enough to place a comforting hand on Tessa's shoulder.

Tillie hurried over to Tessa. She slipped her arms around her friend and held her without speaking. Tessa's shoulders began to shake.

"Oh Tillie, where could she be?" Tessa broke into sobs. "I just want my little girl back. We were going to take her out to the Hamiltons' ranch tomorrow so she could pick out a lamb. She's talked of nothing else for the past week." She squeezed her eyes shut.

Tillie remembered Susan chattering nonstop about the "baby wams." She gripped Tessa's shoulders. "Tessa, by this time tomorrow you're going to be watching Susan playing with her pet lamb."

Some of the men headed out toward their assigned area, and Tillie looked to see which direction Everett was taking. Instead of tramping toward the hills, he was standing only a few feet away, looking at her and Tessa.

At the sound of galloping hooves, Tillie looked past Everett to see a rider coming in and recognized him as one of the hands from a nearby ranch. The man pulled his lathered mount to a stop in a cloud of dust, and several of the men, including the man's boss, ran over to hear what he had to say.

The young man dismounted and walked up to his boss. "We was out lookin' for strays, and we saw some buzzards circling overhead, so I went to check on it. There was a fresh kill—a young heifer." The ranch hand pulled off his hat and dragged his sleeve across his forehead. "It was a wolf kill. Just thought you'd want to know."

"Wolves?" One of the men sounded as though he didn't believe the report. "Why, there ain't been any wolves sighted around here for more'n a decade."

The rider nodded his head vehemently. "It was wolves all right. No mistakin' those tracks."

Chapter 13

N *oo!"* Tessa's mournful wail pierced the air. *"Susan. . ."*
Tillie wrapped her arms around her rib cage and swallowed back
the nausea that rose in her throat. She watched helplessly as Gideon
crushed his wife to his chest for a long moment before leading her out of
earshot of all the talk of wolves. A cold chill ran through Tillie. An image of
horror tried to manifest itself in her mind, and she slammed the door on it,
refusing to allow such ghastly thoughts.

Several of the men listening to the rider's report expressed skepticism. The
young man's boss squinted at his employee. "You're sure it was wolves?"

The ranch hand nodded. "Yes sir, I'm sure. The tracks resemble those of
a dog, but about twice as big. Couldn't tell for certain, but I'm figurin' there
were at least three or four, maybe more. You want to send some riders out to
track them?"

The owner of the ranch scowled and told his employee about the missing
child, instructing him to send the other hands out to search.

The murmur of voices around Tillie grew to a rumble as the level of
urgency built. She tore her eyes away from the man who had delivered the
grim news and turned around to look for Tessa and Gideon. They stood
on the far side of the church, Tessa weeping against Gideon's shoulder. She
hurried over and put her arm around Tessa, giving her shoulders a squeeze.
Together, she and Tessa watched as Gideon strode to their wagon and
pulled a rifle out from under the seat.

Old Cully stamped up the church steps and yanked on the bell rope. He
cupped his hands around his mouth and hollered. "Some o' you men came
to the picnic with your wagon and team. Iffen you need a saddle horse for
searchin', come by the livery, and I'll loan you a mount. No charge."

"Matilda."

Tillie turned to find Da beside her. "I'm taking your ma and the younger
ones home. Then I'm headin' out to search the area between our place and
town. Phillip is partnerin' with Hubert Behr. Are you comin' home?"

361

Tillie gave Da a quick hug. "No, Da. I want to do what I can to help."

"How will ye be gettin' home?"

Tillie glanced from left to right and took her da's arm, stepping away from Tessa for a moment. "I'm sure I can find a ride from someone, but I might stay in town with the Witherspoons. I want to be close by, in case. . ."

Da patted her shoulder. "All right, daughter." He strode off, calling to her younger siblings to get in the wagon.

Ben Kiefer joined with Fletcher Hamilton, the owner of the sheep ranch, and headed south of the creek. A few of the other men paired up, and others set out alone, but all shared a common goal.

Gideon returned, rifle in hand. Tillie stepped back while he embraced Tessa. "We're going to find her. Hold on to that thought."

Tillie cast her gaze across the churchyard, squinting in the afternoon sun, seeking Everett. She located him standing by her family's wagon, talking with Da. Everett gestured to the northwest, and Da pointed toward the woods and then swept his hand in a southwesterly direction. Da gave Everett a nod and clapped him on the back before climbing into the wagon to drive his family home.

When Everett turned and his eyes met hers, she saw a tapestry of fear, compassion, and raw determination. A fleeting instinct told her his expression reflected the same emotions he'd felt before he entered the burning boarding-house. He appeared to have forgotten about hiding his face.

She watched as Everett sent a pointed stare at Tessa, who wept in her husband's arms, as though he was trying to set in his mind the picture of this heart-sore mother. Gideon kissed his wife and set off at a run toward the livery.

Tillie closed the distance between her and Everett. He met her halfway and snagged her hand. "It's good she has a friend like you by her side while she waits for word. Keep telling her that we won't quit until we find her daughter."

Tillie drew her forehead into pinched furrows. When Everett released her hand, she caught his sleeve. "I'm going with you."

His eyes widened, and then a scowl darkened his expression. He grabbed her shoulders and gave her a little shake. "Oh no you're not."

She opened her mouth to protest, but he laid his finger over her lips. His voice strengthened, and it was clear he would brook no argument. "You absolutely will not go out there. You will stay here—do you hear me?"

She'd never before witnessed in Everett the fervor she now saw in him. She stiffened her jaw and pressed her lips into a tight line. "Now you listen to me. Tessa is my best friend. I owe it to her to do everything I can to help find Susan. Standing around here twiddling my thumbs isn't going to find that little girl."

A flicker of something foreign flashed through Everett's eyes. It didn't stay there long enough for her to put a name on it, but if she had to guess, she'd have to call it a glimmer of panic.

He dropped his hands from her shoulders and took a step backward. Running his hand through his hair, he nailed her in place with his unblinking stare. He lowered the volume of his voice but not the resolute intensity. "Tillie, I don't have time to explain all the reasons it's so important that you remain here. But please listen to me. I need to be 100 percent focused on finding Susan, not worrying about your safety. I can't force you to stay, but I am imploring you. Please, Tillie." His voice cracked. "Please stay here so I'll know you're safe."

It was the first time he'd ever asked anything of her. All the times they'd walked in the shadow of the willows, not once had he stepped beyond the refuge of the defensive wall he'd erected. She'd gotten the impression he felt that allowing vulnerability was unthinkable. Yet here he stood, pleading with her to comply with his request. Held captive by the heartfelt ring in his voice and the depth of his mahogany eyes, Tillie tried to remember how to draw a breath. She gave him a slight nod.

His chest fell with a relieved sigh, and his voice took on a gentler pitch. "Take care of Tessa. Maybe you and a couple of the other ladies could put some of the picnic leftovers together for the men if they return hungry. We'll need lots of coffee." He glanced toward the west. "There's probably about three hours of daylight left. If we don't find Susan by sunset, we're going to need lanterns." He caught her hand and gave it a squeeze. "And I need you to pray."

Tillie nodded numbly. The ache in her heart for Tessa and Gideon, and the foreboding she felt over Susan's disappearance, paled for an instant. Making sure Everett knew he could depend on her became primary in her mind.

"I will—you can be sure of that."

A shadow of a smile relaxed some of the hard lines of Everett's face. "Thank you." He scanned the wooded hills to the north and west. "She's such a little girl. It doesn't seem possible she could have gone farther than we've already looked." He returned his gaze to Tillie. "You don't suppose she's hiding, do you? Might she think this is a game, like hide-and-seek?"

Tillie's chest tightened, and she shook her head. "She can sometimes be a stubborn little thing, but she wouldn't hide for this long."

Everett blew out a hard breath. "Ring the bell if there's any news." He pulled his shoulders straight and tugged on the brim of his hat. He sent her a look she dared not interpret and headed into the woods.

Tillie followed him with her eyes until the sun-dappled autumn foliage swallowed him. She longed to be beside him, tramping through the woods, partnering with him. But this was no leisurely stroll. The mission before him, before all the searchers, could end in either joy or sorrow.

"Please, dear Lord, protect Susan wherever she is, and lead one of the men to her." She wiped away a tear. "And keep Everett from harm, Lord. Bring him back—" She started to ask God to bring him safely back to her, but reality insisted that he wasn't hers. Biting back the words wouldn't fool God. Her heavenly Father already knew her heart. "I love him, Lord. Please keep him safe."

❧

Everett paused beside the same small stream he'd found last Sunday morning when he'd hiked through the wooded hills. Scooping a few handfuls of water to his lips, he relished the coldness as the moisture soothed his throat. He cast another glance at the position of the sun and whispered a prayer that they'd find the child soon.

Instead of following the stream, he pushed deeper into the woods. The underbrush was thicker than he'd anticipated, slowing his progress. Every fifty yards or so, he called out Susan's name and paused briefly to listen.

"It's simply not possible for a child of her age to have come this far." Or was it? What if she was following something, like a dog or a butterfly? How far would she go before she couldn't find her way back to the church? His limited knowledge of small children and their tendencies was a hindrance, but not if he trusted God to direct his steps.

"Lead me, Lord. Where is she?" A recollection prodded him. Hadn't he prayed a similar prayer as he crawled through the burning boardinghouse trying to find his father and Pearl? God had answered that prayer. Surely He'd answer this one.

Cupping his hands around his mouth, he called again, "Susan."

He plodded on, continuing to call her name and praying he would hear either the church bell echoing in the distance or three gunshots. The only sound accompanying him on his trek was the breeze rustling the leaves. If he found the little girl, he'd not be able to alert the others. He didn't own a gun, and looking for one to borrow would have taken precious time he didn't want to waste. Now he questioned the wisdom of hiking through the woods unarmed with the report of wolves in the area, but it was too late to turn back now.

Thorny brush snagged his pant legs and tore a hole in his sleeve as he pushed through a thick patch of blackberry canes. No berries remained on the vines this late in the season, reminding Everett that little Susan would likely be hungry and thirsty by now. But he guessed the first thing she'd want would be her mama.

"That's it!" He thrust out one hand, palm upturned. "I have to try to think like a three-year-old. What would she be looking for? She had to have a reason for wandering off."

He leaned against a birch tree and rested for a minute, rolling the questions over in his mind. What would be so fascinating to a three-year-old that it could entice her to leave her mother?

Daylight was slipping away. Through the trees he could see a slice of the sun sinking lower toward the western hills. This was the time of day he'd watched out the office window, waiting for the sun to hide its face so he could venture out. He'd gotten good at estimating the amount of daylight that remained. How many evenings had he impatiently wished the sun would hurry and disappear? Now he wished he could pray like Joshua did in the Old Testament for the sun to stand still. The fiery yellow sphere continued its downward slide. Once the sun set, finding the child would be nearly impossible, humanly speaking. Everett rejected that idea. Nothing was impossible when God moved in His miraculous way.

"Susan!" He pushed away from the tree trunk and pressed on. "Help me, Lord. Lead me. I don't know if making the sun stand still is in Your plans, but Lord, we need a miracle to find that little girl."

A fat squirrel chattered at him from a cottonwood tree. Everett barely gave the creature a passing glance, but something seemed to tug at him. Just what, he couldn't be sure, but he changed course and followed his instinct. The squirrel continued to scold him, and he wondered if Susan might find a squirrel intriguing enough to be lured into the woods. Most children loved animals, didn't they?

Think like a three-year-old. A thought grabbed hold of him. When Tillie was comforting Tessa, the child's mother had said something about. . .

"Lambs. She wanted to go see the baby lambs." He turned a slow, full circle. What direction would the child go if she thought she could find the lambs? The three-year-old wouldn't know how to find the ranch, but that didn't mean she wouldn't try. She'd probably pick the easiest terrain—flat instead of hilly, grass instead of thick underbrush. If she'd been to the ranch before, would she remember if there were trees or grassy hills along the way? He altered directions toward the edge of the woods.

Just as he started forward again, a rifle shot, fired some distance away, echoed. Everett held his breath, waiting for the second and third shots. *Please, God.* No accompanying shots sounded. A single gunshot. Whoever had fired it was likely shooting *at* something.

"Susan!" His throat was nearly raw from yelling. "Lord, please show me what direction she took." He tramped another fifty yards through the brush and saplings, his eyes scanning from left to right and his ears inclined, listening for a child's voice.

Jagged, splintered wood stuck out of a stump from a fallen tree to his right. Something clinging to one of the spearlike shafts of broken bole caught his eye. At first he thought it to be a common yellow butterfly. But this butterfly was very still. He climbed over the trunk of the tree lying in the midst of the underbrush. When he got closer, he saw it wasn't a butterfly at all. It was a small bit of yellow cloth.

He grabbed the bit of material and examined it, and then he raised his eyes to sweep the area. "Susan! Susan, can you hear me?"

Was the child wearing a yellow dress today at the picnic? He had no idea and couldn't remember if anyone had mentioned how the little girl was dressed. Holding the scrap aloft, he entreated God once again.

"Lord, is this hers? Did she come this way?" He searched the area around the stump to see if he could find anything else to indicate Tessa and Gideon's daughter had passed by there.

The sun hovered at the horizon. It would soon be dusk—usually his favorite time of day. But not today. He whispered the name of Jesus to fend off pangs of despair. Over the past several months, he'd taken to singing whatever hymn he could recall from the previous Sunday to carry him through many difficult days. He racked his brain, trying to retrieve a hymn from his memory. Only one came to mind.

"Just as I am without one plea." He lifted his raspy voice, hoping Susan might hear and respond to the song.

Clutching the yellow scrap in his fingers, he pushed forward. The words of the song arrested his conscious thought. God, in His graciousness, hadn't refused to accept him, even with his past arrogance, deceit, and selfishness. God faithfully cleansed him of sin. But once redeemed, he'd refused to accept his own appearance, convinced he'd never be fit for polite company, and no woman would ever want to spend her life with him. How offensive his attitude must be to God.

"Lord, I'm sorry. I think I understand now. When I came to You just the way I was, You rescued me from my sinful self. But ever since then, I've hated my own reflection. You took me as I am. Now I choose to take me. . .just as I am." Instead of leaving a bitter taste, the notion of accepting himself, scars and all, was sweetly liberating. He slowed his steps and raised his eyes and his hands heavenward.

"Thank You, Lord." Resentment drained from him like water from a sieve. "Thank You."

The last sliver of sun was gone, and all that remained were the fading rays. He came to a small clearing and stopped, slowly scanning for some other indication that Susan had been there. An area of grass was matted flat, perhaps where a deer had lain down. Or a child.

"Susan!"

He listened. Nothing.

A huge orange moon was already rising in the darkening sky. "God, I won't be discouraged. You haven't brought me this far to abandon me. I trust You, Lord."

He judged direction by the waning light from the west. If he circled back toward town now, he could approach the church from a different angle and cover an area he'd not yet searched. Shadows deepened, and the air held a chill. Everett stopped to pull a thorny vine from his sleeve. A high-pitched wail carried on the shifting wind. Everett jerked his head up. Was it the cry of a child? He stood motionless, waiting to hear it again, to determine from which direction it came. When the eerie sound reached his ears once more, a shudder filled his being. It was the howl of a wolf.

Chapter 14

Poison darts of helplessness pierced Tillie's heart as the pastor's wife coaxed Tessa to the parsonage to rest for a while. How she wished there was something more she could do. Not having a child of her own, she could only imagine the searing ache attacking Tessa's heart. Determined to stay busy, she headed toward the long plank table, whispering repeated prayers for strength and courage.

Several ladies remained at the church while their husbands were out searching. Tillie joined them, offering sandwiches and coffee to the men who returned empty-handed but in need of a fresh horse. Regret pinched her. If only she hadn't promised Everett she'd stay put at the church. She knew this countryside far better than Everett did. Standing around handing out cups of coffee felt so. . . "Useless."

Pearl Behr slipped over and touched Tillie's shoulder. "Before Hubert left to go searching, he gave me the key to the mercantile and told me to take anything out of the storeroom that was needed. Would you mind coming along and helping me carry some lanterns and coal oil?"

Pearl's request sent an involuntary shiver down her spine as she glanced toward the west. The sun's fading rays set the sky afire with red and purple. The men would need lanterns soon. How she wished to hear three shots echoing across the hills. Nausea tightened her throat, but she nodded. "Of course."

Pearl patted her shoulder, and the two of them hurried off toward the mercantile. Tillie peered at Pearl's profile as they walked. "Tessa told me that you've been like a second mother to her."

The woman gave Tillie a tiny smile. "I suppose." Her voice sounded tight. "Little Susan is like the grandchild I never had." The distress that grew hour by hour showed in the deepened lines on Pearl's face, and Tillie's heart longed to offer comfort, but the words wouldn't form in the right order.

"I heard Cully say he was going to make some torches to put around the churchyard in case. . ." She bit back the words she didn't want to speak.

368

As they stepped up onto the boardwalk in front of the store, Tillie noted the lengthening shadows and the dipping temperature. Another whispered entreaty—part of her continuous prayer—winged toward the throne of heaven. While she appreciated Cully's thoughtfulness in supplying the torches, she prayed Susan would be found before darkness set in, and neither the torches nor the lanterns would be necessary.

Pearl slid the key into the lock and pushed the door open. "Hubert and your brother Phillip went east. He said they planned to go as far as Rock Creek and zigzag back through the hills."

Tillie frowned. "Rock Creek is almost two miles from here. Susan never could have gotten that far. She has to be somewhere close, somewhere we haven't looked." They paused for a moment to look at each other. "But where haven't we already looked?"

Pearl began pulling lanterns off the storeroom shelf and handing them to Tillie. "Some of the ladies got tired of waiting and went to retrace their steps over many of the places around town that have already been searched. Maybe someone will find her curled up asleep."

They each took as many lanterns as they could carry, along with a can of coal oil, and made their way back to the church. No rifle shots or the church bell ringing had called to them while on their errand. They arranged the lanterns on the plank table opposite the coffeepots.

Since Tessa was in Mrs. Witherspoon's capable hands, Tillie felt free to slip into the church for a solitary moment of prayer. Muted noises and voices from the churchyard followed her, but none carried the joyful excitement of good news.

The hours since Everett left had crawled by. She tried to fill the time, keeping her hands occupied with helpful tasks, but more important than brewing pots of coffee or making sandwiches was keeping her promise to Everett. The only thing he'd requested, other than for her to remain at the church, was for prayer, and she set her heart to honor his request. Intercession for Everett's protection and Susan's safe return flowed between her lips and heaven. The imploring tone of his voice and the memory of his face when he'd insisted she stay behind where she'd be safe brushed her senses. So much of their time together over the past months she'd spent looking at only his profile in the shadows—she'd never had the opportunity to look into the depth of his eyes. Most of the time he'd kept his heart as guarded as his countenance, but there were a few moments that had revealed brief glimpses into the things that molded Everett's character. Only on rare occasions had Everett shared anything of a more personal nature. Vulnerability wasn't something he allowed, and to finally see uncloaked emotion on his face had left her breathless.

She sank to her knees and leaned her elbows on a pew, holding her head in her hands. The moment she closed her eyes, images of Everett and Susan— and wolves—emerged in her mind.

"He's doing the same thing he did the day he ran into the burning boardinghouse, Lord. He's hidden his face for a year, and what drew him out from behind his defensive stronghold was hearing a child was in danger. It's like he's running into a burning building again, except this time he's tramping around in the woods and hills unarmed, with wolves in the area." Tears burned her eyes, and she swiped at her nose with her sleeve. "He's not thinking of himself at all. Lord, please keep him safe. He didn't even take a gun."

Her chest tightened. "Lord, of course my heart is burdened for Susan's safety and Tessa's anguish. But as always, I'm lifting Everett up to You. Everything I have ever felt for this man is magnified.

"You've heard my prayers asking You to put Everett and me together. I even ran ahead of You and tried to make it happen using my own selfish devices, because I wasn't willing to wait for You to reveal Your plan to me. Lord, that was wrong. Please forgive my impatience and impulsiveness. There are no secrets from You. You already know I love Everett, and I ask You now, if my love for him isn't Your will, then please remove this love from my heart. And if Everett doesn't love me, please give me the grace to accept it."

Tears welled and spilled over. Uttering the words, even to God, impacted her with such force it nearly knocked the breath from her. Rushing headlong into her own plans had ended in disaster. Waiting for God's plan to unfold stretched her trust further than she had believed possible.

"Dear God, my heart is in Your hands. You are everything I need. The longing of my heart is for Everett and me to be together, but even more than that I want to be obedient to You." She took a deep breath and swallowed hard. "You are my rock, Lord Jesus."

She dug in her pocket for her handkerchief and dabbed at her eyes and blew her nose. "Please be with Everett as he searches. Be with all the men, watch over them, and please, dear Lord, please let one of them find Susan soon. Prayer is the most important thing I can do. I'm sorry for feeling so impatient, wanting to do more."

Tillie continued in prayer, begging God for His mercy and protection for Susan, comfort for Tessa, and strength for the men searching. She opened her eyes and raised her head off the pew at which she was kneeling. The air had turned chilly, and the fading light that had accompanied her into the church was gone. She pushed away from the pew and rose from her knees. There were lanterns to fill.

❧

Everett tipped his head up and watched with appreciation as the moon slowly rose higher in the inky sky, gradually changing from orange to gold to bright white as it ascended. He couldn't remember ever seeing such a large, bright moon, bathing the countryside in silver. Tillie's father had said something about a harvest moon. Everett didn't know the difference between a regular moon and a harvest moon, but as he gazed across the illuminated landscape, he whispered his gratefulness to God for supplying just what he needed to pick his way through the darkness.

The underbrush gave way to meadow grass as he emerged from the woods. He hoped he would come across another stream or spring. Why hadn't he thought to bring a canteen with him? His throat was parched with thirst and raw from yelling Susan's name.

"If I'd used common sense, I'd have taken a few minutes to borrow a canteen and a gun." He shook his head at his foolish impulsiveness.

His feet throbbed and legs ached from hours of hiking, and weariness dogged him. Oh, how he'd love to lie down in the grass and indulge in blessed sleep. But the memory of the wolf howl he'd heard earlier continued to send chilling echoes through his mind. He pushed on.

A few clouds drifted lazily, occasionally obscuring the pale light. Everett paused, waiting for the spooky veil that slowed his progress to move away from the moon. Maybe he should take a few minutes to rest. No, the picture he'd burned into his mind of Susan's distraught mother wouldn't let him stop.

A few trees dotted the meadow, and many of them had shed much of their foliage. Drizzled with mottled moonlight, the branches created curious patterns overhead. The temperature had dropped rapidly once the sun disappeared, and the scent of frost piqued his awareness. It was unlikely Susan wore a coat, and he imagined the little tyke shivering in the cold.

Quiescence reigned over the landscape. Only an occasional breeze rattled the remaining leaves, but even the slight wafting made the air feel colder. At least when there was no wind, he could hear more clearly.

A rustling sound stopped him in his tracks. He turned his head in the direction from which he thought the noise had come, only to hear it again, this time coming from near the woods. The clouds chose that moment to draw their shroud over the moon, plunging him into near blackness. His heart pounded in his ears, and despite the chill in the air, beads of sweat popped out on his upper lip. He tried to hold his breath, but his lungs betrayed him by sucking in a raspy hiss.

Another crackling sound behind him, like stepping on fallen leaves, sent a shudder through him. It might simply be a raccoon or opossum. How did one tell the difference between the sounds made by a foraging animal and a stalking animal? He held his breath and listened hard, praying he wouldn't hear growling. It was impossible to calculate the size or weight of the animal by the rustle of grasses and leaves. The sound seemed to come from more than one direction. Was his mind playing tricks on him, or did the stillness of the cold night air alter the sound? There it was again, this time to his left.

What if it was Susan? Should he call out to her?

What if it isn't Susan? A drop of sweat ran down his neck into the collar of his shirt.

A slight breeze stirred, and an owl hooted from a nearby tree. An explosion of noise erupted from the grass. His heart seized with a jolt, and he instinctively threw his arms up in front of his face. Two or three animals bounded into the woods, the sound of their feet leaping through the brush growing fainter as they retreated. Deer, most likely. Everett's knees wobbled, and his stomach twisted with nausea. The breath he struggled to control moments earlier now came in great gulps. He bent at the waist and propped his hands on his knees.

"Thank You, God."

He waited until his pulse returned to almost normal and the moonlight once again befriended him before he straightened. The owl hooted again, and Everett squinted up through the tree branches. "I suppose you're amused by that." He sent an accusing glare into the trees limbs, and the owl replied with a series of doleful *whoo-whoos*.

The sound reminded Everett of the prayer he'd prayed a few weeks ago for God to make something beautiful of his life. *Something beautiful, beautiful. . .*

He pressed on through the meadow, moonlight and clouds creating a strange patchwork of silver and shadow. The owl's hoots followed him, floating on the still night air. Instead of sounding like a taunt, it fell on his ears in a soothing reminder of God's hand liberating him from his self-made prison.

Everett smiled. "Lord, I don't know what direction You will take me or how You plan to work in my life. I only know the best place, the safest place, for me to be is within Your hand. If I stay there, I believe You *will* make something beautiful happen. Guide me, Lord, through this night. Whatever path You've charted for me, keep me close to You."

Something beautiful. Something beautiful. Heaven spilled affirmation over him, as if God was agreeing with his prayer. Weariness drained away. A fresh spurt of energy flowed. Uplifted, Everett called out again. "Susan. Susan."

What was that? An unidentifiable sound reached him. Another animal? He stopped, all of his senses piqued. The breeze picked up again and stirred the leaves and grass.

There it was again. A frail squeak filtered through the soft whooshing of the wind. Did Gray follow him out here? Silly cat.

He was about to move on when the muted mewing sound penetrated the darkness once more. "Gray? Is that you?"

When no meow replied, he shook his head, chagrined. Perhaps his imagination was getting carried away. He ran a hand through his hair. How long had he been out here? Four hours? Longer? With the light of the moon, he moved on in what he hoped was the direction of the church. His foot stumbled on a low spot, and he realized he'd come across a tiny rivulet, no doubt coming from a spring somewhere higher. Grateful, he bent on one knee to quench his thirst. As he was sucking in the third handful of water, the squeaky cry reached him again, but this time it was closer. And it spoke.

"Mama."

The water slipped through his fingers, and he jerked his head up. "Susan?" He pushed to his feet. "Susan?"

He heard a tiny sob and hiccup. "Mama."

Joy stirred in his middle and rose up, much like the joy he'd felt last year after the fire when he'd learned his father and Pearl were safe. "Susan, where are you? Keep calling so I can find you."

Another weak cry rode on the breeze to his ears. "Mama."

"I'm coming, Susan. I'm coming."

"Mama." Her voice grew stronger.

As the air currents moved the clouds away from the moon, a shaft of radiance like a beam from heaven widened across the meadow and revealed a patch of pale yellow at the base of a tree. Everett headed toward it. "I'm coming, Susan."

"I want Mama."

A grin split Everett's face. He'd never heard such sweet words. A few more strides and he lowered himself to one knee in front of the little girl in the yellow dress. "Hey, do you know how many people are out looking for you?"

Susan tipped her face up and stared at him. She shook her head.

"Are you all right? Are you hurt anywhere?" He sent an anxious scan over her face and arms. No visible blood.

She held out one arm and twisted it around, pointing to a place near her elbow. "Ow."

Everett couldn't see much in the pale light, but based on Susan's description of her injury, it was minor. A wave of relief washed over him.

The little girl chattered her teeth. "I cold." She reached out her arms, and Everett gathered her close to his chest. She snuggled her head onto his shoulder.

He pulled his chin back and looked down at her. "I'll bet you want to go home, don't you?"

Moonlight shimmered off the tears on her plump cheeks. "I want Mama." She locked her arms around his neck.

"I know, honey." He patted her back. "Can I put you down for a minute?" He set her in front of him, and she leaned against his bent knee. A mixture of fatigue and exhilaration made his fingers fumble with the buttons on his shirt, but he pulled the garment off and wrapped it around her. It wasn't a blanket, but it was the best he could do. He tugged the collar higher around her neck and face, and then adjusted his suspenders over the shoulders of his long johns.

"Let's go back over here and get a drink of water. Then we'll go home."

He carried her back a few paces where the tiny stream cut through the meadow. Cupping his hand, he scooped up several handfuls of water for the little tyke, who slurped at the moisture noisily.

She leaned forward and peered up at his face. "Are you a angel?"

Everett chuckled and dabbed at her wet face with the tail of the shirt. "No, honey. My name is Everett, and I'm going to take you home."

"Ever." She wrapped her arms around his neck again.

He rose with the little girl safely snuggled in his arms. She felt like an aspen leaf quivering in the wind. Shivers rippled through her tiny, lithe body. Everett positioned his arms to cover as much of her as he could, hoping he could give her some of his warmth. Again he berated himself for not bringing a gun. The other searchers and those waiting at the church wouldn't know he'd found Susan until he arrived back at Willow Creek with her.

If he kept the woods to his left and followed them, he should eventually find the town. With a prayer of gratitude on his lips, he headed toward the church with as much speed as his limited vision and small burden would allow. The very thought of placing the little girl in her mother's arms filled him with unspeakable joy.

Chapter 15

Tillie's chest tightened at the sound of Tessa's soft weeping. Mrs. Witherspoon sat beside the distraught mother, holding Tessa's hand. Tillie rolled her head from side to side, working out the kinks in her neck and easing the tension in her shoulders. If only she could do the same for Tessa's heart.

Tillie poured three cups of coffee and served sandwiches to the trio of men who'd dragged in minutes earlier, reporting they'd seen no sign of the little girl. With apologetic glances in Tessa's direction, the men spoke quietly of the ground they'd covered and the thoroughness of their search. Tillie listened to their exchange with a sinking heart as they gulped down their food.

One of the men talked around the bite of sandwich in his mouth. "We heard that one rifle shot. Hoped it meant the little one had been found, but"—he shrugged—"there weren't but one shot, so we kept lookin'."

The other men nodded, and one of them jerked his thumb toward another pair of searchers. "Todd Finnigan said he took a shot at a wolf he saw in the distance, but the critter was out of range."

Tillie glanced toward Mr. Finnigan, who was filling a lantern with coal oil. Though discouraged over not having found Susan yet, none of the men who'd come back for a fresh horse or something to eat talked of giving up. For that, Tillie was grateful.

Tillie carried a canteen to the pump at the side of the building and worked the handle up and down, filling the vessel. She fastened the closure and crossed the yard to hand the canteen to Todd Finnigan.

"Mr. Finnigan, where was that wolf you saw?"

The dancing light from the torches seemed to deepen the worry lines in the man's face. "Southwest of here, across Devil's Backbone Hill, near the edge of the woods."

Tillie shook her head slightly. "Do you really think Susan could have wandered that far?"

He accepted the canteen and shrugged. "Who knows? I've seen little ones move faster than the parents thought they could." He slung the canteen onto his shoulder. "Personally, I hope she's found right here, holed up in some little out-of-the-way nook no one thought to check. I know you ladies are still looking all over town." He tugged the brim of his hat and picked up the lantern. "Thanks for the water and the grub."

The man stepped beyond the torchlight and disappeared into the darkness. With a sigh, Tillie poured another cup of coffee and picked up the old quilt she and Ben had sat upon hours earlier. So much had transpired—the picnic was a faded memory. She crossed the yard to the church steps and handed Tessa the cup. Tessa shook her head, but Tillie nudged it toward her insistently. "Drink it. You need something in your stomach." She unfolded the quilt and draped it around Tessa's trembling shoulders. "Mrs. Witherspoon, why don't you go get yourself something to eat. I'll stay with Tessa."

The pastor's wife smiled and rose, nodding toward the church door. "Some of the ladies have started a continuous prayer time inside. Two or three are in there praying right now. After a while some others will spell them."

Tillie nodded. "I'll join them in a bit." She sat down and slipped her arm around Tessa. "Did you get any sleep?"

Tessa shook her head. "No, but Mrs. Witherspoon made me rest even if I couldn't sleep." She released a shaky sigh. "Oh Tillie, what if—"

"Stop!" Tillie held up her hand. "Don't even think like that. There are dozens of men out there combing every inch of the woods and meadows and hills." She rubbed Tessa's back. "Mr. Finnigan said she's probably right around here somewhere in a place we haven't looked. She'll wake up hungry and start crying for you, and wonder what all the fuss is about."

Tessa nodded and took a swallow of coffee. "Has Everett come back yet?"

At the mention of his name, a rush of warmth filled Tillie's chest and traveled up her neck. She shook her head. "No, not yet. I'm sure he's just being thorough." She didn't voice the fear that had run through her head a dozen times already. *He's not as familiar with these hills as the other men. What if he got turned around and can't find his way back to the church?*

Tessa's soft voice broke into her thoughts. "I'm sure he'll come in anytime now."

Tillie blinked at her friend's insight and unselfish expression of comfort. "Of course he's fine. So is Susan. We're the ones who have the hardest job of all—waiting."

"Matilda."

Tillie glanced up to see her father trudging across the yard. "Da." She trotted over to greet him, clutching his arm the instant they met. There was no need to ask the question that burned in her heart. Da's weary eyes and discouraged countenance gave her all the answers she needed. "Da, come and sit down. I'll bring you some coffee and a sandwich."

"'Twould be a blessin', for sure." He sat on the grass and leaned back on his elbows.

Tillie hurried to the table and assembled a sandwich from leftover chicken. Having a task to occupy her hands vented some of her nervous energy, but her mind and heart still yearned to see Everett emerge from the darkness. Immediately, her conscience was smitten. "Lord, it's selfish to think of my own feelings for Everett at a time like this." She glanced over her shoulder at Tessa, who remained on the church steps, looking forlorn with Tillie's quilt draped around her. "Lord, please surround little Susan with Your angels, and bring her back home to Tessa and Gideon." She put the sandwich on a tin plate. "Since You're already working in the midst of this crisis, I beg You, heavenly Father, to bring Everett back safely as well."

She took her father the food and coffee and sat next to him while he ate. He took a noisy slurp. "Ah, 'tis good coffee. It'll warm up me innards."

Tillie scanned the yard, taking in the handful of men, some of whom had just arrived and others who were preparing to go back out. Her gaze moved from left to right until it landed on Tessa. Every time she looked at her friend, Tillie's heart cramped. Da also glanced in Tessa's direction, a deep furrow in his brow.

"Poor girl." He shook his head.

"Da, do you have any idea what areas the men have covered?"

Da munched on his sandwich and chased it down with a swallow of coffee. "Hubert Behr said he and Phillip planned to cover the area from his house south and east. Jed Brewer said he and his boy would go straight east from town to the Clermont road and then circle back toward the north. I covered the stretch between here and our place. Then I headed west a ways and crossed back to that rocky place in the hills where you kids used to go and play." He took another bite. "Has Everett been back yet?"

Tillie shook her head. "When he left here, he was going toward the woods."

Da stuffed the last bite of sandwich into his mouth, chewing thoughtfully. "Mm. He planned to search through the woods. I told him a bit about the lay of the land, him bein' here only a year. Showed him on a sketch how the woods curve to the northwest and meet Devil's Backbone Hill. That's the area he was searchin'. You say he ain't been back in? He should have covered that area by now."

The blood in Tillie's veins froze, and a quiver shuddered through her that had nothing to do with the chill in the air. "Devil's Backbone?"

"Aye." Da hoisted himself to his feet.

Tillie scrambled to snatch Da's sleeve before he could take a step. "Da, Mr. Finnigan said he spotted a wolf near there. He took a shot at it, but it was too far away."

"Ah, that must've been the shot I heard." He slipped his arm around her. "Don't fret, daughter. Everett can take care of himself."

"But Da, he didn't take a gun with him."

Da halted his steps and turned to face her. "Why in heaven's name not?"

She lifted her shoulders. "I don't think he owns one, but that's not important now. Da, he's out there tramping around in the dark, unarmed, in an area where a wolf was sighted."

Da's lips thinned into a grim line, and he cast a hard squint toward the woods. "Fetch me a lantern, daughter. Is Finnigan still here?"

Tillie shook her head. "He left about fifteen minutes before you came in." She pointed in the direction the man headed when he left. "He went that way."

Her father blew out a stiff breath and crossed the yard where two other men with lanterns were preparing to head back out. Tillie scurried to the makeshift table to do her father's bidding. Her hands shook as she tilted the can to pour coal oil into the lantern reservoir, and she spilled some on the table. The acrid odor of the lantern fuel burned her nose, but it was the image in her mind of Everett encountering a wolf in the dark that brought tears to her eyes.

❧

The image in Everett's mind of Tillie's wide green eyes the last time he saw her accompanied him as he tramped through the dark with little Susan in his arms. The moon continued to play hide-and-seek, at times casting the hillside in brightness, sometimes shedding just enough light for him to take a few steps, and sometimes slipping behind a cloud, encasing him in blackness.

He paused, waiting for the nocturnal light to make its appearance again.

Susan whimpered against his shoulder and tightened her grip around his neck. He patted her back.

"It's all right. The moon is just playing a game with us. It will peek out again in a minute." To soothe the child, he started to sing.

"Rock of Ages, cleft for me; let me hide myself in Thee." The words spilled comfort over him, reminding him once again of the only hiding place he ever wanted to seek for the rest of his life. When he couldn't remember all the words to the hymn, he hummed the melody.

Susan raised her head off his shoulder. "Ever, where's my mama?"

Despite their precarious situation, Everett smiled. "She's probably at the church waiting for us, honey." He patted her again, and she laid her head back down.

He continued humming. A moment later the moon reemerged, spilling pocketfuls of pale radiance across the meadow. The trees at the edge of the woods had mostly lost their leaves, casting grotesque shadows like dancing skeletons. Everett peeked down at Susan and was glad to see her head faced away from the spooky patterns.

"Rock of Ages, cleft for me; let me hide myself in Thee. Hmm-mm, hmm-mm."

The wind picked up again, raising gooseflesh on his arms and across the back of his neck. Everett couldn't be sure of the time. He hadn't bothered to wear his watch and chain when he dressed for the picnic, not that he could have dug it out of his pocket without disturbing Susan anyway. How long had it been since the sun had set? Two hours? Three? Curious how being far from town and enveloped in darkness skewed one's judgment of the passing of time. As chilled as he was, it felt like he'd been walking all night.

Using the edge of the woods as his guide, he pressed forward, praying he was heading in the right direction. What if he was headed away from town? *Please, Lord, lead me home.*

Weariness made his feet feel like they were wading through a snowbank. His stomach growled, reminding him he'd not eaten for hours. How much longer had it been since Susan had eaten? His arms tightened around the little girl. She wasn't complaining. Of course, he guessed she was more tired than hungry. His own fatigue was beginning to toy with his sense of direction, not to mention his ability to think straight. Even the sounds of the night teased him into imagining things, like the eerie howl he thought he heard a moment ago. Nonsense. It was just the wind.

The rifle shot he'd heard—how long ago had that been?—seemed to echo through the woods. It was impossible to tell from which direction it had come. Was it the darkness or exhaustion that made him so disoriented?

He took a step, and the ground beneath his foot gave way. His ankle turned, shooting pain up his leg as his balance faltered. He stiffened his back to keep from falling. Steadying himself with his left foot, he pulled the right one free of the gaping burrow—probably a gopher hole. He gritted his teeth and took several deep breaths, waiting for the throbbing to recede. After a few minutes he tried putting weight on the injured foot. Sharp spasms wrapped around his ankle, but he managed to walk. His uneven gait jostled Susan, but she didn't protest.

His body cried out for rest. When he'd first gathered Susan into his arms and snuggled her onto his shoulder to keep her warm, she had been light as a feather. Now she felt like some of the crates he hauled on and off the freight wagon every day. How could one small girl weigh so much? His back ached, and the scars on his shoulder burned as they stretched under his precious burden.

Just put one foot in front of the other.

Susan stirred in his arms, and he peeked down at her. "Are you all right, Susan?"

No response.

"Susan?" He angled his head and tried to see if her eyes were closed, but judging by her limp form, she'd fallen asleep. Good. At least if she was asleep, she wouldn't be frightened. Hopefully, the next time she opened her eyes, he would be handing her to her mother.

The moon disappeared behind a cloud again, forcing him to stop. He needed to rest his ankle anyway. He tugged the collar of his shirt up a little higher around Susan's neck. While he waited for the cloud to ride across the sky and reveal the moon again, he tried to train his eyes to pierce through the darkness. A tiny pinpoint of light floated across his bleary vision. A firefly? He fixed his stare on the friendly insect.

"How nice of you to keep us company in the middle of the night," he said. But not only did this firefly stay in one place; its glow also didn't fade. Everett frowned. Fireflies were plentiful in the warm months of summer, but in late September in the brisk autumn temperatures? The firefly still didn't move.

"That's not a firefly." His pulse picked up. Was he so drained of strength he was seeing things? He glanced at the sky and was rewarded with a glimpse of the moon's glow at the edge of the cloud. In a few moments he could proceed again.

A flash of panic struck him. He'd taken his eyes off the firefly—or whatever it was—to search for the moon. He jerked his eyes forward again. There it was. His breath deepened with a stirring of hope.

Thin moonlight once again splashed softly across the hillside. The pinpoint of light shone like a beacon through the edge of the woods. He set his course straight in its direction, like a ship toward a lighthouse. Periodically the firefly disappeared as he picked his way through the trees, but it always reappeared. Underbrush snagged his trouser legs and threatened to trip him, but he limped on.

Two fireflies now winked ahead of him. His heart accelerated. It had to be the town. His ankle ached with every step, and Susan still lay like deadweight on his shoulder, stretching the scarred tissue, but the discomfort no longer mattered. Fresh determination propelled him through the woods.

Two lights became three, peeking in and out of the brush. He became vaguely aware that he was panting. He stubbed his foot against something hard and unforgiving. A rock? Without shifting Susan, he extended his leg, poking the obstacle with his foot. A fallen tree.

Not wishing to lose sight of the lights, he slid his left leg over the tree trunk, but doing so meant putting all his weight on his painful right ankle. He clamped his teeth and bit back the groan that tried to escape. Lowering his torso to straddle the tree, he carefully swung the other leg over and rose. Susan remained slumped against him. As he stood, his eyes searched through the woods for the lights to anchor his position. Was it his imagination, or did he smell coffee?

His throbbing ankle begged him to stop, but the flickering lights drew him. They grew and danced between the trees. A soft glow outlined a rooftop and a steeple. He'd found the church. A joy-filled shout gathered deep within his chest, but his throat constricted, preventing the expression of exultation from escaping. It was just as well. He didn't want to frighten Susan. He limped past the edge of the woods and came to the feathery cedar trees that lined the churchyard—the same cedars he'd used as a hiding place countless times. With a prayer of thanksgiving on his lips, he stepped beyond the refuge of the cedars and into the torch and lantern light.

Chapter 16

Tillie tipped the can of coal oil to extract the last few drops into the reservoir of the lantern. Her brother Phillip stood a few paces away, blowing on a cup of coffee and taking tentative sips. All the men who'd straggled in throughout the evening looked just the way Phillip did, bedraggled and discouraged, hungry and tired.

"Can I get something to eat, Tillie? I'm starved."

If she hadn't felt so emotionally battered, she'd have grinned. Phillip was always starved.

"All the picnic leftovers are gone. The women made sandwiches until we ran out of ham, chicken, and bread." She set the coal oil can aside. "Mr. Kyle at the hotel said we could use the hotel kitchen to prepare food for everyone. As soon as I'm finished filling these lanterns—"

Her words were drowned out by a shout that rang through the still night air. In her distracted state, Tillie wasn't sure she'd heard the words correctly, but she could have sworn it sounded like the person was praising God. She looked up and saw several people running. Another shout, then another. A jolt shot through her.

"Mercy, what's happened?" She and Phillip both spun in the direction the folks were running. A jubilant chorus split the air. The sight that greeted her buckled her knees. When she opened her mouth, she couldn't push out a single syllable, but her lips formed one silent word. *Everett*.

She was afraid to blink. Indescribable joy welled up within her and could not be contained. Grateful tears and pure laughter blended like a fine tapestry in her soul.

All the shouting awakened the sleeping child snuggled in Everett's arms, and, apparently startled, Susan shrank closer and clung to him as he crossed the yard to the church steps. Tessa rose, her expression a mixture of elation and solace, gratitude and relief. Tears poured down her face as she reached out to receive her child.

Tillie slipped her hand up to cover her mouth, holding in the sobs as

Everett placed Susan in her mother's arms. Was that Everett's shirt wrapped around the tyke? Unchecked tears seeped through her fingers as she witnessed the reunion for which they'd so fervently prayed. Instead of doing what she longed to do—running and throwing her arms around Everett's neck—she stood nailed in place, watching others thump him on the back and pump his hand. Some of the ladies squeezed his arm, and Pearl stood on tiptoe and kissed his cheek.

Susan wiggled and pulled back from her mother's tight hug and pointed at Everett. "Look, Mama. God sended me a angel. His name is Ever."

Amid the chuckles, Tessa stepped over to Everett with grateful tears in her eyes. "How can I thank you? You gave me my little girl back. You *are* an angel." Susan, now cocooned in the old quilt that had earlier draped Tessa's shoulders, sent Everett a sleepy smile.

Someone leaped up the church steps and began pulling on the bell rope, sending peals of jubilation ringing through the town and surrounding hills and calling in the searchers. Each happy clang of the bell resounded with good news. Across the countryside, trios of rifle shots echoed in response, proclaiming to everyone within hearing radius that God had answered their prayers.

Pastor Witherspoon climbed the steps and called for everyone's attention. He led the gathering in a prayer of praise and thanksgiving for Susan's safe return. As soon as everyone whooped, "Amen!" he raised both hands.

"I think I speak for all of us when I express how grateful we are to Everett Behr, and to all the folks who helped search for little Susan. Everett, you're a bona fide hero." More "amens" rose among those gathered, along with shouts of affirmation.

Tillie couldn't take her eyes off Everett. Normally he ducked his head or covered his face and fled from the presence of a large group like this. But he was hemmed in by the townsfolk and couldn't escape even if he wanted to. The public praise brought a flush to his cheeks, but there was something else—something normally absent from his face: a smile. Her heart accelerated. Her hungry eyes took in every plane of his dear countenance.

Pastor Witherspoon continued, "I think you'll agree we're all too tired for a barn dance." A few murmurs and groans of concurrence resonated. "So if it's all right with everyone, and if it's all right with Dan Miller, whose barn we planned to use, we'll hold the harvest dance next Saturday night." More nods and hums of agreement rippled through the group.

A few pairs of searchers came galloping in, among them Gideon Maxwell, who leaped off his horse and ran to embrace his wife and daughter. Tillie wrapped her arms around herself to contain the happy shiver dancing in her chest, and enjoyed the scene as Gideon added his thanks to Everett.

The feelings that swelled her heart went far beyond admiration. Tillie's feet itched to run to Everett, and her fingers trembled in anticipation of touching his hand. Still she held back, waiting for people to disperse. What she wished to tell Everett was best said in quiet and privacy.

Tillie remained off to the side, her gaze locked on the man in the center of the gathering. If she could communicate silently across the space that separated them, she'd already spoken volumes. Finding the words to vocalize her thoughts and feelings to him, however, was a different matter. If only he could simply read her heart.

Everett turned his head from one side to the other. He appeared to be searching the crowd. At no time since he walked in with Susan in his arms had Tillie seen him attempt to hide his scars, and he wasn't doing so now. He craned his neck and turned around. The moment his gaze met hers, she felt the impact. A tiny smile hooked the corner of his mouth and stretched the scars on the right side of his face. Her heart thumped out a rhythm she was certain he could hear, even over the celebration taking place around them. Neither of them looked away. Did he know what she was thinking? Could he hear with his heart what her lips couldn't speak?

Gradually the people called out their final good nights to each other, patting Susan on the head and shaking Everett's hand. A few of the ladies began packing the last of their picnic items away in baskets and crates. All but a few had taken their leave. Before the men took the makeshift table apart and carried the sawhorses away, Tillie turned and poured two cups of coffee.

"Thank you for praying."

Tillie turned to find Everett standing behind her. She noticed he'd donned his shirt once again, covering his long johns. Tillie handed him one of the coffee mugs. His fingers lingered on hers for a few extra moments as he accepted the steaming brew. At his touch, her breathing became more rapid. Tillie studied his dark brown eyes, looking into their depths. She was too filled with wonder to speak.

Weariness etched its mark across his face. "Would you mind if we sat down?" He led the way over to the steps, and it was then Tillie noticed he was limping.

"Everett, you're hurt."

He shook his head as he lowered himself to the step beside her. "It's nothing. I twisted my foot a bit. It'll be fine." He turned and looked fully into her face. "It won't leave a scar."

His tone held no bitterness. She dropped her gaze to her shoe tops for a moment. "Everett Behr, you are an extraordinary man." She returned her shy glance to him.

He shrugged. "There were a lot of men out searching. I was only one of many. God let me find her."

Tillie sipped her coffee and then ran her finger around the rim of the mug. "I noticed little Susan didn't find you repulsive at all. In fact, she clung to you and didn't want to let go when everyone started shouting."

"Tillie, it was amazing." He reached over and picked up her hand, but he didn't seem to realize he'd done so. Torchlight flickered off his face, highlighting his scars. Awe filled his expression, as if he was relating a miracle. "The moonlight came and went as the clouds moved, but when I heard her crying, it was as if God flooded the area with light." He waved his hand, gesturing toward the torches. "The moon was brighter than it had been the entire evening. She looked up at me and climbed right into my arms. She wasn't afraid at all."

"Mm, she thought you were an angel." The smile that began in the depths of her heart grew and rose to fill her entire being. "Everett, your scars are the result of an entirely selfless, love-filled act. Remember, Jesus bore scars from an ultimate act of love. By His scars, we have the hope of heaven. Scars aren't ugly, Everett." She tightened her fingers around his, pulling them toward her. He glanced down at their joined hands and returned the squeeze. When his gaze rose back to meet hers, he lifted his other hand and ran his fingertips over his scars.

Tillie reached out and gently took his hand, pulling it away from his face. "Your scars are beautiful to me."

❧

The warmth permeating Everett's being wasn't the result of sipping the hot coffee. Tillie's nearness quickened his pulse and deepened each breath. The autumn wind sighed through the cedars and flickered the torchlight into ripples across the churchyard. The weariness that had dogged him as he'd made his way through the darkness with little Susan vanished, replaced by revived freshness in Tillie's company. He wanted to stare at her, to take in every nuance of her image and forever commit this moment to memory. She stole his very breath. There was so much he wanted—no, *needed* to say to her. Where should he begin?

"Where's Ben?" *Where's Ben!* He groaned within himself and wanted to yank the words back the instant they escaped. What a stupid thing to say. Where was the comfortable camaraderie they'd enjoyed walking among the willows?

One of her eyebrows arched slightly. "He went out searching with Fletcher Hamilton. They came back a little while ago, after the bell was rung. I don't expect you noticed them in all the commotion."

He hadn't. He only had eyes for Tillie. Another wagon pulled out of the churchyard, its occupants calling out their good nights to the men disassembling the tables and the women finishing the cleanup. He raised his hand to wave in response but quickly returned his focus on Tillie and the moment God was allowing them to share.

Tillie's soft voice intertwined with the song of the night wind. "Ben told me he could see how I felt about you, and he said I wouldn't find a finer man than you. And he's right."

"He did? He is?"

Her laugh reminded him of raindrops falling softly on the fields. Such a sweet sound. But the smile faded from her face, and she lowered her gaze, twisting her fingers into a knot. "I have to ask you something."

He reached over and disentangled her fingers, holding them gently within his. "You can ask me anything."

She took a deep breath, as if the question on her lips needed a push. "Everett, are you planning on leaving?"

Her inquiry so startled him that he tightened his grip on her hands lest they slip from his grasp. Did she know about the letter? Before he could tell her all the things his heart wanted to say, he needed to begin by being honest.

"I've received an offer of a position back east. How did you know?"

She lifted her shoulders. "My brother Phillip was at work in your father's store. He overheard your father and Miss Pearl talking about you moving back to Baltimore. Phillip said he didn't think your parents knew he was in the storeroom." A tiny smile pulled a dimple into her cheek. "Even though he's my younger brother, he thinks he has to protect me. He didn't mean any harm." The smile fell away. "He told me he heard your parents praying that God would work it out for you to stay in Willow Creek." Her green eyes filled with pain, and she repeated her question. "So are you planning on leaving?"

She pulled one hand away to push back her hair, but Everett held the other one captive. "Honestly? I haven't decided yet. I only received the letter a week ago, and it caught me by surprise. I will admit that I've been thinking about it. In the past couple of weeks, I've found it harder than I believed possible to watch you and Ben together."

"But you were the one who kept telling me I should accept Ben's attention."

Everett pursed his lips and nodded. "I know. I truly believed I was doing the right thing. These scars. . . How could I expect. . . ? Tillie, I never meant to hurt you. My only thought was to see you happy. I couldn't ask you to spend your life with someone who looks like a freak."

"You stop right there, Everett Behr." A stubborn scowl took up residence on her beautiful face. "I never want to hear you utter those words again." She pulled her hand away from him and plunked both hands on her hips. "You haven't answered my question."

"Yes, I did. I said I haven't decided yet."

She rolled her eyes heavenward. "Angels preserve us!" Those crystal-green eyes returned to earth and nailed him where he sat. "Don't you think it's high time you *do* decide? Because I have something I want to say to you, but not until I know if you're planning on staying or leaving."

A bubble of laughter formed in his belly and rose into his chest. He clamped his lips shut. Something told him he'd best hold it in. If the feisty expression on her face was any indication, she might not take it kindly if he laughed.

He sucked in a breath. "I was seriously considering the offer, but circumstances have changed, and it appears God wants me to stay where I am."

The light from the torches burned a bit lower. They'd need to say good night soon. Only two men remained at the church, loading up the last of the sawhorses and planks.

The stubborn look in her eye waned like the torchlight. "What circumstances have changed?"

He reached over and hooked the errant lock of hair back behind her ear once again, his fingers grazing the side of her face. Her soft smile invited his hand to linger there as she tipped her head to nestle into his palm. His rib cage prevented his heart from soaring out of his chest. Sorrow pinched him when he removed his hand from her face.

"God has broken through this thick head of mine and shown me how foolish I've been." How should he explain the dawn of understanding? "For months I told myself the friendship you offered me was simply because of your compassion, and I didn't want anyone feeling sorry for me. Especially you."

She opened her mouth, an expression of protest on her face, but he laid his finger on her lips. Complete honesty demanded he finish his explanation.

"I couldn't see myself asking you to be with someone who looked like me. I truly believed I was sparing you from a lifetime of pain."

He captured her hand again. "Tillie, God has shown me your heart. He's allowed me to glimpse the pure, unspoiled love you have to share." He lifted her fingers to his lips. "Once God pulled the blindfold from my eyes and I understood the depth of your feelings, all those excuses I kept calling reasons fell away."

She reached across the space that separated them and touched his scars, a tiny smile tipping the corners of her mouth. "This is the face I want to see every morning for the rest of my life."

His heart leaped with a freedom he'd never known before, and he couldn't keep the grin from stretching across his face. "Why, Tillie O'Dell, are you asking me to marry you?"

The cockiness he'd come to adore danced in her sparkling eyes. "Unless you ask me first, yes."

Laughter rose up from the delight in his heart and spilled over. "Well, in that case, I accept. But just to make it conventional. . ." He slid off the church step and lowered himself to one knee, taking her hand in his. The flickering light of the torch played over her face and reflected off her eyes. "Tillie, I love you. I've loved you for months and didn't realize it. With God's help, I plan to love you until the day He takes me home. I believe you are the partner He has ordained for me, and I for you. Will you marry me?"

Tillie leaned forward and framed his face with her hands. "I've always wanted my very own angel, and now God has sent me one. . .named Ever."

Epilogue

Willow Creek, Iowa, 1887

O h Everett, it's beautiful." Tillie ran her fingers over the pattern of leaded glass in the front door of the house they were building. Sunlight caught the beveled edges of the intricate design. "But isn't it too costly?"

Everett squeezed his wife's shoulders. "Tillie, my love, you are so easy to please, and you never ask for anything. I wanted you to have a little touch of extravagance." He took her hand and led her up the newly painted steps to the wide front porch. "Father has ordered some rocking chairs from a furniture maker in Ohio. I thought we could set them here on the porch and watch the sunset in the evenings."

Tillie smiled up at him. "Sunset always was your favorite time of day." She walked to one end of the porch where a willow tree draped its curtain across the corner of the railing, close enough to reach out and weave her fingers through the dangling green withes. When Everett had shown her the parcel of land at the edge of town that he wanted to purchase, she'd immediately fallen in love with the two willow trees that stood silently beckoning an invitation to hide away in their curtained sanctuaries. Everett had agreed their house should be built right in between them—a giant willow at each end of the sprawling porch.

Tillie smiled and glanced at her husband over her shoulder. "Do you remember how we used to walk in the evenings and watch the fireflies play hide-and-seek through the willow trees?"

Everett's teasing chuckle made her heart flutter. "I seem to recall you taking off your shoes and stockings and dangling your feet in the creek."

A warm blush filled Tillie's face despite the fact they'd been married for almost two years. "How scandalous!"

Everett grinned. "I couldn't see your ankles. Between the twilight and the shadows from the willow trees, it was too dark."

Tillie filled her eyes with the sight of their new house, almost ready for them to move in. "I still can't believe you've had this house built for us. Don't misunderstand—I love the house. It's beautiful, but I'd have been happy living in the apartment over your father's store."

"So you've told me." He placed a gentle kiss on her lips. "I wanted to give you a house of your own. A place where we could grow and establish our own family traditions and memories, a refuge to come home to and a haven for our children. . .someday."

Tillie dipped her head and smiled a private smile over the secret she shared with the Lord. She laid her hand over her abdomen, awe filling her over the tiny life that grew there in its wondrous hiding place. Perhaps this was a good time to tell Everett her news.

"I saw Tessa and Susan today. Susan wanted to know if Uncle Ever was coming to her birthday party."

Everett inspected the framing around the front windows. "She's having another birthday? She must be. . .what, four?"

"She's going to be five years old this Saturday."

"Time sure flies."

"Mm. She's going to be a big sister soon, too. Gideon and Tessa are expecting again."

Everett's face lit up. "That's wonderful. I'll remember to congratulate Gideon when I see him." He laid his hand on the small of her back. "Come on, let's go see how the new kitchen is coming along. Fred Cummings does excellent cabinetry work."

Tillie allowed him to lead her to the front door. "I'm more anxious to see the upstairs."

Everett paused with his hand on the doorknob. "I thought we agreed to wait and finish the upstairs later."

"I believe we said. . .as the need arises."

"Well, yes, but—" Everett's eyes widened.

"Didn't you say there would be enough room for two large bedrooms upstairs?"

"Yes, but—"

"Of course, the room doesn't have to be ready right away. We can wait. . . five, maybe six months."

"But—"

"Won't it be fun for Gideon and Tessa's new baby to have a playmate the same age?"

Her husband stood with his feet anchored in place as he stared unblinking at her.

Tillie gave him her sweetest smile and slid her arms around his neck. "You're going to be a wonderful papa." She watched an expression of absolute rapture sweep across his face.

"Oh, my sweet Tillie." He held her face in both hands and lowered his lips to hers. He pulled his head back and smoothed his fingers over her hair, then raised his eyes to heaven. "Lord, what a marvelous gift You've given us. Every gift from You is perfect. Thank You, Father."

He kissed her again until she was breathless and then wrapped her in his arms. "I can't wait to hold him."

"Him? You know it could be a girl."

Everett blew out his breath tentatively, as if trying not to break the sweet spell of awestruck joy. "A little girl."

She giggled at the look of wonder in her husband's eyes and snuggled into his embrace. A moment later, she found herself scooped up into Everett's arms. Joyous laughter bubbled out of both of them as Everett whooped and whirled her around.

He set her down carefully and grabbed her hand, tugging her down the steps. "Come on!"

"I thought you wanted to look at the house and see how the kitchen was turning out."

"At a time like this? Are you crazy, woman?" He helped her climb into the buggy. "I can't wait to see the expressions on my father's and Pearl's faces when we tell them they're going to be grandparents!"

Pure bliss found expression in her laugh. "My da will do an Irish jig all the way down the main street." She pictured her father's reaction and exclaimed at the image. "Mercy!"

Everett climbed up beside her and unwound the reins from the brake lever. He paused before releasing the brake and pulled her into a tight hug. "Tillie, I love you so much. You are exactly right. God has certainly poured out His mercy on us!"

"Aye," she whispered, adopting her father's vernacular. "His mercy and blessings and love and faithfulness and grace and—"

Everett silenced her list with a kiss.

About the Author

Connie Stevens lives with her husband of forty-plus years in north Georgia, within sight of her beloved mountains. She and her husband are both active in a variety of ministries at their church. A lifelong reader, Connie began creating stories by the time she was ten. Her office manager and writing muse is a cat, but she's never more than a phone call or email away from her critique partners. She enjoys gardening and quilting, but one of her favorite pastimes is browsing antique shops where story ideas often take root in her imagination. Connie has been a member of American Christian Fiction Writers since 2000.

If You Liked This Book, You'll Also Like. . .

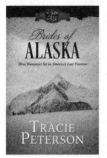

Brides of Alaska
by Tracie Peterson
Three classic romances from bestselling author Tracie Peterson take readers into the wilds of Alaska. The bleak wilderness of America's 49th state challenges three generations of women in the Erikson family in different ways, but overcoming the odds through faith will lead each to lasting love.
Paperback / 978-1-63409-214-2 / $12.99

Brides of Texas
by Cathy Marie Hake
A father's last gifts to his sons accompany three young men from the hills of Scotland to the plains of Texas. The Gregor brothers—Robert, a doctor; Duncan, a cobbler; and Christopher, a lawman—set up shop in a small Texas town and quickly make the acquaintance of local women.
Paperback / 978-1-63409-669-0 / $12.99

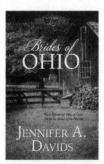

Brides of Ohio
by Jennifer A. Davids
Author Jennifer A. Davids has spun three stories from historic Ohio where hope has been shattered for three women. A Southern belle's life is displaced. A widow takes a risk to save an old friend. A spinster librarian harbors a secret. Between past hurts and present trials, is there room for love?
Paperback / 978-1-63058-152-7 / $12.99